Alone again, Jabari lifted his glass. "To an evening of good company, great conversation and a whole lot of fun."

Alisha touched her glass to his. "Amen." She took a small sip. "How does it feel to be out of the military after so many years?"

"It took a lot of adjusting at first, not having to be up before the crack of dawn, drills, deployments, but my nine to five at the tech company where I work is a welcome change."

"Do you miss it?"

"Sometimes. It's the only life I knew for the past twenty years."

"You never married?"

"Nah. There aren't a lot of women who can handle their husbands being away for a year or two at a time. Michelle said you were divorced."

She had expected the subject to come up, and she supposed it was better to get it out of the way early and move on. "For over three years. He decided one day that he didn't want to be a husband or father and had the women to prove it." Alisha took another sip of her wine, a larger one this time.

"I'm sorry."

"Don't be. It's over and done."

Jabari shook his head. "The man must be out of his mind."

Sheryl Lister is a multi-award-winning author and has enjoyed reading and writing for as long as she can remember. She is a former pediatric occupational therapist with over twenty years of experience and resides in California. Sheryl is a wife, mother of three daughters and a son-in-love, and grandmother to two special little boys. When she's not writing, Sheryl can be found on a date with her husband or in the kitchen creating appetizers. For more information, visit her website at www.sheryllister.com.

Books by Sheryl Lister

Harlequin Kimani Romance

It's Only You
Tender Kisses
Places in My Heart
Giving My All to You
A Touch of Love
Still Loving You
Sweet Love

Visit the Author Profile page at Harlequin.com for more titles.

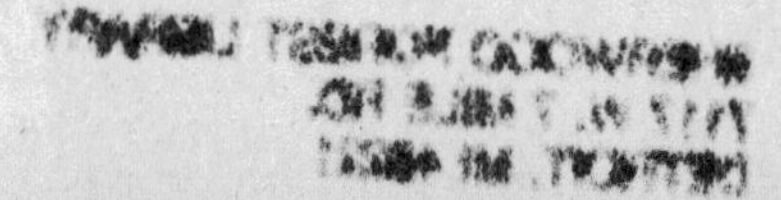

SHERYL LISTER
and
ELLE WRIGHT

Sweet Love & Because of You

ISBN-13: 978-1-335-99881-1

Sweet Love & Because of You

Recycling programs for this product may not exist in your area.

This edition published by arrangement with Harlequin Books S.A.

For questions and comments about the quality of this book, please contact us at CustomerService@Harlequin.com.

Printed in U.S.A.

CONTENTS

For all those looking for love a second time.
It's coming.

Acknowledgments

My Heavenly Father, thank You for my life. You never cease to amaze me with Your blessings!

To my husband, Lance—you continue to show me why you'll always be my #1 hero!

To my children, family and friends, thank you for your continued support. I appreciate and love you!

They always say to find your tribe and I've found mine. They know who they are. I love y'all and can't imagine being on this journey without you.

A very special thank-you to my agent, Sarah E. Younger. I can't tell you how much I appreciate having you in my corner.

SWEET LOVE

Sheryl Lister

Dear Reader,

They say that our youthful years are for making mistakes, particularly when it comes to matters of the heart. This is certainly true for Alisha Hunter. But she isn't ready for the likes of Jabari Sutton, a man who's ready to find Mrs. Right. Of course, the road to happily-ever-after is never an easy one, but throw in a compassionate man, a dose of passion and a little bit of massage oil (if you've read *A Love of My Own*, you know what I mean) and they just might find the sweetest love either has known. Enjoy their journey!

As always, I so appreciate all your love and support. Without you, I couldn't do this.

Much love,

Sheryl

Website: SherylLister.com

Email: sheryllister@gmail.com

Facebook: Facebook.com/SherylListerauthor

Twitter: Twitter.com/1Slynne

Instagram: Instagram.com/SherylLister

Chapter 1

"I can't believe I let you talk me into this."

Jabari Sutton paused in affixing a wheel and grinned at his brother-in-law, Chris Frazier. "Hey, this is for your daughter's birthday party." He had been searching the internet and had come across little cardboard "cars" for watching an outdoor movie, like at the drive-in.

"I'm sure Jade will appreciate all this hard work at four years old," Chris said sarcastically. "Why can't we just make them like the picture? It's just a painted box with black paper plate wheels and a little fake license plate in the back."

"You know I don't do anything by half." Jabari had added a cupholder and tray table for the snacks. "Besides, you can't just watch a movie without food and drinks." He tightened the screw on the cupholder and jiggled it to make sure it was secure.

"Thank goodness there are only eight."

Jabari laughed. "Man, Jade is going to love this. You won't be able to pry her out of it. And just think, at those times when you want five minutes of peace from her thousand and one questions, you can pop in one of those educational videos or Disney movies, fix her a snack and enjoy the silence. Hey, it might also give you and Michelle a few minutes." Chris had been married to Jabari's sister, Michelle, for five years.

Chris glanced up. "Say no more. Think we can sell these to the parents afterward?"

"Maybe." They burst out laughing.

After a few minutes, Chris asked, "How are you adjusting to civilian life?"

Jabari had retired from twenty years in the air force eight months ago. "Easier than I anticipated. Having a job waiting made the transition much smoother."

"Tell me about it. Not everyone can walk out of the military and into a six-figure job with one of the fastest-growing tech companies."

"I didn't just *walk* into it. I worked my butt off during leave times and whenever Martin and I could get a videoconference in." When Jabari's high school buddy Martin Walters had been ready to leave the large company he worked for and strike out on his own, Jabari hadn't hesitated over Martin's offer to be a partner. As teenagers, the two of them had often talked about starting a company and becoming rich. When Jabari got accepted into the United States Air Force Academy and Martin went the business and computer engineering route, Jabari had chalked it up to just two kids dreaming and immersed himself in the realities of life. It had taken the two of them over two years of planning and researching before they launched M & J Technologies three years ago. As a cybersecurity specialist, Jabari had put a system in place and monitored it remotely while on active duty. "I've already seen a return on my investment, though."

Chris finished the car he'd been working on and moved it to the other side of the garage with six others that had been completed. "And the other parts of your life?"

Jabari shrugged. "Nothing. I feel like dating has changed a lot in twenty years."

"Man, the entire world has changed since you went in," Chris said with a laugh. "What happened to the woman you were seeing three months ago?"

"I left her where she was three months ago." Jabari scrubbed a hand over his head. "It's like I'm finding all the women who want nothing more than to be wined and dined constantly and who are only interested in a bed partner. I mean, don't get me wrong, I have no problem with the whole wine-and-dine thing, but I'm looking for more than that."

Chris chuckled. "Well, you are getting on up there in age."

"Shut up. Seriously, though, I'm ready to settle down and have a family." Jabari recalled all the letters, packages, phone calls and videoconferences his fellow soldiers received from their wives or significant others and how happy they'd be. He could count on one hand the number of women he'd dated who took the time to send him something. Most of them couldn't handle the long deployments and, after a while, he'd stopped trying. Now he wanted what his sister and brother-in-law had, what his parents had.

"Knock, knock. Can I come in? You two have had my garage blocked up all week and wouldn't let me see what's going on."

Jabari and Chris shared a look. Jabari affixed the last tray to the car and stood. "Come on in, Chelle. You always were nosy."

Michelle entered the garage fully and put her hand on her hip. "I was not. You were just always keeping secrets from me." She smiled.

He shook his head. At nine years his junior, Michelle had wanted to go with him everywhere, but he hadn't minded. When he left for the academy, she had cried so hard he'd almost changed his mind. Leaving her had been the hardest thing he'd done in his life. But they had both survived and were now closer than ever. "Come look."

"Oh, my goodness! These are fabulous. The kids are going to love these." She took a slow tour through the boxes, pausing to touch the tray and cupholder. "I cannot believe it. And it's supposed to be in the upper seventies tomorrow."

"Perfect for an outdoor movie." The late September temperatures had been in the eighties for the past couple of weeks and had even reached ninety twice.

She walked over and slid her arm around Chris. "So how much did my brother pay you to help him do this?"

Chris leaned away and gave her an incredulous look. "What makes you think it wasn't the other way around?"

Michelle kissed his cheek and patted his chest. "You're handy, baby, but this is way out of your sphere. And I know Jay."

"I slave in this garage all week *after* I get home from eight hours of dealing with a bunch of college students, and this is the thanks I get?"

Jabari laughed. "He helped a lot."

She came over and hugged Jabari. "Thanks. You're

the best big brother a girl could ever have. Always have been."

He kissed the top of her head. "You're welcome. What time is the party again?"

"It starts at noon. I was thinking about going for an hour or so, but with these..." She waved a hand in the direction of the cars. "It'll be the perfect wind-down for them."

"I'll put a sheet up under the canopy and project the movie from the laptop," Chris said.

Michelle rubbed her hands together. "I'm so excited. This is going to be the best party ever. I'm getting ready to make some tea. Do you guys want some? Or coffee?"

"No, baby. I'm fine."

"None for me, either, sis. I'm going to head home. Do you need me to come early to help set up anything?"

She looked to Chris, who shook his head. "I think we have everything, and my friend is coming a little early to help with the food."

"Okay." Jabari followed them inside to the kitchen.

Chris leaned against the counter. "Jay, maybe you should get here a little early. Michelle has a couple of single friends who plan to attend."

He leveled Chris with a glare.

"What? You said you were ready to settle down. I'm just trying to help you out."

Michelle got a mug from the cabinet, placed it on the counter and dropped a tea bag inside. "I thought you were seeing someone." She filled the teakettle and set it on the stove to boil.

"No. We went out to a bar and grill and she'd apparently told a few of her friends. I didn't have a problem with it until my date decided to go sit with the three of them. They had all ordered drinks—several rounds—and she had the nerve to be upset when I said I had no intentions of paying. I told her since she enjoyed their company so much, she could go home with them. I left and blocked her number immediately."

Chris doubled over in laughter. "I would've given anything to see that. I can just imagine the look on her face. Drinks aren't cheap and that tab was probably somewhere near a hundred bucks."

Michelle tried to stifle her laughter and failed. "That is unbelievable. She really couldn't have believed you would pay for those other women's drinks, let alone her own after deserting you like that. I promise you not all women are like that. You may have to relax some of your exacting standards to find her, though."

Jabari lifted a brow. "What exacting standards?" True, he didn't plan to settle for any woman who came along, but he didn't think that fell into the category of *exacting standards*.

"Jabari, you are the pickiest guy I've ever known when it comes to women. No one ever seems to measure up."

"That's not true. I'm just careful about who I get involved with. I like to take my time and get to know a woman first and get a sense of who she is as a person before jumping in headfirst. That's sound judgment, don't you think, Chris?"

Chris held his hands up in mock surrender. "No way are you going to get me to comment on this. I'm trying to have a good night."

Michelle swatted Chris on his arm and rolled her eyes.

He hugged her. "Baby, you know I didn't need more than a minute to realize you were the woman for me."

"Mmm-hmm. All this sweet talking isn't going to get you any closer to the goodies."

"Wait. What?"

Jabari chuckled. "On that note, I'm out of here. See you tomorrow." He and Chris shared a one-arm hug, then he kissed his sister on the forehead. "You don't need to walk me out."

"Okay. Thanks for everything. Love you."

"Love you, too, Chelle." He walked through the house to the front door and loped down the driveway to his car. Jabari slid behind the wheel and sat for a moment. He envied the playful banter and love so evident between Chelle and Chris. He'd been batting a big fat zero in the relationship department and, at thirty-eight, wondered if he would ever find that *one*.

"Mommy, wake up. We're gonna be late."

Alisha Hunter cracked one eye open and saw her six-year-old son, Corey, standing there fully dressed, with his backpack strapped on. She groaned and stared bleary-eyed over at the clock on her nightstand. "Corey, it is only seven. The sleepover doesn't start for another five hours." He had been driving her crazy with excitement from the moment he received the invitation four days ago. Since then, he'd asked every day, "Is it Saturday yet?" Had she known he'd be waking her up at the crack of dawn, she might have changed her answer when he asked last night as she tucked him into bed.

"*Mom*, come on." Corey bounced up and down.

"Baby, it's too early to go to the party. Devon is probably still asleep, and so are his parents." She dragged herself to a sitting position. "I promise you won't miss one minute of the party." While Corey had the sleepover, Lia had been invited to a birthday party for the daughter of Alisha's best friend from college. Both she and Michelle had gotten bachelor's degrees in nursing and ended up working at the same hospital.

Corey viewed her skeptically for a moment and then finally nodded. "Okay."

Alisha smiled and kissed his forehead. "How about you go read one of your books while I get dressed? I'll make you some breakfast in a minute."

He grinned, showing off the gap left from the tooth he'd lost two weeks ago. "Can I have pancakes? Lia likes pancakes, too."

"Yes. And I know she does." Her three-year-old daughter could devour two pancakes in the blink of an eye. Alisha wondered where she put it all. After Corey left, Alisha stretched, stood and trudged to the bathroom. She had worked overtime three days this past week and had hoped to sleep until at least eight this morning. She loved her job as a surgical nurse, but the hours were sometimes long. Thankfully, she had recently transferred to the same-day surgery unit, which meant no more working on weekends or holidays.

After a quick shower, Alisha dressed and went to the kitchen to start breakfast. On the way, she poked her head in Corey's room and found him curled up in his beanbag chair, reading. A soft smile curved her lips. She had always been a voracious reader and couldn't be happier that both of her children seemed to love reading as much as she did. By the time she cooked the bacon, Lia toddled in and wrapped her arms around Alisha's legs.

"Mama, up, please."

Alisha wiped her hand on a towel and bent to pick up her daughter. She kissed her cheek. "Good morning."

Lia laid her head on Alisha's shoulder. "Hi, Mama."

"Are you hungry?"

"Yes."

"I'm going to make some pancakes."

Her head popped up. "Yay!"

Alisha laughed and set the little girl on her feet. "Okay. They'll be ready in a minute." Lia ran off calling her brother's name. Alisha hoped they would be as close as she and Lorenzo. Although Lorenzo was five years older, he'd always made time for her and had never minded when she followed him around. While the griddle heated, she cracked eggs in a bowl and took out a skillet. Working efficiently, she timed it so that both foods were done at the same moment. She fixed their plates, added some of her mother's homemade vanilla maple syrup and placed them on the table.

"Corey and Lia, time to eat." Alisha fixed her own plate and placed it on the table. Both children raced into the kitchen. Corey climbed into his chair while Alisha strapped Lia into her booster seat. She recited a blessing and they dug in.

While eating, she sifted through the mail she'd been too tired to look at last night. She paused at an envelope from the court and frowned. Alisha put her fork down and opened it. She could feel her anger rising with each word she read. Her no-good ex-husband had filed to relinquish his parental rights. As far as she was concerned, he'd done that over three years ago. She scanned the document and saw a court date set for early November, two months from now. Not wanting to ruin her day, she shoved it back in the envelope and tossed it aside.

"Can I have another pancake?" Corey asked.

"May I," she corrected.

"May I have another pancake?"

"Yes." Alisha stood and retrieved one of the last two left on the plate. She cut it into pieces and poured the syrup. Only a small amount of syrup remained in the container and she made a mental note to ask her mom for more.

After breakfast, she cleaned up the kitchen, made sure Corey had everything he needed in his backpack and packed a bag for Lia. She'd promised Michelle she would come a little early for the noon party to help set up, so, after wrapping Jade's present, they left.

"Hey, girl," Michelle said when she opened the door. She bent and hugged both children. "Corey, I think you grew again."

Corey nodded. "That's because I'm a big boy. I'm going to a sleepover."

"Wow. That sounds like fun."

Alisha smiled. "Hey, Chelle." They embraced.

"Come on back. I have Jade in the family room watching a Disney movie. I'm hoping that will keep her occupied for at least thirty minutes so we can get the decorations up outside."

"Lia!" Jade jumped up from the floor and ran across the room. She and Lia hugged each other like they hadn't seen each other in years. "Look." She pointed to the television and clapped. *"The Princess and the Frog."*

Alisha chuckled as Lia, Jade and Corey settled themselves in front of the screen. She turned to Michelle. "What do you need me to do?"

"Follow me. We can keep an eye on them through the sliding glass door." She led Alisha outside to the backyard, where her husband, Chris, was setting up tables.

Chris paused in his task to greet Alisha. "Hey, Alisha. How's it going?"

"Crazy busy, as always. How's college life?"

"About to kick into full gear. I already have students coming up to me, asking if they have to read *all* the pages from the chapters listed on the syllabus." He shook his head. "It's going to be a long semester."

She laughed. "Maybe all those first-year chemistry students will get it together."

"And maybe I'll win the lottery this weekend." He went back to the tables.

Alisha and Michelle covered the tables with plastic tablecloths, hung streamers and balloons, and placed the Doc McStuffins–themed centerpieces on the tables.

"Oh, I have to show you what my brother and Chris made for the kids." Michelle nearly dragged Alisha to the garage. She gestured with a flourish. "Aren't they amazing? I hadn't planned on having all the kids here long enough to show a short movie, but I can't let all their hard work go to waste."

Alisha stared at the eight cardboard cars in awe. "They made these?" She walked over to view them more closely. "And there's a cupholder and food tray. I didn't know Chris was so talented."

Michelle snorted. "He's not. Jabari is. Chris just followed directions."

"I thought Jabari was in the service."

"I didn't tell you he retired eight months ago and is home for good?"

"No." She remembered Michelle's brother being much older from the pictures her friend had shared of the handsome air force officer over the years. "I know you're happy." Michelle had had a hard time with him being gone so long.

"I am. He'll be here later, so you'll finally get to meet him."

"Okay. Oh, I need to leave for a short time to drop Corey off at his friend's house for a sleepover that starts at noon."

"That's fine. Lia probably won't even notice you're gone."

They went back inside, peeked in on the kids and then went to prepare the food. Michelle had decided on mini hot dogs, mini pizzas with cheese or pepperoni, and fruit.

"They'll have Goldfish crackers, pretzels and juice boxes while watching the movie. I'm thinking about letting them take the cupcakes home. Their parents can deal with the sugar high," Michelle added with a chuckle.

"Well, if they eat them near the end of the party, the parent will still have to deal with it. So either way works. Do you want me to put these pizzas in the oven now, or wait until closer to the time you plan to serve the food?"

Michelle tapped her finger on the counter. "Let's wait. I'm sure everyone won't be here right at twelve, so they can play a few of the games."

"Okay." Alisha washed her hands. "I'll start on the fruit." She cut pineapple and strawberries into bite-size pieces, washed grapes and divided them into small cups. The individual portions would make it easier to control and prevent little hands from touching everything on the platter.

Chris called out to Michelle through the screen door. "Let me go see what he wants."

Alisha rinsed the cutting board and knife and disposed of the empty strawberry containers and pineapple skin. On the way to the trash, she dropped a couple of pieces. She bent to pick them up.

"Well, hello."

She whirled around at the sound of the deep, masculine voice. Anything she planned to say died on her tongue. Standing in front of her was over six feet of pure rich chocolate fineness. The pictures she had seen of Michelle's brother hadn't come close to capturing his good looks. The upright posture and low haircut spoke to his military background, as did the well-defined muscles of his chest and arms. She shook herself. Grabbing a towel, she quickly wiped her hands and extended the right one. "I'm Alisha, Michelle's friend. Sorry about the backside introduction. I usually start with the face first."

He threw his head back and laughed. "Believe me, I don't have a problem with either. Jabari Sutton. It's a pleasure to meet you, Alisha." He grasped her hand and smiled.

As if the sound of his voice and the glint of desire in his dark eyes hadn't been enough, the moment he touched her, sparks of awareness shot up her arm and her heart skipped a beat. That had *never* happened before. The last thing she needed in her life right now was a smooth-talking man. A slow grin made its way over his face. Alisha snatched her hand back. Not good. *So* not good.

Chapter 2

Jabari hadn't been prepared for the sight that greeted him when he walked into his sister's kitchen. Seeing the sweet curve of Alisha's backside encased in those body-hugging jeans had sent a jolt straight to his groin. Her beautiful coffee-with-cream face, wide brown eyes and engaging smile had him staring like a lovestruck teen. And like he'd told her, he would take any view, front or back. He observed her as she wiped the same spot on the counter for the umpteenth time. Had he made her nervous? Before he could ask her about it, his sister came in.

"Jabari, I didn't hear you come in." Michelle rushed over and hugged him.

"Hey, Chelle."

"Have you met my friend Alisha?"

His gaze locked on Alisha's, he said, "We've already taken care of the introductions."

"Really? I see." She smiled knowingly. "Hmm…" The doorbell rang. "I'll be right back."

He followed her departure and then shifted his attention back to Alisha. "How long have you and Chelle known each other?"

"We met in college."

"Oh, so you're her friend from nursing school." That put her closer to his sister's age and almost a decade younger than him. He didn't typically date women more than a couple of years younger than him because, at his age, he wanted someone already stable and settled into a career. Michelle's words about him being picky rang in his ears. He'd concede her a point on this issue. However, since Alisha had gone to school with Michelle, she would reasonably be well into her career. A plus in his book.

"Yep, that's me." Alisha placed cups of fruit on a tray.

Michelle came back with two women who had three children between them and made the introductions. "I'm going to take them outside."

"I'll be right behind you after I put these hot dogs on the buns," Alisha said.

"Thanks." Michelle exited, chatting with the two women.

Jabari continued to stare at Alisha.

"I guess the party's starting."

"Yeah, I guess so." He stood there a moment longer. "I'm going to find Chris." It took several seconds before he could get his feet to move. He finally forced himself to leave. *I'm almost forty. Why am I acting like someone half my age?* He shook his head and went out the sliding glass door off the family room. A small girl ran past him and Jabari almost tripped over her.

He reached out to steady her. "Whoa, little one. Be careful." She smiled up at him and resumed her play with the other two children he'd seen. His four-year-old niece spotted him and ran toward him as fast as her legs could carry her.

"Uncle Jay!"

Jabari scooped her up and kissed her cheek. "Hey, birthday girl. You've got a lot of friends here for your party." For the first time, he noticed another little girl about Jade's age with an older boy holding her hand. They favored one another enough to be siblings. He didn't see another parent and wondered if their mother had dropped them off earlier.

"Yes." Jade squirmed in his arms. "Down, please."

He set her on her feet and she went over to the little girl and hugged her.

The purity and innocence of the relationship made Jabari smile. No pretense, no games. Life seemed to be so much simpler at that age.

"Corey, your mom is ready," Michelle called out.

"Yes!" The older boy kissed his sister and waved as he hurried inside.

Jabari made his way over to where Chris was removing a canopy from a box. "What's up?"

"Hey, Jay. You're just in time to help me put this up. The box says it's an easy up, but I can't remember one time when it took less than twenty minutes."

He laughed. "Yeah, well." He grabbed the other end of the box and held it while Chris pulled the canopy out.

"Chelle, I'm leaving."

Jabari turned at the sound of Alisha's voice. She glanced his way briefly and then focused on Chelle, who stood in the doorway talking and nodding. He didn't even want to think about why he felt disappointed by Alisha's leaving.

"All right, you take the end closest to you and I'll get this one. Maybe we can have it up before the party ends."

"Chris, I've done this a hundred times alone and it doesn't take long." They worked in tandem and, true to Jabari's prediction, had it in place five minutes later.

Chris stepped back and surveyed the covering. "Michelle is right. You are handy to have around." He gestured to a folding table leaning against a column. "We can use this table for the projector."

He assembled the table. "What are you going to use as a screen?"

"Your sister had me up at the crack of dawn running around looking for something *appropriate*. I tried to tell her we could just use one of those white sheets in the house, but no. She said that was tacky."

Jabari laughed. He could imagine the look on Chelle's face at Chris's suggestion. She often called Jabari anal, picky and precise, but when it came to throwing a party, she could be the same way.

"We ended up at a fabric store and bought the stuff they used for window shades back in the day." He shook his head. "Man, the next time she wants to throw a party, I'm leaving town."

"Hey, that's my sister you're talking about."

"Yeah, and she's my wife. Speaking of women, see that one who just walked in with the blue top and jeans?"

"What about her?"

"She works with Michelle and is single."

"Hmm." She looked nice, but he didn't feel any of the same interest he'd felt with Alisha.

"That's all you have to say?"

Jabari shrugged. "She's a beautiful woman. What do you know about Chelle's friend Alisha?"

"Alisha is cool people and like a sister."

"What—"

"Can you guys come help with the bubbles while I get the face painting going?" Michelle asked, interrupting his next question.

Chris groaned. "Baby, this was supposed to be a simple little get-together where the kids ran around and played for a while, ate, had cake and opened presents. When did you decide on face painting, bubbles and all these other games you have set up?"

She patted his cheek. "It's just a few little fun games to keep them engaged." She took his hand and led him over to the table.

Jabari followed, chuckling. A couple more children had arrived and all clamored for one of the small bottles of bubbles. He and Chris removed the inner seals and handed each child one, taking time to help the youngest ones, including Jade. It brought to mind a question he'd been wondering about. "Chelle, what happened to the older boy? I saw him leaving."

"Oh, he's gone to a sleepover at his friend's house. He was just here for a short time. This is his sister, Lia." She touched the shoulder of the little girl his niece seemed so fond of. "She and Jade are like two peas in a pod and would spend every day together if we let them," she added with a smile. "Oh, good, Alisha's back. I'll have her help me assemble the pizzas and put them in the oven."

He tried to keep his features neutral, but inside his level of excitement rose a notch. Once again, he didn't stop to analyze his reaction to her.

"Can you and Chris handle this?"

He snorted. "Girl, please. You do remember what I've been doing for the past twenty years? I'm not bubble-challenged. Watch?" He demonstrated blowing a large bubble and caught it on the end of the wand.

"Ooh, look! It's big," one of the children said.

Jabari turned Michelle's way. "I rest my case."

Chris and Michelle laughed and Michelle said, "Show-off," as she walked away.

He and Chris entertained the children for a good five minutes before they were off to some other activity manned by one of the mothers. They moved from table to table, never staying at one for more than a few minutes. A short while later, Alisha and Michelle came out with platters of food. He studied Alisha's interaction with the children. She was a natural. "Alisha's pretty good with the kids."

Chris laughed. "I should hope so, since she has two of her own."

Jabari couldn't disguise his surprise or the momentary wave of disappointment. He'd thought she was just there to help Michelle. Then again, it was a kids' party, so he shouldn't have been shocked to find out she had children, even though he had been hoping the former. He made it a practice of steering clear of women with kids because somewhere there was a father, absent or not, and he would rather not add that kind of drama to his life.

"What?" Chris scrutinized Jabari. "I take it she's caught your attention."

"Maybe, but now—"

"Alisha's not married. She's been divorced a little over three years."

He frowned. He'd guessed her to be around Chelle's

age, so how old had she been when she got married? He shouldn't care, yet he couldn't stop staring at her.

Alisha kept sneaking peeks at Jabari throughout the party. She marveled at his patience when showing one of the little boys how to blow a bubble. He'd even gotten down on all fours on the grass and given "horsie-back" rides to the children. Lia had gone back for a second ride. When it came time for the movie, he helped the excited children into their cars and even passed out the snacks.

"Is everybody ready for the movie?" Chris asked.

"Yes," they all shouted.

Twenty minutes into the *Mickey Mouse Clubhouse* movie, Michelle sidled up next to Alisha. "Would you look at this? They haven't been still the entire day and now their eyes are glued to the screen."

Alisha smiled. "You're going to have to pry them out of those cars when it's over."

"My brother is a genius."

Alisha glanced over at Jabari, who sat on the other side of the yard, talking to Chris. "That he is." As if sensing her scrutiny, he turned her way. A slow smile inched its way across his face. "He's really good with the kids. Does he have any?"

"Yes, he is, and no. I know he wants them. Oh, and don't think I didn't notice all those sparks between you two."

"What sparks? Now, he is a cutie, but I told you that a long time ago."

"Mmm-hmm, whatever you say."

"Girl, I don't even want to hear the word *spark*," she mumbled. "I just received papers from the court and Wayne is trying to relinquish his parental rights."

"You have got to be kidding me. The only reason he's doing it is so he'll be off the hook for the child support he's never paid."

"You've got that right. I don't think the judge will let that happen, though it would make my life so much easier. I don't need his money and my babies won't ever have to worry about whether their sorry excuse for a father is going show up after making a promise." Alisha got angry all over again thinking about the many times Wayne had promised to pick up Corey and take him out, but never showed. Less than a year after their divorce, he'd stopped coming around altogether. And Corey had stopped asking.

"If you need any support, you know I'm there."

"I know and I appreciate it. We should probably start on the cleanup while they're engrossed in the movie."

"Good idea. Not that there's a lot to do since you've already washed up most of the dishes." Michelle spoke quietly to the three other mothers, and then she and Alisha collected the empty platters and bowls and took them inside.

By the time they finished, the movie had ended and it was time for cake and presents. The entire party lasted a little over two hours, and just about all of the children looked as if they would be asleep before their parents could strap them into their car seats. Alisha picked up Lia. "Did you have fun?"

"Yes," Lia said, yawning and laying her head on Alisha's shoulder.

"Ready for a nap?"

"No."

She chuckled. Her baby would be out in less than two minutes. She rubbed Lia's back and felt when her daughter's breathing pattern changed.

Chris came in carrying a sleeping Jade. "I guess they partied too hard."

Michelle made two pallets on the floor in the family room. "They can sleep in here."

Alisha and Chris laid the sleeping girls down and Michelle covered them with a light blanket. The adults tiptoed out and went into the kitchen.

"Well, we survived," Michelle said. "And, honey, you and Jay were so wonderful letting the kids go for rides on your backs. You never let me go for a ride."

Chris grinned. "Sure I do. How do you think—?"

"Okay, you two," Alisha cut in. "Remember, I'm standing here. I do not need to hear any of this." She didn't need to be reminded of everything she'd been missing—though, as of late, she hadn't had time to think about anything except work and family.

Jabari came in a moment later. "They are out like a light."

"I'm going to let Lia sleep for a little while before I leave. She gets cranky when she doesn't get her nap in," Alisha said, taking a seat at the table.

Michelle joined her. "You should just let her spend the night. That way you can have an evening to yourself."

"Thanks for the offer, but I know you're tired from all the work you did on the party."

Michelle waved Alisha off. "Girl, Lia's no trouble. Besides, she and Jade will probably sleep hard tonight."

Chris placed a hand on his wife's shoulder. "She's right, Alisha. You know we don't mind keeping her."

"And the offer is only good for the next—" Michelle glanced down at her watch "—five minutes. After that, it's gone."

Alisha smiled. "In that case, I'll take it. But it's

been so long since I had an evening to myself I have no idea what to do. If I had known earlier, I would've gone to Desiree's shop and bought at least one of those bath bombs." Her sister-in-law owned a bath and body shop in Old Sacramento and she had promised Corey she'd get him another bar of the soap with the animals inside. It would be the perfect time to go. "Hmm, dinner without a little hand grabbing food off my plate, a nice glass of wine, candles and a long soak in the tub would be perfect."

"That sounds good, but what would be even better is having a nice guy take you out for a night on the town."

"You might be right, Chelle, but, unless you have one stashed in your back pocket, tonight I'll be rolling solo." They all laughed.

"A beautiful woman like you shouldn't have to roll solo," Jabari said.

Alisha shifted in her chair to face him. "That may be true, but sometimes that's how it is."

He leaned on the bar and clasped his hands together. "But tonight doesn't have to be one of those times."

The way he stared at her had her heart beating a mile a minute. What was he saying? "What does that mean?"

"It means I'd like to take you out to dinner."

Alisha took a quick glimpse over her shoulder and saw both Michelle and Chris with their mouths hanging open.

Michelle jumped up from her chair. "We're going to check on the girls." She grabbed Chris by the hand and dragged him out.

Jabari came around the bar and took the chair Michelle had vacated. "So what do you say?"

She was so shocked it took her a moment to find her voice. "Are you serious?"

"Of course. Why wouldn't I be?"

"Let's see, you don't know me and I don't know you."

"Not true. We had a very memorable introduction."

Alisha felt her cheeks warm.

"And what better way to get to know each other than over a nice dinner."

She mentally went through her mind to recall the last time she'd gone out with a man and, for the life of her, she couldn't remember. Was it this year or last? Her last two dates had turned out to be a complete waste of time and she had decided to push relationships to the back burner and focus on her children. Besides, she had no intentions of parading a string of men through her house.

"What do you say?"

"Sure" tumbled out of her mouth before she could stop it.

Jabari gave her a sexy smile. "Dinner was just a suggestion, but we can do whatever you like."

"No, no, dinner is fine." He really needed to stop smiling at her like that. He made her body react in ways she had long forgotten.

He whipped out his cell. "What's your address and phone number?"

Alisha rattled off the information.

"You mentioned wanting to stop at a shop in Old Sac?"

"My sister-in-law's store."

"What time does it close?"

"Six or six thirty, I can't remember."

Jabari pocketed the phone. "If you want, we can stop by there before dinner."

She really wanted to go, but if Desiree saw them, she

would tell Lorenzo. The last thing Alisha needed was her overprotective brother showing up on her doorstep first thing in the morning looking for answers. Then again, Desiree most likely would be in the back, so if they got in and out quickly…

"Alisha?"

Jabari calling her name snapped her out of her thoughts. "Sorry, I was just thinking. That would be fine. It won't take me long to find what I want."

He stood and extended his hand. "You're a free woman tonight. We have all evening."

She hesitated briefly before putting her hand in his and letting him help her to her feet.

He glimpsed at his watch. "It's two fifteen now. If I picked you up at four, would that be enough time for you to get ready?"

Alisha nodded. In reality, she had no idea what to wear. And her hair…she'd thrown it up in a ponytail and would have to flat-iron it. The drive from Folsom to Roseville would take about twenty minutes. "I'd better get going."

"Me, too. I don't want to mess up the first date by being late."

She smiled. "Well, with all the rides you let the kids have on your back, I'll be willing to give you a fifteen-minute grace period."

Jabari chuckled. "I appreciate that. Hopefully, it won't be necessary."

They fell silent. Belatedly, Alisha realized he was still holding her hand. She gently pulled away. "Um, I'm going to tell Chelle I'm leaving."

"I'm sure my sister is right around the corner listening, so you won't have to go far." To prove his point, he took four steps to where the kitchen opened into the family room, leaned around the corner and laughed. He pulled Michelle into the kitchen. "Busted. I told you she'd be listening."

Michelle didn't look guilty at all. "Hey, you are two of my favorite people and I needed to make sure everything was okay."

Alisha shook her head. "Since you were listening, you know I have a short window to get ready. Lia has a couple changes of clothes in her bag, but I didn't pack any pajamas."

"She can wear a pair of Jade's. They're about the same size. I'll walk you out." As soon as they were out of earshot, she squealed. "I can't believe you and Jay are going out. It would be so cool if you got together."

She rolled her eyes. "It's one date, Chelle. He probably offered because you made that comment about me needing to go out."

Michelle shrugged. "You do need to go out. Your entire life has revolved around the hospital and the kids for the past four years. Even before your divorce, he was out running around while you were stuck at home with *his* son. And those dates afterward—if you can call them that—weren't worth the time it took for you to get dressed."

Her friend had a point. "You're right. See you later." One night, one date. She could do that.

Chapter 3

"I see you're not wasting any time, Jay," Chris said, leaning against the kitchen entryway. "I know you're getting older and all, but you met the woman three hours ago."

Jabari smiled. "You said she was cool people and I trust your judgment. It's just one date."

"It may be just one date," Michelle said, joining them, "but she's been through too much already to have her heart broken by another man. You're my brother and I love you. However, if you hurt her, I will never speak to you again."

"That's pretty harsh, sis. And you know I don't make it a practice of running through women or playing those kinds of games. What happened with her ex?" He wasn't sure he wanted to know, but he also didn't want to be blindsided by any potential issues, like the man wanting to come back and reclaim his family.

"It's not my place to say. If things go well tonight, maybe she'll share."

Jabari stared at her incredulously. "First you tell me she's been through too much, and now you're saying you won't tell me what happened. How're you going to leave me hanging like that?"

Chris chuckled.

"Chris, help me out, man."

Michelle turned to her husband. "Don't you say one word, Chris. We're staying out of this."

Chris shook his head. "Sorry, bro."

She smiled. "Thanks, baby." She came up on tiptoe to kiss Jabari's cheek. "You'd better get going. You don't want to be late for your date. El Dorado Hills isn't down the street from Roseville, and you know there's always a little traffic." She pushed him toward the front.

"I took care of you and this is how you treat me?" Jabari said with a laugh. He glanced over his shoulder at Chris, who had followed them to the door.

Chris mouthed, "I'll text you."

He nodded. "See you guys later. Kiss Jade for me when she wakes up." He loped down the walkway to his car, parked in the driveway.

Michelle smiled sweetly and waved as he got into his car. "Have fun."

He planned to. Though he still had a few reservations, he was looking forward to the evening. Now he needed to figure out which restaurant to choose. While he drove, he had a hard time remembering any. He'd been away for two decades and things had changed considerably. The area where he resided hadn't even existed ten years ago. Much of the drive up Highway 50 had been open land back then.

Jabari made it home in less than twenty minutes and headed straight for the shower. Afterward, he powered up his laptop and searched for restaurants. Since Alisha had mentioned going to Old Sacramento, he started there. After clicking on several and checking out the menus, he settled on Dawson's Steakhouse in the Hyatt Hotel. It was a little pricey, but for some reason, he wanted to do things differently with Alisha. Besides, it sounded like she needed to have a good time.

His mind went back to Michelle's statement about not wanting Alisha to be hurt again. The text from his brother-in-law was short and to the point: Her ex is a jerk. Cheated and left her when she was 8 months pregnant with Lia. Jabari couldn't even imagine how hard it must be for her to work and manage two kids alone, though he knew women did it every day.

Jabari stood and went to the closet. Since he hadn't had to worry about clothing for so long, his wardrobe was seriously lacking. He'd purchased a couple of suits, a few dress shirts and slacks, but if he planned to date more often, he would need a major overhaul. He selected his charcoal gray suit and white silk tee, not wanting to bother with a tie. While he dressed, his thoughts went back to Alisha and what Chris had said about her ex. Jabari's idea of settling down had never included a ready-made family. He'd witnessed several of his friends become embroiled in one drama after another brought on by an ex, and he had made it a practice to steer clear of those types of relationships. Alisha fell squarely into that category, yet he'd asked her out anyway.

Grabbing his keys, he bounded down the stairs to the garage. He typed her address into the navigation system and backed out. As his sister had pointed out, there was some traffic. He parked in front of Alisha's one-story house with one minute to spare. Jabari took in the well-manicured lawn while waiting for her to open the door and wondered if she had done it herself or had hired a service. He turned when the door opened. All the reasons why he shouldn't pursue anything with this woman fell away when she smiled at him. He had thought her beautiful in the jeans and ponytail. But the woman standing before him now rendered him momentarily speechless. Her hair flowed around her shoulders, and she wore a long-sleeved off-the-shoulder purple dress that skimmed her curves and stopped just above the knee, revealing long, toned legs and a pair of killer black heels.

"Hey, Jabari. Four o'clock on the dot. Come on in," Alisha said with a smile, stepping aside so he could enter.

Jabari returned her smile. "Blame it on the military. I've never liked being late, and even more so now." In his mind, anything less than ten minutes before the appointed time constituted being late. "Nice place." The living room was decorated in neutral colors, with plush, golden brown carpeting.

"Thanks. Have a seat and I'll be right back."

He watched her strut off and smiled again. While waiting, he walked over to the walls where several pictures hung of her and the children at various ages. He saw one of her with an older couple and a man he assumed to be her brother, and another one of her and Chelle in their caps and gowns. Jabari had been saddened that he couldn't attend his sister's graduation. He didn't see any of Alisha's ex with the children and he speculated on just how involved the man was in their lives. That gave Jabari hope that there wouldn't be any interference.

"I'm ready."

He spun around at the sound of Alisha's voice. "So am I." He gestured her toward the door, waited until she locked it and led her to his car.

"Nice ride," Alisha said as he helped her in.

Even in her heels, he still eclipsed her height by a good six inches. The soft scent of her perfume wafted into his nose. It smelled warm and comforting, with a hint of sensuality. "Thanks." Jabari closed the door, rounded the fender and slid in on the driver's side. "After driving the same car for the past fifteen years, I thought it was time for something new. And because I don't spend recklessly, I figured I could splurge a little." He had purchased the new Audi sedan a month after his retirement.

She turned in her seat. "Or being a miser, according to your sister."

He chuckled and shook his head. "Family. Gotta love 'em." He started the engine and drove off. "I hope you don't mind Dawson's Steakhouse in the Hyatt downtown. I made a reservation for five forty-five. It was either that or nine and I opted for the earlier time in case we wanted to do something else later, if that's okay. And we can stop at your sister-in-law's store first."

"It's just fine. Thank you."

Jabari's eyes left the road briefly to glance her way. She sat looking out the window and clasping and unclasping her hands. Did he make her nervous? he wondered again. "Are you okay?"

"Fine, why?"

"You seem nervous."

She continued to stare out the window. "It's been a really long time since I've gone out, that's all."

"That makes two of us," he murmured.

Alisha whipped her head around. "Are the women around here crazy? Or is it you? You're not one of those men with a long laundry list of qualities a woman needs to have, are you?"

He laughed. "Honestly, probably a little bit of both." Since she and Michelle were friends, his sister had more than likely told Alisha he was picky. He preferred the term *selective.*

"I guess I should I be happy I made the cut, then, huh?"

"I could say the same thing. I'm sure you have standards when it comes to men."

"Yeah, I do," she said softly.

Jabari thought he heard something that sounded like regret in her voice and wanted to ask about it, but he didn't press. That was a conversation for a later time. "So, now that we've gotten that out of the way, we can relax and enjoy each other's company. It's been a while for both of us, so let's have some fun. Deal?" He held out his hand.

"Deal." She placed her hand in his palm.

He brought it to his lips, placed a soft kiss on the back and smiled. *It's going to be a good night.*

The spot on Alisha's hand Jabari had kissed was still tingling by the time they reached Old Sac. She told him to park in the underground garage near the Railroad Museum, rather than bother with searching for parking on the street.

"Is the store nearby?"

"It's about a block and a half away, but with all these people out here, you probably won't find any parking."

Jabari got into the line leading into the garage. "Will you be okay walking in those shoes?"

Alisha waved him off. "They're not that high, and as long as we're not planning to walk around for the next three hours, I'll be good." Her shoes were the least of her concerns. She just hoped to get in and out without Desiree seeing her. If she hadn't promised Corey more of the soap her sister-in-law had made, she would have postponed the trip for another time. Somehow, Desiree had created a clear bar that had a small toy inside, only reachable once the soap was almost completely used. Alisha hadn't had to coerce her son into the tub once since the first night he'd used it.

Jabari found a spot on the second level and they walked back downstairs and started up the walk. He reached for her hand and entwined their fingers as if it was the most natural thing. Her hopes were dashed as soon as she walked through the door. Desiree stood less than three feet away. Her gaze drifted down to Alisha's and Jabari's hands, then back up.

She came toward them with a curious smile. "Hey, girl."

"Hey, Desiree."

She hugged her sister-in-law and said in a low murmur that only Alisha could hear, "I will be calling you to find out all about Mr. Tall, Dark and Fine." Stepping back, she gave Alisha a look.

"Desiree, this is Jabari Sutton. Jabari, my sister-in-law, Desiree Hunter."

"It's a pleasure to meet you, Desiree. You have a nice place."

"Nice to meet you, too, and thank you. We have a

section for men you're welcome to check out. Casey can answer any questions you might have." Desiree called the young woman over and she led Jabari away. "Now, where did you meet him and how long have you two been dating? Does Lorenzo know about him?"

"I met him today at Jade's birthday party. He's Michelle's brother." Desiree had met Michelle at the bridal shower Alisha had coordinated for Desiree. "We were sitting around talking after the party and Michelle offered to keep Lia for the night since Corey is at his friend's sleepover, so I can have a free night."

Desiree's brows knitted in confusion. "How does that translate to a date?"

Alisha told her about the conversation they'd had and Michelle's comment about Alisha needing a date. "Jabari happened to be standing there and he asked me out."

"Just like that."

"Yep." She shifted her gaze to Jabari and saw him sniffing a couple of the products. She still couldn't believe she had agreed to the date. She had turned down men over the past several months without batting an eye but had barely hesitated when he asked.

"Well, the brother is fine with a capital *F.* If you need anything to spice up your evening just let me know," Desiree added with a smile.

"Dinner. That's it. I came to get more soap for Corey. The boy won't bathe with anything else. That soap is about the size of a quarter and he insists on using it. He got the toy out two weeks ago, but I guess he figures I won't buy more until it's gone."

She laughed. "I have my nephew covered. He told me he likes cars, so I made some in his favorite blue color. I'll get them. Oh, and I know how much Lia loves her bubbles, so I have something for her, too."

Alisha shook her head. In less than two months, Desiree had both children spoiled rotten. "What about me?"

"I told you…massage oils, body paint…"

"I just met the man four hours ago," she whispered, making sure Jabari hadn't heard. "A bath bomb. That's all I want. Since I'll have the house to myself tonight, I'm going to finally take that long-overdue soak in the tub." She had been excited about the master bathroom when she bought the house because the tub had spa jets. She could count on one hand the number of times she had been able to use it. Alisha planned to take full advantage of her "me time."

Desiree laughed as she walked away.

Alisha shook her head and went over to where Jabari still stood. "Find anything?"

"Actually, yes. I've never thought about coming into one of these places because I considered them women's-only spaces, but Desiree has a nice selection." He picked up two bars of citrus basil soap and a bottle of the shower gel. "Are you getting anything?"

"Yes. Corey's soap, some bubble bath for Lia and a bath bomb for me."

"Bath bomb?"

She chuckled at his puzzled expression. "You put it in your bath and it dissolves, leaving a nice fragrance and softening the water."

Desiree came back and handed her the items in a small basket. "I chose the vanilla and ylang-ylang bath bomb for you. It has cocoa butter, and the fragrance is soft and relaxing." She held it up for Alisha to smell.

"Oh, this does smell good. I think I want two." Alisha went over to the tub and grabbed another one.

Jabari relieved her of the basket and headed for the checkout.

"You might want to hold on to that one, sis," Desiree said. "Four hours, and he's paying."

Alisha hadn't intended for him to pay and hurried to catch up with him. "What are you doing?"

"Paying for our stuff." He handed Casey his credit card.

"I can pay for mine." She reached into her purse for her wallet.

"I know you can pay for it. Put your money away, Alisha. I've got it this time."

His softly spoken words and compassionate expression made her heart flip. To cover her rising attraction, she averted her eyes and shoved her wallet back into her purse. Alisha chanced a glance over her shoulder and saw Desiree viewing the exchange with mild amusement.

Jabari checked his watch. "We should probably head over to the restaurant."

"Okay. See you later, Desiree."

"Enjoy your evening. Hope to see you again, Jabari."

"I'll definitely have to stop in again. Thanks."

As they walked back to the parking garage, Alisha said, "You really didn't have to pay, you know."

"Think of it as a thank-you for agreeing to go out with me tonight." He moved closer to her to let some people pass. "I haven't been down here in years. Maybe we can come back another time whenever your schedule is free."

"I'll let you know." She wasn't ready to commit to anything past this evening.

"Fair enough." Once on the road again, he said, "I forgot about all these one-way streets. I hope I don't turn down one going the wrong way."

"It does take some getting used to."

He pulled into the valet lane at the Hyatt a couple of minutes later and handed the car off. Alisha silently admired his lean, muscular frame in the tailored slacks and silk tee. Jabari slipped into his suit coat, then helped her out of the car.

"I've never been here, so I hope it's okay. If not, we can go somewhere else."

Alisha patted his arm. "I'm sure it'll be fine. You can't go wrong with a steakhouse." The moment she stepped into the restaurant, she sent up a silent thank-you that she had chosen a dress. She didn't know what she had expected—maybe a moderately priced place—but certainly not this high-end restaurant. It took a lot to impress her, but Jabari had done it twice in the past half hour.

Jabari gave his name to the hostess and she led them to a booth.

"This is lovely." Alisha picked up her menu and scanned the selections.

"What looks good?"

"Everything," she answered with a chuckle. A server came to take their drink order and they both ordered glasses of chardonnay.

The server came back a few minutes later and placed a glass in front of each of them. "Are you ready to order?"

Jabari glanced at Alisha and she nodded. "Yes."

She chose the six-ounce fillet, while Jabari opted for the salt-crusted prime rib. They decided to share the asparagus and the lobster mac and cheese.

When they were alone again, Jabari lifted his glass. "To an evening of good company, great conversation and a whole lot of fun."

Alisha touched her glass to his. "Amen." She took a small sip. "How does it feel to be out of the military after so many years?"

"It took a lot of adjusting at first, not having to be up before the crack of dawn, and not having drills or deployments, but my nine-to-five at the tech company where I work is a welcome change."

"Do you miss it?"

"Sometimes. It's the only life I knew for the past twenty years."

"You never married?"

"Nah. There aren't a lot of women who can handle their husbands being away for a year or two at a time. Michelle said you were divorced."

She had expected the subject to come up, and she supposed it was better to get it out of the way early and move on. "For over three years. He decided one day that he didn't want to be a husband or father and had the women to prove it." Alisha took another sip of her wine, a larger one this time.

"I'm sorry."

"Don't be. It's over and done."

Jabari shook his head. "The man must be out of his mind."

A smile played around the corners of her mouth. "According to my mother, yes. My brother, on the other hand… Well, let's just say it took a whole lot of convincing to keep him and my two male cousins who live here from doing my ex bodily harm."

"Had it been my sister, no amount of convincing would've kept him safe," he said, his jaw tight.

"I know." Alisha covered his hand with hers. "Michelle is lucky to have you as her brother." She instinctively knew that he would make some woman a great husband and protect her with his life, if necessary.

"We're lucky to have each other."

"You were a natural with the kids," she said, changing the subject. "Jade seems to have gotten used to you being around."

"I had only seen Jade twice before I retired. Getting to know her has been one of the best things in my life. I love that little girl."

Her heart melted. "It's obvious that she loves you, too. All the kids did."

Jabari chuckled. "I'm sure crawling around the grass on all fours with a couple of kids on my back yelling 'go, go' probably had a lot to do with it."

She smiled. "You're probably right." The server returned with their food. For the first few minutes they ate in silence and then continued the conversation.

"I admit I give in to Jade way too easily. She looks at me with those big sad eyes and I let her have whatever she wants."

Alisha pointed her fork his way. "Wait until you have your own. You'll become immune to begging in all forms—sad eyes, constant pleas, promises to act nice, tears—and walk away. You're going to learn quick how to say *no*." While eating, they swapped stories about his niece and her two children. She found herself relaxing and thoroughly enjoying his company and, as they finished the meal, she didn't want the evening to end.

He placed his fork on the empty plate. "Would you like something else? Dessert?"

"No, thank you. Everything was delicious."

"I think I want to get the chocolate dome to go."

"You don't have to get it to go. We can stay here and eat it."

"I'm a little too full right now. Besides, if I save it for later, maybe I can convince you to share it with me."

"Well, I've never been known to turn down chocolate."

Jabari laughed softly and signaled the server. After placing the order, he clasped his hands together on the table. "Is there any place you'd like to go?"

"I can't think of anywhere. Pretty much everything in my life revolves around Corey and Lia."

The server returned with the bagged dessert. Jabari thanked him. To Alisha he said, "Would you be okay with going back over to Old Sac to walk around? We won't stay too long." He leaned forward and a sexy grin tilted the corner of his mouth. "Although I can always carry you if your feet start to hurt."

An image of being cradled in in his strong arms flashed in her mind and her pulse skipped. "I…um… That won't be necessary," Alisha said with a nervous chuckle.

Jabari settled the bill, stood and helped Alisha to her feet. "We'll save it for another time, then."

I'm not touching that comment. Nope, no way, no how. They drove back, parked in the same garage and strolled leisurely down the street. The night crowd had descended on the area and they had to walk closer together. He held her hand and the same warmth she'd felt in Michelle's kitchen flowed up her arm. Lively chatter surrounded them, rhythmic music spilled out of buildings and the smell of sweet treats permeated the air.

"This is nice. I didn't realize this place was so popular."

"This crowd is nothing. You should see it in the summer. No way would we have found parking in the garage this late."

"I'll have to make a point of coming back then."

They walked two blocks, went up another one and ended up on the cobblestoned street, stopping inside several shops to look around.

When they turned the corner leading back toward the garage, Jabari asked, "Are your feet okay?"

"Yes." In reality, her feet were killing her. These days she rarely wore heels, with the last time being her brother's wedding at the beginning of the month. But she couldn't tell Jabari that, not with his suggestion of carrying her. Alisha had no doubts that he would make good on it. With the current technology, a photo of her being carried through Old Sacramento would be uploaded to every social media outlet and turned into the latest meme before they left the parking lot. As soon as she got in the car, she toed off the shoes and released a deep sigh of relief.

"You know, we could have shortened the walk if you'd told me your feet were hurting." Jabari slanted her an amused glance.

She burst out laughing. "You knew?"

"Of course. I could tell before I asked. Why do you think I turned the corner and didn't keep going down the block?"

"I can't believe you."

He shrugged and exited the lot.

Alisha remained silent for most of the ride, agonizing over whether she should invite him in once they reached her house. In the two years since moving there, no men except those in her family had been there. But she had already sort of told him that she would share the dessert. By the time he pulled into her driveway and they got to her front door, she still hadn't decided. It would be easy to decline, close the door and enjoy her solitary evening. She unlocked the door and faced him, ready to tell him just that. "Would you like to come in for a few minutes?" tumbled out instead.

Jabari held up the bag. "Absolutely. We have to eat our dessert." He followed her inside and chuckled when she immediately removed her shoes.

"Hey, working in the hospital doesn't require heels. We can take the cake into the family room." She led him through the kitchen, where she deposited the bag from Desiree's shop and retrieved two saucers and forks before continuing to the family room on the opposite side. She sat on the sofa and placed the dishes on the table.

He sat next to her and removed the cake from the bag. "We don't need to mess up any dishes." He moved the plates aside, eased one of the forks from her hand and held the container between them. "Go ahead."

Alisha hesitantly forked up a portion and brought it to her mouth. The combination of chocolate mousse and bourbon caramel center on top of chocolate cake exploded on her tongue and she stifled a moan.

"How is it?"

"*So* good."

Jabari dug out a portion and brought it to his mouth. He nodded. "Oh, this is good."

He licked the remaining chocolate off the fork and the sight sent a shock of desire through her. She tried to ignore it and stuck her fork into the container. Two bites in, she realized the intimacy of sharing the slice of cake did nothing to calm the surge of heat thrumming through her body. Her gaze dropped to Jabari's mouth and the way he slid the fork in and out. It had been a long time since she responded to a man this way. If she were being honest, she would acknowledge that it had never happened. Not even with her ex-husband.

"You should stop looking at me that way."

She jerked her gaze up. "Huh? What? Looking at you how?"

"Like you want to be kissed," he said, his voice low and seductive. "Do you?"

Alisha couldn't respond if her life depended on it. A thousand and one reasons why she should send him and his sinful cake packing rushed through her mind. Yet, she couldn't push the words past her lips. Once again, she glanced down at his full, sexy lips. One kiss. What could it hurt? She tilted her head.

Jabari leaned closer, leaving less than an inch between their mouths. "Do you?"

"Yes," she whispered. He captured her mouth with lightning speed, sending her senses spiraling out of control. He tasted of chocolate and his own unique flavor and teased and swirled his tongue around hers with a sensual finesse that left her weak. She had no idea how he accomplished it, but the cake and forks were gone and she ended up straddling his lap with her dress hiked around her hips. His hands blazed a path over her thighs and she moaned.

At length, he eased back. "I could easily become addicted to your kiss."

She could say the same but needed to put the brakes on whatever was happening between them.

"What are you doing next weekend?" he asked.

Alisha left his lap and reclaimed her seat on the sofa. "I had a really good time tonight, but I'm not sure if I'm ready to get involved with someone right now."

"I can understand that with what you've gone through, but I'd like to get to know you, Alisha. We can go as slow as you need."

She couldn't deny the chemistry between them, but she was also intrigued by his gentleness. "Okay."

Jabari leaned over and touched his mouth to hers. "I should get going. I'll call you and we can talk about our next date."

She nodded and placed the lid on the unfinished cake. "Don't forget this."

He stood. "No, you finish the rest. There isn't much left."

As she'd told him earlier, she never turned down chocolate. Alisha pushed to her feet and walked him to the door.

He slid an arm around her waist. "Thank you for spending the evening with me. I hope you enjoyed it as much as I did."

"I did. Thank you."

He lowered his head and slid his tongue between her parted lips in a long, drugging kiss.

"Good night, Alisha." And he was gone.

Alisha locked the door and rested her forehead against it. She'd told herself one kiss couldn't hurt. She was wrong. It could change everything.

Chapter 4

Monday afternoon, Jabari sat in his office staring out of the window, thinking about Alisha. It had been the best date he'd had in a long while. He had enjoyed laughing and conversing over dinner and walking around downtown. However, the highlight of the evening for him had been the sweet kisses they'd shared. He'd wanted to keep right on kissing her all night but sensed her pulling back. She'd voiced her hesitations and he understood them. He had some of his own with regard to dating a woman with children, but that didn't stop him from asking her out again.

"You can't protect my company from data breaches if you're staring out the window all day."

Jabari slowly rotated in his chair and saw his best friend, Martin Walters, leaning against the doorframe. "*Your* company? As I recall, a good portion of my money is invested, too."

Martin smiled, entered the office and sat across from Jabari. "I wanted to get an update on the red flags you found." Someone had tried accessing the system last week.

"So far nothing more than what I told you on Friday. Whoever it is tried to log on at least four times but didn't get in because they weren't able to bypass the extra security we put in place." The company planned to unveil new wireless technology to improve wave signals to smartphones and other mobile devices at the start of next year and Jabari had installed more firewalls.

"Good. I made some improvements to our existing design and I'm thinking about hiring a couple of guys I used to work with to work on the specs off-site. I don't want anyone to get wind of what's coming. This is going to revolutionize the range and coverage of wireless signals."

"Can you trust these guys?"

"Yes. I'm going to try to set up a meeting with them for later this week and I want you to be there."

"I assume it won't be here," Jabari guessed.

"No."

"In the meantime, I'll make sure my team is monitoring the system closely. Also, I wanted to let you know that I'm going to be conducting the quarterly security check." In an effort to ensure that the company's best practices were being applied, Jabari sent fake phishing emails to the employees once a quarter. If an employee clicked on the pseudo-malicious link, it would redirect them to an internal portal and his security team would explain what they did wrong and how to correct it in the future.

"Okay. How are we doing this year?"

"Since the beginning of the year, we've reduced the click rate by 55 percent. It's not where I want to be, but it's better than last year. How're things with Dena?"

Martin scrubbed a hand down his face. "I don't know what I was thinking when I gave her carte blanche for this wedding. Every week she has some new idea, the latest...*whatever*." He waved a hand. "Lately, she's been talking about a destination wedding."

Jabari's brows knitted in confusion. "I thought she wanted a large wedding."

"That hasn't changed. Apparently, a couple of her friends suggested that she ask me about using the jet to fly everyone over." Martin had purchased the fourteen-passenger jet six years ago when he'd made a fortune on one of his investments.

Jabari laughed. "And you said?"

Martin looked at Jabari as if he had lost his mind. "What do you think I said? Make sure the woman you end up with doesn't try to send you to the poorhouse."

"You're rich as a king. What's the problem?"

"And I'd like to stay that way. Hell, you are, too."

Jabari had invested wisely, saved his money and could live comfortably, but he didn't believe in being wasteful. "Well, I don't think I have to worry about the woman I'm dating falling into that category." Alisha didn't strike him as a woman who spent frivolously.

"Wait. What? When did you start seeing someone?"

"I met her Saturday at my niece's birthday party and we went out that night. She's Michelle's best friend."

Martin shook his head, as if to clear his confusion. "Let me get this straight. You met a woman at a birthday party for your sister's daughter and asked her out. And she's your sister's best friend."

"That about covers it."

"That would put her almost a decade younger than you. And she was there helping out?"

"Not exactly. She brought her three-year-old daughter to the party."

Martin's eyes widened. "I thought you said you wouldn't date a woman with kids."

"I know. She also has a six-year-old son. And is divorced."

"Sounds like a recipe for drama if you ask me."

"Yeah." Jabari had told himself the same thing. "But I like her."

"And the ex?" he asked, crossing his ankle over his knee.

"Apparently, he cheated on her and decided he didn't want to be married anymore. We didn't get into how involved he is with the kids. Chelle is being pretty closemouthed about it and said she's staying out of it."

"Does she know what you do?"

"I just told her I work for a tech company." He hadn't said more than that at the time because he didn't typically share that kind of personal information on a first date. After serving as a cyber operations officer in the air force, the transition to chief information security officer here had been smooth.

Martin rose to his feet. "Do you think she has potential to be the future Mrs. Sutton?"

"We'll see. I'll let you know if there's another attempted breach."

"And I'll keep you posted on when I get the meeting set up."

"I have a meeting with the security team on Wednesday morning and I don't want to push that out. But I can work around everything else."

Martin nodded and headed for the door.

Jabari turned his attention back to the computer. After an hour, his thoughts went back to Alisha. He had purposely not called her yesterday to give himself time to assess his feelings. But he wanted to hear her voice tonight, and they needed to discuss their next date. He picked up his cell and sent her a text to let her know he was thinking about her and looking forward to seeing her again. He asked if she'd be up for a conversation later tonight. He didn't expect her to respond right away because he knew her job kept her busy.

He set up the phishing email and sent it to all one hundred and fifteen employees. With any luck, this quarter would show a greater decrease in clicks. Jabari's phone buzzed. He picked it up and read the text from Alisha: Should be free to talk after 8:30. He smiled. No, he couldn't seem to stay away from her, but he would proceed with caution. And he would hit up his brother-in-law for more information on Alisha's ex. He wanted to be prepared for anything.

"Come on in, Alisha."

"Hey, Miss Georgia." Alisha hugged her ex-mother-in-law.

"Mommy!" Corey came barreling toward Alisha and launched himself into her arms.

She caught him up and planted a kiss on his cheek. "Hi, sweetheart. How was your day?"

"Good. We got a new spelling list and I know all the words already."

Alisha smiled. "That is fabulous. I'm so proud of you."

"Mama, up, please," Lia said with her arms raised.

She picked Lia up and kissed her temple. "Did you have fun at school?"

"Yes." Lia launched into a discussion of every detail of the day.

Georgia laughed. "She's been talking nonstop since I picked them up."

"She loves to talk," Alisha said, tickling Lia.

"They're such good kids. I sure wish you and Wayne would get back together."

Her smile faded. Alisha placed Lia on her feet. "You guys go get your backpacks." For the first couple of years after the divorce, Georgia had been angry with her son and his behavior. However, over the past month, she had been on this you-two-should-get-back-together kick. Alisha saw no reason to keep saying it would never happen—she'd stated her position more than once. She wondered if the woman knew her son had decided to try to relinquish his parental rights. Though Alisha had no intentions of *ever* taking Wayne back, this latest stunt guaranteed his place in hell from her standpoint. "You already know my answer." Alisha smiled at Corey and Lia when they returned. "Tell Grammy goodbye." She hurried the children through their farewells and hustled them out to the car.

Five minutes into the drive, Corey asked, "Mommy, why doesn't Daddy come to see us?"

Alisha groaned. Her son had a vague recollection of his father, whereas Lia had never seen him. "Honey, sometimes, people aren't ready to be dads." She wanted to add that Wayne wanted to have his cake and eat it, too. Being a husband and father cut into his social time. Wayne liked going to clubs and hanging out with his boys. She had been fine with occasionally going out to the dance clubs when they were dating, but once she started nursing school, her focus had changed. Even more so once they married and she became pregnant.

"Oh," he said, dejectedly.

"Corey, it has nothing to do with you, baby." She hated these conversations and knew her son was starting to see the difference at school with some of his friends. She had been blessed that Lorenzo always stepped in to take up the slack. Her cousins Cedric and Jeremy pitched in, as well. But it wasn't the same, and the older Corey got, the more he'd begun to realize it. Lorenzo was a married man now and, although she knew he wouldn't hesitate to do more, she didn't want to ask.

Alisha glanced in her rearview mirror at Corey's sad face. "How about we have make-your-own pizza tonight for dinner?"

His face lit up. "Yay, pizza! I want lots of pepperonis."

"Pizza," Lia echoed, clapping her hands.

Smiling, Alisha refocused on the road. She stopped at the store to pick up the ingredients and headed home. As soon as she turned into the driveway, she saw Lorenzo's SUV pull up behind her. "Speaking of." She got out and took Lia out of her car seat. Lia ran to Lorenzo. Corey undid his own, hopped out and did the same.

Lorenzo came toward Alisha, holding both children in his arms, and kissed her cheek. "Hey, sis."

"Hey. Your ears must have been burning." She got the backpacks and grocery bags out of the car.

"Whatever it is, I didn't do it," he said with a laugh, following her into the house through the garage.

"What are you doing here? You never leave the office before five and it's a quarter to." She placed the grocery bags on the kitchen counter and then told the children to put their backpacks into their rooms. Lorenzo and their cousin Cedric had recently taken over the family's construction company started by their father and his twin brother.

"Trying to learn to delegate a little more, and I haven't had a chance to hang out with you since we got back from Paris." Lorenzo and Desiree had spent two weeks in the city of love.

He put the children down. Corey asked, "Uncle Lorenzo, we're having pizza for dinner. Are you going to eat with us?"

"Your uncle may not have time to stay tonight. Remember he has to go home to see Aunt Desiree." Alisha had had a hard time explaining that Lorenzo couldn't come over as often as he used to.

"Actually, I'm all in for pizza," Lorenzo said. "Aunt Desiree is working late tonight."

Alisha went to the sink and washed her hands. "It's make-your-own pizza, so you'll be working for your supper."

"Nothing wrong with a little work. As long as you have some mushrooms in that bag, I'm good."

She laughed. "You know I do." They both loved pepperoni-and-mushroom pizza.

Lorenzo picked up Lia and put his hand on Corey's shoulder. "Let's go wash your hands."

By the time Lorenzo returned with Corey and Lia, Alisha had the sauce, cheese and toppings laid out on the table. She helped Lia, while Lorenzo did the same for Corey. The sight made Alisha feel a little melancholy. She had envisioned married life to be something like this, where she and her husband would spend time together with their children.

While the pizzas baked, Alisha checked the backpacks for any notices and helped Corey finish his homework. Thankfully, Georgia had gotten him started and he only had a small amount of math left to do. Dinner turned out to be a lively affair. Lorenzo kept the children entertained and got them to eat every piece of crust on their plates. He stayed around to help with baths and put them to bed.

Lorenzo dropped down on the sofa. "I missed them."

Alisha sat next to him, released her hair and finger-combed it. "They missed you, too. How's married life?"

He grinned. "Better than I ever thought."

"I'm really happy for you."

"What's been going on? Just like you've always been able to read me, I can do the same with you. Don't think I haven't noticed that a few times you've had this sad look on your face."

She blew out a long breath and told him about what Georgia had said and about the conversation with Corey in the car. "He looked so sad and there's nothing I can do about it."

"And now with all the school activities, I'm sure he's seeing all his friends and their fathers together."

"Exactly."

"I'll make a point of coming to spend more time with him."

"I love you for offering, but I can't ask you to do that. You're a newlywed and you need to be spending that time with Desiree."

Lorenzo patted her knee. "Spending time with my niece and nephew won't interfere in the least. Remember all that talk about balance Dad's been drilling into my head and how family is always the priority? This qualifies."

Alisha could always count on her big brother and wouldn't trade him for the world. She glanced down at her watch and noticed it was almost eight thirty. Jabari had said he'd call and she wanted Lorenzo to be gone by then. No doubt he'd have a million questions. The fact that he hadn't mentioned something already meant that Desiree hadn't told him about Alisha's date on Saturday. "Don't you need to be going home to your wife?"

"She's putting together some gifts for a bridal shower this weekend and said she'd be home around nine."

"Oh."

He studied her. "You have something to do?"

"Yeah. Go to bed. I had back-to-back surgeries today."

"That's right. You transferred to another unit. Do you like it?"

She chuckled. "I just traded one surgery unit for another, so that didn't change. I do like the fact that I won't have to work weekends or holidays now." The doorbell rang.

Lorenzo frowned and started to stand. "Are you expecting someone?"

"No, and sit down. I can answer my own door." She stood.

"Do you think Georgia is sending Wayne over here to try to convince you to take him back?"

Alisha whirled around. "She'd better not. If it's him, you'll know it." She headed toward the door.

"If it is, I'm kicking his ass," Lorenzo called out.

She shook her head. This time she might let him. She looked through the peephole and felt her eyes widen. *What is he doing here?* Alisha opened the door. "Jabari, hey? What are you doing here? I thought you were going to call."

Jabari smiled. "Hello to you, too. I had planned to call, but I wanted to see you again." He moved closer.

"I also can't kiss you over the phone," he murmured close to her lips. "And I do want to kiss you."

His lips touched hers.

"Who is it, Lisha?" Lorenzo called.

Alisha jumped back just as Lorenzo appeared, a deep scowl lining his face. "Lorenzo, this is Jabari. Jabari, this is my brother, Lorenzo."

"Nice to meet you, Lorenzo."

Lorenzo shook Jabari's hand. "Same here. How do you know my sister?"

"We met on Saturday."

Alisha stepped back. "Come on in, Jabari. My brother was just leaving." Lorenzo gave her a look that said he wasn't going anywhere, but she ignored it. She led Jabari to the family room but turned back and mouthed to her brother, "Stay right there."

He shook his head and took a step.

She sent a lethal glare his way and motioned for him to stop. Thankfully, he did. She let out a deep breath.

"Your brother doesn't look too happy about me being here," Jabari said as he took a seat on the sofa.

"Yeah, well, he'll have to get over it. I'm not sixteen anymore. Be right back." Alisha went back to the front where Lorenzo paced back and forth, still frowning. He started in with rapid-fire questions about where she met Jabari, where he worked and whether Lorenzo needed to do a background check on him. "He's Michelle's brother and I met him at Jade's party on Saturday, so you can relax."

"Is this the brother who was in the military?"

"Yes. He recently retired." That was absolutely the wrong thing to say. She realized it as soon as the words left her mouth. Her brother would pick up on the age difference immediately.

"If he retired, that means he has at least twenty years in and that makes him at least thirty-eight and far too old for you."

Alisha rolled her eyes and pushed him toward the door. "Go home."

"Call me when he leaves."

She gave him an incredulous look. "I will not. You don't need to be in my business like that. I'm not a kid."

"That's *exactly* why you need to call me. He's probably way more experienced when it comes to women and—"

"And I can take care of myself." She smiled. "But if I need you, you know I'll call."

Lorenzo stared for a long moment and then ran a hand over his locs. "Fine. Call me tomorrow."

"I will. Love you."

"Love you, too." He tilted her chin. "Be careful. I won't stand for another man breaking your heart." He pressed a brotherly kiss to her forehead and walked out.

She inhaled deeply and let it out slowly. She was all for not having her heart broken again.

Jabari stood when Alisha came into the room. "Is everything okay?"

Alisha waved him off. "Yes. He's just being his overprotective self." She sat on the sofa.

He lowered himself next to her. "I can't blame him. I was the same way with Chelle. Just ask Chris. Me being away in the military didn't change that."

"Oh, I know all about how much you hassled Chris. Chelle wanted you to be shipped out to some unheard of foreign country until the wedding."

He chuckled. "What can I say? I had to know that Chris was going to love and protect her the way he's supposed to. I'm happy to say that he has."

She was happy, too, that her friend had found a man who did all the things her own lousy ex hadn't. She also wondered if Jabari's protectiveness would extend to whatever woman he ended up marrying. Alisha shook off the crazy thought. She had no business worrying about that. "What did you want to talk about?"

"Nothing specific. I did want to talk to you about our next date."

"What did you have in mind?" She mentally tried to remember if her parents would be available to babysit over the weekend. Since her father's retirement, they tended to take more short trips.

Jabari draped his arm around her. "I have a proposal I hope you'll agree to."

"What?" she asked warily.

"I'd like to have a picnic on Saturday…and I want Corey and Lia to come."

"What?" Her heart started pounding. She did not bring men around her children. The two men she had dated since her divorce hadn't even seen the inside of her house. Technically, he had already met her children and Lia was still talking about her "horsie" ride. But this would be different. Just the four of them. Like they were a family. "I don't know. No offense, but I don't typically bring dates around my children."

"I understand that completely. But I want you to understand that if we plan to date exclusively, they are part of this equation and I don't want to exclude them. Besides, they've already met me and since you and Chelle regularly get together, I'll be there, too." He grasped her hand. "But I want you to be comfortable with it."

She didn't know what to say. He had voiced one of her concerns. One of the guys she had gone out with had told her he didn't plan to step in and be daddy to anyone's kids except his own. She had an unspoken rule that she wouldn't hide the fact that she had children, but a man couldn't meet them until he and Alisha had been dating for at least three months. But Jabari had a point. She was bound to run into him at any gatherings she attended at Chris and Michelle's. She weighed it over in her mind a moment longer and then finally said, "Okay."

"Are you sure?"

"Yes."

Jabari grinned. "Now that that's out of the way, may I kiss you?"

Alisha couldn't stop the smile that spread across her lips. She nodded. When his lips touched hers, she knew she was in trouble. Big trouble.

Chapter 5

Jabari pulled Alisha close. He could get used to being with her like this. His family would say he was moving too fast, but he had come to appreciate that tomorrow wasn't promised and had vowed to live each day as such.

"Can I get you something to eat or drink?"

"I'm good, thanks. What do you typically do after the kids go to bed?"

"Take a few minutes to unwind. I might read or watch TV if I can find something good. Tonight, I was going to watch *Coming to America* again."

"What time does it come on?"

"Nine."

Part of him didn't want to intrude on her time because he knew she didn't have much downtime. The other part of him wanted to spend as much time with her as he could. "Would you like some company?"

Alisha sat up. “Sure. I’m making popcorn. Do you want some, too?”

“Can’t watch a movie without snacks.” They shared a smile. “I’ll help make it.”

“There’s nothing to do but toss the bag in the microwave,” she said, standing and starting for the kitchen.

Jabari followed. “We’ll do movie night at my place next time and I’ll make you my special movie snack.”

She got two bags of popcorn from the pantry and placed one in the microwave. “What’s in it?”

“Popcorn and a couple of other things.”

Alisha viewed him skeptically. “It’s not some crazy mix of stuff, is it?”

“No,” he answered laughingly. “You’ll like it.”

“Hmm...we’ll see.” She went to the refrigerator and took out a pitcher of lemonade and then went to a cabinet to retrieve two glasses. “I really want an orange freeze, but I don’t have any ice cream, so this will have to do.”

Jabari eased the pitcher from her hand and filled the glasses. “How do you make it?”

“Just like a root beer float, except I use orange soda.”

“I’ll have to try it.” He made a mental note to purchase orange soda and vanilla ice cream for when she came to his house. When she got ready to open the second bag of popcorn, he placed a staying hand on hers. “We don’t need two.”

She continued opening the plastic covering and eyed him. “We do if you plan to eat some.”

“Oh, it’s like that?”

“It’s exactly like that.” She stuck it in the microwave. “I do not share my bag of popcorn. With *anyone*.”

He laughed and lifted his hands in mock surrender.

"I don't want to mess things up before they get started, so I promise not to take one kernel of your popcorn."

Alisha rolled her eyes playfully. "Whatever," she muttered. But she was smiling.

When the popcorn finished, they took everything into the family room and Alisha turned on the movie. They laughed from the first scene, quoting lines from the movie and reminding themselves several times to be quiet, so as not to wake up the children. They finished the popcorn halfway through and he reclined. Alisha laid her head in his lap and he felt a contentment that made him smile. Later, as the credits rolled across the screen, he said, "It's been a long time since I've relaxed like this. Thanks for letting me hang out with you during your wind-down time."

"It's been a while for me, too."

"What do your evenings typically look like?"

She laughed. "My evenings revolve around homework, dinner, mediating 'that's mine' arguments, baths, story time and listening to all the reasons why Corey can't go to sleep. His foot hurts, he forgot to tell me something, or he needs water…the list goes on and on. By the time that's over, I take a quick shower, fall into bed and then I get up and do it all again."

Jabari had had both his parents growing up and couldn't imagine how difficult it was for her to do it alone. "You don't have anyone to help you?"

Alisha rolled her head in his direction. "My parents help out, and my brother is a godsend."

"Do you ever get tired of it all?"

"Sometimes, and I'd love to take a vacation. But I wouldn't trade my babies for anything. I don't know what I'd do without them. They enrich my life in ways I can't begin to explain."

"Where would you go for your vacation?"

She angled her head thoughtfully. "My cousin Malcolm went to Belize and showed me some of the pictures he took. They were gorgeous. Maybe there or anywhere in the Caribbean. My passport is ready, so I just need the time. Have you been there?"

"No, but it's on my list." He had traveled to several countries, but not much of it was for pleasure. He had planned to take a trip after leaving the air force but had jumped straight into his job. "What about your ex?" He wasn't sure he wanted the answer but decided to ask anyway.

"No."

Her abrupt answer made him wonder how often the man came around, but not enough to ask. Besides, her tone gave him the impression that she didn't want to talk about it. He stroked a finger down her cheek. "If you ever need anything, *anything*, call me, no matter what time it is, and I'll come."

Alisha stared up at him with a strange look, as if she was trying to determine whether he had an ulterior motive.

"No strings attached. Wait, maybe one—a kiss every now and again. What?" he asked when she shook her head. "Don't you think that's fair compensation?"

Alisha smiled and shook her head again. "You are such a nut." She sobered. "But I appreciate the offer."

The sweet kiss that followed made Jabari's heart beat faster. Their eyes held a moment longer, and then she resumed her position on his lap. They sat quietly and he idly massaged her scalp. He didn't know how much time passed before he detected a change in Alisha's breathing pattern. He peered down and saw that she had fallen asleep. He laid his head back and smiled inwardly. *This is what I want.* Now he had to decide whether she was worth the risk.

"Yes, he's your brother, but I need to know what kind of guy he is. I mean, he seems really nice, but… I don't know what I'm trying to say." Alisha cradled the phone against her ear as she talked to Michelle while packing snacks for the picnic.

"I'm not going to lie—it would totally make my day if you became my sister-in-law. But, like I told Jay, I'm staying out of it."

Alisha added string cheese and Goldfish crackers to the bag. "You're not helping, Chelle."

Michelle laughed. "I just said that. Honestly, he's a great guy. Picky, but great. So are you two still seeing each other?"

"We're supposed to be having a picnic today…with the kids. I'm a little nervous because I have never brought another man around them. Technically, he met them—well Lia, anyway—at your house." Alisha released a deep sigh. "Corey's been asking about why his dad is MIA lately and remember I told you that Wayne has filed to end his parental rights. I'm not sure introducing another man is a good idea right now." She groaned. "I feel so weird talking to you about your brother."

"Wait. Back up. Never mind Jabari. He's still going to try and go through with that?"

"Yep. The court date is set for November."

"He is such an idiot. Ugh. I wish you had never married him. Sorry."

"Don't be. Sometimes, I feel the same way." Alisha could look back and see that there were several indications that she should have done something differently, but Wayne had promised he'd been ready for their life together and had kept up a good front for a solid two years. "Anyway, Jabari will be here in a little while, so I need to go."

"You kids have fun," Michelle said with a little laugh.

"Yeah, we'll see how it goes." They disconnected, and Alisha leaned against the counter. She couldn't deny the chemistry between them or that his touch left her breathless. As much as she enjoyed being with him, she didn't want to risk another man walking away and breaking her heart. She also didn't want to bring a man into her children's lives, only to leave them with unkept promises, just like their father had done on countless occasions.

Alisha finished packing the bag and then went to get the children ready. She had decided not to tell them about the picnic before now because Corey would have bugged her the entire week. "Hey, guys. We're going to go to the park in a little while."

"Can we play on the playground?" Corey asked.

"Yes. But someone else is going to go with us. He's Aunt Michelle's brother." Michelle and Chris were godparents to both of Alisha's children and Alisha was Jade's godmother.

"Is he going to play on the playground with us?" Corey asked.

She smiled. "We'll have to ask him. Can you put your shoes on, please?"

"Okay." He raced off down the hallway to his room. She didn't bother telling him to walk. He had two speeds—sleep and run. "Come on," she said to Lia, picking her up and heading to the bedroom. "Let's get your shoes." Alisha paused in Corey's door. "Is that the right foot?"

Corey looked down at the shoe. "Oh." He grinned and put the shoe on the correct foot.

She smiled and continued to Lia's room. After putting on her daughter's shoes, she put a change of clothes into her backpack and did the same for Corey. Every time she took the kids out for the day, it looked like she was packing for a week. But Alisha liked to be prepared for any- and everything. The doorbell rang and her heart rate kicked up. She drew in a calming breath and went to answer the door.

"Hi. Come on in."

"Hey." Jabari brushed a kiss over her lips and followed her in.

Lia was standing in the living room but ran to Jabari. "I wanna ride." She obviously remembered him from the party.

Alisha chuckled. "You know you're never going to be able to go anywhere without some kid asking for a horseback ride."

Jabari smiled and picked up Lia. "We'll ride later, okay?"

"Okay."

Corey stood off to the side, viewing Jabari warily.

Alisha extended her hand. "Corey, this is Mr. Sutton." He came over, grasped her hand and partially hid behind her.

"Hi."

Jabari hunkered down in front of him. "Hi, Corey. It's nice to meet you." He reached out to shake Corey's hand.

Corey gave him a shy smile.

"Do you like to play ball?" Jabari asked.

The boy nodded.

"Good. I brought a baseball, basketball and football, so we can play."

Corey's eyes lit up. He glanced up at Alisha and then back at Jabari. "I have to get my baseball cap and my bat." He ran off excitedly.

Lia ran behind him.

Jabari stood and smiled. "He has your eyes and beautiful smile."

His gaze dropped to her mouth and she saw the hint of desire. She wanted the kiss but not in front of her children. "I…I need to get jackets and we can go." Alisha turned and fled. She hadn't even thought about kissing a man in months, but every time she saw Jabari, it was the first thing on her mind. She retrieved the jackets. "Let's go." Corey came out of his room with his bat and wearing the black baseball cap that her cousin Cedric had given him at one of their family gatherings. When she came back with the three bags, Jabari briefly raised a brow. "Snacks and changes of clothes," she explained.

"I didn't say anything."

"You didn't have to. I saw the look."

Jabari smiled and reached for them. "I'll put these in the car."

Alisha ushered Corey and Lia out the door. "Speaking of cars, it might be easier to take mine so we don't have to worry about transferring the car seats."

He stopped walking and turned to face her. "We'll take my car. It's no big deal to transfer the seats." He popped the trunk by remote, put the bags inside and closed it. "I'll help you get them." He strode past Alisha back up the driveway as if she hadn't made the suggestion and gestured to the garage.

She didn't know whether to be flattered or annoyed. Flattery won out. He reminded her of the men in her family. They all would have responded the same way. With Jabari's help, they made the transfer quickly and strapped the children in their seats and were on the way. It turned out to be a perfect day for a picnic. October was a few days away and the temperatures still hovered near the eighty-degree mark, but the days cooled considerably in the afternoon. "This car definitely hasn't seen too many kids," Alisha said, checking out the spotless interior. She managed to keep her Highlander relatively clean, but it took some effort.

"Jade has been in a few times and if you look in the glove compartment, you'll find a book or two," Jabari said.

Corey and Lia kept up a steady stream of conversation as they drove and Alisha was glad for the buffer. A few minutes later, Jabari drove into a newer park not far from her house.

"I hope I have everything." Jabari removed a large cooler with wheels and stacked two picnic baskets on top, along with her cooler tote. Next came a net bag holding all of the balls and a blanket.

"And you were talking about how much stuff I had," Alisha teased. "There's only four of us."

He laughed. "Yeah, well, you'll learn that I don't do anything by half." He held her gaze. "I go all the way."

Oh, my! The intensity of his gaze let her know he meant more than the food. Several people had the same idea of enjoying the good weather and it took a moment to find a spot. All of the covered tables were taken.

Jabari scanned the park. "Maybe we should have come earlier."

"Apparently." Alisha had assumed arriving around

noon would be a good time. "Look, there's a spot over there." She pointed to a grassy area not too far from the playground that was shaded by a large tree.

"Let me get over there before someone else claims it." He quickened his pace.

"Mommy, where is Mr. Sutton going?" Corey asked.

"He went to save our spot." She and the kids joined Jabari a moment later. He unfolded the blanket and Alisha grabbed an end. While they were spreading it out, Lia jumped in the middle, rolled around and giggled.

Laughing, Corey followed. "Jump, Lia!"

"No, don't jump," Alisha said. "Can you wait until we're done?"

Jabari merely smiled.

Once they'd straightened out the blanket, Corey asked, "Can we go play ball now, Mommy?"

"Ask Mr. Sutton."

He glanced over at Jabari. "Can we go play, Mr. Sutton?" he asked, barely audible.

She shook her head. Corey hadn't been shy a day in his life and she always had to remind him to lower his voice, but today he acted like he couldn't talk above a whisper.

Jabari ruffled Corey's cap. "Sure. What do you want to play first?"

"Baseball, because I already have my baseball cap and my bat."

"Baseball it is." He reached into the bag and pulled out two baseballs, a tee and two gloves. He helped Corey put on one of the gloves. "Okay, let's go see what you've got."

They moved a short distance away and Alisha marveled at Jabari's patience. When Corey started to get frustrated, he encouraged him and when Corey hit the ball, he yelled even louder than her son. They practiced throwing the football and running plays, and Corey's laughter filled her ears. Tears stung Alisha's eyes. She had never realized how much her baby needed a father in his life. She played all those games with him, but the light in his eyes and the grin on his face today were different. The smile on Jabari's handsome face seemed to match Corey's. She took a moment to study the lean, hard lines of his body. He had the speed and agility of a twenty-year-old and his muscles flexed with every movement. Nothing about him said he was approaching the forty-year mark and, not for the first time, she wondered what he'd look like without that shirt. "Okay, girl, you're getting way ahead of yourself," she muttered. To distract herself, she slung her small cross-body bag over her head and scooped Lia up. "Do you want to go play?"

"Yes." Lia was up in a flash and started toward the playground.

Alisha quickly caught Lia by the hand. "Not so fast, little girl." She gestured to Jabari where they were going and he nodded. She helped Lia climb the structures, played peek-a-boo and held her hand as she came down the slide, all while keeping an eye on their belongings. Alisha noticed Jabari doing the same. More than once, their eyes connected and he smiled, making her heart race.

"Mommy, eat."

"Okay. We need to go wash your hands first." They went to the bathroom and met Corey and Jabari coming as they approached the blanket.

"We're going to wash up and then we can eat," Jabari said, standing close to her.

"Okay." His heat surrounded her and neither of them

moved, the air around them thickening. The feel of Lia banging on Alisha's leg broke the spell. "Um…we'll be waiting." She took Lia's hand and continued toward their spot and dared herself not to turn around. She lost the battle three steps in and glimpsed over her shoulder to find Jabari still standing there watching her. A smile curved his lips. She whipped her head around and kept walking. *Get a grip, girl.* He came back a couple of minutes later carrying Corey on his shoulders. Both wore big grins and Alisha's fears about Corey getting attached surfaced again. She tried to force it down and concentrate on enjoying the day. "So, what are we eating?" Jabari had insisted on preparing the food.

He unearthed fried chicken wings, veggies and dip, cut fruit, rolls, sparkling lemonade for them and juice boxes for the kids. "This is my mom's fried chicken and it's good."

Alisha laughed. "You had your mother make the food?"

"Of course not," he said, looking at her as if he were offended. "It's her recipe. I know how to cook."

"Mmm-hmm, we'll see." She added food to Corey's and Lia's plates and fixed her own. "Okay, let's check out this chicken." She took a bite and her gaze flew to his.

He tossed her a bold wink. "Told you. Good, huh?"

She'd thought no chicken recipe tasted as good as her mother's, but she grudgingly admitted his did. "Yeah, yeah, it's good." Evidently, the children agreed, because both asked for more. They laughed and ate and the idyllic family scene stirred a longing in her she didn't realize had existed. She could easily get used to this and that scared her to death.

Chapter 6

Jabari couldn't believe how much fun he was having with Alisha's children. And Alisha. His attraction was steadily growing. Even now, as they sat watching Corey rolling the ball to Lia, he found himself staring at her.

"I have a surprise dessert."

Alisha shifted her gaze from the kids. "What is it?"

"Ice cream."

"Ice cream? It's probably melted in all this heat, even in the cooler." She leaned over to stop the ball and handed it to Lia.

"It's hasn't melted because I haven't made it yet," he said with a wink.

Her head whipped around. "Are you talking about making homemade ice cream?"

"Yes, ma'am."

"I didn't see an ice cream maker."

"It's in the car." He stood. "I'll be back." As he

walked away, Jabari heard Corey ask where he was going and smiled. At the car, he got the other cooler and the ice cream maker and retraced his steps.

"What's that?" Corey asked, dropping the ball and coming to stand next to Jabari.

"It's an ice cream maker. We're going to make vanilla ice cream." He had purchased an old-fashioned maker with the hand crank, just like his father used to own. Jabari remembered how excited he had been to help his father.

Corey's mouth fell open. "Mommy, we're making ice cream," he said, grinning.

Alisha smiled. "I heard."

"Ice cream is my favorite."

"Along with cookies, cupcakes and any other sweet you can get your hands on," she said, tickling him.

Corey dissolved into a fit of laughter. Lia came over and joined in on the fun and Jabari observed the happy scene with a smile. "Corey, do you want to help me?"

"Ooh, yes."

He had already made the base for the sweet treat, and he now let Corey help pour it into the aluminum can. "Okay. Now we need to place it in the bucket." He set it in the bucket, put the paddle in and closed it up. They worked together, alternating the ice and rock salt, and even Lia helped. Jabari stood behind Corey and showed him how to turn it.

"Look, Mommy. I'm making the ice cream."

"You're doing such a great job and I can't wait to taste it."

"I do it," Lia repeated over and over, trying to insert herself between her brother and the handle.

"Let's give your sister a turn," Jabari suggested. Corey moved aside without complaint, which Jabari found amazing. "Stand right here, Lia." He and Alisha stifled chuckles watching the little girl trying to turn a machine that was nearly the same size as she was. After about four revolutions, she walked away, lifted her arms and twisted her hands back and forth.

His confusion must have shown on his face, because Alisha said, "That means all done in sign language. My cousins taught their children some basic signs—more, all done, milk, eat, tired—and I started doing the same. It really helps fill in the some of the baby talk gaps."

"I bet. That's amazing. I wonder if Chelle is teaching Jade." Corey resumed his position and Jabari let the little boy turn it alone until it became too difficult.

"I can take a turn," Alisha volunteered.

"Nope. We men can handle it."

"Yeah, Mommy, the men can handle it," Corey chimed in.

She smiled and mouthed, "Thank you."

Jabari nodded. "If you and Lia want to go back over to the playground, we'll join you when we're done."

"Okay. Come on, Lia. Let's go swing." She got to her feet. "On your marks, get set...go!" She took off, and Lia toddled after, as fast as her little legs could carry her. Her sounds of delight echoed in the air.

He turned his attention back to the ice cream. After a while, it started to freeze and the crank became stiff.

"My arms are tired, Mr. Sutton." Corey dropped down on the blanket.

Jabari patted Corey's back. "I'll finish it. You did a great job." He added more ice and salt before continuing. Once it was ready, he dug into one of the picnic baskets for the spatula and scraped the cream from the paddle, repacked everything and covered it with the towel he'd brought.

"Can we eat it now?"

"Not yet. It's too soft. We can go play with your mom and Lia. By the time we get back it'll be ready, okay?"

"Okay."

He made sure he secured everything, and then they went over to the playground. Corey immediately ran over to the climbing structure. All of Jabari's apprehensions about dating a woman with children had disappeared five minutes after arriving at the park. At almost forty, he would be too old to play with his own children if his search for a wife took much longer. He studied Alisha pushing Lia on the swing. Their smiles and laughter tugged at his heart. Each time Alisha leaned forward, the shorts she wore stretched taut and made him want to caress every inch of her delectable behind. He didn't know whether things would work out between them, but he began to hope. She made him smile. They played for a while and, instead of going to the bathroom to wash their hands, Alisha pulled out some antibacterial hand wipes from her bag.

"You are prepared," Jabari said.

"Hey, with kids, I have to be prepared for everything."

"Ready for ice cream?"

"Yes!" Corey said, jumping up and down.

"Yes!" Lia echoed.

He dished up the dessert and they all dug in.

"Oh, my goodness. I'd forgotten how good homemade ice cream tasted." Alisha groaned. "You know you're now the official ice cream maker, right?"

"Baby, I'll make you ice cream and anything else you want…whenever you want."

She gasped softly and their eyes locked.

"Can I have more ice cream?" Corey asked, breaking the spell.

Jabari had momentarily forgotten he and Alisha weren't alone.

"It's '*May* I have more ice cream, *please*?'" Alisha corrected Corey.

Corey repeated the request and she scooped him up another small portion.

They finished eating without speaking, but the sexual tension remained between them. He cleaned up while Alisha took Lia to the bathroom.

"Corey, you should go to the bathroom, too. Come on."

Corey grasped Jabari's hand. "Can Mr. Sutton take me?"

She shot a glance at Jabari and he nodded. "Um… sure."

"We'll go when you and Lia get back." While they were gone, he chatted with Corey about school and found out the boy liked math, reading and playing kickball with his friends. They took their turn in the bathroom and returned to find Lia asleep in Alisha's arms.

"Wow. She went to sleep fast."

Alisha laughed softly. "When she's sleepy, she goes out like a light."

"Are you having a good time?"

"I am. Thank you for being so patient with Corey. I really appreciate it."

Jabari glanced down at the little boy cuddled next to him. "He's a great kid." Aside from his niece, he had never spent much time around children. "Do you have a busy week coming up?"

"Every week is a busy one." She laid Lia on the blanket next to her.

"Do you and Chelle work in the same area?"

"No. I'm a surgical nurse and I recently moved to the same-day surgery unit, which means no work on weekends and holidays. It also means things move at lightning speed. Sometimes, surgeries last longer than expected and I end up being there until six or seven, instead of getting off at my normal three-thirty time."

And then she came home and worked another full-time job. Alone. "What happens to Corey and Lia?"

"My mother or brother will pick them up." Alisha pointed to Corey. "Somebody else is tired, too."

Jabari smiled. "It was all that work he put into making ice cream."

"Probably. They have about ten more minutes to sleep, then I'm waking them up."

He frowned. "Why? I thought you said Lia gets cranky when she doesn't get a nap."

"She does, but it's after four and if I let her sleep long, she'll be ready to play tonight when it's bedtime."

Alisha woke them up after a short time, but both children fell asleep again on the ride home and nothing she did could keep them awake for long, including offering their favorite snack.

"I'm going to put her down and I'll be out," Alisha said, pointing to Corey's room.

Jabari laid Corey in his bed and removed his shoes. Corey stirred for a moment, then flipped over and continued to sleep. Jabari tiptoed out and went back to the car to bring in her tote and the container of ice cream. He had just come inside when Alisha returned.

She reached out for the bag and container. "Thanks. Let me put this in the freezer. Can't have my ice cream melting. I think I'm going to have a little more after the kids go to bed tonight."

He'd give anything to be there when she did. Earlier, he'd had a hard time keeping his eyes off her while she ate. The way she slid the spoon in and out of her mouth and her soft groans had him so aroused it was all he could do to sit still. Unable to resist any longer, Jabari fitted himself behind her in the kitchen and trailed kisses along the column of her neck. "I've been waiting to kiss you all day," he murmured. She closed the freezer and he turned her in his arms as his head descended and covered her mouth in a deep, passionate kiss. The contact skyrocketed his desire. He tried to remind himself that he'd only recently met her, but his body didn't care. Her soft moan made him deepen the kiss and swirl his tongue around hers. At length, she tore her mouth away.

"Jabari," Alisha said breathlessly, her eyes still closed and her chest heaving with her ragged breathing.

"Yeah, baby."

"I… This is moving a little too fast for me."

He rested his forehead against hers. "I know. I didn't expect this." She stared up at him, and he saw desire, longing and a hint of fear. He recalled what Chris had told him and told himself to slow down. He needed to be gentle with her and build her trust. "Thank you for spending the day with me."

She smiled. "Thank you. I had a really good time and I'm sure you could tell how much Corey and Lia enjoyed themselves."

Jabari chuckled. "Yeah, I could tell. Maybe we can do it again before it gets too cool."

"I'd like that."

He released her, took her hand and walked to the front door. "I'll call you tomorrow." He kissed her once more and stepped out. Jabari agreed with her assessment. Things between them were moving fast, but he couldn't do anything about it. Truthfully, he didn't want to. For the first time, everything felt right.

Early Wednesday morning, Alisha stood counting everything in the OR for the first surgery—instruments, sponges, needles—everything. For her noon surgery, she had been paired with the one surgeon who drove everyone crazy. Dr. Gill was one of the best orthopedic surgeons around, but timeliness had never been his strong point. He had been known to show up one to two hours late for surgery and stroll in like he had all the time in the world or sometimes acting like everyone else was holding him up. She finished her task and helped the scrub nurse into his gown.

"How late do you think Dr. Gill will be this time?"

Alisha rolled her eyes. "Please don't jinx me. I want to get out of here on time today." She had left past her regular time all week and she was exhausted. The ACL surgery would last about an hour and a half, and if the doctor showed up as scheduled, she could leave close to on time. So far, she had only stayed less than an hour later, so she hadn't had to rely on her family to pick up Corey and Lia from the afterschool care center this week.

The nurse laughed. "Hey, we have a pool going. You should get in. At least you'll have some compensation, if you win."

She smiled. "I might just do that. See you in a few." She left to go greet the patient and ran into Dr. Kovo, whom she would be working with in the first surgery. He always arrived early and she appreciated it. They conferred for a moment and continued to the patient.

Twenty minutes later, she wheeled the woman into the OR. Everything ran smoothly and after transferring the patient to post-op, Alisha went down for a quick lunch.

She opted to sit outside on a bench. She checked her messages and saw a text from Michelle. Alisha had been avoiding her all week because she knew her friend would want an update on Alisha and Jabari's relationship, despite all her talk about staying out of it. She picked at her salad and thought about Saturday's picnic. It had been perfect from start to finish, including the kisses at the end of the day. What had started out as casual had quickly turned into something a little more serious in only a week, and she didn't know what to do. She stood and tossed the container and what was left of her food in the trash. She had more pressing things to deal with now, like praying that Dr. Gill made an appearance before the sun went down.

By some miracle, the man arrived only fifteen minutes late and she made it out of the hospital on time.

"Hey, Alisha." Michelle caught up to her as she exited the front doors. "I've been looking for you all week."

"Hey, girl. It's been crazy and I've left late every day."

"Are you going out for a break now or leaving?"

"Leaving, thank goodness." Unlike Alisha, whose shift could run over, Michelle worked on a progressive care floor and rarely left late, unless she was covering someone else's shift. They started toward the parking lot.

"So, how's it going with Jay?"

She slanted Michelle a look. "I thought you said you were staying out of it."

"I am…as his sister. But as your BFF, I need the 411." They laughed.

"You are so crazy. I don't know how I put up with you all these years."

Still laughing, Michelle said, "You know you love me, girl. So, come on, spill it."

"We had a really great time and he was so good with Corey. They played baseball, basketball and football, and Jabari let him help make ice cream."

"Jay has always been like that. Even with our nine-year age difference, he always made time for me and never had a problem with me following him around. I told you he's a great guy."

"Then why hasn't he ever been married?" The question had been bugging her. With all his stellar qualities, surely some woman would have snapped him up by now. The man was pushing forty and had apparently never come close to the altar, and she needed to know why.

"Not many women are cut out to handle their husbands being in the military. All the moving around and deployments can take a toll on a relationship. I remember one woman he dated broke it off for that reason. He doesn't really say much about it, but I know she hurt him. They'd been together almost two years." A smile played around the corners of her mouth. "And then, like I told you, he can be very picky."

"Great."

She chuckled "Not in a bad way. He knows what he likes and goes after it, and doesn't bother with stuff he doesn't. And he likes you."

Alisha didn't comment. She stopped at her car. "I'll see you later." They embraced.

"Keep me posted." Michelle threw up a wave and continued to her car.

Inside the car, Alisha turned the volume up on her phone and immediately saw a message. She read: Just thinking about you and hoping your day is going well. Looking forward to more of your kisses. Soon. J. She leaned her head against the seat and groaned. This man made it hard to maintain some level of distance. She didn't know how to deal with this. She started the car and went to pick up her babies.

Later that evening, she sat reading with Corey before bedtime, as she did every night.

When she finished the story, he said, "I like Mr. Sutton. Is he going to come over and play ball with me again?"

"I don't know, sweetheart. We'll see. Right now, you need to go to sleep. You have school in the morning." She placed a kiss on his brow and rose from the bed. "Good night. I love you."

"Love you, too, Mommy." Corey scooted down in the bed and she covered him with the sheet.

Alisha flipped on the night-light and turned off the lamp. She poked her head into Lia's room to check on her once more and then continued to her bedroom. She picked up the phone and dialed her mother's number. The two of them had always been close and Alisha knew she could talk to her mom about anything. She needed some advice.

"Hi, baby," her mother said when she answered the phone.

"Hi, Mom. You have a minute?"

"Of course. Is everything okay? There's nothing wrong with my babies, is there?"

"They're fine. Both are in bed. I'm okay. Tired, as usual, but that's nothing new. I wanted to ask—" Her phone beeped, signaling another call. She checked the display and saw Jabari's name. "Mom, I have another call coming in."

"Go answer it and call me back."

"Okay." She clicked over. "Hi, Jabari."

"Hey. Did I catch you at a bad time?"

Just the sound of his voice made her pulse skip. "No. I was talking to my mom."

"I'm sorry. I can call you back."

"It's okay. I'll talk to her later. Sorry I didn't return your text. I got it when I was leaving work this afternoon."

"You didn't have to respond. I knew you were busy. I just wanted you to know you were in my thoughts. Long day?"

Alisha closed her eyes. His thoughtfulness moved her in a way she couldn't explain. "Not too bad. I actually left work on time today. What about you?"

"Back-to-back meetings and writing reports. I won't keep you long because I know you're tired. I wanted to know if you'd be available to go out on Saturday evening. A local R&B artist will be playing at a restaurant club. He's supposed to be pretty good."

"Can I get back to you tomorrow after I check with my parents?" Part of her felt guilty for going out and leaving them, but the other part realized she couldn't stay locked in the house until they were grown and gone.

"Yep. If they're busy, don't worry about it. We'll do something another time."

"I appreciate that."

"Go rest, sweetheart, and we can talk tomorrow."

"Good night."

"Night."

Alisha disconnected and held the phone against her chest. She had to keep from falling for him.

Chapter 7

Friday morning, Jabari sat with his security staff discussing the extra precautions that had been put in place. "We've already flagged a couple hits with someone trying to bypass the system and log into classified information. We need to be especially vigilant with the new wireless technology scheduled for release at the beginning of next year. I don't have to remind you of the confidentiality clause you've all signed. Nothing goes beyond this building, not even in pillow talk." He paused and met the eyes of each of the seven individuals. Two wouldn't meet his and one woman's eyes widened for the briefest of moments. The casual observer might have missed it but not him. He made a mental note to check more closely into their backgrounds. "Are there any questions?"

"Will this require us to work overtime?"

"No. You'll continue with your current shift. Martin and I have taken care of hiring someone to cover nights. Anything else?" No one said anything. Jabari stood. "Okay. Thanks. Be sure to let me know if you notice anything suspicious." They all filed out of the small conference room and Jabari headed directly to Martin's office.

"Hi, Colleen. Is Martin available?"

Martin's very efficient assistant, Colleen Davis, smiled. "He said he didn't want to be disturbed, but I don't think that includes you."

He chuckled. "Well, how about you check, just to be on the safe side. I'd rather he take your head off than mine."

She stood and laughed. "Of course you would." She knocked on Martin's closed door and then poked her head in. "Jabari's here. I told him he wasn't included in your do-not-disturb edict."

"He's at the top of the list," Jabari heard Martin say.

Colleen waved a dismissive hand. "Whatever you say. Jabari, go on in."

"Thanks." He entered, closed the door and took one of the chairs across from Martin's desk. "So I'm at the top of the list, huh?"

Martin grinned. "Hey, it sounded good." He leaned back in his seat and propped an elbow on the desk. "What's up?"

"I just met with my staff and I need some background information on three of them." Jabari shared what he had told them. "When I mentioned the pillow talk part, there were a few things that jumped out at me." He rattled off the names of the three people in question." All had been hired before he took over as chief information security officer. Before then, Martin had played both Jabari's role and that of CEO.

"All of their backgrounds checked out and I've never had any concerns or problems with any of them. You're welcome to look at their files." Martin sat up, buzzed Colleen and asked her to pull the files. "That's why you should've gotten your butt out of the air force when we first started the company."

Jabari let out a short bark of laughter. "Maybe you should have waited until I got out."

"Whatever, man. Gallivanting all across the globe, when you knew I needed you here. Security in any form, especially cybersecurity, is not my area of expertise."

"The only reason I'm here now is because of how much you're paying me." Martin opened his mouth for what Jabari knew would be a string of expletives that would singe Jabari's ears off, but he cut Martin off. "Ah, watch your mouth."

"You're lucky we have this product launch coming. Otherwise, I'd fire your ass," Martin mumbled, leaning forward.

Jabari grinned and crossed a long leg over his knee. "I'm not worried. You want the best, and I'm it. Besides, you can't fire me from my own company. You do remember this is a fifty-fifty venture." They had always teased each other, but both would give his life for the other.

"Modest, too, I see."

He shrugged. "What can I say? Anyway, I'll check the files, do some digging, if necessary, and see if anything else turns up."

"Sounds good. So how's it going with your new lady friend?"

"It's going pretty well, I think. We went on a picnic Saturday with her kids." Jabari shared the details of the outing, including how much he had enjoyed playing with Corey and allowing him and his sister to help make the ice cream.

"All your talk about not jumping into a ready-made family seems to be less of an issue. What about her ex? Is he in the picture? Are you sure this is what you want to do?"

He had asked himself the last question more than once and the answer kept coming back *yes*. "I really like her and the kids. As for the ex, he's nowhere to be found."

"What if he shows up wanting to get his family back?"

"Then I'm out." As much as he liked Alisha, he refused to be in the middle of that kind of drama.

"So you say, and you didn't answer my question—is this what you want?"

He hesitated for a moment. "Yes, she's who I want."

"Then I hope it works out for the best."

"Me, too." He stood. "I'll keep you posted on what turns up." On his way out, he picked up the files from Colleen and took them to his office.

Jabari spent the next two hours reviewing each of the employees' backgrounds and found nothing that might raise a red flag. That didn't mean anything. He'd learned early in his military career that people weren't always who they presented when another cybersecurity officer he'd respected had been caught stealing secrets. He closed the last file and rotated in his chair toward the computer to see how their phishing test was going. So far, only 15 percent of the employees had clicked on the link. Several people had forwarded the email to him as "suspicious" and that was a good thing.

By the end of the day, he had written four reports

and met with the group of analysts. Instead of going straight home, he decided to make a visit to his sister's house to see if he could flush out more information about Alisha's ex. With them getting closer, he needed to know what he would be up against. On the surface, Alisha seemed to be exactly the type of woman he could settle down with, but as he'd recalled earlier, some people didn't always turn out to be who he thought they were. He just hoped she'd be the woman he was growing to care about.

"Hey, big brother," Michelle said when she opened the door to him.

He kissed her cheek. "Hi."

"What are you doing here? As if I didn't know," she added with a smile.

Jabari returned her smile. "I need answers, Chelle."

She blew out a long breath. "Come on back. We're just finishing dinner."

Chris was wiping Jade's hands and face when they entered the kitchen. "What's up, Jay?"

"Hey." He reached down, lifted his niece into his arms and placed a kiss on her soft cheek. "How's Uncle Jay's big girl?"

"Good," Jade said with a big grin.

"What brings you by on a Friday night?" Chris asked. "I thought you'd be out on a date or something."

"He's here to grill me again about Alisha."

"I'm not here to *grill* you, Chelle. I just have a couple of questions about Alisha's ex. I know that he walked out on her, but do you think he's going to try coming back into the picture?"

Michelle placed a hand on her hip. "He can try all he wants, but it won't be happening, not in this lifetime or the next."

Jabari lifted a brow. "That bad?"

"He's a jerk."

"What if you're wrong and he does start popping up again? I don't think I could deal with that."

She studied him intently. "You're really into her, aren't you?"

"I am. She's a lot younger than the women I usually date, but she's also settled and an all-around great person." He enjoyed laughing and talking to her as much as he did kissing her.

"Do. Not. Break. Her. Heart." She punctuated each word with a poke in Jabari's chest. "She's like a sister to me and watching her suffer the first time was hard. I won't do it again."

He grabbed her hand. "Can you not poke a hole in my chest? I don't plan to break her heart. And what about my heart?"

Jade laughed and mimicked poking him.

"Is yours involved in this?" Michelle asked pointedly.

"Inquiring minds want to know," Chris spoke up.

Jabari shot a lethal glare at him. "No. I mean… I don't know. We've only been dating a couple of weeks. I will say that I'm not looking for a hookup. I'm too old for that. You know me, Chelle. I have never hopped from woman to woman, mistreated or played games with one. I've already said that I want what you and Chris have, what Mom and Dad have. Whether Alisha is that person remains to be seen. But you also know how I feel about keeping my life drama free. I'm too old for that kind of mess."

"I know. You have such a good heart and I really am rooting for the two of you."

"Thanks." He handed Jade to his sister. "I'm going

home now." He had some thinking to do. Michelle's comment about Alisha's ex being a nonfactor bolstered his hope. However, he reminded himself that he had only known this woman two weeks and she might not have told Michelle every detail. He said his goodbyes and got on the road.

Even though it was after seven, a fair amount of traffic remained. Jabari started his Jill Scott playlist and let her sultry voice take him home. Once there, he reheated some leftover pasta and sifted through the mail while eating at the bar. He glanced over at the microwave clock. He told himself he needed to think about the direction he wanted his relationship with Alisha to go and that he wouldn't call her tonight. They'd talked almost every night this week and they would be going to the concert tomorrow.

That rationale lasted about thirty minutes and he picked up the phone to call. When she greeted him with her smooth-as-honey voice, he knew he was fighting a losing battle.

Late Saturday afternoon, Alisha ran around the room getting ready for her date with Jabari.

"Mommy, are we going with you and Mr. Sutton?"

"Not this time, Corey. You and Lia are going to stay with Grandma and Papa." She and Jabari had agreed—more like Jabari had insisted—that it would be a waste of time for her to drive to her parents' to drop the kids off and then come back home. So they'd decided to stop at her parents' on their way to Rancho Cordova. "If you want to take a book or movie, go ahead and get it now." Corey ran off and she smiled. Alisha continued applying light makeup and then combed her hair. She stepped around Lia, who sat in the middle of the floor scribbling in a coloring book, and went into the closet to slip into her dress. Tonight she'd chosen a navy sheath with a network of straps crisscrossing the upper back.

She wondered what her parents would think of Jabari. She hadn't planned for them to meet him yet and hadn't brought another man to meet them since Wayne. After her divorce, she hadn't even wanted to speak to a man and pretty much ignored every attempt at one trying to gain her attention. Alisha had only started dating again a year ago, and those occasions were few and far between. She didn't have time for the bull and had no intentions of becoming a bed partner five minutes after the greeting. She had dated one guy for three months and they'd slept together once, but she'd broken it off when he announced that he only wanted a "friends with benefits" relationship.

Corey came back into the room with a movie and two *Jake and the Never Land Pirates* books. "When are we going on another picnic?"

He'd been asking the question all week and she'd given him the same answer. "I don't know, honey." Alisha had been second-guessing her decision to bring Jabari around them, but she couldn't be mad because the man had been amazing. "Let's go make sure you have everything in your bag," she said to distract him. She picked up Lia and left the bedroom.

She packed their pajamas so she wouldn't have to worry about waking them to change once she got home. She didn't bother about adding toys because her mother had purchased enough to start her own toy store.

Jabari arrived precisely at five. He greeted Corey and Lia, and then kissed Alisha on the cheek. "Hey, baby. I'll save the rest for later."

His seductive tone sent heat skittering through her and she resisted the urge to fan herself. "I'm ready."

He smiled knowingly but didn't comment.

They transferred the car seats and Alisha grabbed the backpacks.

"Wait, Mommy. I have to get my soap," Corey said.

At Jabari's confused look, she explained. "Desiree made it and he loves it. That's what I went to get at her shop that night."

"Ah."

Corey came back with the soap and held it up. "See, Mr. Sutton. It has a car."

"Hey, that's pretty cool. I might have to ask your aunt Desiree to make me one."

Corey grinned. "She can make you one with dinosaurs, too."

"Really? I love dinosaurs."

"Me, too."

Alisha held up a Ziploc bag. "Put your soap in here." Corey dropped it in and she closed it and stuck it in his backpack. "Okay. I think we're ready now."

She was nervous the entire drive and considered having Jabari wait in the car. Her hopes were dashed when her mother stepped out onto the porch as soon as they pulled up. *Just great.* They got out and the kids ran to greet their grandmother.

Her mother wore a curious smile.

"Mom, this is Jabari Sutton. Jabari, my mom, LaVerne Hunter."

"It's an honor to meet you, Mrs. Hunter," Jabari said.

"Same here. Please, come in."

"Um, Mom, we don't want to be late for the concert."

Her mother waved a hand. "Two minutes won't hurt, and I'm sure you want to introduce him to your father."

No, actually, she didn't. Sighing inwardly, she followed her mother inside.

"Papa!" Corey and Lia ran to their grandfather and he immediately wrapped them up in a big bear hug.

"How're you two doing?" Her father laughed at their exuberant replies. He stood from his favorite recliner in the family room and divided a glance between Alisha and Jabari. "Hey, baby girl."

"Hi, Dad. This is Jabari Sutton. Jabari, this is my father, Russell Hunter."

Jabari immediately extended his hand. "It's a pleasure to meet you, sir."

"Nice to meet you, too. Why don't you have a seat?" He gestured to the sofa.

"Ah, Dad, we're going to a concert, so we really need to get going."

Her father scrutinized her a lengthy minute, then said to Jabari, "Son, I'm sure we'll have time to talk another time."

Alisha understood the tone. It wasn't a suggestion.

Jabari's gaze never wavered. "I'm looking forward to it."

She squatted down and opened her arms. "Give Mommy a hug and I'll see you guys later." She embraced her children. "Be good for Grandma and Papa."

"Okay," Corey said.

Lia just smiled.

"Thanks for watching them."

"Oh, honey, it's our pleasure." Her mother hugged her and whispered, "He's very handsome."

She didn't reply to the comment. "We'll see you later." She made a hasty exit.

"You okay over there?" Jabari asked when they were in the car.

"Yes. Sorry about all that."

He nodded.

It dawned on her that she might have hurt his feelings and she tried to make amends. Alisha laid a hand on his arm. "Please don't think I didn't want you to meet my parents. It's just that—"

"It's a little early in the relationship. I understand it, though as crazy as it may sound, I wondered if there was another reason."

"No. No other reason. So far, you've proven to be a man a woman would be happy to take home to her parents." *Girl, that was* not *what you were supposed to say.* Alisha clamped her jaws shut before something else tumbled out, like how much she enjoyed being with him, how much she wanted him to kiss her.

"Glad to hear it. And just so you know, the same goes for you." Jabari started the car and eased onto the road. A few minutes into the drive, he said, "I hope you're okay with eating at the venue. The restaurant seems to be pretty nice. I thought we'd get there a little early so we can get a good seat."

"Dinner and music in one place sounds fabulous to me. Do you know about the artist?"

"No. Just that he's someone local and up-and-coming. I happened to hear an interview with him on the radio. They played one of his songs, and it sounded pretty good, so I thought it would be nice to support the brother." He slanted Alisha a glance. "And it gives me another opportunity to spend time with you."

Though brief, his gaze seared her. Alisha didn't have a comeback. She usually could hold her own, but she didn't know how to play these games. Wayne had been her first and only boyfriend and her mother's advice years ago rang loudly in her ears now: *Don't get so serious about one boy right now. You have a lot of learning and growing to do when it comes to male friendships.* She hadn't listened. And she hadn't learned. She and her mother needed to have that conversation again and soon.

They arrived an hour before the show and were able to get a table close to the stage and with a center view.

"I like your style, Jabari Sutton," she said. She felt the deep rumble of his laughter against her back as he seated her.

He sat across from her. "I'm glad you like it."

A hostess brought them menus and took their drink order.

Alisha scanned the room before looking at the menu. "I didn't even know this place existed. It's nice." The lounge area had comfortable leather seating and a stone fireplace. The restaurant area provided an intimate atmosphere. A stage sat in the front and behind it, a rock wall.

"I agree. I've been away for so long I sometimes feel like I'm in a new city."

She lowered the menu. "I've never thought about it that way. It has changed significantly in twenty years."

"Tell me about it," he said with a chuckle. "I'm pretty much acclimated now, but if I need a tour guide, can I count on you?"

Alisha smiled sweetly. "Sure, if you promise to make more of that ice cream."

Jabari laughed. "You're on."

She thoroughly enjoyed herself. The artist's vocals were on point, as were the background singers', and the beat had her dancing in her seat. They stayed around afterward to purchase an autographed copy of the CD and, once in the car, Alisha pulled out her phone and followed the singer on social media.

"What are you doing?"

"Following him on Twitter and Instagram and liking his Facebook page. If he's performing again, we don't want to miss it."

Jabari chuckled. "We, huh?"

Had she said *we*?

"I like the sound of that." He reclined his seat and carefully guided her over the gearshift onto his lap.

"What...what are you doing?"

He traced a finger over her lips. "Finally getting the kiss I've been craving all night."

Before she could blink, his mouth was on hers. His lips were incredibly warm and soft and his tongue stroked hers with the confidence of a man who had perfected the art of pleasing a woman. His hand slid up her thigh, taking her dress with it and sending shock waves of desire humming through her veins. She ran her hand over the hard planes of his broad chest and around to his nape, holding him in place.

"I can't get enough of kissing you," Jabari murmured, transferring his kisses to her throat, while his hand came up to caress her breasts.

Alisha felt the solid ridge of his erection beneath her. Her head fell back and her breaths came in short gasps. He had her body so on fire she lost all sense of time and space. Nothing else mattered except this moment with him. She moaned his name, grabbed his head and kissed him.

At length, he eased back. "We should probably stop before we get arrested."

"Mmm. Probably." Alisha's body trembled and the

space between her thighs throbbed. *Thank goodness for tinted windows.*

"We could always take this back to my place."

"I need to pick up the kids," she murmured as he trailed kisses along her jaw.

"Oh, yeah. Can we have movie night next weekend at my house?"

She was tempted to tell him he could have *all* night. She knew that movie night wouldn't be the only thing that happened if she went to his house. Was she ready to take this next step? Her mind said it was too soon. Her body argued that it wasn't soon enough. "Yeah. Movie night sounds perfect."

Chapter 8

Jabari's week went by in a blur. From a series of meetings with the IT team to identify weaknesses and maintain a high level of data protection in the upcoming new technology and tracking activity on the network of computers, to meeting with each department, he barely had time to breathe. He got home every night after nine and was back in the office by six in the morning. By Friday, he was more than looking forward to movie night with Alisha. With any luck, he would be able to leave work on time.

He finished going over the various projects that had been finalized, along with the security controls that needed to be put in place, and then left the office to meet his mentor for lunch. Jabari tried to schedule at least one meeting with his former supervisor each month. Robert Burdett had retired from the air force a decade before Jabari, but they'd kept in touch regularly.

Until now, all their discussions had been done over the phone or by videoconference. He'd been happy to know that the man had moved to the Sacramento area to be close to his aging mother.

Jabari searched the restaurant and spotted Robert standing near a table and waving. He crossed the room and the two men shared a rough hug. Robert stood a good five inches shorter than Jabari's six-foot-four-inch height. There was a little added girth around his middle, but his dark brown face remained unlined.

"Retirement looks good on you, Jabari," Robert said as they took their seats.

"And you don't look a day older than the last time I saw you."

Robert laughed. "Still trying to eat right and exercise, and I'm feeling good for someone pushing sixty. How are you enjoying civilian life?"

"More than I thought I would." Jabari had been concerned that after being accustomed to military life, he would get bored easily. "I've finally seen my four-year-old niece and my mom doesn't worry so much."

Robert nodded. "It's a heavy burden for our families, but I'm glad to be out in one piece."

"Tell me about it." For the next forty-five minutes, they discussed the newest innovations in cybersecurity. Jabari wanted to continually challenge himself to learn more about his field and stay at the top of his game. Even more so now that he and Martin had a lot riding on their company. Robert possessed a wealth of information and never hesitated to share what he knew. Jabari hoped to be able to pay it forward someday.

As the meal came to a close, Robert said, "I'm glad to hear the company is growing and doing well. I've been keeping up with it."

"Thanks. I can't tell you how much I appreciate your help all these years. How's Ms. Diane? Is she ready to throw you out of the house yet?" Robert's wife, Diane, said she had gotten used to having time away from her husband and didn't know how she was going to deal with him being underfoot all the time. She'd teased that she might have to send him on another deployment to get some peace.

Robert chuckled. "You know she's all talk. It's been nice traveling together without having to worry about it being interrupted. What about you? Any closer to walking down the aisle?"

"No, but I just started seeing someone. We're still getting to know each other, so I'll keep you posted." Jabari checked his watch. "I need to head back to the office. I want to try to leave on time today."

"Hot date?"

He grinned. "Something like that." He signaled the server and settled the bill. They walked out to the parking lot, made plans to meet again and went their separate ways.

Any hopes Jabari had of leaving on time were dashed when he returned and found that an outage had occurred with one of their critical applications. He immediately went into action, checking all the protocols and making sure the outage wasn't the result of the system being hacked. They hadn't found the problem by five and he realized he would, most likely, have to cancel movie night.

He went back to his office and made the call. "Hey, baby. Bad news," he said when she greeted him.

"Something happen at work?"

"Yes. We have a system outage and I can't leave until it's back online. I'm not sure how long it's going to take, so we're going to have to postpone our movie night. I'm sorry."

"I won't lie—I'm disappointed," Alisha said. "But I understand and I'm glad you called."

"I'm disappointed, too. If you're available, we can do it tomorrow."

"I can't. We're having a family dinner to celebrate Lorenzo and Desiree."

That meant he would have to wait another week before seeing her. "Let's plan for next weekend, Friday or Saturday."

"That works. I'll reschedule babysitting with my mom when I hang up."

"I'll call you tonight, if I get home early enough."

"I'll be up late, since it's Friday. Hope you can get it figured out."

"Thanks. Talk to you soon."

It took another three hours to find the infected computer. Jabari and his team had gone through each one and found that an employee had used the company computer to log on to his personal account and clicked on an email containing a link to a strain of malware. Because of the protocols he'd put in place, the system immediately alerted him.

"The good news is it wasn't someone trying to steal information," Jabari told Martin as they sat in Jabari's office. "No data was compromised and we were able to get rid of the virus. I just finished a scan and the system is clean."

"Thank goodness," Martin muttered. "That's the last thing I need right now. I'll have Colleen send out a memo to everyone tomorrow reminding them not to access outside email accounts. We have too much at stake for it to be compromised."

"Already done."

Martin smiled for the first time since all the mess began. "Thanks, man." He pushed to his feet. "Let's go home."

"I'm going to run one more scan and I'll be right behind you. Enjoy your weekend."

"I plan to," Martin called over his shoulder as he exited.

At least one of them would. Jabari ran the scan and made sure everything had been secured before heading home. Once there, he took out the steak he had left marinating in his special dry rub and heated the stovetop grill. His stomach growled, reminding him that he hadn't eaten since lunch. He added a baked yam and a green salad, and after the steak finished cooking, took everything to his family room. While eating, he channel surfed until settling on a baseball playoff game. When Jabari finished, he stretched out on the sofa and released a weary sigh. They had dodged a bullet today and he'd had to keep his irritation in check when they confronted the man responsible for losing over four productive work hours—and costing Jabari his movie night.

He lay there for a few more minutes and then decided to call Alisha. She'd said she would be up late and ten thirty qualified in his book, especially for a single mother.

"Well, hello, Mr. Sutton. Did you get everything straightened out at work?" Alisha said when she answered.

Jabari smiled. "Hey, and yes. Thankfully, it turned out to be nothing that would compromise our work."

"I'm glad to hear it. Are you just getting home?"

"I've been here about forty-five minutes. Long

enough to eat dinner. So, which day is better for movie night next weekend?"

"Friday works better for me."

"Then Friday it is. I may have to make a midweek visit to get at least one kiss, though. I've missed those kisses."

"I've kind of missed yours, too. Two weeks is a long time not to have your lips on mine," Alisha said in a low, sexy voice.

That was music to his ears. "Be careful, or I might just be on your doorstep in thirty minutes." With no traffic, he might even be able to shave off at least five of those minutes.

She laughed. "Yeah, right. You aren't leaving your house at almost eleven o'clock at night to drive all the way across town."

"You never know. Those kisses are a powerful motivator." His phone beeped, signaling another call. "Can you hang on for a minute? I have another call."

"Yep."

He clicked over to answer Martin's call. "What's up?"

"I forgot to ask you if we're still going running tomorrow or Sunday."

"We can do either day, but let's make it Sunday. I have Alisha on the line, so I'll text you with a time," Jabari said.

"Okay, later."

When Jabari went back to his call with Alisha, an idea popped into his head. "Hey, baby. I need to take this. How late are you going to be up?"

"Probably another hour or so."

"Okay. I'll call you back." He sat up, turned off the TV and took his dishes to the kitchen. He grabbed his keys off the hook and smiled. Alisha didn't think he'd leave his house for a kiss. She thought wrong.

Jabari made it to her house in twenty-eight minutes, including a stop at a nearby grocery store that had a large floral department. His plan had been to give the flowers to her, but when he saw she had left her car in the driveway, he decided to leave them on the windshield for her to find tomorrow. He scribbled a quick note, tucked it into the bouquet of red roses and placed them on the driver's side of the windshield. Then he went to ring the doorbell. A moment later the light came on and the door swung open.

"*Jabari?* What are you doing here?"

The shocked look on her face was priceless. "I'm here to deliver those kisses you said you missed." He swept her into his arms, kicked the door shut and carried her inside.

Alisha went through her day on Saturday with a smile on her face. She still couldn't believe Jabari had driven clear across town last night for kisses. She'd been even more shocked by the fact that she had told him she'd missed his kisses. No, she hadn't wanted to wait two weeks to see him, and his visit more than solidified that in her mind. He'd kissed her in ways and places that still had her body tingling and she couldn't wait until next Friday's movie night.

Remembering she had a pedicure appointment before the visit to her parents' house, she got ready to leave. She searched all over for the flip-flops she usually wore, finally recalling that she'd put them in her car. They were far more comfortable to drive in than her heels.

Alisha got her keys and opened the garage door. She

hadn't pulled the car inside because she had planned to drop the children off before her date with Jabari last night. The door rose and she froze. "What in the...?" On her windshield sat a dozen of the reddest roses she'd ever seen, accented with baby's breath, wrapped in silver paper and tied with a sheer red ribbon. She picked them up and saw the card. Alisha unlocked the car, got her flip-flops, relocked the doors and carried her flowers inside. She took them to the kitchen and opened the card. *Alisha, the kisses were worth every mile of the drive and more. Enjoy your day, beautiful. J.*

She braced her hands on the counter and lowered her head as emotions she couldn't name surged through her with such force that it brought tears to her eyes.

"Mommy, what's the matter?"

Alisha looked down at Corey, whose face was lined with worry. "Nothing, baby. I'm fine. I'm going to put my pretty flowers in a vase and then we'll leave. Did you remember we're going over to Grandma and Papa's house later?"

"Oh, yeah. I have to show Grandma my new book."

"Yes, you do. And don't forget to tell her thank-you." When her mother had found out that she could now purchase Scholastic Books online, she'd been beyond excited and had ordered him three books. The books had been delivered to Corey's classroom yesterday. Alisha recalled feeling the same excitement when her teachers used to send home the three-page book listing. She had wanted to buy every book in the catalogue.

After she arranged the flowers, Alisha went to her bedroom to call Jabari. She tried to hide her disappointment when the call went to voice mail. She left him a message telling him how much she liked the flowers, thanked him and hung up. Michelle had offered to watch the kids while Alisha went to get her pedicure. Alisha dropped them off at her friend's, picked them up an hour later and then drove to her parents' house. Alisha wanted to get there a little early to talk to her mother before the rest of the family arrived.

Letting herself into her parents' house, she called out, "Mom, Dad."

Her mother rounded the corner, wiping her hands on a towel.

"Grandma!" Corey and Lia ran into her outstretched arms.

She squatted down, wrapped them up in a hug and kissed their foreheads. "How're Grandma's babies?"

"I'm good," Lia said.

"Good." Corey held up his new book. "Thank you for my books."

"You're welcome. We'll have to read it before you leave." Still smiling, she straightened and hugged Alisha. "Hi, baby. You're here early. Dinner's not for another hour."

Alisha nodded. "I know. I wanted to talk to you before everyone got here."

"Is everything all right?"

"I'm okay." Not exactly the truth.

Her mom viewed Alisha skeptically. "Your dad's outside cooking on the grill. Corey and Lia can play out there, and you and I can talk." They cut through the kitchen, where a sliding glass door led to the backyard.

Alisha walked out on the deck toward her father. "Hey, Dad."

Russell Hunter turned from the grill and a wide smile creased his face. As always, Corey and Lia showered him with the same affection that they'd done their grandmother. He engulfed Alisha in a strong hug. "How are you, sweetheart?"

"I'm good. It smells good out here."

"And it'll taste good, too," he said with a laugh. "You still seeing that young man?"

"Yes."

"Is he treating you all right?"

She couldn't hide her smile. "Yes, Dad."

He grunted.

Her father continued to be as protective of her now as he had been when she was a little girl. "Can Corey and Lia play out here? I'm going to talk to Mom."

"Of course." He smiled down at his grandchildren. "Come on, you two. Let's get the golf set out and see if you can beat me this time."

Alisha shook her head and left them to their game. She found her mother standing at the kitchen island slicing pineapples for the fruit salad. "What do you want me to do?" She went over to the sink to wash her hands.

"I want you to sit right there and tell me what's going on," her mother said, gesturing to one of the barstools on the other side of the island.

The look on her face left no doubt that any assistance Alisha planned to offer would be turned down. LaVerne Hunter was known to be direct and, sometimes, bordering on blunt. Alisha could be the same way. Except now.

"I assume this is about Jabari."

"Yes." She didn't know where to begin. "I'm confused, Mom."

"He seemed like a nice young man. Where did you meet him and why are you confused?"

"He is very nice." Which was part of her concern.

She wondered how long it would be before he changed. "Jabari is Michelle's brother and I met him at Jade's birthday party. I like him…a lot," she added softly.

Her mother paused in her chopping. "Doesn't sound like you're confused to me. I didn't realize Michelle had a brother."

"He's nine years older and has been in the military for the past twenty years."

"Hmm, I see. So, what's really the problem, Alisha?"

"I don't know. This is the first guy I've really liked since Wayne and I feel like a fish out of water."

"I bet now you wish you'd listened when I told you not to get so wrapped up in one boy," she said with a chuckle. "Back then, nothing we said made a difference where Wayne was concerned."

Yeah, Alisha sincerely wished she had listened. "Is this the 'I told you so' moment you've been waiting for?"

"No, baby. It broke our hearts to see you going through all that mess. Lord knows I wanted to intervene before you two got married, but we all had to let you learn on your own." She added diced cantaloupe, grapes and strawberries to the salad.

"I sure wish you had said something, *anything*," Alisha said, thinking back. In hindsight, there had been a few red flags she should have heeded. Wayne's decision to drop out of college after they became engaged—he cited a need to get a "real" job to provide for them—topped the list. She had told him they should wait to get married until after graduating and finding jobs in their fields, but she'd fallen for the I-don't-want-to-wait-because-I-love-you spiel and relented.

"If I had, we wouldn't have those two precious ones running around outside."

She smiled. "You're right." No matter what, she loved her babies. "But I don't know what to do about Jabari. He makes me feel… I can't explain it. I mean, he open doors, stands when I come into the room and when I went out to the car today, he'd left roses on my car windshield."

"Roses?"

"A dozen red ones. He's incredible, almost too good to be true."

"Well, now. Is he still in the military?"

"No. He retired at the beginning of the year and now works in cybersecurity at a tech company."

"Smart and a gentleman." Her mother washed and dried her hands, and then came around the bar and draped an arm around Alisha's shoulders. "Sounds to me like you're falling in love."

Alisha jerked her head around. "What? No, I can't be. I just met the man like two, three weeks ago. I like him and all, but I'm definitely not falling in love with him."

"Why not?"

"Because."

"Because what?" When Alisha didn't answer, her mom said, "Because you're afraid."

She had verbalized what Alisha didn't want to acknowledge. Back when Lorenzo first met Desiree she'd told him that just because her marriage hadn't worked out it didn't mean she wouldn't try again. She'd talked a good game, and now that those familiar emotions had crept into the mix, she wanted to run as far and as fast as she could.

"Honey, it's okay to be afraid and I understand why.

Don't let that stop you from finding the happiness and love you deserve. That may or may not be with Jabari, but you won't know that until you open yourself to the possibility."

Tears misted Alisha's eyes. "What if the same thing happens again?"

"What if it doesn't? You can't worry about the what-ifs. Otherwise, they'll keep you from truly living."

"I know, but it's so hard."

"Mom, are you in here?"

Alisha heard Lorenzo's voice and quickly wiped away her tears. Apparently, she hadn't done a good job, if the expression on his face was any indication.

"What happened?"

Before she could answer, the doorbell rang and she breathed a sigh of relief.

"Lorenzo, that's probably Reuben and Theresa. Can you get the door?" LaVerne said.

Lorenzo kept his gaze fixed on Alisha, his expression clearly indicating that he'd rather stay and get answers. After a few seconds, he finally said, "Sure, Mom."

"Thanks. Desiree, how are you, honey?"

"Fine. Hey, sis," Desiree said to Alisha. The two shared a hug.

"Did you work today?"

"Yes, but I left a couple hours early." She turned to her mother-in-law. "Do you need help with anything, Mom?"

"No. As soon as Russell brings in the meat, we'll be ready to eat."

Lorenzo came back with their aunt and uncle, as well as their two sons, Cedric and Jeremy. Cedric worked with Lorenzo, heading up the family's construction business, while Jeremy had recently started his own robotics engineering company. As the greetings began, Corey and Lia bounded into the kitchen, followed by Alisha's father, who was carrying a large pan of ribs, chicken and salmon.

Everyone gathered around the dining room table, her father recited a blessing, and they talked and laughed while filling plates and throughout the duration of the meal. Every time Alisha glanced up, she found Lorenzo's gaze locked on hers, seemingly searching for some reason for the tears he had seen. With the entire family present, there hadn't been any time for him to interrogate her, but Alisha knew she would be hearing from him soon.

It took until Wednesday of the following week for Lorenzo to catch up with Alisha. When she walked out of the hospital to her car and saw his name on her phone's display, she sighed.

"Are you working late?" Lorenzo said as soon as she answered the call.

She started to lie in an effort to postpone his cross-examination but decided to tell the truth. "No, just leaving. Hang on while I connect the Bluetooth." She turned on the car and waited for the phone to pair. "Okay, I'm back."

"What happened on Saturday? And don't try to tell me it was *nothing* because I could tell you'd been crying."

Alisha repeated what she had told their mother. "I just don't want to go through the same thing again. Jabari hasn't done anything yet, but—"

Lorenzo's heavy sigh came through the line. "I know where you're coming from. I felt the same way because of what Veronica had done." His ex-girlfriend had hidden drugs in his home and stolen money from him. As a result, Lorenzo had stayed away from women and relationships. "Don't do like I did and punish Jabari for what Wayne did. And you know how much Desiree had been hurt in her past. Our fears almost caused us to lose each other." He shared the details of what had happened between them. "Now, I can't imagine my life without her."

Alisha knew how much her brother loved his wife, just not all the details of what they'd gone through. "I hear you. I have to go. I'm here at Georgia's to pick up the kids."

"Okay. Keep me posted. Oh, and if he turns out *not* to be the man he's presenting, we *will* kick his butt."

She smiled. She had no doubts that Lorenzo meant what he'd said and Cedric and Jeremy wouldn't hesitate to back him up. "I know. Love you, big brother, and thanks."

"Love you, too."

She disconnected and got out of the car. Georgia had called and asked if she could pick up Corey and Lia from school and take them to the bookstore. As much as Alisha had wanted to say no, she'd okayed the outing, reminding herself that Georgia was their grandmother. With any luck, she would be able to get in and out without any impertinent comments from Georgia. She had been fighting a bug all week and was too tired to deal with the woman today.

"Come on in, Alisha," Georgia said when she opened the door. "We had fun at the bookstore and I hope you don't mind that I treated them to some ice cream."

"No, it's fine. I'm glad you guys had a good time."

Both children ran to greet her, excitedly talking about all they had done. She passed out hugs and kisses and then helped them gather their belongings. “You can show me your new books when we get home.”

Georgia walked them out and waited while Alisha strapped them into their seats. “Who is this *Mr. Sutton* Corey’s been talking about? He mentioned something about helping this man make ice cream.”

Alisha went still. Corey’s eyes widened. She smiled at her son and closed the door.

“I don’t think it’s wise for you to start bringing all these strange men around my grandchildren,” Georgia said.

Alisha turned to face Georgia, smile now gone. “With all due respect, who I choose to see is my personal business.”

“I don’t want them to get confused about who their real father is.”

Alisha snorted. “No confusion there. They don’t have a father. They have a sperm donor.” She clamped her jaws shut to keep herself from giving the woman the set-down she rightly deserved. Ignoring the stunned look on Georgia’s face, Alisha rounded the fender, got in and drove off.

“I wasn’t supposed to tell Grammy about Mr. Sutton, Mommy?” Corey asked glumly. “She asked me if a man came to visit you and I did like you said and told the truth.”

She could imagine what else Georgia had asked and wanted to strangle the woman. “You did the right thing, Corey. It’s okay.”

“You’re not mad?”

“No, baby. I’m not mad at you.”

“Good, because I like Mr. Sutton.”

So did she. She liked Jabari far more than she had ever thought she would. Each moment they spent together chipped away at the layers over her heart and challenged her resolve to do the one thing she had promised she'd never do again.

Chapter 9

Jabari navigated the Friday evening traffic to pick up Alisha. By the time he arrived, his heart was racing with the excitement of a child on Christmas morning. And when she opened the door to him with the radiant smile he'd come to look for, he knew he wanted her to become a bigger part of his life.

Alisha came up on tiptoe and kissed him. "Come in."

He stepped inside. "Where are the kids?"

"I dropped them off at my parents' already."

A pang of disappointment hit him. He had been looking forward to seeing them again. "Ready?"

"Yep." She picked up her purse and jacket. "I usually prefer going to the theater, but I'm finding I like these home movie nights."

Jabari grinned. "Glad to hear it. We'll have to put them in the regular rotation." He would take being alone with her over a crowded theater any day. He led her out to his car and got them underway. They rode the first few miles in companionable silence, the only sounds coming from the soft music being played on one of the satellite stations. "How are Corey and Lia enjoying school?"

"They love it. Corey's adjusting to the increased work in first grade and Lia loves preschool."

"What time do you need to pick them up tonight?"

Alisha shifted in her seat to face him. "I don't. They're spending the night, so I can stay out as long as I like."

The implication sent a jolt directly to his groin. "I'll have to make sure you enjoy every second of your free night."

She chuckled. "I'd expect nothing less. You've been setting the bar pretty high." She resettled in her seat and started humming along with the song.

Jabari wanted the bar to be high enough that no other man would be able to climb it. Twenty-five minutes later, he parked in his driveway and escorted her to the front door.

"Wow," she said when she walked into the foyer. "This is gorgeous."

"Thanks. Let me show you around." He pointed out the formal living and dining rooms, guest bedroom and two first-floor bathrooms, and then took the stairs to the upper level.

Alisha stuck her head in two unfurnished bedrooms, each with its own bathroom. "This is not your usual bachelor pad. Seems a little big for one person. Looks more suited for a good-sized family."

"Yes, it is." She whipped her head around and he met her gaze steadily. He had purchased the home with the intent of filling it with a wife and two or three children. "One more room to go." Jabari gestured toward his bedroom. The master suite had been one of the things that heavily influenced his decision to buy the house. It had a sitting area connected by an archway that he'd furnished with two loungers and a small table positioned to view the fireplace or backyard, and a desk where he could work.

"I love this stone fireplace." She ran her hand along the sides. "Balcony?" she asked, gesturing to the French doors.

"Yes." He opened the doors so she could go out.

"You have a huge backyard. I wish I could see it."

Aside from the solar lights around the deck, the yard was shrouded in darkness. "You can see it the next time you're here." He took her hand and led her back downstairs to the family room, where they would watch the movie. She had asked to see *Black Panther.* He was a fan of the Marvel Comics character as well as the movie, and had no problem with her suggestion.

Alisha laughed and pointed at the seventy-two-inch television mounted on the wall. "You don't need to go to the theater. You've got your own right here."

"And I have the theater sound to go with it," Jabari said. They shared a smile. "Make yourself comfortable. I'll get the snacks ready and start the movie."

Instead of sitting, she followed him to the kitchen. "I love this kitchen. There's enough room to cook a Christmas dinner without anyone bumping into each other."

He laughed as he turned on the oven. "I can't speak to that. Christmas has always been at my parents' house and I don't see my mother changing her tradition, at least for a while."

"Same with my mom." She climbed onto a barstool. "What kind of snacks are we having? You know I need my popcorn."

"I have your popcorn. It's a kicked-up version my mother used to make for us. I also have some more of that homemade vanilla ice cream and orange Crush soda to make that freeze you mentioned."

Alisha hopped down from the stool, rushed around the bar and threw her arms around him. "Ooh, *yes*! Thank you. I think that bar just went up another notch." She pulled his head down and kissed him. "I like you, Jabari."

"I like you, too." A lot. Jabari eased her closer and captured her lips again. He took his time feeding from the sweetness of her mouth, tasting and absorbing her essence into his. She pressed her soft curves against him and he heard himself groan. He finally dragged his mouth away but continued to place fleeting kisses along her jaw. At length, Jabari lifted his head. The desire he saw in her eyes had him close to saying they should forget about watching the movie and instead create one of their own.

She backed out of his arms, her breathing as ragged as his. "Um...do you need help with anything?"

"No. It'll be ready in a few minutes." He stood there a moment longer before going over to the other side of the kitchen where he'd left everything. He poured the popcorn he had already made into a bowl, added mini pretzels, Cheezits, Worcestershire sauce and cheese-flavored seasoning. Jabari mixed it all together, poured it onto a cookie sheet and slid it into the oven. "It'll be ready in about fifteen minutes." While waiting, he went into the family room and stuck the movie into the Blu-ray player.

"I can't get over the size of this TV. I thought my brother's was big, but this is *huge*. And the picture looks almost 3-D. I'm going to be salty having to go back to my little screen."

He smiled. "Your TV isn't that small. It's what, about forty inches?"

"Yes, but it looks like a tablet compared to yours."

He shook his head. "Come on and we'll make your orange freeze." The smile she gave him had him contemplating buying a case of the soda and making at least two gallons of the ice cream. He got two large glasses from the cabinet, the ice cream scooper from the drawer and placed them on the counter. Then he got the ice cream and soda. Although Alisha didn't say anything, she studied him closely, as if making sure he added the ingredients in the right amounts. When he was done, he placed a long spoon and straw in each glass and handed her one. "Well?"

Alisha took a sip, angled her head, took another one, then gave him a thumbs-up. "You can make this for me anytime. It's perfect. Thank you."

Jabari took a sip of his own and nodded. "This is good."

"You've never had one before?" she asked with surprise.

"Nope. Only root beer or Coke."

She rolled her eyes playfully. "I can't believe you've never had the best drink ever. It's a good thing I'm here."

"It's a very good thing you're here." He stroked a finger down her cheek. Just like that the mood went from playful to something else. Their gazes held and their attraction rose. The oven timer went off, breaking the sensual spell. Jabari turned off the oven and, using an oven mitt, removed the pan and poured everything into a large bowl. "Can you grab some napkins?" Alisha pulled a few from the holder and followed him into the family room. They sat in an oversize recliner that comfortably fit two people and Jabari started the movie.

Alisha ate some of the popcorn snack. "Oh, my goodness. This is so good. You'll have to give me the recipe. Corey and Lia would love this."

"I'm glad you like it. I'll write it down for you." They ate, laughed and recited their favorite lines. He'd seen the movie once before but enjoyed it more this time. When the movie ended, Jabari placed the empty bowl and their glasses on the end table and gathered her closer to him. He closed his eyes as contentment washed over him. He tilted Alisha's chin, touched his lips to hers and then slid his tongue inside. He deepened the kiss, wanting her to feel how much he wanted her. She reciprocated by grabbing his head and holding him in place. Her hand traveled over his face, down his chest and under his shirt. Feeling her hand on his bare skin skyrocketed his desire. Without breaking the seal of their mouths, Jabari straddled her across his lap, reached under her top and caressed her back. He undid the clasp on her bra, pushed her top up and cupped her full breasts.

Alisha tore her mouth away and moaned.

With her head thrown back, she made an alluring picture. The sight made him grow harder. He transferred his kisses to her breasts, suckling first one erect nipple, then the other. He was quickly losing control. "Baby, if you're not ready for this, I need you to tell me now."

She met his eyes. "I'm ready."

It was all he needed to hear. Jabari put down the recliner and carried her up to his bedroom. He planned to gift her with a night that neither of them would forget.

Alisha didn't stop to analyze her decision. If she did, she might be running away as fast as she could. Sleeping with Jabari would only add to the complex emotions she had, but tonight, she wanted him. Wanted to *feel* him. She would deal with the ramifications later.

He laid her on his bed, turned on a table lamp and removed her shoes. "Are you sure about this, Alisha? I don't want you to have any regrets."

She placed a finger to his lips. "No regrets." She replaced her finger with her mouth and he kissed her down on the bed. With lightning speed, he had her shirt and bra off. He trailed butterfly kisses down her neck and the valley between her breasts, while his hand skimmed over her thighs and up to unfasten her pants.

Jabari came up on his knees and hooked his fingers in the waistband of her crop pants. "Ease up, baby."

She lifted her hips and he slid her pants and panties down and off. The kisses began again, this time from her ankle, up to her knees and higher to her inner thighs. He spent an inordinate amount of time just touching and kissing her everywhere. Alisha's breath stacked up in her throat. She cried out when he slid one finger inside of her. "Jabari," she called on a ragged groan. She arched against his hand, urging him to give her more. Kissing her again, he added another finger and thrust in and out.

"Do you like this, baby?"

"I…oh, *yes*." She more than liked it. He changed the tempo and she gripped his shoulders as his fingers moved faster. Her breath came in short gasps as the pressure built and she screamed his name. Bolts of pleasure tore through her body and she trembled as waves of pleasure consumed her. He withdrew his fingers and she moaned at the loss.

"Don't worry, we're not done, sweetheart. I'm not close to being done." Jabari stood, removed his clothes and donned a condom.

Alisha had known he had a great body, but she couldn't take her eyes off him. Her gaze roamed over every smooth brown inch of him, from his bulging biceps and rock-solid chest, to his strong, muscular thighs and thick erection. He was a pure work of art. He came back to the bed and stretched his body over hers. She sighed with pleasure.

Jabari stared into her eyes. "You're beautiful and I want you to know that I don't take lightly what we're doing. This isn't some one-nighter, Alisha. It's more. I want more."

He didn't give her time to process his statement before he covered her mouth in a searing kiss that snatched her breath and sent a shiver down her spine.

"I can't get enough of touching and kissing you," he murmured as he charted a path with his hands and tongue all over her body.

Alisha couldn't get enough of it, either...being touched *and* touching him. He alternately kissed and suckled her neck, shoulders and breasts. Jabari continued his sensuous torture until she was writhing and moaning. Just when she thought she couldn't take anymore, he used his knee to part her thighs and teased the head of his erection at her entrance. Their eyes locked and he guided himself slowly inside until he was fully embedded. They both moaned. Keeping his gaze focused on her, he withdrew to the tip and slowly thrust back in, delving deeper with each rhythmic push. He guided her hips as he kept up the measured, insistent rhythm. Alisha shuddered at the feel of him sliding in and out of her at an unhurried pace. She wrapped her legs around his waist and locked her ankles behind his back as he kept up the sensual tempo.

"Do you feel this?"

She felt him everywhere, and the sensations were so staggering she thought she might pass out. His strokes came faster and harder, and she moaned with pleasure. She met and matched his thrusts, their passionate cries echoing in the quiet space. Jabari changed the tempo and slowed, the deep subtle movements burning her up from the inside out. And suddenly her body was shaking, and she came with a soul-shattering intensity.

Moments later, Jabari went rigid against her, threw his head back and exploded with a shout. His body shuddered above hers, his breathing harsh and uneven.

Alisha opened her eyes and found him staring at her with a look of tenderness that brought tears to her eyes. He kissed her softly, tenderly and with a passion that stirred the emotions she had kept locked away. *I cannot fall in love with this man.*

Alisha woke up Saturday morning with a smile. Despite her misgivings, she'd thoroughly enjoyed being with Jabari last night. They had made love a second time while showering and her core pulsed at the memory of him thrusting deeply inside her from behind as she stood with her hands braced on the shower wall that was large enough for three people. He'd brought her home around three and she'd fallen into bed and gone promptly to sleep. Her morning would be perfect if it weren't for the slight sore throat and body aches.

Alisha didn't know if they stemmed from some kind of virus or all the screaming she had done last night, along with the sensual workout. Most likely it was a combination of both. She thought she had successfully kept the bug at bay, but it seemed as if it might be coming back. Since her mother wouldn't be bringing Corey and Lia home until noon, she took more cold medicine and slept another two hours.

Alisha felt only marginally better when she woke up. Determined to power through like always, she managed to get two loads of laundry done before her mother arrived.

"Mommy!" Lia said with her arms outstretched.

She hugged her baby and placed a kiss on her hair but didn't pick her up. She repeated the same with Corey. Alisha didn't want them to get the same infection. "Were you guys good for Grandma and Papa?"

"Yes, but my stomach hurts."

She rubbed Corey's back. "Why don't you go lie down for a while."

"Okay."

When he slowly walked out of the room instead of running, Alisha knew he really didn't feel well. She turned to her mom. "Did he eat a lot?"

"No. In fact the only thing they had that was even remotely sweet was graham crackers. This morning, he only ate a few bites of his pancake, while little Miss Lia devoured two." She handed Alisha a bag. "Corey said you were almost out of syrup."

"Thanks, Mom. If I felt like it, I'd make me some pancakes."

Her mother frowned. "What's wrong?"

"I think I'm coming down with something. I've been

trying to fight it all week." She turned to watch Lia walk down the hallway to Corey's room.

"I can hear it."

"I know. My throat hurts." She was starting to lose her voice.

"How was your date?"

"We had a great time." They'd had a better than great time, but she didn't think her mother needed to have those details.

"Sounds like you guys are getting serious."

"I don't know."

"Well, he seems far more settled than Wayne ever was." She rolled her eyes.

Alisha recalled Jabari's response when she'd mentioned his house being suited for a family. There was something about the way he'd said it. She'd tried not to read anything into it but couldn't help wondering what he had meant. "He is. I didn't tell you, but Wayne filed to terminate his parental rights," she said quietly, glancing over her shoulder to make sure the kids weren't in hearing range.

"It's not like he's been a father anyway," her mother mumbled. "Sorry, baby. How are you feeling about it?"

"On one hand, if the judge allows it, I'll be totally free from him. On the other, I'd feel bad for Corey. He's been asking a lot more questions."

"And I bet Georgia is filling his head with a bunch of nonsense about her no-account son."

Alisha scrubbed a hand over her forehead and released a deep sigh. "Apparently, she's been asking him whether I'm seeing someone."

Her mother placed a hand on her hip. "That's none of her business."

"I don't want to keep them from going to see her,

but if she keeps this up, I will. My baby felt so bad and thought he'd done something wrong."

"That woman needs to keep her mouth shut."

Alisha rubbed her temples.

"You don't look so good, honey. Your father and I are supposed to be going up to Tahoe in a little while for a dinner cruise and overnight stay. But if you need me to stay and help you, I can cancel."

She waved her off. "Go on your trip, Mom, I'll be fine. I'm going to take it slow."

"What about Corey?"

"I'm sure he'll be okay." She had done this countless times alone and had always managed.

"If you're sure."

"I am."

"Okay. I'll check on you tomorrow when we get back."

"You guys have fun." Alisha saw her mother to the door and went to check on Corey. He lay in bed curled up in a ball. Lia, seemingly sensing something was wrong with her big brother, sat next to him. Alisha checked Corey's forehead and sent up a silent thank-you that he didn't have a fever. She figured that with a little rest and light eating, he would back to his usual self soon.

As the day progressed, Alisha moved more and more slowly, and by late afternoon, her hoarseness, sore throat and body aches had worsened. She didn't need a thermometer to tell her what she already knew—she had a fever. To make matters worse, Corey's stomachache hadn't gone away. Her homemade chicken noodle soup always worked wonders for colds or bellyaches, but she could barely heat a can of soup, let alone stand in the kitchen for the time it would take to make her concoction. She and Corey only managed to eat a small portion. Lia, on the other hand, was her usual ball of energy. Alisha wished she could bottle it and take a couple of sips. She needed all the energy she could get at the moment.

Afterward, she gathered them on her bed and turned on a movie. It was easier than having to get up and down to check on them. Alisha fought to keep her eyes open. She was ready to fall out and contemplated calling Lorenzo to come over. But she had to keep reminding herself that her brother was a married man and she couldn't rely on him as much as she used to. He most likely wouldn't agree with Alisha's assessment, but Alisha respected Desiree's position in Lorenzo's life.

The phone rang. She picked up her phone and saw Jabari's name on the display. She answered and greeted him.

"Alisha? Baby, are you all right?" he asked, concern lining his voice.

"I think I'm coming down with the flu or some type of cold."

"Do you want me to come over and help with the kids?"

"Thanks, but no. I don't want you to catch whatever I have. Besides, I do this all the time. As soon as I put them to bed, I'll be right behind them." She didn't want to start relying on him and then have him disappear just like her ex.

"I don't like this. You shouldn't be alone."

"I'll be fine after I get some rest." Although she said the words, she wasn't fine.

His heavy sigh came through the line. "Promise me you'll call me if you need me."

"I promise." Alisha hung up and dropped the phone

on the bed. Common sense said she probably should have accepted his offer, but as she'd told him, she always did this alone and managed. Also, allowing him to come over and take care of her and her son spoke of an intimacy she wasn't ready to open herself to yet.

She dragged herself up and got both children bathed and into bed. What normally took her less than thirty minutes to do, tonight required more than double because she had to stop and catch her breath several times. Her entire body ached as if she'd been run over by an eighteen-wheeler. Alisha contemplated skipping her own shower, but between the hot and cold sweats, her skin felt clammy. She took some daytime cold medicine—with the kids home, she couldn't risk not being able to function with the nighttime version—then hopped into the shower. It was all she could do to lift her arms and wash. Ten minutes later, she fell across the bed and promptly drifted off.

"Mommy!"

Alisha jerked upright in the bed and immediately regretted the sudden movement. She groaned and pressed her hands against her head to ease the throbbing pain and dizziness. She glanced over at the clock—midnight. After getting her bearings, she stumbled down the hallway to Corey's room. "Your stomach is still hurting?"

Corey nodded, clutching his midsection as tears ran down his face.

"I'm so sorry, honey." Before she could say anything else, he vomited, projectile-style, all over himself, her, the bed and the carpet. Ignoring her own pain, she grabbed him up and hurried to the bathroom, where he continued to empty his stomach into the toilet between sobs. Alisha turned on the shower and adjusted the temperature.

Corey slumped to the floor.

She stroked his forehead. "Is it better now?"

He barely nodded.

"Let's get you cleaned up, okay?" Alisha stripped off his soiled pajamas and washed him off. "It's all right, sweetheart," she said to him as he continued to cry. She wrapped him in a towel. "Stay right here and I'll get you another pair of pajamas." She stepped out and heard Lia crying. *Not tonight.* "What's wrong?" Alisha tried to console her, but Lia kept right on crying.

"Mama, up, please."

She paused in midreach, remembering that she still needed to change her own clothes. "Hold on, baby. I can't pick you up right now. I'll be right back." She rushed out of the room and into Corey's to get his pajamas, then back to the bathroom to help him dress. She led him into the family room. "Lie down right here until I clean up your bed." His cries had softened to a whimper, but he clung to her.

"*Noo*, Mommy."

"I'll be right back. I have to change my clothes, too." Alisha did a quick change, went to get Lia, who hadn't stopped crying, and sat in the rocking chair with her. "It's okay, Lia." After a few minutes of rocking, Lia stopped crying but started up again every time Alisha tried to put her down. Resignedly, Alisha stood and carried her to the family room, being careful to avoid the trail of vomit in the hallway. "How about you watch *Mickey Mouse Clubhouse* while I go clean up Corey's room?" She had recorded several of the episodes for moments like this.

Alisha finally got Corey and Lia to settle down enough for her to tackle the big mess. She filled a bucket with warm water, got towels, liquid soap and carpet cleaner, and started in. Her throat was on fire and every movement of her head made her light-headed and increased the pain. She gritted her teeth. Tears stung her eyes and she thought about calling Lorenzo and asking him to come over but nixed the idea. With her parents out of town, she didn't have anyone else to rely on. She wiped away the tears that wouldn't stop with the back of her hand and continued to scrub the hall carpet. *Promise me you'll call me if you need me.* Jabari's words came back to her. As much as she didn't want to drop something like this on him—what man would want to take on a sick woman and kid who wasn't his—she needed help.

Alisha trudged to her bedroom and searched in the rumpled covers for her cell. She found it, scrolled to Jabari's number and pressed Call.

"Hello," came the groggy greeting.

"Jabari," Alisha croaked, "I'm sorry to bother you, but you said to call. I… Can you…?"

"I'm on my way."

She sighed in relief. Tonight her pride would take a back seat.

Chapter 10

Jabari pulled up to Alisha's house exactly twenty-five minutes after her call. He mentally berated himself for not following his first mind and coming immediately after their earlier conversation. He'd broken every speed limit and sent thanks to heaven that he hadn't been stopped. He jumped out of the car and hurried up the walkway to ring the bell. When she opened the door holding Lia in her arms and he saw both their tearstained faces, his heart constricted. "Hey, baby." Jabari immediately relieved her of the baby and draped an arm around Alisha's shoulder. "What do you need me to do?"

"Corey's room."

As soon as they reached the hall, the pungent smell of vomit assailed him. He saw a bucket, carpet cleaner and towels on the floor. "Where is he?"

"Lying on the sofa in the family room."

Jabari followed the trail into Corey's room. "Where do you keep the sheets?"

She showed him the laundry room, where she kept sheets and towels. "Thank you so much for being here."

He placed a soft kiss on her brow. "Sweetheart, I would've been here hours ago if you'd called." He barely made out her words with her hoarse voice and felt the heat radiating from her. He was glad he'd had the foresight to bring something for her cold and fever. "You go get in bed and I'll take care of everything else."

"But Corey—"

"I've got it, baby. I'll be in to check on you in a little bit." Jabari watched Alisha's slow steps as she made her way to the bedroom at the end of the hall. He shifted his attention to the little girl in his arms. "You worried about your mama, baby girl?" He kissed her forehead and rubbed her back. "Let's go see about your big brother." He cut through the kitchen and rounded the corner to the family room. Some Mickey Mouse show played on the television. Corey's sad eyes met Jabari's.

"Hi, Mr. Sutton. I don't feel good."

Jabari lowered himself to the sofa next to Corey. "I know. I'm going to get your bed all cleaned up so you can get in it."

"Okay," Corey said quietly.

He sat Lia next to Corey and she began to fuss. "I'll be right back." He tried to reassure her, but her little hands gripped his shirt and wouldn't let go. He had no other choice but to take her with him. Jabari went to the kitchen, poured a small amount of water in a glass and took it to Alisha's room. She had already fallen asleep. He didn't want to wake her, but he knew she needed the medicine. He coaxed her awake and got her to swallow the two cold tablets, then covered her with the sheet. "Okay, Lia, are you going to help me clean up?" She stared at him with sleepy eyes.

He had no idea how Alisha managed situations like this alone. He could have had everything cleaned up in a short amount of time, but running between both children made the task take much longer. Lia finally fell asleep on his shoulder and he carefully placed her in her bed. He went back to the family room, picked up Corey and carried the half-asleep little boy to his room.

Corey moaned. "My stomach…" He gagged and started crying.

Jabari quickly changed directions and deposited Corey in front of the toilet just as he started throwing up. "It's okay, little man. You're going to be all right," he said, trying to assure the boy. When he was certain the episode had ended, Jabari carried Corey's listless body to bed, changed his pajamas and then went back to sanitize the bathroom. He took all the dirty towels and clothes and put them in the washer. While they washed, he flipped through the television channels but found nothing to hold his interest for long. Once the washer stopped, he tossed the clothes in the dryer and went to check on Corey.

When he came out, he heard Lia calling for her mother and went to get her before she could wake Alisha. "Hey, you're awake again?" He figured she had been awakened by Corey's crying. Jabari took her to the family room, stretched out on the sofa and laid her on his chest. He was exhausted and couldn't imagine Alisha doing this while sick. It made his admiration for her soar through the roof. While lying there, he gently patted Lia's back and contemplated the direction this relationship seemed to be headed. Tonight, he'd done everything a husband and father would do, and he was neither. But strangely enough, he hadn't minded. In fact, it solidified the feeling in his mind that this was exactly where he wanted to be. In the back of his mind, a nagging voice reminded him that Alisha had an ex-husband whom he still didn't know much about, but he pushed the thought aside. She'd told him the guy wasn't in the picture and he believed her. After several minutes, he angled his head and noticed that Lia had finally gone to sleep. He lay there awhile longer just to make sure she stayed asleep, then carefully rose and put her to bed. He checked on Corey and gave him a few sips of some Pedialyte he'd found in the pantry to keep him from getting dehydrated.

Jabari crept silently down the hall to Alisha's bedroom and crossed the room to where she lay sleeping. He gently touched his lips to her forehead, pleased to find it much cooler. He stood there and studied her. She drew him like no other woman and he had to find a way to keep her in his life. He still sensed her hesitancy and knew it stemmed from her ex, but last night, she'd given him all of herself and he had done the same.

As much as he wanted to climb into bed and hold her through the night, it wouldn't be good for her children to see. He had more respect for Alisha than that. He stroked a gentle finger down her cheek and brushed his lips over the spot. Emotions swirled in his chest. *I'm falling in love with her. And her children.*

Alisha woke with a start and glanced over at the nightstand clock. It was already after eight. Though her head and throat still ached, she felt a little better. *Corey!* She flipped the covers back, jumped to her feet and started from the room. She remembered trying to clean up, but nothing after that. Alisha went still. Jabari. She'd called him and he'd come. She frowned. She didn't recall walking him to the door. *I must've really been out of it.* She ran a hand through her hair, trying to tame the wild mess. Last night, she hadn't cared one bit about wrapping it.

She walked down the hall, poked her head in Lia's room and smiled upon seeing Lia lying on her back with her arms and legs spread. She covered her with the light blanket, which would most likely be kicked off again in the next five minutes, and then checked on Corey.

He seemed to be sleeping soundly and didn't have a fever. Alisha paused. He wore a different pair of pajamas. She gently stroked his head and smiled. Hopefully, whatever bug he'd contracted had passed. On her way out, she noticed the carpet had been cleaned in Corey's room and the hallway. Curious, she went into the bathroom and saw that it, too, had been left spotless. She would have to call Jabari later to thank him. He'd done far more than she expected.

After brushing her teeth and pulling on a pair of sweatpants and a tee, Alisha put her hair into a ponytail and made her way to the kitchen. The babies would be awake soon and Lia would definitely be hungry. She would start with something light and see how Corey's system reacted before progressing to his normal diet. She turned the corner and froze in her tracks. Jabari lay sprawled on the sofa with one hand on his belly and the other thrown over his face. His soft snores floated across the space. She came closer and noticed the tired lines etched in his face. She couldn't believe he'd stayed all night. Emotion welled up inside her. As if sensing her perusal, he opened his eyes.

Jabari eased his hand down and sat up. “Hey, baby. How are you feeling?”

“Much better. Thank you for everything.” It had been a long time since she’d had a man other than her father and brother come to her rescue, but she didn’t want to get her hopes up that it would always be this way in case their relationship didn’t last.

He stood and dragged a hand down his face. “Let me go grab my bag out of the car and get cleaned up. Then I’ll help you.”

Bag? Had he planned to stay the night? She nodded and watched his sexy stroll until he disappeared. Turning her attention to breakfast, Alisha searched the pantry for the spare bottle of Pedialyte she always kept on hand but didn’t see it. She could have sworn that she had at least one or two bottles. She decided that she would just dilute some orange juice, since she couldn’t find it. Alisha went to the refrigerator, took out eggs, milk and butter. She saw the electrolyte drink on the top shelf and shook her head. Jabari must have opened it. Once again, he had surprised her. One would think he had a couple of kids stashed somewhere given the way he’d handled last night’s circumstances.

A few minutes later, Jabari came into the kitchen wearing a different pair of jeans and shirt. He wrapped his arms around her. “What do you need me to do?”

“Nothing. You look exhausted. I’m just going to make scrambled eggs and toast. I can fix you something a little more substantial if you want.”

“I’m good.”

She laid her head on his chest and hugged him. “I’ll make it up to you.”

A sexy grin curved his lips. “Only if it’s in a bed and you’re lying with me.”

She snapped her head up and her mouth fell open.

"Seriously, though, there's nothing to make up. I'll be here to help you anytime you need me. All you have to do is ask." He eased back. "Do you think I can have a good-morning kiss?"

Alisha smiled. "You sure you want a kiss? I know you don't want this bug I have." Her voice still hadn't returned to normal.

"I'm willing to chance it," Jabari said as his mouth connected with hers.

She melted in his arms. His tongue moved slowly, provocatively, curling around hers. She came up on her tiptoes and gripped his shoulders. Too soon, it ended.

"Good morning."

This had been a better than good morning in her estimation. A big part of her wanted to start all her mornings this way. "Good morning." She backed out of his embrace and started breakfast.

Lia came into the kitchen a few minutes later, yawning and rubbing her eyes. Corey followed shortly after.

Jabari sat at the kitchen table with Corey on one knee and Lia on the other, chatting. When breakfast was ready, he helped bring the plates to the table.

Alisha observed the interaction between Jabari and the kids as they laughed and ate. Family meals had been one of the things she'd wanted in her marriage, but they had rarely happened. She'd grown up with them and wanted to continue the tradition with her own family. Those dinners served as check-in times and opportunities for fun conversation.

When they finished, she started to get up and Jabari said, "You stay put. I'll take care of these. I don't want you relapsing and all my hard work nursing you back to health going to waste." He tossed her a wink and cleared the table.

She laughed, though with her being hoarse, it sounded more like a wheeze. The doorbell rang and, still chuckling, she went to answer it. She figured her parents had returned early and come to check on her. Either that or her mother had told Lorenzo and sent him. It had happened on more than one occasion. She opened the door and couldn't have been more wrong.

"What are you doing here, Wayne?" She hadn't seen her ex in over two years and he had never been to her house. Georgia immediately came to mind.

"I came to see my kids."

Alisha looked him up and down. At just under six feet, he'd seemed to her the best-looking boy in her high school class. But now, as he stood there, she couldn't find one thing to like about him. "You mean the kids you plan to throw away like yesterday's old trash?"

"Are you going to let me in?"

"Absolutely not. I told you a long time ago that you were not going to walk in and out of their lives like a revolving door, popping up every time the urge hits you."

Wayne banged on the locked screen door. "You can't just keep me from seeing them."

"You've done just fine on your own with that one," she said with a snort. "And I assume since you're here, you have the $13,684.97 you owe in child support, right?" Their voices steadily rose.

"What's going on here?" Jabari appeared at the door and divided a glance between Alisha and Wayne.

"I guess my mother was right about you bringing all kinds of men around my kids."

"Your mother needs to mind her own damn business," Alisha said. She went to unlock the screen. She was going to punch this fool's lights out.

Jabari stepped between her and the door. "Do you want him here?"

"No!"

He turned to Wayne. "You have thirty seconds to walk away."

"Or what?" Wayne tried to puff himself up, but with Jabari towering over him by a good four or five inches, he looked comical, at best.

"Or I'm going to unlock the screen door and show you exactly how I feel about cowards who disrespect women."

For a moment, Wayne looked like he was going to challenge Jabari, but he obviously thought better of it. He sent a hostile glare Alisha's way. "You're not getting rid of me that easy. These are *my* kids and I'll be back. You can count on it."

"For your continued good health, I wouldn't advise it," Jabari said with lethal calmness.

Alisha reached around him and slammed the door. "Sorry about that. Thanks for coming to my rescue again."

"Does he do this often?"

"No. This is the first time I've seen him in over two years. My guess is that his mother told him about you." At his confused look, she explained. "She kept the kids a couple of times recently and I found out she'd been asking Corey whether I'm seeing someone. Corey mentioned the picnic to her."

"I see. So, he's going to start coming around again?"

"He's going to do the same thing he's been doing… *nothing*."

"Didn't sound that way just now." Jabari scrubbed

a hand over his head. "I should probably head out." He stepped around her and strode off.

Alisha stood there, stunned. Less than five minutes later, Jabari left. She was mad at him for leaving, mad at Wayne for showing up out of the blue and disrupting her life and mad at herself for getting mixed up with both of them. Any chance she had with a new relationship had been just shot to hell. Not that she could blame Jabari. What man would want to be embroiled in the kind of mess she knew Wayne could cause? *And this is why I don't rely on a man.*

Alisha spent the rest of the afternoon taking it easy. She had to endure questions from Corey about when Jabari would return and she didn't have an answer for him. She didn't have one for herself. She hoped that he would call, but as the hours passed, she accepted the fact that whatever they had shared was maybe over. She should have stuck with her first mind and walked away from Jabari after that first date.

Chapter 11

Sunday afternoon, Jabari tried to concentrate on his breathing while running. He couldn't stop thinking about what had happened at Alisha's house that morning. Seeing her ex had brought back all the reasons why he never dated women with children. He had been confused and hurt and a jumble of other emotions he didn't quite understand. He increased his pace, the slip-slap of his running shoes hitting the pavement with a steady rhythm. Beside him, he could hear Martin panting. They made it back to the starting point and Jabari slowed, then stopped.

Martin collapsed on a nearby bench, winded. "So there's trouble in paradise, I take it."

Jabari sat on the other end of the bench. "What makes you think that?"

"You nearly killed me with this run. I consider myself in decent shape, since we've been doing this for the past eight months, but today I felt like I'd stumbled into boot camp. Besides, you've been quieter than usual."

Jabari couldn't deny that he hadn't had much to say. He tended to be somewhere on the introvert scale, but he'd learned to put himself out there when necessary. He had considered canceling but didn't want to explain why, and he'd needed to work off his frustration.

"Well? After all this, you owe me. I thought things were going well and you were meeting Friday night."

"We did. And we had a great time watching a movie at my place." They'd had an even better time after the movie.

"With the way you're feeling about this woman and how you're acting now, something more than movie night happened," Martin said perceptively.

"Yeah, it did."

"Are you ready to take it to the next level and she's not?"

"We've already taken it to the next level. She got sick on Saturday and so did her son. She called me around midnight asking for help and I went. I don't know how she does it by herself all the time." He told Martin about Corey throwing up, Lia crying, Alisha's fever and how he'd cleaned up and stayed overnight.

"Wait. You spent the night at her house with her kids there?"

"On the couch."

Martin shook his head. "You're a better man than me."

"I wasn't there to sleep with her. She was sick and needed my help. After breakfast this morning, her ex showed up demanding to see the kids. She refused and he acted like he might do something, banging on the door and whatnot. He tried to get into my face and I sent him packing. Then I left," he added. "I didn't want to get in the middle." More than that, his insecurities had gotten the best of him. She said she had no plans to take him back, but they had a history and two children, and Jabari didn't want to end up being the odd man out.

"It wouldn't bother you if you didn't care about her. What about her kids? How do you feel about them?"

"They're great." He recalled Lia not wanting to let him go and sleeping on his chest, playing ball with Corey and the way the little boy had laid his head on Jabari's shoulder last night as if he trusted Jabari with his life. Those things were exactly what he had hoped to share with his own children. He was getting attached to Corey and Lia and didn't want to risk them being ripped out of his life.

"Have you talked to Alisha since leaving this morning?"

He glanced over at the trees blowing in the slight breeze. "No."

"You're going to walk away?"

"I don't know. I thought about it." But not having Alisha in his life brought on another set of emotions that made the churning in his gut worsen. Jabari had to decide whether to stick it out or get out before investing any more of his heart.

"Don't wait too long to decide, bro. It's not a good choice for either of you."

"No, probably not." Not wanting to talk about it anymore, he shifted the conversation to work. "I'm going to the office after we're done here to put trackers on all the computers."

Martin frowned. "I thought you guys did that already."

"We did. I'm adding an additional one that not even my team knows about. If someone is trying to bypass the current known firewalls, they'll have to get by another gate."

"I assume this is something you picked up in the military?"

Jabari smiled. "Something like that."

"I'm all for anything that keeps my data safe."

"How are those two guys you hired working out?" He had done extensive background checks on both men after their meeting last week and hadn't found any red flags.

"So far, so good. I've decided to do more of the final programming myself and I've updated a few things."

"Which means they don't have all the pieces, either."

"No." Martin glanced Jabari's way. "I've learned not to give away all my secrets."

He understood. Back in high school, Martin had been paired with another classmate for a project and shared his plans. The guy had ended up asking for another partner and doing the same project. It had taken Martin weeks to prove that he had, indeed, been the mastermind. After that, Martin had never trusted anyone completely.

"I'll do everything in my power to make sure your secrets stay yours. I'm watching everyone," Jabari assured him.

"You think it's internal?"

"I'm leaning that way." Jabari stood and Martin followed suit. "It's getting late and I don't want to be there all night." They walked to the parking lot, said their goodbyes and went their separate ways.

Once at the office, Jabari took over three hours to set up the firewalls on all the computers. When he finished, he contemplated installing additional cameras in the workspaces and made a mental note to reach out to an old army buddy. Due to the sensitive nature of the company's data, employees, when hired, were notified that the premises would be under surveillance, so it wouldn't be breaking any laws. He went back to his office and shut down everything. A glimpse at the wall clock showed the time to be nine fifteen. He toyed with the idea of calling Alisha, but he didn't know what to say other than to ask about her and Corey's health. In the end he sent a text. Her reply came back a short while later with one word: Fine.

Jabari tossed the phone on his desk, leaned back in the chair and let out a frustrated sigh. Everything inside him said he should drive over and talk to her, but her reply let him know that she might not be happy to see him. In the end, he drove home. Thoughts of her remained on his mind for the rest of the night and each time he reasoned that walking away might be the best course of action, his heart wouldn't allow him to entertain the idea. Now what was he supposed to do?

By Wednesday, Alisha was back to herself. She had taken Monday off to be on the safe side and it turned out to be a good thing. Her energy level had increased, and physically, she felt better than she had in the past week. However, she couldn't say the same about her emotional health. She was still incensed that Georgia had told Wayne about her relationship with Jabari. Neither had a say in how she lived her life and *who* she chose to live it with. She had been trying to maintain the kids' relationship with Georgia, but after this latest stunt, she seriously considered telling the woman they were off-limits to her. Alisha would not tolerate any interference in their lives, even if it meant keeping Corey and Lia away from Georgia.

Then there was Jabari. Outside of the text he'd sent Sunday night, she hadn't heard from him. It bothered her, but as she had told herself before, she couldn't blame him for not wanting to be embroiled in Wayne's drama. And drama would be the only thing Wayne brought. She hoped the judge would grant him his wish. He wanted to play games, but he would have to do it somewhere else far away from her.

Alisha tried to tell herself that she could easily move on from Jabari—they had only known each other a few weeks—but deep inside she knew it was a lie. She missed him and his easygoing manner, their phone calls. She wanted to talk to someone about her dilemma but didn't know whom to call. She usually shared her relationship woes with Michelle, but with Jabari being her brother, she didn't think it would be a good idea. As a result, Alisha avoided her best friend all week. Whenever Michelle texted or called her floor to see if they could have lunch, Alisha made an excuse. Today Michelle hadn't called and Alisha breathed a sigh of relief.

She decided to have lunch outside near the grassy area. She found an empty bench beneath a shade tree. With the October temperatures in the seventies, she could enjoy the weather before it turned cold. Before she could take a bite of her food, she saw Michelle approaching.

"Hey, girl," Michelle said, sitting next to Alisha. "I've been trying to catch up with you all week. I heard you called in sick Monday. Was it one of the kids?"

Alisha made room on the bench. "Corey had a stomach bug over the weekend, but I was the sick one."

"You should've called me so I could help by keeping Lia."

"It worked out okay."

Michelle ate some of her trail mix. "How are things between you and Jabari?"

She chuckled. "For someone who's supposed to be staying out of it, you sure ask a lot of questions."

Michelle shrugged. "What can I say? We've been sharing secrets for over a decade. Old habits are hard to break."

"That might be true if you were trying to actually break them."

"True. So?"

She didn't speak for a few seconds. Then she said, "I haven't talked to him since Sunday." Alisha told her friend how Jabari had come over and helped her Saturday night. "I couldn't believe how he took care of everything. Apparently, Lia woke up crying a couple of times and I never knew it until he told me. He even washed the dirty sheets and towels." She had discovered them in the dryer later that evening. "Everything was fine until Wayne showed up after breakfast Sunday morning talking about how he wanted to see *his kids*."

Michelle whipped her head around. "He *what*? He hasn't come around in the last what…two years or longer? And has he even seen Lia?"

"Yeah." Alisha pushed the salad around in her bowl.

"Ugh! I can't stand that idiot. You should've let Lorenzo kick his butt, like he wanted."

"Maybe." When Lorenzo found out that Wayne had cheated on Alisha and left her, it had taken both her father and Uncle Reuben to keep her brother and cousins from hunting Wayne down. Alisha had cried and pleaded with them because she hadn't wanted them going to jail. "Anyway, I wouldn't let him in. Jabari came to the door and told Wayne to leave. After that, Jabari said he should probably leave and that was it."

Michelle paused. "Wait a minute. It just dawned on me that you said my brother spent the night at your house."

She eyed her friend. "Yes, on the *sofa*. I doubt he got much sleep because he stayed up checking on everybody all night long. I still can't believe how amazing he was. But now? I mean, I kind of understand. I wouldn't want to add that kind of hassle to my life, either."

"I hate to say this, but Jay does not do well with drama. At all. Never has, and he will walk away in a heartbeat if he gets even a hint of it. On the flip side, he's really into you. I've never seen him so interested in a woman before."

"That was before." But would he walk away again? Alisha didn't want to put either of them through that and began to believe it might be better for her to cut her losses now.

"I think he'll come around," Michelle remarked.

Alisha did not respond. She finished as much of her salad as she could stomach and replaced the lid. Her appetite had waned considerably. "I need to get back."

Michelle stood. "So do I."

They headed up the path toward the hospital entrance. Inside, they parted. "I'll see you later."

"I really hope things turn around for you and Jay. You are two of my favorite people and both deserve to be happy."

Alisha didn't comment. She wasn't holding her breath.

Thursday, Jabari sat in his office compiling several reports for the afternoon's board meeting. He hit the print button and spun in his chair to stare out the window. It had been five days since he walked out of

Alisha's house and he missed her more than he'd ever thought possible. It had taken her only a short few weeks to work her way into his psyche. If he were being truthful, he would admit that she had been knocking on the door of his heart from the moment he stumbled upon her shapely backside in Chelle's kitchen.

He had always been very selective in his love life, especially when it came to women who carried as much baggage as Alisha seemed to. However, instead of wanting to get as far away as possible, this time, he wanted to help shoulder her load. He didn't know where she stood with her ex, but her tone suggested that she had no interest in reconciling. Jabari would know for sure once he talked to her tonight. He had sent her a text asking if he could stop by. As much as he wanted to see Corey and Lia, he thought it best that he and Alisha have their conversation after the kids had gone to bed. If they weren't on the same page about the direction of the relationship, it would make it easier on Jabari to not see them or have to say goodbye.

The printer stopped and he gathered and collated the sheets. A beep sounded on his computer, alerting him to suspect activity. He quickly went back to his machine. Jabari sighed when he saw that an employee had bypassed the normal firewall and logged onto a pornography site. The man had no idea that Jabari had installed another layer and most likely thought he had gotten away with violating office policy.

Jabari pushed back from his desk and made his way to the man's cubicle. *Time for a little surprise.* He stood behind the employee, just out of sight, for a good two minutes before making his presence known. The man's eyes widened and he hastily tried to shut down the page. "My office, *now*," Jabari said, pivoting on his heel and leaving the employee to follow.

"I—" Donald started as soon as he entered Jabari's office.

"I don't care what you do on your personal computer, but the rules are very clear and this is not your first time."

"It's my lunch hour, so I wasn't on company time."

"You were using a company computer, so it doesn't matter. Company policy clearly states that unapproved websites may not be visited at any time. This is your last warning. The next time you'll be on probation." Jabari reached into his drawer and pulled out a copy of the written warning and slid it across the desk for him to sign.

Donald reluctantly penned his name on paper and shoved it back across the desk.

"If you need help, we have employee services available."

"I don't need any help!" Donald jumped to his feet and stormed out.

Jabari sighed. He had hoped to find the person or persons responsible for trying to hack into their system. He finished the reports and headed to the conference room for the meeting.

Two hours later, he and Martin came back to Jabari's office. He explained what had happened with Donald.

Martin stood leaning against the door and shook his head. "I heard his wife divorced him six months ago. I guess he's trying to get it in the best way he can," he added with a chuckle. "You want to grab dinner and a beer later? Dena is gone to a management conference this week." His fiancée owned a chain of jewelry stores.

"Can I take a rain check? I'm going to talk to Alisha tonight."

"Are you guys going to try to work it out?"

"Maybe. I need to see what she's feeling. I'm still not sure I want to put myself out there, but I can't stay away from her. She's... I don't know. I just really like being with her."

"I wish you luck. I'm going to head out and do some work from home."

"Thanks."

Jabari decided to drive to Alisha's straight from work, rather than going home and coming back down the hill. Their Folsom office was slightly closer to Roseville than his house and it would save him time and gas.

By the time he arrived at Alisha's that evening, Jabari's anxiety levels had increased tenfold and every what-if question had run through his mind. When she opened the door, it took him a moment to find his voice, much like the first time they'd met. His gaze roamed over her lovely face and down to the snug long-sleeved tee and spandex crop pants. "Hi."

"Hey." Alisha moved aside for him to enter and started toward the family room.

He followed, his eyes riveted by the sway of her hips. The pants she wore outlined every sensuous curve.

"Can I get you something to drink?"

"No, thanks." He wanted nothing more than to haul her into his arms and reacquaint himself with the taste of her sweet kisses, but they needed to talk first.

She perched on the edge of the sofa.

Jabari lowered himself next to her. "How's Corey doing?"

She gave him a small smile. "Back to his usual boisterous self."

He nodded. "Good. And you?"

"Fine."

He covered her hand with his. "I've missed you."

Alisha moved her hand. "Is that why you left?"

"Alisha, I've spent my life avoiding drama as much as possible and I don't like being in the middle of something—"

"Michelle told me all about your no-drama policy— that you'll walk away if there's even a hint of it."

"Chelle talks too damn much," he muttered. He was having a hard enough time explaining why he'd left without his sister interjecting her thoughts.

"So?"

"I have done that a couple of times. But this time was different. While the conflict played a part, so did jealousy." Jabari had finally admitted to himself that part of his problem stemmed from the fact that she and Wayne shared an intimate history. Irrational, but the truth.

Alisha stared at him incredulously. "Jealous? Of Wayne?"

"Yes. I like you, Alisha Hunter, and want to be with you, but I don't want to wonder whether there will be a day when you decide to take him back for the children or..." He didn't want to think about the possibility that Alisha would want the man for herself. "I have to know if there's a chance that you two will get back together."

"Hell, no!" She rolled her eyes. "He spent the last six months of our marriage out with his *boys* more than he did at home. He cheated on me and walked out when I was eight months pregnant with his daughter. He hasn't paid one dime in child support. No, I will *never* take him back for *any* reason."

The tears in her eyes were Jabari's undoing. He

lifted her onto his lap and wrapped his arms around her. "I'm so sorry, baby." He pressed a kiss to her temple.

"I don't want you to be sorry, Jabari. I just need to know that I don't have to worry about you doing the same thing. I've already broken my rule by introducing you to my children. My son has been hurt enough and I will not allow him to be hurt by another man."

"I wouldn't hurt Corey or Lia, and I don't envision walking away from you."

"You say that now, but what about later?"

"Now or later, makes no difference. I want you in my life and you can trust that I'll be here for you and the kids."

"I don't know."

He could hear the uncertainty in her voice and figured that what she had just revealed to him about her marriage was only the tip of the iceberg. "Let's just take it slow. I don't want to give you up."

"Even with all my drama?" Alisha said, giving him the side-eye.

Jabari chuckled. "Yeah, baby. Even with the drama." She finally smiled at him and it felt as if a heavy weight had been lifted from his heart. He brought his hands up to frame her face and did what he had been wanting to from the moment he arrived. With his kiss, he tried to communicate everything he'd just told her. It was time to prove to her that he was a man of his word and would be there for her no matter what.

Chapter 12

"It is only Tuesday and I'm worn out," Alisha mumbled after she finished giving discharge instructions to her patient. She'd hit the ground running on Monday and they'd had an emergency surgery that lasted twice the estimated length of time. She hadn't got out of the building until after eight that evening. It didn't look like she would be leaving on time today, either. On her way to prep for the next surgery, she took a moment to call and ask her mother to pick up the kids. As she stuck the phone back into her drawer, it buzzed with a text message from Jabari: *I know you've had a long couple of days and I wanted to let you know that I'm thinking about you. I meant what I said last week.* She reread the message once more and put the phone away. He had told her that he'd be there for her, but she had been lied to so many times by Wayne it was hard to believe any such promise. Putting him out of her mind, she went about her preparations.

Four hours later, Alisha dragged herself out to the car and drove to her parents' house.

After a round of greetings, her mother said, "The kids have already had dinner and Corey finished his homework."

"Thank you so much, Mom."

"Come on into the kitchen and fix your plate. No sense in you going home to cook something when I have all this food on the stove."

She hugged her mother. "You're the best mother ever." She didn't know what she would do without her family. "Can I take it to go?"

"Of course, baby. Are you going to have to work late tomorrow?"

"No, thank goodness. I checked the schedule and I should be out on time." Her mother handed her a to-go container and Alisha filled it with a barbecue pork chop, mashed potatoes and green beans. She licked the sauce off her fingers and groaned. It tasted so good.

"How are the other parts of your life?"

"Okay. Still taking it one day at a time." She hadn't told them about Wayne's visit or the resulting issues with Jabari. If they got wind of her ex trying to insert himself back into her life, all hell would break loose.

Her father had packed the kids' backpacks and had their jackets on by the time Alisha finished. Both parents walked her out and helped strap Corey and Lia into their car seats. With a wave, she backed out the driveway and headed home. The kids kept up a steady stream of conversation between singing the songs from the children's playlist she had made. She couldn't help smiling.

When they got home, she spent the first half an hour talking to them about their days.

"Look, Mommy." Lia held up a fall leaf she had colored so close to Alisha's face Alisha had to jerk back.

She eased it away. "It's so pretty. Do you know what color this is? It's orange." They had started working on colors and shapes.

"Orange," Lia repeated.

"Good job."

Alisha called out a few addition problems and sight words for Corey and he answered them all correctly.

"I know all my words," Corey said proudly.

"Yes, you do. I'm so proud of you." She hugged him, then Lia. "I'm proud of you, too, Lia. Okay, it's bath time. Then you can have your snack."

With her leaving work so late, she ended up getting the children to bed twenty minutes past their normal eight o'clock bedtime. Her stomach rumbled and she went to heat up her dinner. While eating, Alisha sat at the kitchen table and sifted through the mail. She smiled seeing an envelope from her cousin Siobhan Cartwright in Los Angeles. Siobhan was the oldest of the five Gray siblings and worked as the PR director for their family's home safety company. Siobhan had married a really nice guy. She opened it and saw the photos of her two children, Christian and Nyla, along with a note saying that they were overdue for a visit and that Corey and Lia needed to spend some time with their cousins. Alisha agreed. Growing up, she, Lorenzo, Cedric and Jeremy had always spent part of their summer vacation at the Grays' and vice versa, and all nine cousins were very close as a result. They needed to ensure this next generation enjoyed the same closeness.

She went to the refrigerator for water and then continued eating. Her phone rang. Alisha wiped her hand on a napkin and answered. "Hey, Jabari."

"Hey, sweetheart. You sound tired."

"I am way past tired," she said with a little laugh. "I got off late again."

"You just got over a nasty bug. Be careful that you don't get run down so quickly. I don't want you to get sick again."

His concern always touched her. "As soon as I finish dinner, I'm going to bed early."

"I wish I had known. I would've brought you dinner so you wouldn't have had to cook."

"You're so sweet, but my mother picked the kids up and she cooked. All I had to do was eat. How was your day?"

"Long, but not as long as yours."

"Have you resolved that security issue at your job yet?"

"No," Jabari answered with a sigh.

Alisha was admittedly curious about it but knew he couldn't and wouldn't share any secrets. Because he worked at a tech company, she assumed it had to do with data protection. "I hope you get to the bottom of it soon."

"So do I. Between our schedules, we both have been putting in extra hours. We need to find some time for us soon. Let me know what your weekend schedule looks like and we'll figure something out."

"Okay. Oh, I got your text earlier, but I didn't get a chance to respond." She took a sip of her water.

"I wasn't expecting a response because I know how crazy your day can be. I just wanted you to think about what I'm offering."

Alisha almost choked on her water. "What exactly are you offering?" she asked tentatively.

"To give you whatever you need…whenever you need it."

She melted in her chair. She had only dated two guys since Wayne and none of them had made her feel the way Jabari did or said anything remotely close to this.

"I know he hurt you."

"You can't possibly know," she said quietly. She hadn't even told her family the depths of Wayne's deception—how for the last six months of their marriage he had stopped paying most of their household bills and opened another credit card that he maxed out, leaving her to pay. The only saving grace had been that because of his low credit score, he could only get a thousand dollars. Wayne had tried bullying her into signing for a joint card, but she'd refused and threatened to call Lorenzo. He'd packed up and left that night. She said, "I finally have my life the way I want it and—"

"You don't have room for someone else who cares about you?"

"I'm not saying that." But she had learned to take care of herself independent of a man and didn't want to fall into the same trap again, only to be left holding the bag.

"Then I can show you why we'll be good together. I'm not going to keep you, but know this. I'm going to prove my case every chance I get. Sleep well, baby."

Alisha sat stunned, her heart racing a mile a minute. What did that mean? Then she smiled.

Jabari's week hadn't gone anywhere near the way he had planned. Since his discussion with Alisha on Tuesday, they had only talked once briefly in the past four days, and he couldn't call the "Hey, how are you, I gotta go" they'd had the next evening a conversation.

He had hoped to spend his entire Saturday with her, but his mother had called that morning and asked him and Chris to help move his aunt's belongings from Vallejo to his parents' house. His aunt had lost her husband a year ago and his mother had been concerned about her older sister being alone. Of course, there had to be traffic on Highway 80 on the way back to Sacramento. He had been on the road for close to two hours in the truck he'd rented and still had another twenty miles before reaching their Elk Grove home.

"That's like the fifth time I've heard you groan," Chris said from the passenger seat. "What's the problem?"

"There should not be this much traffic on a Saturday at noon."

He laughed. "Traffic has been like this for years now. Unless you're on the road before ten in the morning or after eight at night, there's going to be traffic. You have someplace to be? Never mind. Forget I asked. There's only one person who could have Mr. Easygoing so uptight—Alisha."

"Yes. We've been trying to coordinate our schedules for over a week."

"I'm glad things seem to be working out for you two. Michelle told me about Wayne showing up. She wanted to call you, but I told her to stay out of it."

"Thanks. Has he always been a jerk?"

"Yeah. Honestly, I never understood what Alisha saw in him."

"She said she's over him."

"You don't believe her?"

"I do, but I also see how much he's hurt her and I feel like it's going to impact whatever we're trying to build."

"Look, Jay, I know you don't do drama, but don't blame Alisha for Wayne's ignorance. She's sweet, a good person, and loyal."

"I don't blame her." Jabari had found that the lure of Alisha overshadowed his issues with drama. "We're taking it day by day." Although, with all these interruptions, they hadn't been able to take anything anywhere.

They finally made it to his parents' house. He and Chris unloaded the truck, set up the furniture his aunt would be using in the guest room, and then took the rest to a storage unit.

When they got back, Jabari showered and prepared to leave.

"Jabari, I made dinner to welcome your aunt Phyllis, so don't run off."

He sighed inwardly.

Chris chuckled and clapped him on the shoulder. "Guess that visit is going to have to wait a little longer, huh, bro?" he said under his breath.

The look on his mother's face said she wouldn't take no for an answer. Louis and Rose Sutton had taught them the importance of family first. He loved his family, but his mother believed in practicing what she preached and expected everyone else to fall in line. He met his father's smiling face. "Sure, Mom."

She beamed. "We'll have everything on the table in a few minutes. Come on, Michelle."

When they went into the kitchen, Jabari dug his phone out of his pocket and called Alisha to let her know he would be later than he anticipated. He turned and saw his mother standing there with a smile on her face. Evidently, she'd heard the tail end of his conversation.

"You're dating someone?"

"Yes." He gave Michelle a quick shake of the head, not wanting her to say anything. His mother knew Alisha and he didn't want her to do or say anything that might make Alisha any more skittish. He already had his work cut out for him and he didn't need any interference.

"That's wonderful, sweetheart." She placed the platter on the table. "What's her name and where did you meet her?"

His sister must have seen the panic on his face, because she said, "Mom, can you come show me which bowl to use for the baked beans. I don't see the matching white one."

"I swear I have more dishes disappearing these days." She turned and went into the kitchen.

Jabari sent a grateful smile to his sister.

Michelle winked and followed her mother.

A few minutes later, they all gathered around the table. Jade sat next to him in her high chair and kept trying to feed him off her plate, which kept everyone laughing. Even his aunt, who had been quiet all day, joined in the lively conversation. When dinner ended, Jabari declined dessert and said his goodbyes.

It was already after eight when he arrived at Alisha's house and, as much as he missed Corey and Lia, he hoped they would be in bed, because tonight, he didn't want one more thing to intrude on his time with Alisha. As soon as she opened the door, he hauled her into his arms, kicked the door closed and placed her against it. "Kids?"

"In bed."

"Good. All week, I've had to be everywhere except where I wanted to be." Jabari's mouth came down on hers and he kissed her with an intensity that bordered on obsession. She locked her legs around his waist and he continued to devour her mouth one erotic stroke at a time. Her soft moans sent his arousal spiraling. His phone buzzed in his pocket but he ignored it. The buzzing came back again and again. Breathing harshly, he rested his forehead against hers and muttered a curse. Still holding her in place, Jabari dug the phone out and saw a text from the weekend security supervisor: Hacking attempt.

"What is it?"

Sighing heavily, he lowered Alisha to the floor. "Security alert from work. I have to go." He stroked a finger down her cheek. "I'll call you if it's not too late." He kissed her once more. "We're going to have some uninterrupted time soon, I promise. These constant interruptions are getting old."

"Well, it won't be tonight," Alisha said with a chuckle. She cupped his jaw and smiled. "Go handle your business, baby. We'll get that time."

He stilled. It was the first time she had ever used any kind of endearment. He nodded and reluctantly left. In the car, he flipped the air conditioner on its highest setting and drew in several breaths to calm the raging fire in his body. By the time he made it to the office, the throbbing behind his zipper had lessened, but the remnants of arousal still hummed in his veins.

Jabari inputted the code to unlock the door, made sure it closed behind him and strode down the hallway to Stacey Tolbert's office. His mentor had introduced him to the former army intelligence officer, and hiring her had proven to be one of his best decisions. She was the only one he trusted.

"Sorry to interrupt your evening, boss, but I thought

you'd want to know that Brooks is trying to download some of the specs for the new wireless technology we're working on."

"Does he know he's being watched?"

"Nope. He hasn't gotten hold of any important data as yet, but I want to see how far he goes. I'm tracking his digital footprint so when we drop down on him he won't have a leg to stand on."

Jabari pulled out his phone, pressed a few buttons and held it up for her to see. "And having the video can't hurt, either."

Stacey smiled. "He's gone back to the same files a couple of times and tried to cover his tracks, but not well enough."

He reached for the phone on Stacey's desk and dialed. "Martin. It's Jay. You might want to get over to the office. Brooks is trying to get into the system."

Martin cursed. "I'll be there in fifteen minutes."

They continued to monitor the man until Martin arrived. Grim-faced, they all walked down to the office James Brooks had been using. The man's wide-eyed, deer-in-the-headlights expression would have been comical if the matter weren't so serious.

Jabari marched around the desk and hauled him to his feet. "Hand over the two flash drives." They had watched him put them in his pocket five minutes ago.

"I was just finishing up some work. I know you want this tech to hit the market in time for the new year, M-Martin," he stammered.

"Cut the bull, Brooks." Martin held out his hand. "You have no reason to be in the files you've accessed."

When he hesitated, Jabari pulled out his phone and called the police.

James shoved the drives into Martin's hand. "That's everything. I…I don't have anything else. I swear. We don't need to involve the police, right?"

"Wrong," Jabari said. "You were caught stealing files and this isn't even your office. Did you think we're going to just give you a slap on the wrist and let it go?"

Martin scrubbed a frustrated hand down his face. "I need to know why. You've been with the company almost from the beginning."

"I've got debts," James finally confessed, slumping back down into the chair.

Jabari raised a brow. "What kind of debt?"

"Gambling." The amount he quoted made them all shake their heads.

"And you thought you could sell the information to the highest bidder."

He didn't comment.

"You do know that you're fired. As of this moment, all of your access has been revoked. I'll have Payroll cut your final check on Monday." Martin strode out.

While Stacey went through the process of deactivating his access codes, Jabari escorted Brooks to his cubicle and waited while the man gathered his personal belongings. He made sure nothing that belonged to M & J Technologies made it into the bag. The police arrived shortly after and escorted James off the property in handcuffs. It took another hour to make sure no other files had been compromised.

Jabari climbed into his car, started the engine and glanced at the dash clock. It was nearly midnight, far too late to call Alisha or drive back over and continue what they'd started. His mind went back to the feel of her in his arms, the taste of her kiss, and the slide of her body against his. His groin stirred. He had to get her alone. A smile curved his mouth. He knew exactly what to do.

Chapter 13

It had been a week since Alisha had seen Jabari. Memories of him holding her against the door while he literally devoured her had constantly replayed in her mind, along with his previous statement about what he'd offer her—*to give you whatever you need...whenever you need it.* She tried to tell herself what she felt was only strong physical desire but knew it had to be more. No way could she resist falling for him. Even though he had a lot going on at his job, he always sent a text or left her a voice mail to tell her she was on his mind. He called almost every night and she looked forward to hearing his voice, even for a moment. Knowing she would see him today sent excitement flowing through her. A tap on her side interrupted her thoughts.

"Mommy, are we going to Aunt Desiree's today to get more soap?"

She smiled down at Corey. He had finally used the

soap enough to reach the car in the middle. "Yes." He'd been bugging her about it all morning. "We'll go as soon as Mr. Sutton gets here."

Corey's eyes lit up. "Yay! Mr. Sutton's going, too?"

She nodded.

"I like him." He did a little dance and ran off.

She liked him, too. Alisha shook her head and smiled. Her smile faded suddenly. Her son was quickly becoming attached to Jabari and, despite Jabari's promise that he wouldn't hurt Corey, she couldn't help being concerned. She'd have to be the one to explain the lies and broken promises, just like before. Thoughts of the impending court date surfaced in her mind. With Wayne showing up and now wanting to lay claim to "his kids," would he change his mind and drop the petition? She didn't think so, but she also didn't think the judge would allow Wayne to let go of his rights just because he was an irresponsible jerk.

Not wanting to ruin her day, Alisha pushed the irritating thoughts from her mind. *I'm not giving him another millimeter of space in my head.* She bent to pick up a stray block and tossed it into the toy crate in the corner of the family room. The doorbell rang and Corey came flying out of his room, with Lia close behind. She couldn't tell who was more excited about seeing Jabari, her or the kids. And Jabari, bless his heart, demonstrated the patience of a saint as Corey asked him a hundred questions.

"Let's let Mr. Sutton in the house, guys."

They finally moved back enough for Jabari to enter, but the questions and vying for his attention didn't end. It took a good five minutes before he greeted her. Up to this point, they had been very careful about any displays of affection, but this time Jabari placed a quick kiss on her lips.

"Hey, baby."

Corey brought his hands up to his mouth and giggled.

Jabari chuckled.

"Go get your jacket," Alisha said. Over the past week the mid-October temperatures had dropped a few degrees and hovered near seventy. She smiled at Jabari. "Took you long enough to say hello. I feel like I'm at a concert trying to get the music star's attention."

He returned her smile. "What can I say? Can't let my fans down."

She swatted him on the arm. "Whatever."

"Give me your keys and I'll transfer the car seats."

"They're in the kitchen on the wall next to the door leading to the garage. Just go through that door. I'm going to get the bags and we'll be out in a minute." Alisha's smile was still in place a few minutes later when she joined him outside. He was still struggling to put the first seat in. She grabbed the other one and had it done in no time.

"You do that so fast. I'm still trying to get this one in," Jabari groused.

"I've been doing it for six years. The more you do it, the faster you'll get." She stopped, realizing what she had said. Him doing it often would imply that he'd be around awhile. "Here, let me help you." Alisha reached in and felt him staring at her but wouldn't meet his eyes. Once she finished, she moved back and Corey hopped into the seat and buckled himself in. She tightened the straps and watched as Jabari buckled Lia's harness. It took him a few minutes to get them all done.

He smiled at her. "Practice makes perfect."

She got in without replying. As he drove off, she said, "You never said where we were going."

"The Jelly Belly Factory in Fairfield. I saw it on my way back from moving my aunt last weekend and looked it up. The workers are off on the weekend, but the tour includes videos of them making the candy."

Yep, thoughtful. "They've never been, so it should be fun."

"And since it's not peak season, I hope we won't have a long wait."

"Do you know how long the tour is?"

Jabari squinted as if trying to remember. "Forty minutes, I believe. Will that be too long for them?"

"We'll see," she said.

"Mr. Sutton, can you take me to my aunt Desiree's shop so I can get some more soap?"

Alisha whirled around in her seat. Jabari placed his hand on her thigh and gave it a gentle pat.

Jabari glanced in the rearview mirror. "We sure can. You'll have to show me what kind she has."

"Okay."

He said to Alisha. "I need to get another bar of the citrus basil. I really like it."

She had smelled it a few times and, on him, it came off as an aphrodisiac. Downtown, they were fortunate enough to find parking a few doors away from Desiree's shop. Jabari carried Lia and Alisha held Corey's hand. "When we go inside, I don't want you to touch anything unless Aunt Desiree says it's okay."

"I won't."

Corey said the words, but she knew her son. In his excitement, he would forget her admonition two seconds after they crossed the threshold.

"Hey, guys," Desiree said, coming toward them.

"Aunt Desiree!" Corey snatched away from Alisha and wrapped his arms around Desiree's waist.

She placed a kiss on his head. "Hi. I bet you need some more soap."

He nodded vigorously.

"Hey, Lia." She kissed Lia's hand. "Good to see you again, Jabari."

"Same here."

Desiree turned to Alisha and embraced her. "You two look good together, like a real family," she whispered.

Alisha hazarded a glance Jabari's way. He looked like a natural, holding Lia and chatting with Corey about the soap.

"You're falling in love with him, aren't you?"

"It's hard not to," she confessed.

Desiree squeezed her hand. "That's a good thing. Come on, Corey. I have some new soaps with sea animals."

Alisha smiled as Corey skipped off with Desiree. "Are you going to get your soap?"

"Yep." Jabari walked over to the table holding the men's products and picked up two bars. "Did you use your bath bombs?"

"One of them. I haven't had time for a long bath lately."

"I'll have to make sure you get some time, then. If you see something you want, let me know."

"I don't need anything right now." She wanted to ask how he planned to ensure she had time for that bath but decided she didn't really want to know right now. The scales in her heart were slowly tilting toward him.

Corey came back with a bag and a big smile. "Look

at my soap, Mommy. I have a dolphin, a fish and a whale."

"Wow, those are cool. Did you say thank you?"

"Yes, he did," Desiree said. "And I got a hug and a kiss."

"How much do I owe you?"

"Girl, nothing. It's my treat." She handed a small bag to Alisha. "Because I know you need five minutes."

Alisha peeked inside the bag and saw the shower bath bombs. She could place them on the floor of the shower and they would dissolve and give off a relaxing scent. "My brother is so lucky." Her sister-in-law had the most generous heart.

"No, I'm the lucky one."

The peace and contentment reflected in Desiree's face sent a pang of envy through Alisha.

"I just need to pay for this and we can go," Jabari said, coming over to where they stood.

Desiree took the soap from him and dropped it in Alisha's bag. "It's on the house. Next time, I hope I can convince you to try a few of my other products. I have some great things for couples."

He grinned. "Is that right?"

"We have to go." Alisha pushed Jabari to the door. "Bye, Desiree."

Jabari laughed as they walked to the car. "Why are you in such a rush? I think we should see what she has."

"I bet you do. Don't we need to get on the road? You know there's going to be traffic."

"Don't remind me. That's why I wanted to leave early in the day. The last tour is at three and they close at four. It's noon now and I'm hoping we don't run into too much."

Aside from a slight bottleneck at one of the freeway

interchanges and a couple of slowdowns, they made it to the factory in a little over an hour.

Alisha didn't know whose mouth gaped the most, hers or Corey's. She saw every flavor of jelly bean imaginable, including buttered popcorn, cappuccino, and pancake and maple syrup. She thought the kids would get bored when they took the tour, but they watched each video. Jabari pointed out different things and, once again, Alisha found herself longing for that family Desiree mentioned.

"Okay, now we need to go taste some jelly beans," Jabari said after the tour ended.

They followed their group back downstairs to the store area. She and Jabari decided to try the pancake and maple syrup one first. "It smells like syrup." She put it in her mouth and chewed.

"I think my mouth is confused."

Alisha laughed. "I know, right? It's weird to be eating a candy breakfast food."

Corey wrinkled his nose. "I don't like it, Mommy."

Lia promptly spit it out.

"Oo-kay," Alisha said, wrapping it up in a napkin she'd taken from her purse. "I think we should stick with a few regular flavors." Corey and Lia liked the watermelon, strawberry jam and red apple.

"Now this is what I'm talking about." Jabari fed her one.

She chewed slowly. "I've found my flavor." She grabbed a plastic bag and added a scoop of the margarita-flavored candy.

"Put some in there for me, too. I'll get them when we get home."

"Okay." They also got cream soda, root beer and Sunkist orange.

"Eat," Lia said.

Jabari, who was still carrying Lia since she refused to get down or go to Alisha, asked, "Are you hungry?"

"Yes."

"They have a café on the other side. We can see if there's something they like after I pay for the candy," he said.

"I'll pay. You drove." Not giving him a chance to protest, she walked off. Alisha appreciated his willingness to foot the bill each time they went somewhere, but she had been paying her own way and didn't want him to think she expected him to do it. When she came back, Jabari was frowning. "What happened?" she asked.

"If I invite you to go out, I don't expect you to pay."

"I know. Stop frowning. It was just a few dollars. If it'll make you feel better, I'll let you take care of the food." She smiled up at him.

He shook his head and smiled. "Come on."

Alisha took Corey's hand and they went to the café. Corey couldn't contain his excitement over seeing the jelly bean–shaped pepperoni pizza.

"Wait, we have to take a picture." Jabari whipped out his phone and took photos of Corey and Lia smiling in front of the pizza.

"Can you send them to me?" Alisha asked.

"Yeah."

Over the meal, they continued to talk about what they'd seen. Before they left, he had another guest take a picture of the four of them, wearing their paper hats bearing the store's logo and seated on a bench with a wall of jelly beans behind them. When she saw the photo, the longing came back again and she had to look away.

"They're out like a light," Jabari said a mile into the drive.

Alisha turned in her seat. "It's hard having all that fun." She laid a hand on Jabari's arm. "Thank you for this. They had a great time and so did I."

"It was my pleasure. Made me feel like a kid again. I have a proposal for you. What do you think about the two of us going away for an overnighter next weekend, if you can find a babysitter?"

Her heart started pounding. Overnight meant things were becoming a little more serious. "Where are you thinking of going?"

He shrugged. "No idea. Wherever we go won't be more than a couple of hours away. Since it'll only be one night, I'd rather not spend most of our time driving. I just want us to have some time together without having to worry about jobs and phone calls. If we do it on Saturday, we can leave early and have the whole day."

"I'll check with my family, see who's available and let you know."

"Do you have a preference where?"

"No." She hadn't been anywhere that resembled a vacation in years. Her only getaways had been to LA to attend all her cousins' weddings.

He grasped her hand. "I'm looking forward to having you all to myself."

Yeah. So was she. More than she cared to admit.

Monday evening, after all the employees had gone home, Jabari and Stacey sat in his office tying up loose ends on James Brooks.

"I think we may have a second person involved," Stacey said, not looking up from her laptop. "There were three instances where someone logged on to James's account when he wasn't here."

His head came up sharply. He'd known that multiple entities would be interested in getting their hands on their latest advances in wireless technology, and just about anyone could be bought with a price. "Let's see who else was working on those days and cross-reference with the date and time stamp." For the next several minutes, only the sounds of clicking on the keyboards could be heard. "Only two people were here each time—Horace and Joy."

Stacey continued typing. "Horace has worked here for sixteen months, and Joy started not long after Martin—and, as quiet as it's kept, you—started the company."

Jabari smiled. "And we're going to continue to keep it quiet." Outside of his family, no one knew that he was part owner of the company. He had always been a private person and only shared personal details on a need-to-know basis. He hadn't even told Alisha, but thought if things continued to become more serious, he would. He refocused his attention on the task in front of him. "What have you two been up to?" he murmured.

"Horace only accessed a few files but didn't download anything. Can't say the same for Joy. Oh, she's good. She tried to cover her tracks well. She must have realized what James was doing and figured she'd just use him as a cover in case things went south. The woman utilized some sophisticated tech to mask her activities, but she didn't count on you," Stacey added with a chuckle. "I can't wait to see her face when we bust her."

He couldn't, either. Joy had gotten only the old specs because of the precautions they'd put in place. Martin had been right to take it out of house. Jabari picked up the phone and dialed. "You might want to come to my office."

Martin appeared a moment later. "You found something else? Hey, Stacey."

Stacey nodded his way. "Martin."

"Yeah, man." He told Martin what they'd found. "She's gotten her hands on a lot of the old data. We need to know more about her background."

Stacey stood. "I'll see what I can dig up tomorrow. I have an old friend who is good at finding information."

Jabari nodded. "Night."

"Thanks. Good night." Martin waited until she'd walked out the door before a string of expletives erupted from his mouth. He slammed his hand down on the desk. "I can't believe Joy would do something like this."

"How well do you know her?"

"We go way back. Met her at some function our families attended when I was about nineteen or twenty, and we struck up a conversation. We've been friends ever since. I went to her wedding."

"What about the husband?"

He shrugged "Nice enough guy. He's in the computer field, too. Not sure what he does exactly, though."

Jabari leaned back in his chair and stroked his chin. "Where did she work before?"

"Some Fortune 500 company. She wasn't getting promoted and her salary was crap. I needed her level of expertise as an analyst, so I brought her on."

"I guess you told her about starting the company beforehand."

"Yes. We had a couple of conversations and she was encouraging." Martin frowned. "Which is why I don't understand why she would do something like this." He ran a hand over his face. "Why now?"

"I don't, either." He hoped she had a good reason, though he couldn't imagine one scenario that would warrant betraying a friend. "I know she's your friend, so how do you want to handle this?"

Martin's eyes went cold. "The same way we'd handle it with anyone else."

"I'm sorry."

"Yeah, so am I. But not sorry enough not to have her met by the police when she walks in the door tomorrow."

"She's actually on vacation until next week. I'll check with HR in the morning to see exactly when and let you know."

"Fine. I'm going home."

"I'll be right behind you." Jabari sighed as his friend walked out. He powered off his laptop and placed it in his bag, then made sure he locked up everything. Taking one last look around, he hefted the bag on his shoulder and left. As soon as he got into the car, his cell buzzed. He smiled upon seeing Alisha's name on the display. He read her text: Desiree and Lorenzo agreed to watch the kids both Friday and Saturday night. His smile widened. That meant he'd have her for two nights instead of one. Even better.

Chapter 14

"Be sure to follow all the instructions on the discharge summary. If you have any questions or problems, call this number here." Alisha circled the hospital phone number on the sheet. She went over all the details, had the woman pen her signature and placed a copy into the drawstring bag with her other belongings. "Do you have any questions?"

"No. Thank you. You've been so sweet."

She smiled at the older woman, then glanced over her shoulder and saw the young orderly approaching with a wheelchair. "Your chariot awaits. Your husband should be waiting for you at the entrance." Alisha helped her into the chair.

The woman gave Alisha's hand a gentle squeeze and waved as she was wheeled out of the recovery area.

Alisha finished charting, washed her hands and checked Monday's schedule. Then she headed to the locker room to change out of her scrubs. She stuffed everything into a duffel bag, slung it and her purse on her shoulder and turned on her phone. It immediately chimed with two messages. She listened to the first one from Georgia: *Alisha, I can't believe you kept Wayne from seeing his children, and to have that man threaten him... I expected better from you. There's no telling what kind of influence he'll have on my grandchildren and I'm thinking we might have to discuss this legally.* Alisha's heart started pounding. What was this woman up to? She did not need any more mess from Georgia and Wayne.

The next message was from Jabari, and hearing his voice calmed her a little: *I can't wait to have you all to myself. Two days, just you, just me.* She smiled, even as the butterflies danced in her belly.

"You and my brother must've straightened things out."

She spun around and saw Michelle lounging in the doorway with a smile on her face. "What makes you say that? Has he said anything to you?" Alisha hadn't told Michelle about her conversation with Jabari or their decision to continue seeing each other.

Michelle pushed off the wall and came to where Alisha still stood. "Nope, but I saw you smiling at your phone. And it was *not* the smile when it's one of the kids. It was kind of like the one I have when Chris sends me a sexy text. So?"

It still felt strange confiding in her about Jabari. "He's taking me away for the weekend," she said finally.

"He's doing what?" Michelle asked with her mouth hanging open. "My nitpicky, cheap brother is paying for a weekender?"

"Cheap?" That word never came to mind when she thought about him. More like generous. He had paid for everything from their first date, aside from those jelly beans. Even then, he had pouted for several minutes. He went out of his way to make sure she and the kids always had a great time.

"Jay doesn't spend anything unless he totally researches it, right down to silverware and towels. That's why he's in such good financial shape."

It certainly shed some light on how he had been able to afford his El Dorado Hills home and the brand-new Audi sedan. "I'm sure Jabari won't appreciate you spreading his personal business around."

Michelle waved her off. "You'll know all of it soon enough. Mark my words. Where are you guys going?"

"Sonoma." When Jabari had suggested it, she thought it the perfect getaway spot. They had also tossed around going to Lake Tahoe, but with the weather forecast predicting partly cloudy skies and temperatures barely reaching sixty degrees, they'd decided eighty degrees in wine country might be better. "We'll be there around eight."

"Ooh, sounds like fun."

"I hope so. I haven't been alone with a man for this long in I don't remember how many years." She and Wayne had rarely done overnight trips, and when they did, he complained about it being a waste of money. Over the past couple of months, since being with Jabari, Alisha realized that with Wayne, she had settled for a lot of things she shouldn't have. She chalked it up to being a naive twenty-one-year-old. She would not make the same mistake again. She debated whether to tell her about the message from Georgia but decided she would wait until after her weekend trip. "I'd better get going. I need to pack and Lorenzo will be over to pick up the kids around five thirty."

"Have a great time."

"We will."

"Oh, and I'll need all the details."

"I'm not telling you anything, Miss I'm-Staying-Out-Of-It." Alisha gave her friend an amused smile and walked away, Michelle's laughter following.

When Alisha arrived home with the children and told them that they would be staying with their uncle and aunt, one would have thought she'd promised them a trip to Disneyland. Corey was beside himself with excitement. Lia followed whatever her brother did. So while they both danced and clapped, Alisha packed their clothes, making sure to take Corey's soap. Then she packed her own. Jabari had told her they'd be doing a casual weekend, so there was no need for her to dress up.

Alisha placed her toiletries in the case and put it in her rolling tote. She went back to the closet for her jacket. Even though it would reach eighty during the day, the night temperatures were predicted to be in the upper forties. As she carried everything into the living room, she heard the doorbell. She let her brother in.

"Hey, sis." Lorenzo bent to kiss her cheek.

"How are you?"

"Good."

"And things at work?"

"Settling down finally." He closed the door and followed her to the family room. "We're looking into promoting a couple of supervisors to help out with our old positions."

She smiled. "I know how hard that is for both of you." They were anal when it came to work.

"Yeah. We're still going to be closely monitoring everything."

"Unca Wenzo." Lia ran in. "Up, please."

"Hey, baby girl." Lorenzo picked her up and planted a kiss on her cheek. "Where's Corey?"

She pointed and called his name.

Corey came in and hugged Lorenzo. "Hi, Uncle Lorenzo. We're going to stay at your house."

"What's up, little man? Yep, you guys get to hang with Aunt Desiree and me. You can bring a movie and some books, if you want."

"Okay."

Lorenzo placed Lia on her feet and the two children hurried off. "Are you sure this is what you want to do? He's much older than you and way more experienced when it comes to women."

"I'm sure and you said all that before."

"I just don't want him taking advantage of you, like Wayne."

Alisha rolled her eyes. "He's not." She debated on whether to tell him about Wayne's visit and, after waging an inner battle, decided to go ahead. Before speaking, she made sure the kids were out of hearing range and lowered her voice. "Wayne showed up here a couple of weeks ago wanting to see the kids. I think he only came because his mama told him I was seeing someone." She related the details, leaving out the part about Jabari being there.

Anger clouded Lorenzo's face. "Wayne better keep his distance if he knows what's good for him. If he's bent on starting trouble, he's going to find it and, this time, I'm not holding back."

"He also filed papers to terminate his parental rights."

"But he's going to show up here." Lorenzo shook his

head. "Yeah, he'd better not show up over here again." He glanced at his watch. "Corey and Lia, time to go."

They came running. Alisha put their jackets on, hugged and kissed them. "Be good."

"Okay."

She walked out with them.

Lorenzo gave Alisha a strong hug. "Be careful and have a good time."

"I will." She could see him having a hard time leaving. "I'll be fine. Go, and don't give my babies too much junk food."

He smiled. "No promises." He got in and backed out.

Alisha waved until they were out of sight and then went back inside. She showered and changed into a pair of jeans, a long-sleeved tee and ballet flats. The closer it came to eight, the more nervous she became, and when Jabari arrived, she had to take several deep breaths before opening the door. He looked good in his jeans and a US Air Force T-shirt that stretched taut against his muscular chest. The smile he gave her eased some of her tension. "Hi."

"How are you?" Jabari captured her mouth in a gentle kiss.

"Good. I'm all ready."

"So am I," he said, not taking his eyes off her.

Her pulse skipped.

"Where's your bag?"

She pointed to the chair.

He picked it up and they walked out to his car. He helped her in, placed her bag on the back seat and got in on the driver's side. "We should make good time. I checked the traffic and it's clear."

For the first several miles they made small talk.

The conversation tapered off and Alisha folded and unfolded her hands in her lap.

Jabari asked, "Are you okay?"

"Just a little nervous."

"Do I make you nervous?"

"No, it's been a while since…" She trailed off.

He covered her hand with his warm one. "This weekend is for you, sweetheart. Whatever you want to do…or not do, I'm good with it, so relax."

He entwined their fingers and she felt her anxiety slowly decrease. Her phone buzzed in her pocket and startled her. She pulled it out and saw Siobhan's name on the display. "Excuse me, this is my cousin." She connected. "Hey, Vonnie."

"Hey, girl. Did you get the pictures?"

"I did. I can't believe how much Christian and Nyla have grown. We definitely need to get the kids together. Can I call you next week sometime? Um… I'm actually on my way out of town for the weekend."

"With a guy?"

"Yes."

"Oh, honey, yes. We'll have to do a three-way with Morgan. If you don't call by Tuesday, expect me to be blowing up your phone."

Alisha laughed. Siobhan was the most outspoken of the family and the oldest, and Alisha knew Siobhan meant every word. Her sister, Morgan, worked as a sports agent and was almost as blunt. "I'll call."

"Have a great time. Love you."

"Thanks. Love you, too." She disconnected. "Sorry. That was my cousin from LA."

"You could've talked to her. We still have another fifteen minutes or so to go."

No, she couldn't have, because Siobhan would have

been asking questions about Jabari and Alisha had no intentions of letting him hear anything she had to say. "I didn't want to be rude. We'll just talk next week."

"More like you didn't want to talk about me while I'm sitting here," Jabari said, not taking his eyes off the road.

She burst out laughing.

He slanted her an amused glance. "That's what I thought. I want to know what you would've told her."

"I would have said you're a great guy, handsome, intelligent." And that he could melt her with his kiss and his touch.

"And?"

"That's it." Alisha smiled, turned her head and pretended to watch the scenery.

Twenty minutes later, they pulled up to the hotel entrance and entrusted the car to the valet. It only took a few minutes to check in and he led her to a second-story room with a king-size bed, balcony and a shower big enough for two.

"Is this okay?"

"It's lovely. I think I'm going to enjoy myself."

Jabari placed their bags on a bench and wrapped his arms around her. "My only job this weekend is to make sure you do." He captured her mouth with his in a sweet, tender kiss that quickly changed to hot and demanding.

He's off to a good start was the only thing in her mind.

Jabari had meant for them to take things slow, but he could no more stop kissing her than he could stop breathing. He took his time tasting every centimeter of her delectable mouth. He slid his hands over her hips, down her thighs and up again to caress her shapely backside. She ran her hands over his chest, her touch igniting a blaze inside him. He had never been driven to this point from a simple kiss, but the way Alisha's tongue swirled around his had him on the brink of losing control. Jabari left her mouth briefly to remove her shirt, then transferred his kisses to her exposed throat, shoulders and the valley between her breasts. He reached around her back, unclasped her bra and dragged the straps down. He latched on to a dark nipple and sucked in into his mouth.

"Ohh..."

The sound of her soft moans and the feel of her nails digging into his shoulders turned him on even more and he grew harder with each sensual second. He circled his tongue around the hardened tip and lavished the same treatment on its twin. Her knees buckled and he tightened his grip on her waist. Jabari straightened and reclaimed her mouth. He unfastened her jeans, hooked his thumbs in the waistband and pushed them, along with her panties, down. "Step out, baby," he said, dropping to his knees. He tossed them aside. Jabari trailed his tongue along her inner thigh to her warm, moist center, then mirrored his actions on her right leg. He repeated the action until she trembled and writhed beneath him, then plunged his tongue into her slick, wet heat.

Alisha called his name and gripped the back of his head, holding him in place.

Jabari made one long swipe across her clit and she cried out again. He slid two fingers inside and kept up the sensual pleasure until she convulsed all around him. He stood and, within seconds, had stripped. He dug a condom from his wallet, rolled it on, then picked her up and carried her to the nearest wall. "Ever since that night at your house against the door, I've fantasized about having you this way." He eased his engorged erection inside her and gritted his teeth to keep from exploding.

"So have I." Alisha wrapped her legs around his waist and her head fell back. She moaned again. She lifted her head and stared into his eyes. "You make me feel so good."

"And I'm going to make you feel even better." Jabari started with slow, deep thrusts. The familiar emotions welled up and he tried to push them down and concentrate on only drawing out as much pleasure as he could from this interlude, but they kept coming back. So finally, he let them come. She locked her legs tighter around his back and tilted her hips to meet his. He delved deeper with each measured stroke, then eased out to the tip and thrust again, establishing an easy rhythm. "So good. How do you feel?"

"Good. So good."

He increased the pace, his strokes coming faster. "I love how your body fits mine," he murmured, not slowing. He felt her walls clutching him and grasped her hips, thrusting harder.

She threw back her head and screamed as she climaxed. *"Jabari!"*

Jabari went rigid against her, then bucked and shuddered as he came right behind her, yelling her name loud enough to be heard throughout the entire building. He collapsed against her with a harsh groan of satisfaction. Slowly he drew them down to the bed with her on top of him. Their harsh breathing magnified in the room and he held her close. His heart pounded in his chest and the magnitude of what he felt for her rose sharply. *I love her.* He drifted off with a smile on his face.

When Jabari woke up the next morning, it took him a moment to get his bearings. He glanced down at Alisha cuddled in his arms. The sheet half covered their naked bodies and he had no recollection of when or how it happened. He studied her relaxed features and resisted the urge to caress her face. She rarely had an opportunity to rest and, as he had told her, relaxation would be their only goal this weekend. He was still blown away by their lovemaking and the realization that he loved her. He debated whether he should tell her. Letting her know his feelings might go a long way toward making her more secure, but it could also frighten her even more. Jabari still sensed her holding back. He glanced over at the nightstand clock and saw it was a few minutes past seven. They had a busy day, but he'd made sure to schedule their first appointment a little later so she could sleep in. Jabari shifted Alisha's head onto the pillow. She stirred for a moment and then turned over. He eased off the bed, pulled the sheet higher on her body and headed to the bathroom.

Fifteen minutes later, showered and dressed, he pulled his sweatshirt on and went to sit on the balcony. The sun had already risen, but the morning was cool and crisp. He inhaled deeply and let it out slowly. After being in the military for so long, he had a hard time sleeping late. Most mornings he got up at six to go running or work out in the shed in his backyard, which he'd turned into a home gym. The hotel had a fitness center, but he needed to learn to relax, too. So Jabari sat listening to the sounds of the morning and thinking about how he was going to convince Alisha to be part of his life permanently.

Jabari turned at the sound of the door opening. "Good morning."

"Good morning." Alisha stepped out onto the balcony wearing one of the hotel robes.

The smile she gave him went straight to his heart. "Did you sleep well?"

"Very, but I'm starving."

"After you get dressed, we can go over to the restaurant for breakfast. We have an appointment at ten and one later today at three."

Alisha lifted a brow. "Where are we going?"

He smiled. "You'll see." He stood and kissed her. "Go ahead and get dressed."

She stood there a moment longer as if trying to figure out what he had planned. "I hope it's nothing too crazy."

He chuckled. "How are we going to do something crazy when I told you it's going to be all about us relaxing?"

"All right. I'm trusting you." She stepped back inside and closed the door.

I'm trusting you. Jabari wanted her to trust him for more than just a weekend. He remained out on the balcony until she was ready.

They walked hand in hand across the courtyard to the building housing the front desk and restaurant.

"This place is beautiful," Alisha said. "How did you find it?"

"Google search." The manicured lawns, colorful flowers and strategically placed benches along the walking path fitted perfectly with what he wanted to do. In front of the main building, several cushioned sofas had been placed around a firepit.

"I'm glad you chose this one. It would be nice to sit out here later, if we have time."

"We'll have plenty of time." Inside they were immediately shown to a table.

She opened the menu and scanned it for a minute. "You know, if we didn't have an appointment in an hour, we'd be eating somewhere else."

Jabari frowned. "Why? You don't see anything you want?"

"Oh, I see plenty. But at these prices, those eggs had better have been laid by golden hens."

He laughed so hard he almost choked. "You are too much."

"I'm just sayin'."

He was still chuckling when the server came to take their order. After she departed, he clasped his hands on the table. "Are you enjoying yourself so far?"

"Yes. You started the weekend with a…bang." Alisha tossed him a saucy smile.

Until now, she had never engaged in this sort of wordplay, and he liked it. "I'd like to end with a bang, too."

"I'll hold you to it."

His body reacted with lightning speed. "You know you're about a millisecond away from me throwing you over my shoulder and carrying you back to the room."

Alisha opened her mouth to speak but the server returned with their food. "Guess we'll have to save this conversation for later."

Jabari thanked the woman, who smiled and walked away. He picked up his fork. "I would've never guessed you could be such a tease."

"I never have been. Must be the company I'm keeping." She ate a bite of her eggs.

He had a difficult time focusing on his breakfast and not on the woman sitting across from him. He reminded himself he had plans that didn't include keeping her inside the hotel room until it was time to leave tomorrow.

Alisha finished the last bite of her potatoes and leaned back in the chair. "That was good. How long will it take to get to our appointment? It's nine forty-five."

"Only a few minutes." Jabari settled the bill and escorted her out. They took a different path and ended up at the spa. "When was the last time you had a massage?"

"When Chelle and I treated ourselves to a day of pampering after graduating from nursing school."

"Then it's been too long." He gave their names to the receptionist and she gave them directions on where to go. They passed a shop and swimming pool on the way to the spa area. Once there, they were given a tour of the mineral pools, saunas and lounging areas, then directed to lockers to change into robes. He and Alisha met in a waiting area where they had tea, water and fruit available.

A few minutes later, a massage therapist came and escorted them upstairs to the room for their couple's massage. "You can undress and lie facedown on the table. We'll be back in a few minutes." She exited and closed the door softly.

Alisha turned his way with tears in her eyes. "I don't know how to thank you for doing this, Jabari."

"Baby, I told you I want to give you whatever you need, *whenever* you need it, and I meant it." Jabari touched his mouth to hers, then removed her robe and helped her onto the table. He took off his own and climbed onto the table next to hers. The massage would be a first for him and he wasn't exactly sure what to expect having a stranger touching him so intimately.

"Hmm, I don't think I can move," Alisha said when it was over. "My body has never felt so relaxed and loose. Can we just stay here?"

He laughed softly. "I don't think so, but another few minutes won't hurt."

"In another few minutes, I'll be asleep, so I'd better get up now." She sat up and slid off the table.

Jabari fitted himself behind her and couldn't resist touching her. He let his hands travel over her oil-slicked skin and placed fleeting kisses along her bare shoulder.

"We shouldn't…mmm."

"I know, and I'm trying to stop." He reluctantly lifted his head. "To be continued." They donned their robes and went to continue their recreational respite out on the verandah where a row of loungers had been placed. He held her hand, but they didn't speak for several minutes. "We'll need to leave around one forty-five to get to our next appointment. We can eat here or leave a little earlier and eat there."

"Let's eat there."

He and Alisha stayed there awhile longer before strolling along the gardens and leaving for lunch and their wine tour, and later, dinner.

After returning, they took another walk around the property. The moon shone in a clear sky and the mild temperatures made it a perfect night. Jabari stopped walking and turned her to face him. "I need to tell you something."

"What is it?" Alisha placed her hand on his chest. "Is something wrong?"

He covered her hand with his. "Nothing is wrong.

Everything is right. These past weeks with you have been the best of my life. I love you, Alisha."

She gasped softly. "Jabari. I don't know what to say. It's all going very fast."

"I know we've only known each other a short time, but it doesn't change what I feel." He tilted her chin and covered her mouth in a deep, passionate kiss, filling it with everything he tried to say—that he would be here for her, protect her, care for her and love her. Forever.

Chapter 15

It had been two days since Jabari's weekend with Alisha. Two days since he had told her he loved her. Though he suspected she felt the same, she hadn't reciprocated and he tried not to be disappointed. He'd seen the split second of fear in her eyes when he shared what lay in his heart. No, he didn't particularly care for drama, and yes, he'd messed up initially by leaving that first time, but he thought that by telling her, he could make her understand she could count on him to be in the relationship for the duration. Apparently, it had backfired, because she had been pulling away from him ever since. Jabari had sensed it when they'd made love again on Saturday night and when he kissed her goodbye on Sunday. He had sent her a text message and left a voice mail, and she had yet to respond to either.

A knock sounded on his door and Martin stuck his

head inside. "Come on in. Did you see the video I sent you?"

Martin dropped down heavily in the chair across from Jabari and blew out a long breath. "Yes, and I still can't figure out why Joy would do something like this."

Jabari had sent him a recording of Joy entering the building one evening during her vacation and leaving an hour later with a thick folder. "I reached out to a friend of mine at the FBI and he's coming by this morning."

"Good. The sooner he gets here, the sooner she'll be off my property. She's back from vacation now, right?" Martin said.

"Yes. Today is her first day back."

"And her last day working for me. How was your weekend, by the way?"

Jabari smiled.

"That good, huh?"

"Better. I'm in love with her."

Martin stared. "Wow. Okay. That's not what I expected you to say. Don't you think it's kind of sudden? You've only been dating her a couple of months, if that."

"Thereabouts."

"I've never known you to be impulsive when it comes to women and relationships, or hell, anything, for that matter."

"And I'm not starting now." He had tried to rationalize that it might be too soon, as well. However, he had no illusions about what his heart had already decided. He loved Alisha, and no amount of reasoning would change that fact. "I know it seems too early in the relationship, but it's right. I'm almost forty, not some indecisive twenty-year-old. I know what I want." Jabari stared out the window. “I just need to convince her of the same thing. Her ex really did a number on her. I just didn’t realize how much he’d hurt her until now. I’ve got my work cut out for me.”

“Wait, are you saying you don’t know if she loves you back?” Martin asked. “I don’t know, Jay. She might not be worth all this drama. And didn’t you tell me she has kids?”

He nodded. “Two amazing kids, and yes, she’s worth it. I—” The intercom buzzed. Jabari reached over and hit the button.

“There’s a Brent Trevino here to see you, Mr. Sutton,” the receptionist said.

“Thanks. I’ll be right out.” Because of the sensitive nature of their information, all visitors needed an escort to enter any area outside of the lobby. “Be back,” he said to Martin, rising and walking out to the front. He came back a minute later and made the introductions. They filled Brent in on what had happened.

After hearing everything, Brent asked, “Is she back from vacation?”

Martin nodded. “She just got back today.”

Brent shifted his position. “Gentlemen, let’s invite Ms. Pennington to the party and see what she has to say.”

Martin picked up the phone and dialed her extension. “Joy, it’s Martin. I need to see you in Jabari’s office.” He paused for a moment. “Thanks.” He hung up. “She’ll be here.”

They all moved to the small conference table and waited.

A few minutes later, Martin answered Joy’s knock.

“Hey, Martin,” Joy said, entering with a smile. Her

smile faded when she saw Jabari and Brent sitting at the table. "What's going on? Did something happen?"

"That's what I'd like to know. Have a seat, Joy." Martin gestured her to the table. He started to reclaim his chair next to her, then shot her a glare, rounded the table and took the one farthest from her.

She frowned. "Martin, what's this about? I'm not following."

Jabari placed a series of photos in front of her—images showing Joy entering the building during off-hours, logging onto a computer, leaving with the folder. "You were on vacation and shouldn't have been here after hours. What were you doing?"

Joy laughed and waved a hand. "Is this all? That's not the first time I've come in after hours. I knew I'd be gone for two weeks and wanted to make sure I had everything up to date. Come on, Martin, this isn't news." She smiled.

Martin slid a sheet in front of her containing dates, times and data accessed. "But this is. You aren't on these parts of the project, so you have no reason to access those files."

Joy divided a glance between the three men. "Are you accusing me of something?"

Martin jumped up. "Cut the crap, Joy! We've been friends for too long, which is why I can't understand why you would steal from me." She opened her mouth to say something and he raised a hand. "Save it. We know that you downloaded some of the specs for the new 5G technology slated to be unveiled at the end of the year. All I need to know is why and who you're giving *my* information to." He dropped back down in his chair and released a deep sigh.

Jabari could see the toll this had taken on Martin

and he felt bad. "Joy, I'm sure you remember the confidentiality clause every employee signs and there is a specific intellectual property caveat on the schematics of every file."

Up to this point, Brent had said nothing. He leaned forward and clasped his hands on the table. "Ms. Pennington, are you aware that theft of intellectual property carries a jail sentence and a fine."

Joy's eyes widened. "Martin, you can't be serious. I thought we were friends."

"So did I," Martin murmured. He held her gaze. "But friends don't steal from friends." He turned away.

Joy started to cry and babble.

Jabari wasn't moved in the least, and by the looks on Martin's and Brent's faces, they weren't, either. A moment later, Joy seemed to realize that fact and the waterworks stopped and she dropped the act.

Her light brown face took on a derisive scowl. She tapped a manicured finger on the table. "Martin, when you came to me about starting your company, I encouraged you. I'm the one who said you could do it when other people didn't believe in your dream. I *listened* to your plans and offered suggestions." Her voice rose with each statement. "Yet, when it came time to do it, you did it without me. This was supposed to be *ours*."

"I don't know how you would come to that conclusion based on two or three conversations. I never said anything about a partnership. As for the suggestions, you didn't tell me anything someone starting a business wouldn't have already taken into consideration."

"Were you intending to use the information you stole to start your own company?" Jabari asked. "I assume since your background isn't in engineering, you have a partner or partners."

Brent opened a folder. "I understand that your husband is an engineer."

"Yes."

"We know you downloaded several specs. Where are they?"

Joy didn't answer for a lengthy minute. Finally she said, "On my husband's laptop."

"We'll need that laptop." Brent continued with his interrogation for another hour and when it ended, Joy was escorted off the property in handcuffs.

Jabari and Martin sat in silence. After a long while, Jabari asked, "You okay?"

Martin placed his head in his hands. "I will be. The only good thing is that she doesn't have the updated technology. Even if they were able to piece everything together, it's old tech." He stood. "I'm going to have her desk cleaned off."

He nodded and watched Martin's heavy steps as he left the office. Jabari spent the rest of the afternoon preparing the paperwork to be forwarded to Brent for the formal investigation. Near the end of the day, he received a text from his sister inviting him to dinner. He sent a quick reply letting her know he would be there. He missed seeing Jade and it would give him an opportunity to hit Chelle up for information that would help him in his pursuit.

Jabari made it to his sister's house by six thirty and immediately scooped up his niece. "How's Uncle Jay's girl?"

"Good. See my new shirt." Jade pointed to the purple shirt with a picture of some character.

"I like it. Who's that?"

She tried to explain and he didn't have a clue what she was talking about.

Michelle laughed and explained. "It's a character from the *Doc McStuffins* show."

"Ah." He placed Jade on her feet. "How's it going, sis?"

"We're good. How was *your* weekend?" Michelle's smile widened.

"Great, but something's not right."

She studied him. "I'm putting the food on the table and we can talk."

Jabari followed her to the kitchen and greeted Chris.

"We used to see you all the time, but now that you've got yourself a woman, we can't even get a phone call," Chris teased.

He ignored the comment and went to wash his hands. Afterward, he joined them at the table.

"You said something's not right?" Michelle asked as soon as he picked up his fork.

"Alisha and I had a great time, but I can feel her pulling away. Did something else happen with her ex? We were getting along just fine and now..." Jabari shrugged.

His sister kept her head lowered and pushed the food around on her plate.

"Chelle?" When she finally looked up, he said, "If you know something, please tell me. I love her and want to make this work."

"You what?" Michelle and Chris said at the same time.

"Are you *serious*, Jay?" Michelle asked. "I mean, I'm probably happier than you about it, but I...I'm floored. Have you told her?"

"Yes, over the weekend." He put down his fork. "And she's been pulling away ever since. I figured if I said it first, it would be easier for her to accept." It crossed his mind that she might not believe him, but he'd done everything in his power to *show* her he did. "If you know anything, help me out here, sis. I need to know. I get that she's afraid of history repeating itself, but I thought we'd already crossed that bridge." He sent her a pleading look.

She glanced at Chris, who nodded and said, "I know she's your friend, but he's your brother. You said you wanted Alisha to be happy."

Michelle sighed. "I'm going to tell you what she said yesterday, but you have to promise me, *promise* me that you will not mention it. I mean it, Jay."

"I promise."

"You're right about her being afraid, but it's more than that now. After you guys got back, Wayne's mother had left a second voice mail basically telling her she had no right to keep Wayne from seeing the kids and she was worried about what kind of influence you were having on them. She didn't threaten Alisha with anything, but the implication was there. She'd left a similar one the day you guys left."

"She doesn't have any legal rights to them. How can she—"

"There's more."

Jabari's heart rate kicked up. "More?"

"The last few times she's kept them, the woman was grilling Corey about Alisha's love life, which is how she found out you and Alisha were dating. The icing on the cake is Wayne filed to terminate his parental rights, but after seeing you, he's supposedly thinking about changing his mind. All of this is according to his mother, mind you. So on top of her fears about being in a relationship again, she's now faced with wondering what those two idi—" Michelle cut a quick glance at Jade "—those two are up to."

It took everything inside him to keep his seat. He wished more than ever that he had knocked the hell out of her ex when he had the chance. If he got another chance, he planned to make it abundantly clear that Alisha, Corey and Lia were off-limits.

"I know what you're thinking, Jay," Chris said. "Believe me, I've had the same thoughts. But he's not worth it."

"He is if it's interfering with my life." Silence descended over the table. Jade happily ate her food, but the three adults seemed to have lost their appetites. "Sorry for ruining dinner," Jabari said.

"You didn't. I'm going to say one more thing. If you love her like you say you do, then don't give up on her. Alisha needs you just as much as you need her, but she can't see it right now."

Jabari nodded. He ate a few more bites, then pushed the plate away and stood. "I think I'm going to call it a night."

He kissed Michelle and Jade. "See you later."

Chris leaped to his feet. "I'll walk you out."

He didn't speak until they reached the front door. And then he said, "Hang in there. If you need something, let me know." He pulled Jabari into a one-arm hug and clapped him on the shoulder.

Jabari loped down the walk to his car and sat, debating on whether to call Alisha or wait another day. He pulled out his phone, scrolled to her number and hit the button.

"Hello."

"Hey, baby."

"Jabari, hey. Sorry I haven't had a chance to get back

to you. It's been a busy couple of days and right now I'm making cookies for both Corey's and Lia's classes for tomorrow."

The words had tumbled out of her mouth without her taking a breath and she never responded to him that way. "Sounds like fun. I haven't had homemade cookies in a while. Maybe you can save me a couple."

"Um…they might be gone by the next time I see you."

"Not if I come get them now."

Alisha didn't comment immediately. "Now?"

"I won't stay long. I just need to see you for a few minutes."

After another long pause, "Okay," came the soft reply.

"See you in a bit." He started the car. He had no idea what he would say or how to keep Michelle's confidence, but he would figure out once he got there. Or, at least, he hoped so.

Alisha hung up and tried to concentrate on helping Corey and Lia spread frosting on the sugar cookies. Hearing Jabari's voice had brought back all the emotions she had been trying to keep at bay. Yes, she'd come to realize she really did love him, but dealing with Georgia's and Wayne's veiled threats and knowing how Jabari felt about drama, she was just about at her limit. Her ex and his mother loved to keep up chaos and wouldn't hesitate to use the children in any way possible. Alisha could not allow that to happen, which she knew would create a bigger mess. And she could see Jabari walking away at some point. If it was too much for her, no way could she expect him to deal with it forever. She had tried to figure out a way to make it work—in a perfect world she and Jabari would be together and her ex would drop off the face of the earth—but she hadn't found one scenario that didn't end with one of them getting hurt.

"Not too much, Corey." She took a portion of the frosting off the plastic knife.

"See, I can do it." Corey beamed when he spread it all on.

"Yes, you can." She guided the knife to help Lia.

"No, Mommy. I do, I do."

"You are doing it, Lia. I just need to help you a little bit, okay?" Lia was becoming more independent and Alisha constantly found herself battling with her child when it came to offering assistance. She had let them each do half a dozen and she would finish the rest after they went to bed. "Now we're ready for sprinkles." Corey added his sprinkles, but Alisha had to watch Lia like a hawk because her definition of putting on sprinkles included sprinkling some into her mouth, as well. Once they finished, she bathed them and got them into bed.

Alisha went back to the kitchen to frost the rest of the cookies. When the doorbell rang later, she felt more nervous than she had on their first date. She wiped her hands on a towel and went to open the door. The moment she saw him, she wanted to bury herself in his arms and stay there forever. "Come in." As if he knew she needed it, Jabari closed the door behind him, kissed her softly and wrapped his arms tightly around her. He didn't say anything. He just held her. She didn't know how she would find the strength to let him go, but she had to, for all their sakes.

"You look exhausted."

"It's been a long couple of days." And she'd had

trouble sleeping ever since hearing those messages on her voice mail. "The cookies are in the kitchen. Sorry, they're only sugar cookies."

Jabari smiled. "They're still homemade, so it doesn't matter."

Alisha pointed to the cookie sheet. "Take from this pile over here."

He grabbed two and bit into the first one. "These are really good. They'd be better with some milk."

"Is that your way of asking for a glass of milk?" She got a glass, filled it with milk and handed it to him. To distract herself from his piercing gaze, she picked up a cookie, broke off a piece and popped it into her mouth. She waited for him to say something, but he continued to eat, sip his drink and scrutinize her. She searched her mind for a topic to talk about. "Did you get that problem taken care of at work?"

"Yes, finally."

"I know that's a load off your mind."

Jabari nodded and polished off the second cookie. "My partner and I are glad. We still have to wrap up some things, though."

She paused with a piece of cookie halfway to her mouth. "Partner? I thought you just worked for the company." Alisha had googled M & J Technologies when he told her where he worked and found out that it was one of the fastest growing tech companies in the region.

He laughed. "I do work there. I work my butt off."

"But by partner, do you mean you're part owner?"

"I do, indeed."

"That's great. Now *that's* a second career." She briefly wondered why he'd kept that information from her and what else he might be holding back. Then she tried to chalk it up to her being oversensitive. Alisha reasoned that they had only been dating a short time and she recalled her brother and male cousins doing the same thing when they first started dating a woman for fear she would see dollar signs first.

Jabari drained the last of his drink, placed the glass on the counter and came to where she stood. "What's going on with you, sweetheart?"

Alisha's brows knitted in confusion. "Nothing. I told you this week has been pretty long already. I don't know what else you mean."

He moved closer to her, leaving mere inches between their bodies. "Us. You don't think I feel you retreating? Something happened between the weekend and now and I want to know what it is, so I can help."

She took a step back. "There's nothing you can do." The mess with Wayne and his mother was her problem, not his.

"So you admit to retreating."

"I… That's not what I said."

"You haven't said much of anything." Jabari grasped her hand. "Honey, I love you, and whatever bothers you, bothers me. Talk to me, Alisha. Let me help you."

She wanted to accept his offer so badly, but the thought of him regretting their relationship sometime down the line kept her from telling him everything. "I think we're moving too fast. I have a lot going on right now and I just need some space."

His jaw tightened. "What exactly are you saying?"

"We should… I need…" Alisha couldn't get the words past her throat. "Maybe we should take a break."

"A break?" Jabari asked incredulously. "For how long?"

She averted her eyes. "I don't know."

"Let me see if I understand this correctly. You think we should take a break from this relationship for who knows how long, for a reason you can't or won't tell me."

Alisha couldn't answer.

He braced his hands on the counter next to her. "I know you're afraid that I'll do the same thing as your ex. I'm not him and I won't. So, while we're on this break, what am I supposed to do when I want to talk to you, touch you, kiss you…make love to you?"

She forced back the tears threatening to fall and bit down on her lip to keep from crying.

Jabari stroked a finger down her cheek. "I'll respect your wishes, but I'm not going to wait forever." He brushed his lips across hers and walked out.

Her heart breaking, Alisha wrapped her arms around her midsection and let the tears fall.

Chapter 16

By Thursday, Jabari still hadn't heard from Alisha. He kept trying to remind himself that she was dealing with a mountain of issues, but it still hurt that she wouldn't open up to him, knowing that he loved her. His worry surged with each passing day and he didn't even want to think about what he would do if she decided to make this "break" permanent. He had been staying at the office well past business hours to keep his mind occupied, but nothing had helped. Tonight, he had nothing to hold him at work and went home.

Too wound up to eat, he changed into his running gear and drove to the park where he and Martin jogged. Jabari did a few warm-up liners on the basketball court, then started a slow jog on the trail. He gradually increased his pace until he was full out sprinting. He kept going for another half mile before reducing his speed. He completed four miles, and when he got back to the car, he found that he had only sufficiently worn his body out. His mind continued to sprint. Jabari drove back home and searched his refrigerator for something to eat and settled on the leftover pasta he'd brought home from his dinner with Martin last night. They had ordered in while gathering the remainder of the information Brent requested. Brent had let them know that Joy's husband's laptop had been turned in and they were going through the hard drive and all the flash drives to determine if there were any incriminating files.

Jabari dumped the contents onto a plate, covered it with a paper towel and stuck it into the microwave. The timer went off at the same time as his cell rang. He removed the plate while answering it. "Hey, Chelle."

"Hey. Did you get a chance to talk to Alisha?"

"Yeah." He stirred the food, tasted it and placed the plate back into the microwave for an additional minute. "She wouldn't open up to me and said we needed to take a break."

"Oh, Jay, I'm so sorry. What are you going to do?"

"There's not much I can do." He couldn't force Alisha to talk to him and he had promised his sister he wouldn't divulge the information Alisha had told Michelle in confidence. If he did, it would invariably ruin their friendship and he couldn't do that. "I'm hoping she'll realize that she can trust me and that she doesn't have to handle the stress on her own anymore."

"I hope so, too. Is there anything I can do?"

"No. I don't want you to ask her about us at all. You can't be in the middle."

"But—"

"No buts, Chelle. Stay out of it, please. She's going

to need your friendship and that can't happen if you meddle."

Michelle's heavy sigh came through the line. "I know. I can tell you're miserable and I know she is, too. I feel so helpless."

"Join the club." Jabari retrieved his plate. "I need to go eat before my food gets cold."

"Okay. Keep me posted."

He chuckled. "Like you'd let me do otherwise."

She laughed. "Hey, I have to make sure my favorite brother and my best friend get to the altar."

"Favorite brother? I'm your only brother." He didn't comment on the rest of her statement. "I'll talk to you later." He could still hear her laughter when he hung up.

Jabari got a glass of water and napkin, picked up his plate and took them upstairs to his bedroom. He turned on the television and channel surfed until he came across a showing of *The Equalizer 2*. He had seen the first movie but hadn't gotten around to seeing the sequel. When he finished eating, he stretched out on the bed. Lying there brought back memories of movie nights with Alisha and how much he had enjoyed them. It dawned on him that they were supposed to have another one this weekend. As much as he wanted to call and ask about it, he agreed to give her space. She would have to make the first move.

When the credits started to roll, Jabari muted the sound. He needed to talk to someone and called the one person who always gave him good advice. "Hey, Dad. Are you busy?" he said when his father answered.

"No. I'm just sitting here reading the newspaper. You all right?"

"I need some advice."

"About the young lady you're seeing?"

"Yes. You and Mom know her already. She's Chelle's best friend."

"You and Alisha are dating?" His father's booming laughter came through the line. "What a small world. I didn't realize you two knew each other."

"We didn't. I met her at Jade's birthday party and we've been going out ever since. But she asked for a break earlier this week and I don't know what to do." He told his father about their growing relationship, his bonding with her children and her ex's reappearance. "I know she's afraid that the same thing will happen again, but I've tried to show her that's one thing she doesn't have to worry about. I think she's really overwhelmed, as well, but I can't get her to open up to me."

"I know a little about what happened because of Alisha's friendship with Michelle, and that kind of hurt is hard to get over. How serious are you about her?"

"I'm in love with her."

"That didn't take long. What exactly is it that you want to know?"

"What to do next."

"Son, right now you're going to have to give her the space she needs. But don't remove yourself totally. Send her a message or call her just to let her know you're thinking about her. Just because you're out of sight doesn't mean you have to be out of mind. After about a week or so, see what's she's feeling. If she needs more time, go ahead and give it. But at some point, if she hasn't come around, you're going to have to decide when to walk away. You can't force her to love you."

Jabari groaned. This was not the advice he wanted to hear.

"I take it that's not the advice you were looking for."

"No."

"This is the first time in a long while that you've mentioned being serious about a woman and I hope things turn out the way you want. We already think of Alisha as another daughter and I can tell you that your mother would be beside herself if it became official, as would Michelle, I'm sure."

"Yeah, she's already said as much."

"You know your sister thinks she needs to fix everything, but don't let her get in the middle of your relationship with Alisha."

"We've already had that conversation." He decided not to tell his father that Chelle had given him inside information that would technically qualify as getting in the middle. "Thanks, Dad."

"Anytime. I'm glad you came to me. Your mother is sitting here chomping at the bit to know what's going on."

Jabari chuckled. "And I'm sure you're going to tell her." His parents had been married for forty years and had become each other's confidant.

"It's either that or have her nag me until Christmas."

He laughed. He could hear his mother in the background fussing. "Well, you'd better get it over with. Tell Mom hi."

"Good night, son."

"Night." Jabari sighed wearily. He didn't do waiting well and the thought of having to walk away caused a searing pain in his heart.

Alisha sat on her bed Thursday evening, holding her phone in her hand. Several times over the past two days, she'd started to call Jabari but chickened out because she had no idea what to say. She thought she'd made the right decision, but being without him was harder than dealing with her crazy ex and his mother. Against her better judgment, she clicked on the photos of them at the Jelly Belly Factory. Her favorite had been the one of the four of them. She couldn't remember a time when she had been happier than that day. Corey and Lia were sitting on Jabari's lap and their smiles matched his. She studied Jabari's handsome face. She missed him. *So, while we're on this break, what am I supposed to do when I want to talk to you, touch you, kiss you...make love to you?* His words rushed back to her. She had no answer because she didn't know what to do.

Alisha's phone rang in her hand, startling her. She saw Siobhan's name on the display and sighed. She hadn't called her back. Not wanting to talk about her predicament, she let it go to voice mail and played it back.

Hey, cousin. It's way past Tuesday and I haven't heard from you. It's a weeknight and I know the kids are in bed. So, you can either call me back in the next ten minutes or I can be on the first plane to Sacramento tomorrow morning. Your choice.

She had no doubt Siobhan would make good on her threat, so she hit the call button.

"Oh, good. I thought I was going to have to book a flight. I had the Southwest page already open," Siobhan said when she answered.

Alisha couldn't help smiling. "I figured as much."

"How was the weekend trip?"

"Like something out of this world."

"All righty now. Are you going to be the next to take that trip down the aisle?"

"No," she said softly.

"What happened? I know he didn't do something crazy. Hold on. I'm calling Morgan."

Before she could say anything, the line went quiet. A minute later, Siobhan came back. "Okay, Morgan's on the line."

"Hey, Morgan. How are the Omars doing?"

Morgan laughed. "Both are good, but driving me crazy chasing each other through the house all the time. How are Corey and Lia enjoying school?"

"They love it."

"Okay, okay, we can play catch-up another time," Siobhan cut in. "Something happened with this guy Alisha's been dating."

"Do we need to come up there?" Morgan asked.

"No. Jabari hasn't done anything. It was me. I told him we should take a break." Before she knew it, Alisha had told them everything that had happened since she met Jabari, including the mess surrounding Wayne and his mother. "I'm worried she's going to try to convince him to withdraw his petition for termination and do something else like ask for joint custody. I don't want my babies in the middle of her crap."

Morgan snorted. "First of all, a judge isn't going to terminate his parental rights just because he wants to get out of paying child support, of which I know he hasn't paid one penny." Though she currently worked as a sports agent, she was also an attorney. "When was the last time he saw *his kids*?" she asked sarcastically.

"The day he walked out. He's never seen or held Lia. He came by once over two years ago, but the kids weren't there."

"I can look into it if you want. I also have an attorney friend who is a beast in the courtroom. When he's done with Wayne and his momma, they won't have anything left but the clothes on their backs. If she wants to play hardball, we can play."

"I know that's right," Siobhan said. "They don't want none of this family. Alisha, don't let them keep you from the love of a good man. And from what you've said about Jabari, he's exactly that. I almost let my fears keep me from accepting Justin's love. Don't make the same mistake. Let him love you the way you deserve to be loved."

"I don't know how. I've done everything myself for so long I don't know how else to be. And I'm scared."

"Let go and allow him to help you carry this load. I'm sure he wants to."

Her cousin was right. Jabari had said more than once that he would be there and she knew he had been waiting for her to open up to him. "Yes, he does."

"Good. Girl, go get your man. I'm going to tell you what my mom told me. She said she didn't advocate for women to chase after men, but since you've already got him, it won't hurt to remind him why he chose you in the first place."

Alisha burst out laughing. "Aunt Dee said that?"

"Yes, she did. Honey, I almost fell over. But you'd better believe I took her advice. Had my little bottle of honey and mmm-hmm, he didn't stand a chance."

Alisha couldn't believe Siobhan. For the longest time, she had been so serious, but she was back to the fun cousin she'd known growing up.

"Lisha, you know we've all had our issues trying to navigate this falling-in-love thing, but trust us, the payoff is totally worth it," Morgan said.

"Thanks, guys." She appreciated being able to share everything with them. Typically, all her girl talks had been with Michelle, but there was no way she could involve her this time.

"Let us know how it goes," Siobhan said. "And don't make me have to hop on a plane to get the details."

"I'll be right beside her."

"I hear you and I'll call you. Do you think I've waited too long?"

Siobhan laughed. "Girl, no. He's not falling out of love in a week. Just don't wait much longer to let him know you love him."

"I won't." Jabari had confessed to loving her twice and she hadn't told him once. "I'll talk to you guys soon." They spoke a moment longer before hanging up.

Alisha sat contemplating how to get her man back, as Siobhan had said. She chuckled at what her cousin had said about the honey. An idea popped into her head. She smiled. Just maybe.

Friday, Alisha had a surgery cancellation and it allowed her the opportunity to leave a little early to put her plan into motion. She had some anxiety about how it would all play out and her fears still lingered, but she pushed them aside. She googled M & J Technologies and programmed the address into her GPS. From downtown Sacramento, it would take about thirty minutes to get to the Folsom office without traffic. She didn't have to pick up the children for another two and a half hours, so she had plenty of time to run all her errands. Before going to Folsom, she drove the few blocks to Desiree's shop.

Alisha didn't see her when she walked in, but asked Brenda, Desiree's best friend and business partner, if Desiree was available.

"She's in the back. Let me get her."

"Thanks." She wandered around the shop while waiting and tried out some of the products.

"Alisha?"

She turned. "Hey, sis. I need your help."

"Sure. We can talk in my office," Desiree said, starting in that direction.

Alisha placed a staying hand on her arm. "We can talk here." There were only a few people in the store. They moved to the far side and she quickly explained what had happened.

"Oh, I'm so sorry. You sound just like me." She grabbed Alisha's hand. "I have just the thing." She walked over to a shelf that held a variety of massage oils, body paints and other sensual products. She picked up a tester bottle. "This is a warming massage oil. Hold out your hand." She put a drop on the back of Alisha's hand. "Rub it in."

Alisha did as asked. "It's warming up."

"Now gently blow on it."

She did and it became warmer. Her eyes lit with surprise.

"Taste it. Go ahead," Desiree said when Alisha hesitated.

She put a drop on her finger and licked it off. "It tastes like strawberries."

"I have that one, chocolate, honey, caramel, raspberry. It's edible and you can put it everywhere. *Everywhere.*"

Alisha picked up a small bottle of the strawberry.

"Ah, I think you should just get the four-ounce size. You'll need the whole bottle, trust me. How do you think I got your brother back after I temporarily lost my good sense?"

Her mouth fell open and she giggled. Desiree always seemed so quiet and proper. "The whole bottle?"

"Every time," she answered with a satisfied smile.

Alisha replaced the half-ounce bottle and got the larger size. She started for the cash register, turned back and grabbed a bottle of the chocolate-flavored oil.

Desiree chuckled. "You need us to watch the kids?"

She had planned to ask her mother when she stopped by to talk to her today, but she decided to take her sister-in-law up on her offer. "Tonight around seven?"

"I'll let Lorenzo know. They can stay the night."

She hugged Desiree. "Thank you."

"It's my pleasure. I've seen the way Jabari watches you. It's possessive, but in a good way."

Alisha knew what she meant. When he looked at her, she felt protected, desirable…loved. She paid for the oil, hugged Desiree once more and left. She navigated through downtown and took Highway 50 to Folsom. Instead of going inside the building, she decided to leave a note on the windshield of his car with a single long-stemmed rose. Thankfully, the lot wasn't a large one and she spotted his car almost immediately. She dug in her purse for the travel-sized bottle of her favorite fragrance and sprayed a little on the note. She glanced around to make sure he didn't suddenly appear, and then quickly placed it, along with the flower, on the car.

She got back on the road and went to her parents' house. She had called that morning to make sure her mother would be home.

Her mother pulled her into the house. "Hi, baby. What's going on? You've never taken off work early. Sit down."

Alisha sat on the sofa next to her mother. "I let my fears get the best of me and messed up with Jabari."

"Oh, honey. Have you tried talking to him?"

"Not yet."

"We talked about this before and I thought you were okay."

"We did, but..."

"He loves you, doesn't he?"

"Yes, but I figured if he didn't get close to my heart, he couldn't hurt me."

"Sweetheart, that may be true, but if he can't get close to your heart he can't love you."

"Don't be afraid to love him back, Alisha."

"It's hard not to. Then Georgia started her mess again." She told her mother about the messages she'd left and how she had intimated that she might convince Wayne to seek ways to see the children. "She didn't say it directly, but I'm worried about what she might do."

Her mother jumped up from the sofa. "You know what, I've had just about enough of that woman, always meddling in somebody's life. I'm going over there and knocking her into the middle of next week. Somebody needs to put her in her place and I'm just the woman to do it."

Some things never changed. Her mother didn't play when it came to her children. Alisha remembered the time when one of the neighborhood boys kept harassing Alisha. Her mother had marched down to their house and told his mother in no uncertain terms that her son had better stay away from Alisha. They took it to heart because he never bothered Alisha again. "Mom, it's okay."

"No, it's not. If she spent as much energy teaching her son to be a *real* man as she did worrying about your business, maybe he would've learned something by now." She snorted. "Making my blood pressure go up." She patted Alisha's hand. "Sorry, honey. That woman just irritates me. What are you going to do about Jabari?"

"Hopefully, I'll be able to talk to him tonight. I left him a message, so I'll see if he responds." *Or opens the door when I show up at his house.*

"We can watch the kids."

"Desiree already volunteered, but thanks." She checked her watch. "I'd better get going."

They stood. "Give my babies a hug and I pray everything works out. I happen to think Jabari will be good for you."

"I will and we'll see." Her mother walked her out and stood on the porch waving until Alisha pulled off. As she drove, something her mother said resonated with her. She took a detour. She had one more stop to make before picking up the children.

Twenty minutes later, she parked in front of Georgia's house and went to ring the bell.

"Alisha, what are you doing here?" Georgia glanced around Alisha. "Where are the kids?"

"I haven't picked them up yet. May I come in? I won't keep you long."

Georgia eyed Alisha warily, then unlocked the screen and invited her in. After they were seated, she said, "You wanted to talk? I hope you're reconsidering having that man around my grandchildren. It sets a bad example."

Alisha gave her a side-eye and mentally counted to ten, trying to remind herself to remain somewhat respectful to an elder. She gathered her thoughts and took a deep breath. "Miss Georgia, I've put up with you meddling in my life for long enough, but from here on out it's not happening. You will also not use my children to gain information about my life. What I do and who I do it with is none of your business, nor is it Wayne's." She ignored the shocked look on Georgia's face and plowed on. "If you ask my son one more question, he'll be graduating from college the next time you see him. Do I make myself clear?" She stood. "Oh, and *that man* has been a better example of a father to your grandchildren than your son ever was. If I have my way, he'll be doing it forever. Have a nice day." Alisha left the woman sitting there with her mouth hanging open and strode out of the house. LaVerne Hunter had said she was the woman to put Georgia in her place. Not today. Today, Alisha thought with a smile, *she* was the woman and it felt damn good. Alisha had a good man to apologize to and with any luck, she could convince him to be part of her life for a long time.

Chapter 17

"Have you talked to Alisha since Tuesday?"

Jabari lifted his head from the stack of papers he'd been collating and stared at Martin. "No. We were supposed to do a movie night at her place tonight and something with the kids tomorrow, but now?"

"Maybe you should call to see if you guys are still on."

"She said she needed space. A movie night and picnic isn't exactly the definition of giving *space*." Besides, if he asked and she said no, it would add another dagger to his heart. His pride couldn't handle a second rejection. He was considering sending her a text message like his father had suggested when he got home later. If she didn't respond, it would still hurt, but not as much as hearing it.

"If she's afraid like you said, she's probably waiting for you to make the first move."

He placed the stack of papers in a box. "I told her I loved her, that she can trust me. I've done everything I know how to do to prove I'll be there." Jabari sighed. "This time she has to make the move. She has to believe in me."

"Do you think she loves you?" Martin added another stack of papers to the box.

"She's never said it, but I feel it." The first night they made love in Sonoma, he knew. He couldn't explain it, but he *knew* she loved him. He wondered, though, if he would ever hear her say it.

"What time did Brent say he'd be by today?" Martin asked.

Brent had asked for additional information on Joy, and Jabari and Martin had just finished gathering all the paperwork. "Sometime before five."

"Good. That's only half an hour away. I have to be out of here on time tonight. Dena and I are having dinner with her parents and some out-of-town family members. Some kind of engagement thing or another." Martin waved a dismissive hand. "I'll be so glad when this whole wedding is over. I should've just offered to fly our families over to the Caribbean for an intimate wedding. We'd be already married, instead of having all these dinners and parties. And I have an entire year to wait before it's over," he added wearily. Martin and Dena planned to be married the following fall.

Jabari chuckled. "You're the one who agreed to this long engagement."

"Please don't remind me. Just wait until it's your turn."

"Oh, hell no. I'm not waiting longer than six months, and that's pushing it." He placed the top on the box and sealed it.

"You say that now. Just wait, you're going to be as frustrated as I am."

"Nah, man. I don't think so." If he ever got the chance. His mind went back to Alisha. How long would he have to wait for her to decide? When should he throw in the towel?

Martin picked up the box. "I'll take this back to my office. I want to talk to Brent when he gets here. How late are you staying?"

He glanced over at the wall clock. "It's almost five, so I may just take off. Stacey will be here until six thirty." He hadn't slept more than three hours a night this week and it had begun to wear on him. Jabari had spent twenty years in the military and was used to running on little to no sleep, but this thing with Alisha was draining him physically and mentally.

"Okay. See you on Monday. I hope you'll have some good news by then."

"So do I. Enjoy dinner."

Martin groaned and exited.

Jabari laughed, locked up his office, then stopped to let Stacey know he was leaving. He shook his head at the string of small pumpkin lights she'd hung around the wall to celebrate Halloween next week. Seeing them immediately made him think of Corey and Lia. Did they like dressing up or carving pumpkins? Jabari's heart clenched. He missed them almost as much as he missed their mother.

He pushed through the front doors and a brisk breeze greeted him. The temperatures had dipped to the low sixties in the past week. He crossed the lot to his car and stopped short. In the fading light, he saw a rose and an envelope tucked into the driver's side windshield. He removed them both and a familiar fragrance wafted into his nose. He hastily scanned the lot in hopes of seeing Alisha. He sat in the car and, with shaky hands, opened the envelope, pulled out the folded card and read: *Your house. Tonight. 8p. A.* His heart started pounding in equal parts fear and anticipation. He didn't know whether to plan for a reconciliation or… Jabari halted his train of thought. He didn't even want to consider the alternative.

He drove home, changed into a pair of basketball shorts and a T-shirt and attempted to eat, but with his stomach tied in knots, he gave up. Jabari's mind went into overdrive and nothing—watching television, listening to music, reading—could distract him. He kept checking his watch and it seemed as if time had slowed to a crawl.

By the time his doorbell rang at ten minutes before eight, his anxiety had climbed to a level he'd never experienced. He had to make himself slow down and not all out sprint to answer the door.

Jabari snatched the door open and a mixture of relief and love filled him when he saw Alisha standing there. His gaze roamed over her beautiful, lightly made-up face with her hair flowing around her shoulders, down to the long buttoned-up jacket, bare calves and high-heeled sandals. It took all his control not to touch her and kiss her like he had been dreaming of doing since Sonoma. "You're early."

A small smile touched Alisha's lips. "I decided to take a page out of your book. Is that okay?"

"Absolutely. Come in." He waved her in and closed the door. For a moment, all he could do was stare. "Can I take your coat?"

"I'm fine for now."

"We can talk in the family room." He gestured her forward. "Do you want something to eat or drink?"

"No, thanks," she said over her shoulder. Alisha perched on the edge of the sofa and wrung her hands.

Jabari sat on the other end and waited for her to speak. He sensed her nervousness and covered her hands with his. "How are you, baby?"

"Miserable." She took a deep breath. "I practiced what I was going to say on the drive over and now that I'm here, I don't have a clue where to start."

He gave her hand a gentle squeeze of encouragement.

Alisha lowered her head. "I'm sorry for hurting you, Jabari. For not trusting in you and the love you've offered me. For not opening up to you. I've always had to rely on myself, so I did what came naturally, and in the process, I shut you out. I was also afraid. Afraid of what other kinds of chaos Wayne and his mother are cooking up, afraid of my babies being in the middle of all the mess." She met his eyes. "Afraid that this drama will make you walk away one day." She swiped at an escaped tear. "I'm still afraid of those things, but I need you in my life. I can't begin to explain the feelings I have in my heart for you. You inspire a love inside of me so strong that it overwhelms my every thought." Alisha scooted closer to him and placed his hand over her heart. "I wish you could look inside my soul and see how deep it flows. I love you, Jabari Sutton, with everything in me."

Jabari had no words to describe the emotions overtaking him at this moment. Her impassioned confession moved him like nothing ever had. He crushed his mouth against hers in a deep, sensual kiss and tried to communicate the depths of his love for her. He rested his forehead on hers. "You don't ever have to be afraid of me walking away. I will love and protect you, Corey and Lia from everything and everyone." She stared at him with tearstained eyes. "Anyone who tries to hurt you will have to go through me." He kissed her again, his tongue slowly entwining with hers. Her hands came up to caress his face and the passion simmering just below the surface ignited into a full blaze.

Alisha tore her mouth away. "You asked me what you were supposed to do when you wanted to touch me, kiss me and make love to me. I didn't have an answer then, but I have one now." She eased off the sofa, unbuttoned her jacket and let it drop to the floor.

Jabari gasped sharply. Electricity shot to his groin. All he could do was stare at Alisha in the black strapless dress that molded to each one of her sensuous curves and stopped midthigh. He didn't realize he had been holding his breath until he felt the tightness in his chest.

"I know what I want you to do and what I want to do to you."

He blinked. "What?" She didn't give him time to process her statement before she straddled his lap and fused her mouth with his. She pushed him backward on the sofa until his head hit the armrest. She pushed his shirt up and over his head and tossed it aside, then charted a path with her tongue down the front of his body, placing lingering kisses just below his belly button. She grasped the waistband of his shorts. "What are you doing?"

Alisha gave him a sultry smile. "Showing you what I want to do to you."

"Baby—" Anything he had planned to say died on his tongue when she reached inside his shorts and grasped his shaft, stroking him from base to tip. Jabari's head fell back and his eyes closed. He heard a snap and then felt something wet and warm. The warmth increased as she continued to stroke him. Before he could sit up to see what she had, Alisha took him into her mouth and warm became hot. He jerked upright and swore hoarsely. What she was doing to him felt so good it had his entire body shaking. Knowing he was two seconds away from exploding, he pulled her up onto his lap. Jabari closed his eyes and tried to gain control. "What the hell are you doing to me?" he asked, his breathing ragged. He opened his eyes and met her smiling face.

She held up the bottle. "A little something I picked up from Desiree's shop. Edible massage oil. Do you like it? I sure do."

"*Like it?* I hope you have enough of it because I'm going to show you just how much I like it."

Desire lit in her eyes. She reached into her purse, pulled out another bottle and waved it in the air. "Chocolate. And the kids are spending the night with Desiree and Lorenzo."

That was all he needed to hear. He surged to his feet. "I'm glad you have two. I'm going to use every drop of it."

"That's what I'm counting on."

Jabari picked her up in his arms, strode through the house and up the stairs to his bedroom. He loved this woman and he planned to show her just how much, and also show her why she would never have to be afraid again.

Alisha read the text from Jabari and giggled.

"That's like the fourth time you've done that," Michelle said, seated across from Alisha in her kitchen Saturday morning.

She smiled. "I can't help it." Since they had made up two weeks ago, he'd come by the house almost every evening and spent time with her and the kids. He carved pumpkins for Halloween and organized a little party for Cory, Lia, Jade and a couple of other children who had been at Jade's birthday party. She had opened up to him more about her fears and shared what Morgan had said. Jabari had bluntly told Alisha, "If she can't do it, I'll find a lawyer." It made her love him all the more.

"Well, as your best friend, I'd just like to say I told you so."

She had missed being with her friend this way. She grasped Michelle's hand. "I'm sorry I've been so distant." She had shied away from talking to her because she didn't know how Michelle would respond to the fact that Alisha had hurt Jabari.

"It was hard not being able to be there for you like always, but I understood it. Girl, Chris almost had to tie me down a couple of times because I was on my way over. You and Jay were both miserable and I couldn't do a thing about it. But I'm so glad you guys worked everything out."

"So am I. I love him." Their night with the oil flashed in her mind and her body heated. True to his word, they had used every drop from both bottles.

"Are you ready for your weekend getaway?"

"Yes, but he won't say where we're going. I appreciate you taking care of Corey and Lia." They would be leaving in a few minutes. Jabari had told her to pack a few outfits for day and night and said the temperatures would be somewhere between seventy-five and eighty-five. Because she had no idea what he had planned, she had ended up with enough clothes to last a week.

"Oh, you know I love having them over."

"You ready, baby?" Jabari asked, coming into the kitchen.

Alisha stood. "Yes, as soon as I say bye to my babies." They all went into the family room, where the three were dancing along to a Disney song. Corey and Lia barely acknowledged her hug and kiss and kept right on dancing. "Well, I guess they'll be fine without me," she said with mock sadness.

Jabari chuckled and kissed her temple. "That's all right. I love you."

She smiled up at him. Hearing him declare his love now did not evoke the fear it had previously, but only brought her a sense of peace and contentment.

He escorted her to the car, started the engine and pulled off.

"You're still not telling me where we're going?"

"Nope," he said with a wide grin.

She ran her hand up his thigh. "Pretty please?"

He clamped down on her hand and chuckled. "Quit trying to tempt me. I'm not telling, so just relax."

Alisha rolled her eyes, but she couldn't stop smiling. She made herself comfortable and attempted to figure out where they could be headed. When he took the exit for the airport, she sat up straight in her seat. "The airport?" Her heart rate kicked up.

"Yep. We're going to take a short trip."

Her heart beat even faster when he drove to an area where several private planes sat. She could feel her fears rising but pushed them down. *You can trust him*, she repeated over and over again.

Jabari retrieved their bags from the trunk and

handed them over to the airport staff. “Shall we?” He grasped her hand and led her over to a midsize jet.

She climbed the stairs and gasped at the elegant interior of the plane. It had about a dozen oversize leather seats, a sofa and a worktable in the back.

“You can sit anywhere.”

Trying to quell her nervousness, she sat in the first seat. Jabari took the one next to her.

The smiling flight attendant came over. “Welcome aboard. It’s good to see you again, Mr. Sutton, Miss. We’ll be taking off in a few minutes. Would either of you like something to drink?”

Alisha shook her head.

“No, thank you,” Jabari said.

Minutes later, the plane roared down the runway and lifted off the ground.

“Are you okay?”

“Fine,” she lied. “How long is this trip?”

“We’re flying back Tuesday afternoon.”

“Tuesday?” She thought she might faint. “What about my babies? They have to go to school… And my job… I can’t just take off without calling.” Her voice began to rise. “And my family.”

“Alisha, baby.”

“No, I just met you. I don’t even know you like that. You can’t just take me away and my family not know where I am. What if something happens?”

Jabari cradled her face in his palms. “Sweetheart, calm down. I would never leave without your family knowing. They know exactly where we’re going.”

“Wait. What?” It took her a moment for his words to filter through her jumbled mind.

“Your parents, brother and sister-in-law all know where we’re going. I went over to talk to your parents last Sunday and I stopped by Desiree's shop yesterday for more of that oil. As for your job, that's taken care of, too, with a little help from Michelle." He pulled out his phone, pushed a few buttons and handed it to her.

Michelle was in on it? Alisha read the itinerary. "Belize. We're going to *Belize*?"

"Do you remember what you said when I asked you where you'd like to go, if you had the chance?"

She nodded. They had been talking and relaxing that night, but she had no idea he had paid that much attention.

"And what I told you I'm offering?"

"Yes." She threw her arms around him. "I love you."

"I love you, too," Jabari said with a laugh. "Is this how you're going to be if I decide to surprise you?"

"*Nooo* way."

He lifted a brow.

"Okay, I admit I overreacted just a little bit." Alisha put her thumb and forefinger close together.

Jabari reached over and spread them as far as they could go. "More like a lotta bit."

"Yeah, yeah, okay. You're right. I promise not to overreact and you can surprise me anytime you want." He shook his head and she burst out laughing. "You are so good for me, Jabari. I never knew it could be this way."

"Sweetheart, this *is* the way it'll always be with us."

Smiling, Alisha settled into her seat and enjoyed the rest of the flight. The journey took about five and a half hours and they arrived at the hotel close to four. With the difference in time zone of only two hours, she didn't have to worry about jet lag. The hotel had a stunning view of the Caribbean Sea and she was excited when they had the same view from their suite.

She crossed the marble floors in the room to the private balcony, opened the door and stepped out. Jabari fitted himself behind her and wrapped his arms around her.

"What do you think?"

Alisha turned in his arms. "I think I'm the luckiest woman on the face of the earth to have you. Thank you so much." She came up on tiptoe to kiss him. "So, what do you have planned for this little getaway?"

Jabari grinned. "A little of this and a little of that."

"That's fine. I don't need to know."

"That's my girl. You're getting better at this."

She laughed. "I do have a request, though. Can we find some food and then take a walk on the beach at sunset?"

"You read my mind. We probably should watch the sunset first, since it's getting late."

"That works." They walked hand in hand down to the water and stood silently as the sun dipped below the horizon, painting the sky in vivid reds and purples. "It's amazing. It's been long time since I've taken time to watch the sunset." She turned to see Jabari staring at her with an intensity that made her insides heat up. "What is it?"

Jabari seemed to struggle with his words. He tucked her hair behind her ear. "I had planned to do this later in the weekend, but I can't wait."

"Do wh—" He lowered himself to one knee. Alisha's heart stopped and started up again.

He took her hand. "Alisha, there's nothing halfway about the way I love you. When you kiss me, I feel forever. When you smile at me, I know that the rest of my days will be happy. And when you put your arms around me, I know I'll never be alone. I promise to walk beside you, protect you and love you until I take my last

breath. I will love and protect Corey and Lia as if they were my own. Although, I feel they already are mine. You'll never have to be afraid because my arms will always be there to shelter you. You are my everything, baby, and I want to spend the rest of my life with only you. Will you marry me?"

Alisha was crying so hard she could barely answer. "Yes," she finally managed.

He slid the solitaire onto her finger, rose to his feet, lifted her into his arms and swung her around.

She kissed him with everything she had in her. It wasn't until she heard clapping that she realized they weren't alone. She whipped her head around and saw a small knot of people standing around. "And you are my everything."

Epilogue

Three months later

Alisha couldn't contain her excitement as she waited in the holding room at the historic downtown Sacramento mansion where she and Jabari would be married in a few short minutes.

"If you don't stop bouncing, those curls are going to be flat," Michelle said, coming into the room.

She laughed. "I can't help it."

"I'm glad to see you so happy. It's been a long time coming."

"Yes, it has." They shared a smile. She grasped her friend's hand. Michelle had been there from the beginning and knew what Alisha had gone through. But that was all behind her now. Today, she had a chance to start a new life with the right man. She no longer had to concern herself with Georgia and Wayne interfering in her life. Apparently, after their little *talk*, Georgia had realized she was in danger of missing out on her grandchildren and had had a change of heart. Wayne decided he didn't want the responsibility of being a father after all and continued with his petition. Jabari had walked into that courtroom with her and declared that they would be getting married and he would assume responsibility for raising Corey and Lia. By some miracle, the judge was moved, and Alisha had walked out with the last tie to her past severed.

A knock sounded on the door.

Michelle went to answer it and let Alisha's father in. "Hi, Mr. Hunter. Don't you look handsome?" She turned to Alisha. "I'll see you in a minute."

Her father closed the door behind Michelle and stood silently for a moment. "You look beautiful, baby girl."

"Thanks, Dad." Alisha smoothed a hand over the strapless fit-and-flare ivory gown in soft tulle, with its sweetheart neckline, lace applique and dropped-waist bodice covered in sparkling crystal and beads.

He closed the distance between them. "Jabari is a good man and I'm proud to call him son."

Tears misted her eyes. While in Belize, Jabari had confessed that he'd asked her father's permission to marry her. That he respected her enough to do what many people thought was outdated had earned him a special place in her parents' hearts. "Yes, he is."

He extended his arm. "Ready?"

"Yes!"

They had chosen to have the ceremony inside, rather than worry about the unpredictable February weather. The room had been decorated in her favorite deep shade of purple with cream-colored accents. Lia and Jade in their ivory dresses with a purple band around the waist served as flower girls. Corey wore a miniature tux that matched Jabari's and stood beaming at Jabari's side. Both children had already started calling him "Daddy."

But what held her attention most was the man at the end of the aisle, standing tall and as handsome as she had ever seen him in his off-white tuxedo. Their eyes met and the love and passion she saw there took her breath away.

Her father smiled, kissed her brow and placed her hand in Jabari's. "Be happy, baby."

Jabari stared down at her. "You are exquisite."

They smiled and faced the minister. They repeated their vows and exchanged rings. Her cousin Khalil Gray, one of Siobhan and Morgan's brothers, surprised her by having R&B superstar Monte sing. She had no idea Khalil and Monte were friends, but she planned to thank her cousin for making her day even more special.

"I now pronounce you husband and wife," the minister said. "Jabari, you may kiss your bride."

Jabari wasted no time. He slanted his mouth over hers in a tender but passionate kiss. "Thank you for marrying me."

"I love you, Jabari."

"I love you, too, Mrs. Sutton. I think I was a goner from the moment you introduced yourself, backside first."

Alisha buried her head in Jabari's chest and groaned. She had been so embarrassed that day. Never could she have imagined that incident would lead to this moment. To forever. In him, she'd found the sweetest love she had ever known.

* * * * *

Once again, Ian didn't know how to respond, so he remained quiet.

"Then I met you. And I made a decision based on the way we talked, the way you seemed to see inside me at the bar. It was new and different. But it was also terrifying."

"I feel the same way," he admitted.

"I know you have so much more experience with women." She smiled, a wistful look in her eyes. "But I didn't feel inexperienced with you. I felt powerful, alive. I want that again."

Ian searched her eyes, saw the truth in them. Then he made his decision. He pressed his lips to hers. Her low moan spurred him on, and he pulled her to him.

The kiss was soft yet firm. It was everything it should have been in that moment. She needed something, and he wanted to give it to her. When he broke the kiss, he let out a deep breath and rested his forehead against hers.

There was never a time when **Elle Wright** wasn't about to start a book, already deep in a book or just finishing one. She grew up believing in the importance of reading, and became a lover of all things romance when her mother gave her her first romance novel. She lives in Southeast Michigan.

Books by Elle Wright

Harlequin Kimani Romance

It's Always Been You
Wherever You Are
Because of You

Visit the Author Profile page
at Harlequin.com for more titles.

BECAUSE OF YOU

Elle Wright

To my mother, Regina—you are missed.

Acknowledgments

Without God, I would be nothing.
I thank Him for being everything to me.

To Jason, my children, Asante, Kaia, Masai,
and the rest of my family, I love you all BIG.
There are so many of you, I can't name everyone.
But you know who you are. I learned long ago
that you don't have to be blood to be family.
That couldn't be more true. I appreciate the time,
the talks, the hugs, the tears…everything.
I thank you all for your unwavering support.

To my agent, Sara, I thank you for believing in me.

To the Kimani Family,
thank you for your encouragement.

I wouldn't be on this journey without all of your love
and support. Thank you for being #TeamElle!!!
You all mean the world to me!

Dear Reader,

It's okay to live a little, take time to smell the roses. When I wrote *Because of You*, I knew I wanted it to be fun and flirty, sexy and serious.

I can so relate to Bailee. She has spent her life doing what is expected of her. When the book opens, she's tired of living for everyone else and makes the decision to stop being so "buttoned-up"—if only for one weekend. When she meets Ian, he changes her life. Literally. What starts as something fleeting becomes something lasting.

Because of You is about two people at a crossroads in their lives, on the cusp of big changes. They quickly realize that what they're missing, they have found in each other. I absolutely loved these two. Dr. Ian Jackson is unlike any of his brothers and I enjoyed writing their journey to happily-ever-after.

I hope you enjoy the ride!

Love,

Elle

ElleWright.com

@LWrightAuthor

Chapter 1

Turning thirty was almost like a sudden death. One day, Bailee Sanders was twenty-nine, working as a nurse anesthetist, dating one of the most eligible bachelors in Columbus and living what she thought was her best life. The next day...well, let's just say she panicked when she felt like her "best life" was choking her. So she did what any person would do in that position—quit her job, ended her relationship and purchased a first-class ticket to the Big Easy for a weekend of fun with her bestie.

It couldn't be that easy, though. Hence, her current predicament. In her defense, it was hot in Louisiana—so hot she was pretty sure the New Orleans air had destroyed her brain cells and rendered her incapable of making good decisions. How else could she explain her behavior?

First, she'd knocked back three too many Hand Grenades on Bourbon Street. Two…*or is it second?* Anyway, after her last drink, she'd cozied up to a stranger at the hotel bar. Not only did she chat with him like she'd known him for years, she'd made matters so much worse when she invited Mr. Hottie McHotStuff back to her room after they'd closed down the bar. And—

"Damn, baby, I can't get enough of you," Mr. Hottie whispered as he thrust into her once again. He circled her nose with his before he nipped her chin with his teeth.

Oh God.

Bailee couldn't think straight. Not when his scent seemed to invade her mind. Not when his lips brushed against her neck, her cheeks, her forehead. Not when his body conquered hers in such a way that made her forget all the reasons why it was a bad idea to get busy with a stranger.

Her gaze dropped to his full lips. She'd been the one to set the conditions for the night—no kissing, no love, just sex. Hell, she'd even given him a fake name. And he'd accepted her conditions with no arguments or questions. But his touch sparked something inside her. He'd filled her so completely, she wanted to beg him for more. It was his fault she'd wanted to renege on her own rules. Had he not been so skilled, so adept at knowing what she needed, she wouldn't be imagining how his lips would taste, how his tongue would feel against hers.

Sex had never been quite like this for Bailee. Passion had never threatened to overtake her common sense, or make her want to throw caution to the wind for it. Instead of rolling her eyes and preparing for the orgasmic performance of her life, she was… *Shit.* She was in trouble.

His hooded eyes clouded with lust. "You're so beautiful," he murmured, his breath soft against her face.

He trailed wet kisses up her jaw. She wanted those talented lips on hers. Except she'd told him not to. As if she was channeling Julia Roberts in *Pretty Woman*, trying to protect her heart.

Above her, his brown skin glistened with sweat. They were so in tune with each other, giving and taking in equal measure. It had been years since her body had this type of reaction to anyone.

"Let go, sweetie," he whispered against her cheek before he circled her nose with his. "Give me what I need."

Bailee could do nothing but grunt. Or was that a groan? *A whimper?* Everything about this man set her on fire. He was so hot, so virile, that she forgot to blink. Hell, she forgot to breathe. And even though he hadn't kissed her, she felt even hotter imagining it. And...*oh God.*

Her orgasm was powerful and unexpected, making her feel dizzy as it raced through her. It was good. Too good. So good tears pricked her eyes. He followed soon after, letting out a low groan.

She felt boneless, sated. This release, this man, had been exactly what she needed. He rolled over onto his back and she smiled. The need to sleep overtook her in that moment, and she allowed her eyes to drift closed. Then...

Bailee sat upright as reality dawned on her. She couldn't fall asleep. That's not what this was. In the days since she'd arrived in New Orleans, she'd agreed to let loose. Life had always been a regimented plan for her, and she wanted to do something she'd never done before.

Seeing Mr. Hottie at the bar, looking so fly in jeans and a button-down shirt, had made her decision easy. One-night stand. *Check.* It was something she swore she would never do, and she had to psych herself up for it. Giving him conditions was one thing, but she'd also given herself a short checklist of things not to do. Falling asleep after the act was at the top of the list.

Running a hand through her hair, she scanned the suite for her clothes. Apparently, they'd disappeared with her inhibitions. Her gaze drifted to the bathroom door.

"Are you okay?" he asked.

She jumped and pulled the sheet up to her chin. Nodding rapidly, she said, "I'm fine. Just… I need to go to the bathroom."

Without another word, she bolted from the bed, pulling the sheet with her. She swiped her cell phone off the dresser before stepping into the bathroom and closing the door behind her, sagging against it.

Bailee dialed her friend, and prayed April would pick up.

"Are you thoroughly satisfied, Bai?"

April had been Bailee's lab partner in Anatomy during their freshman year in college. Oddly, the two could barely stand each other during class. It wasn't until their third year of undergrad, when they both pledged the same sorority, that they became friends. Since then, they'd been closer than sisters. April was the devil on Bailee's shoulder, while Bailee played the angel on April's shoulder.

Bailee shushed April. "Be quiet. Are you alone?"

The last time she'd seen her friend was when April was leaving the bar with her vacation boo. "Unfortunately, yes. Me and my vacation boo had to part ways when he insisted on coming to Michigan for a visit. Ain't nobody got time for that."

Bailee couldn't help the giggle that escaped at her friend's words. "You're crazy."

"Hey, I can only be me. Anyway, why are you calling me? Shouldn't you be in post-orgasmic bliss with Mr. HotStuff?"

"Shh."

"You're being weird. Am I on speakerphone or something?"

"No," Bailee whispered. "But I can't talk about this right now."

"What happened? Where are you?"

"In my room," Bailee mumbled.

"Why are you whispering?" April asked. "Is he still there?"

"Yes." Bailee crawled to the other side of the bathroom, away from the door. "I'm in the bathroom."

"Judging by your behavior, I'm guessing he sucked."

"We're not talking about this. I need a favor."

"What is it? Do I need to kick the door down and save you?" April grew up the only girl in a house full of boys, and had learned a few tricks to get herself out of trouble. It had served them well over the years.

"No, you don't have to do anything like that. I just need to know how to tell him to go home."

"Wait, what?"

"How do I end this?"

"Tell his ass to go home," April said. "What's the big deal?"

"You know this is out of my depth. And I don't want to be mean. He's nice."

"Key word. Nice. He's not a killer. Just tell him thanks for the fun time, but bye."

Bailee snickered. “Tell me why I called you again? You’re not helping.”

“Listen.” Bailee heard movement in the background, like April was walking around. “You’re thirty years old. You’re beautiful. You’re intelligent. You can tell a man to kick rocks. It’s not that hard. I’m sure he’ll be just fine. He might even be relieved that he doesn’t have to make that move.”

“You know what? You’re absolutely right. I’m a professional. I can handle this.” She let out a heavy sigh. “Men do it all the time, right?”

“Exactly! You got this, Bai. I’ll give you a few minutes to let him down easy, and then I’ll come down there.”

“Okay. Yes, I got this. Talk to you in a bit.”

“Cool beans. Be direct.”

“Direct,” Bailee repeated. Once she ended the call, though, all the bravado she’d just mustered up seeped out of her body. “Oh, Lord, I can’t do this.”

Sighing, Bailee closed her eyes. This wasn’t how the night was supposed to turn out, with her cowering in the bathroom in an attempt to avoid the man who had just made her see stars.

She’d had hot, amazing sex with a man she barely knew. Actually, barely was an overstatement. Good conversation at the bar, flirty banter...that wasn’t knowing him. That was foreplay. But she didn’t regret it because, for once, she’d lived in the moment. She’d been fun Bailee, not work-too-hard-and-asleep-by-nine Bailee. And she was okay with that. April was right. This wasn’t rocket science. She could put on her big-girl panties—if she could find them—and tell him that it had been fun, but she needed to get some rest. She could tell him to beat it in the nicest way possible.

A soft knock on the door jolted her out of her thoughts.

"Hey," he called from the other side. "Are you good?"

Bailee stood up. "I'm fine. I…I need to get ready for… My friend is probably wondering where I am." She rolled her eyes at her attempt to lie.

"As long as you're okay," he said.

"No need to worry. Um…you don't have to wait. You can let yourself out," Bailee blurted. "I'm just going to take a shower and pack up."

For a minute, she wondered if bringing him back to her hotel room had been a mistake. If she'd been thinking about the aftermath, rather than his body on hers, she would have insisted on getting another room. Or going to his.

"I'll just go," he said.

Relieved, Bailee shouted, "Thanks!"

Thanks? She was worse than she thought. Not only was she rude, but she'd basically treated him like a transaction.

Bailee smacked her forehead with her palm and shuffled to the mirror. Dark circles under her eyes, smeared eye makeup and pale lips greeted her when she stared at her reflection. "Hello, Hot Mess," she grumbled before pulling the makeup remover from her toiletry bag and smearing the cream on her face.

After a few more minutes, she finally opened the door and stepped out of the bathroom. But instead of facing an empty room, Mr. Hottie was sitting on the edge of the bed. Startled by his presence, she yelped and nearly fell on her butt.

Recovering quickly, she tugged at the robe she'd put on. "You're still here."

He smirked. "What's on your face?"

"Oh no." Mortified, she ran into the bathroom, grabbed a clean towel and wiped her face. He stood in the doorway as she scrubbed her cheeks, forehead and chin. "It's makeup remover. I thought you left."

"No worries. I'll be out in a sec."

Once she finished, she dropped the washcloth on the sink and turned to him.

His gaze traveled the length of her body before meeting hers. "Unless you want a repeat."

Just the words, the promise in his eyes, made her want to take him up on the offer. But she wouldn't. She couldn't. "Uh, no. That won't be necessary. I have to go and…" She patted his shoulder as if he were simply a platonic acquaintance. "This is just… I mean, no need to pretend I like you."

"Ouch."

"I didn't mean it like that." She crossed her arms over her breasts. "I meant that we don't need to do this." *Shut up, Bailee.* "You know, the awkward promise to see each other again another time. We both know that won't happen."

He blinked.

"I just… I'm not good at this." The more she talked, the worse she sounded. And strangely, she couldn't stop talking. "I've never had casual relations. I mean, relationships."

He gripped her shoulders and squeezed. "You should stop talking now."

Bailee swallowed. "I'm sorry. I'm not usually rude."

He didn't respond to that. Instead, he stood there just staring at her with those eyes. What else was she supposed to say? Enjoy the rest of your trip? From their earlier conversation, she knew he didn't live in the city, but had traveled there for work.

Finally, he broke the silence. "I'll..." He scratched his neck. "Well, I won't see you around, but I hope you enjoy the rest of your stay here."

"I have a plane to catch in the morning. Remember, it's—"

"Your last night here," he finished for her. "I remember. Okay. Safe travels, Aries."

Bailee winced, tucking a strand of hair behind her ear. At the hotel bar, they'd agreed to keep things simple, so she'd given him an alias. Why she told him her name was Aries, she didn't know. Bailee had never been a good liar, so she'd spouted off the first thing that came to mind. He'd told her his name was Ian, which she suspected was his real name.

With narrowed eyes, he tilted his head. "Is Aries your real name?"

She couldn't even bring herself to say yes. So she simply nodded.

He shot her a disbelieving look. "Yeah...okay."

She couldn't blame him. Unfortunately, she wasn't used to giving fake names or having sex with men she didn't know and had no intention of seeing again.

Clearing his throat, he said, "Good night...Aries."

"Good night, Ian."

He turned and she followed him to the door. When he pulled it open, April was standing there, her hand poised to knock.

"Oh." April dropped her hand to her side. "I'm sorry to interrupt. I didn't realize you still had company."

Ian shot Bailee a look out of the corner of his eye. "I'm on my way out."

April smirked. "Don't leave on my account."

Bailee grabbed April's hand and tugged her into the room. "April, Ian has to go." She gave him a tight smile. "Enjoy the rest of your time here."

His gaze raked over her. "I will."

Then he was gone. Bailee shut the door and turned to April. Her friend was staring, mouth open. "What?"

April pointed at the closed door. "Girl, you're crazy. That man is even hotter up close. And judging by the way he looked at you, he wouldn't have minded staying a little longer."

Bailee tightened her robe. "Shut up." She brushed past her friend and walked into the bathroom. "What would be the point of him staying anyway? It's not like we'll ever see each other again."

"Um, because he's fine. And his arms. Those lips. That—"

"I get it, April." Bailee rolled her eyes. "He's nice looking. You don't have to give me a rundown of his finer attributes."

April eyed Bailee. "Why are you so snappy?"

Bailee didn't know why she felt so irritated all of a sudden. Leaning against the sink, she shrugged. "I don't know."

"You know what I think?"

"No, but I'm sure you're going to tell me."

"I think you're being too hard on yourself. Stop second-guessing your decision. So you let your hair down and had some fun. You're not the first, and certainly won't be the last person to enjoy a little random sex with a stranger."

Bailee let out a heavy sigh. "I know. It's just hard. I had a life, a relationship. And now I have no idea what I'm going home to. Or what I even want anymore."

"Bai, you're not an old maid. You broke up with

Brandon because you knew that he wasn't the type of man you need in your life. It's better to end things now before you end up in divorce court later. Sometimes, you just grow apart. As for your job, I still think you should move to Michigan. We can be roomies again. Fun times."

April lived in Novi, Michigan, one of the fastest growing cities in the state. It was a short twenty-five-minute drive to Ann Arbor, where Bailee's brother, Mason, lived and worked. She couldn't deny she'd thought about making the move many times over the last several months. Although she loved her hometown, there was nothing keeping her in Columbus any longer. Especially since her parents had recently moved to Fort Lauderdale to be close to her mother's family.

"April, it's not that simple. I can't just move. I have a home there."

"True. But you don't have a job."

Glaring at her friend, Bailee crossed her arms. "Really, April? You're going to throw that in my face?"

April lifted her hands in surrender. "Don't kill me, but I still think it's funny. You quit your job without another one. That's so unlike you."

"Don't remind me."

"Fine, but I'm going to need you to stop making excuses. It's the perfect time to make a move. Your place is in a nice neighborhood, and I'm sure you won't have any trouble finding a buyer."

"I guess I'm just scared."

April wrapped an arm around Bailee and pulled her into a hug. "I know."

Bailee allowed herself to relax in her friend's comforting embrace. "What if I made a mistake?"

Bailee had never rocked the boat. She'd made decisions based on expectations. Bailee chose to become a nurse because her mother thought it was the perfect way to honor her grandmother, who'd spent years in the profession. She'd bought a condo because her father told her it was important to purchase her first home at an early age, like he'd done. And she'd spent years trying to make a relationship work with Brandon, because her parents, his parents…hell, their entire community had been invested in the "B&B" wedding.

Going with the flow, doing what others expected had worked well for her. At thirty, she earned a good living and had a pretty impressive investment portfolio. Although she had a trust fund, she'd never had a reason to touch it. From the outside looking in, one might think she had a picture-perfect life.

Yet, Bailee had dreamed of a happiness that seemed just out of reach. She wanted to go to work and love what she did. She wanted to be with a man who made her smile at just the thought of him. She needed more.

"Stop. You're pretty amazing." April pulled back and met Bailee's gaze. "You've already accomplished so much. You're a freakin' DNP, for goodness sake. At thirty."

Bailee had spent the majority of her twenties in school, furthering her education. After she'd graduated from college, she worked a couple of years and then enrolled in an intensive Nurse Anesthesia–Doctor of Nursing Practice program. She'd recently completed her studies.

"Also, it took courage to end your relationship, to walk away," April continued. "I have no doubt you'll be able to flourish in another state."

"You're not going to give up, are you?"

April grinned. "Nope. I've already talked to Mason,

and he agrees. He'd be happy to have you near him. And I'm sure he can get you a job at the hospital."

Bailee's older brother, Mason, worked as a pharmacist for Michigan Medicine, formerly known as the University of Michigan Health System. "Since when do you talk to Mason?"

Her best friend and her brother had a somewhat contentious relationship. Bailee knew it had a lot to do with the little fling they'd had several years ago, against her dire warnings. Bailee knew they weren't right for each other, but neither of them had listened to her. The relationship had ended with hurt feelings and a broken heart for her best friend.

"I don't." April tugged at her ear. "Well, not really. We actually ran into each other at the mall. He was with his fiancée."

Bailee saw the flash of hurt in her bestie's eyes, and gave her a sad smile. "I'm sorry."

April waved a dismissive hand her way. "Stop apologizing. Your brother is a good guy, and he deserves to be happy. And so do you. Since you're going to be in Michigan next weekend for his wedding, you can start planning your move. Then you can come visit me when it's over."

Bailee had to admit, April's plan made sense. Breaking up with Brandon had been her first step in asserting her own will in her life. Quitting her job had been the next power move in her quest for "more."

She'd traveled on a whim to a place she'd always wanted to go, spent much-needed time with her best friend and had a one-night stand with a man who looked like sex on a stick. Bailee wasn't old. She was a woman in her prime, with her entire life ahead of her. She should be having fun, exploring life. And Bailee planned to use her newfound free time to figure out what she really wanted for her life. Instinctively, she knew a move was in her future. But she wasn't sure Michigan was the answer.

"Fine, I'll think about it." April pointed at her friend and issued a warning. "But I'm not making any promises."

April hugged her. "Yes! That's all I ask. Now, enough of the heavy stuff. Tell me all about Mr. Hot-Stuff. And I want details."

Chapter 2

Dr. Ian Jackson couldn't get out of the Detroit Metro Airport fast enough. The lure of his bed and much-needed sleep propelled him through the airport in record time. After giving up his first-class seat on the plane to a disabled elderly woman who'd struggled to make it to her economy seat, he'd been forced to entertain a little girl with stories and weird faces for the entire flight. Little Ashley with her wild curls and toothy grin had prevented his nap, but Mrs. Palmer's grateful smile made his sacrifice worth it.

He pulled his phone out of his pocket and turned it on. Five missed calls, umpteen texts. Once he'd picked up his luggage and was in the safety of the town car he'd hired to take him home, he read through his emails and text messages. Next were his voice mails.

Most were simple one-liners from his brothers, his younger sister, and his best friend, Mia. But the one from his father angered him. It wasn't so much the content of the message, but the tone. Although Ian was a grown man, a doctor, his father still felt comfortable telling him what he should or should not do.

Dr. Lawrence Jackson had not been the best and most supportive father. In fact, Ian's dad was an unbearable control freak. It hadn't been that long ago that it was revealed he had offered Ian's uncle El's girlfriend money to break up with him. Ian's oldest brother, Drake, had recently shared with him all the sordid details about his father's affair with Drake's mother.

Growing up, it was hard being the son of Dr. Lawrence and Monica Jackson. His parents weren't the loving parents his peers thought they were. They were cold and only concerned with appearances. Which was why he suspected his mother spent more time at the plastic surgeon getting Botox and the like than she did with him and his twin brother.

But his life was a cakewalk compared to those he'd seen in his volunteer work. He didn't have to worry about food or clothes or access to water. He never had to wonder how he would get much-needed medication or medical care. That was why he'd signed up to join the American Red Cross as a volunteer in New Orleans and had recently applied to Doctors Without Borders.

Unfortunately, his noble intentions would not be met with enthusiasm from his father. In fact, Ian was sure his father wouldn't be proud of his decision. Which was why he hadn't shared his intentions with him. Ian knew his father wouldn't understand, and he was tired of fighting.

With a heavy sigh, he placed his first return call.

"Ian, where the hell have you been?" Myles asked, cutting right to the chase.

"How are you, brother?"

"I'm fine. Where are you?"

Ian glanced out of the window. Hard to believe he'd been gone for six months. When he'd originally signed up to volunteer, he'd expected to be in Louisiana for three months. But he found that he'd enjoyed the work immensely and spoke with his med school adviser about extending his stay.

"I'm here, on my way home. Just landed. What's up?"

"Dad is on the warpath again. He's been asking to meet with us."

That was the last thing Ian had on his agenda. "Yeah, I'm not doing that. I have to drive up to Traverse City tomorrow anyway. The plan for the next several hours is sleep. After that, I'm going to meet my new niece."

One of the downsides to being gone for so long was Ian had missed key events in his family. His brother Drake and his wife, Lovely, had welcomed their first child. Ian was thrilled to be an uncle, and ready to spoil his little sweetie pie. They'd texted pictures of baby Zoe, and she was adorable.

"Well, he does plan to go to the wedding," Myles told him. "How will you avoid him?"

"I'll figure that out," Ian replied.

"How was the trip?"

As the town car sped down I-94 toward Ann Arbor, he noted the subtle changes in the area. Buildings were sprouting up where lush trees used to stand tall. Construction crews were working the roads, expanding them for the many commuters in the area.

"Good. We did a lot of good work. Wish you had come with me."

Ian knew Myles wasn't interested in being on the

front line. His twin was as straitlaced as they came. They were like night and day. Ian was comfortable in jeans and a T-shirt, while Myles dressed in a suit nearly every day of the week. But there wasn't much Ian didn't know about Myles, and vice versa. And Ian didn't doubt that Myles had his back no matter what. Just like Ian wouldn't hesitate to be there for Myles.

"I probably should have come down to visit, at least," Myles admitted, which surprised Ian. "I need a break from here."

"You could always ride up north early with me."

"I can't. Dad is lecturing tomorrow at the school. I told him I'd be there."

Ian shook his head. "Myles, when are you going to stop trying to fit yourself into the box Dad tries to put you in?"

"Don't start. I'm not like you, ready to leave at any moment. I need stability, and I'm happy where I am."

"Whatever." Ian checked his watch. "Let me go. I have to call Mia before she has a panic attack or something."

"What time are you going to Drake's?"

"In a few hours. Are you going to meet me there?"

Myles agreed to meet him later, and they hung up. Next, Ian called Mia.

"Ian, I hope you know that I'm killing you on sight," Mia said, skipping the pleasantries.

"Hey, Mia. Are you officially turning into a bridezilla now?"

"Ian, you're my man of honor and you haven't been here for anything. You missed my engagement party, the bridal party roundup and my bridal shower. What's up with that?"

"I've been working, Mia. And I'm a man. There's

no way I was coming to your bridal shower and eating cucumber sandwiches and dainty hors d'oeuvres, and watching you open boxes filled with lingerie. That's not what we're about."

Mia laughed. "You're silly."

"No, I'm being serious. When you asked me to stand up with you on your wedding day, I thought you meant that in an honorary way."

"Why would you think that? Stand up with me is pretty clear. Besides, you're my best friend. I need you at my side when I take the biggest step of my life."

Ian smiled. Mia Solomon had given him his first haircut—against his will. She'd made him his first mud pie and had been there through every good and bad thing in his life. Although they weren't related by blood, she was his sister, his best friend.

Ian's and Mia's fathers had been great friends, and the two families had spent a lot of time together, traveling to exotic islands and mountain villas. He'd stayed entire summers at the Solomon estate near Traverse City, Michigan, running the grounds and getting into trouble. And when they moved back to Ann Arbor from Las Vegas during his teenage years, they'd lived on the same street in a wealthy west-side neighborhood.

"You know I can be your best friend in the front row. I don't need to be in the wedding, Mia."

"You promised. It's too late to back out."

Ian didn't remember telling his friend that he'd don a tuxedo and walk down the aisle to music by himself. When they'd first discussed the wedding, she'd told him that she couldn't pick between her sisters for maid of honor. Mia was one of five Solomon women, all of them successful, all them headstrong and all of them bosses. So he could only imagine what would happen if she'd had to pick just one to handle the role.

He'd been friends with Mia long enough to know he'd never win this battle. Ian loved Mia, but she was relentless when she had her mind set on something. Sighing, he said, "What do you need, Mia?"

"How about answer your damn phone when I call you? And get up here as soon as possible. There's so much to do."

"I can't promise I'll answer the phone every single time you call. I do have a job, and a life."

"Speaking of having a life, you sent me a text about a woman the other day. Who is she?"

Ian groaned, recalling how he'd sent Mia a string of emojis when he'd met Aries at the bar. Mia had been texting him about floral arrangements and color swatches when he'd sent the text. It had been his way of telling his friend that his attention was on something else, namely an attractive and available woman.

"We're not talking about me right now, Mia," he told her. "I'll compromise and make sure my phone is on me at all times until you jump over that broom."

Mia thanked him. "I just miss you."

"I miss you, too, Big Head."

She barked out a laugh. "Shut up, Munch."

Ian groaned. "I told you to stop calling me that."

He had picked up the nickname when he was a cute, albeit chubby little boy. Mia's dad had started calling him Munch because he was always munching on food. Somewhere around the age of fourteen, Ian had demanded they stop calling him the name, and had refused to answer to it. Also around the same time, he'd started cycling and dropped his excess weight quickly.

As if on cue, Mia said, "Bring your bike. We can ride the grounds."

Aside from Myles, Mia was the only person who understood him without question. She knew that cycling was a necessary part of his life. Cycling had not only been his way to get in shape, it had also helped him get away with minimal fuss. As a teenager, he didn't have to borrow one of his father's cars to leave the house. All he'd needed was his bike. Even now, he rode his bike into work most days. The unpredictable Michigan weather didn't faze him; he could ride on the coldest or hottest days. He'd cycled across the country, through many different terrains, along the countryside or up a mountain or near the beach. He'd raced in the Tour de France and the one-day Lotoja race from Utah to Wyoming.

Ian smiled. "I knew I loved you for some reason other than your homemade biscuits."

Mia laughed. "You're crazy. Seriously, though, I really need you here, Munch. Come soon."

Something in Mia's voice gave him pause. "Are you okay, Mia? What's going on? Because if Mason—"

"I'm fine," Mia said, cutting him off. "Mason is fine. I'm just stressed. Weddings are hard work. My sisters are driving me crazy, and trying to take over."

Ian chuckled. "That doesn't surprise me, Mia. All of you think you know everything."

"Be quiet. I'm learning to sit back and observe, like you."

The Solomon family had an interesting dynamic, like his family. But Dr. and Mrs. Solomon, or Mama and Pop as he called them, beat his parents hands down in the love department. They'd always shown him nothing but unconditional love and support. When he'd mentioned his desire to go down to New Orleans to work with the American Red Cross, it was Pop's recommendation that placed him above the other candidates. Ian owed them a debt that couldn't be repaid with money. In many ways, he owed them his ability to think for himself—he owed them his life.

"Good. But, Mia, it's your wedding. No one else's opinion matters but yours. And Mason's."

His best friend let out a heavy sigh. "I needed to hear that. Lately, I've felt the pressure because Nonna is getting older, and I'm the first grandchild to marry."

Anna Maria Solomon was eighty-one years young, if you let her tell it. The family matriarch ran a real-estate development business and had amassed quite a fortune over the years. She'd adopted Dr. Solomon at age five, when his mother died. Back then, it had been a bit of a scandal for a white woman to adopt an African American child, but Anna didn't care what people said. She'd made a promise to her best friend to raise her son if something should ever happen to her, and she'd kept that promise.

Recently, Dr. Solomon retired and moved to Traverse City permanently to help his mother. Since he'd made the move, he'd opened an Italian restaurant on the outskirts of their huge estate, bringing the old recipes his mother and grandmother had taught him to the resort town.

"I get it," Ian told Mia. "But Nonna is already proud of you. You're well on your way to becoming a successful neonatal surgeon. You love your family with your whole heart, and you're giving. All things she taught you. Don't put so much pressure on yourself. I'd rather have a centerpiece out of place or a wilted flower in that arch thing than a crazed friend with bald patches in her hair due to stress."

"Oh!" Mia yelped. "I'm hanging up. You took it too far with the bald patches."

Ian laughed. "I had to make the point." The town car pulled up in front of his condominium. "Listen, I'm home. Take a long soak in the tub and go to sleep. I'll be there tomorrow."

"I love you, Munch."

"Love you, too."

Ian ended the call and hopped out.

Big doe eyes, curly black hair and a smile that melted him a little… Ian couldn't help but smile at the squirming baby girl in his arms. His niece, Zoe, gripped his index finger and tried to stuff it into her mouth.

He gently tugged his finger out of Zoe's grasp. "Nah, baby girl. Don't eat that." He gave her a pink-and-blue pacifier. "See, that's better."

"You're smitten, bruh," Drake said from behind him.

Ian ignored his brother and focused on Zoe. "Remember I'm the best uncle in the world, Zoe Bear. Don't even let Uncle Myles or Uncle-Brother El tell you anything different." Zoe let out a cute little gurgle and smiled. "That's right. I'm the greatest."

"Aw, that's so sweet." Ian's sister-in-law, Lovely, squeezed his shoulder. "You're so going to babysit. She loves you."

Ian peered up at Love. "Bring it on." He kissed Zoe's brow and handed her to Love. "I'll keep her anytime you want me to. She's beautiful."

When Ian had arrived at Drake and Love's home earlier, he'd immediately picked his niece up out of the baby swing. He'd never seen anything more perfect. Drake wasn't wrong. Ian *was* smitten.

Love smiled as she rocked the baby. "Isn't she? I can stare at her for hours."

Ian approached Love and ran his finger over Zoe's hand. "Me, too. How are you?"

Love had been part of his life since he was a kid. They'd grown up together in Las Vegas. She and Drake had been platonic best friends until a fated trip to Vegas a couple years ago. In an attempt to console Love after she'd lost a patient, Drake had taken her out to party along The Strip. The following morning, the two had awakened with hangovers and a marriage certificate. While both Drake and Love had been mortified at their drunken choice to marry, the two soon realized that they were better together and fell in love.

"I'm good. Went back to work a couple months ago, which was hard."

"You could have taken more time off, Love." Ian gave his brother the side-eye. "See, you should have gotten drunk and married me. I would have insisted you stay at home longer."

Love giggled. "You're too much."

Drake pushed Ian away. "Get away from my wife, man."

Ian barked out a laugh. "I can't help it. You're an easy mark."

"How was NOLA?" Drake handed Love a clean bib. "I can't tell you how proud I am, Ian. Despite your normal asshole tendencies, your heart to serve is phenomenal."

Drake had been the quintessential older brother in Ian's eyes, even though they were only seven months apart in age. Ian had looked up to Drake, and had followed him everywhere for years. Hearing his brother say he was proud meant everything to Ian.

"Thanks, bruh. I appreciate that."

"I mean it," Drake said. "No matter what Dad says, you're doing great work. Keep doing you."

Ian swallowed. "I've been avoiding his calls. I don't want to hear how disappointed he is in my choices."

"That's right. You're a grown man, creating your own path."

Ian wasn't the first offspring to depart from his father's predetermined field of medicine. It had all started when El, Ian's uncle, dared to become an emergency psychiatrist against Ian's father's wishes. El had been more like an older brother than an uncle to Ian, because he'd been raised by Dr. Law, as everyone called Ian's father. Drake followed El's lead when he declared cardiothoracic surgery instead of Plastics. Since then, Ian's father had been on his head about his specialty.

Working in a hospital was good, but Ian wanted to do more than breast lifts and tummy tucks. He wanted to leave an impact. There were people suffering every day who needed medical assistance, and he could provide that much-needed help. And he would. As far as Ian was concerned, working in a plush, air-conditioned building with his father and brother would be akin to dying slowly.

"Dad isn't going to be happy. But I can't open that practice with him."

Drake waved a dismissive hand. "He'll be all right. He has Myles."

Ian shook his head. "I don't know why Myles is entertaining this. He'd rather be in front of a piano, composing music."

"I'm not sure I believe that."

Ian's twin brother had spent years perfecting his skills. He'd written songs Ian was sure would be mega-hits if Myles followed through with recording them. But Myles would rather not rock the boat with their father. Dr. Law, who'd had an impressive career in Plastics performing necessary and cosmetic surgery for patients, had decided to focus solely on cosmetic surgery and open a practice in the area. Myles was set to join him.

"Well, we'll never find out, right?" Ian said. "You know how steadfast Myles is. He'll go to the grave insisting he's doing what he wants to do."

"You never know. Speaking as someone who thought I'd be living in a high-rise apartment in New York City or Los Angeles, life has a way of taking you way off course. And you know what? Living here with Love and Zoe, working at Michigan Medicine on my dream, is exactly what I need and want."

Ian nodded. "And I'd say this life agrees with you."

Love grinned up at them. "We're happy, Ian. I want you to be as happy as we are."

"He will be," Drake said. "He's on the right track. So…you never did answer my question. How was New Orleans?"

"Did you meet anyone down there?" Love asked.

Ian had thought about Aries several times since they'd spent a few hours getting to know each other intimately. The way her body had responded to his, the feel of her skin under his fingers…just the thought of her made him want to find her. But they'd agreed to one night, one time.

"Uh-oh." Love tilted her head, assessing him. "I think he did meet someone down there."

Ian blinked. "What?"

"I think you're right, baby," Drake said, folding his arms across his chest. "What's that look for, bruh?"

Frowning, Ian scratched the back of his head. "I'm ready for dessert. I saw the box of beignets on the counter. If you think these are good, Love, you definitely have to visit Café Du Monde in New Orleans." He headed toward the kitchen.

Love stood in front of him, blocking his way. "I've had them before, and don't change the subject. Who is she?"

Ian put on his best smile and looked at his sister-in-law. "I met many women in New Orleans. I'm not daydreaming about any one woman. I'm thinking about dough and powdered sugar. Trust me, there's nothing special to tell."

And Ian figured if he kept repeating that to himself, he'd finally believe it.

Chapter 3

"Mason!" Bailee sprinted into her brother's waiting arms and squealed when he lifted her off her feet in a tight embrace. "I missed you so much." Being enveloped in her big brother's arms made her feel safe, like she was home. And she didn't want to let go.

"I missed you, too, Bai."

When Mason finally set Bailee down, she grinned up at him. He looked the same as he looked every time she saw him. Freshly shaven, clothes crisp and eyes sincere. Mason had always been sure and dependable, and she wouldn't change him for the world.

"I'm so happy for you." She hugged him again.

Although Mason was three years older than Bailee, they'd always been extremely close. Growing up, he'd taken her everywhere, to the chagrin of some of his friends, who hated his little sister tagging along on all of their exploits.

"I'm happy, too. Mia is everything to me."

"She's perfect for you, Mase."

Bailee had had the opportunity to hang out with Mia several times over the past few years. Mia had struck her as a genuine woman who cared deeply for Mason, which was all Bailee could ask for.

"I think so, too." Mason kissed Bailee's brow. "Come on. Mom and Dad arrived last night. They want us all to sit down tonight and catch up."

Mason had met Bailee in the long, circular driveway in front of the house. As they headed toward the house, she scanned the area. "This is beautiful, Mase. Wow."

Lush greenery and beautiful flowers surrounded the huge mansion. As she drove up the private driveway, she couldn't help but gush over the expansive estate. She'd passed a huge barn, where Mason told her the ceremony would take place. Off to the side stood a smaller house, with huge white shutters and a wraparound porch. She assumed it was a guesthouse, or a pool house. A gazebo could be seen off in the distance, and Bailee imagined having coffee in the mornings out there. It was obvious the Solomon clan took care of their property.

"I passed the restaurant on my way in. It's beautiful," she said. *Anna's* was the Italian restaurant owned by Dr. Solomon, named after his adoptive mother. According to Mason, the restaurant was known for its authentic Italian cuisine and gorgeous views of Grand Traverse Bay. The stunning building was situated on a hilltop and had floor-to-ceiling windows, dark wood trim and a beautiful brick patio surrounding it. She'd noticed customers enjoying lunch outside, and couldn't wait to try the food.

"The rehearsal dinner will be there, so you'll get to

try it. We have a jam-packed week ahead of us, with activities every single day."

Mason and Mia had decided to invite their closest family and friends up to the estate ahead of the ceremony, which would take place on Saturday evening. The mission was twofold, since the Solomon clan had decided to open up the estate to other families as a wedding resort in the very near future. This wedding would be a trial run of sorts.

"I have a question, though. Where will the family stay once this place is open to the public?"

"Mia's oldest sisters, Marisa and Luna, will stay at the main house and manage it. Dr. and Mrs. Solomon, along with Nonna, have already moved into the lake house on the far west side of the estate. I'll take you on a tour once we get you settled."

"I'm excited. It's like heaven on earth up here."

They approached the door and he turned to her. "Mia's excited to see you. Maybe you can help me keep her calm until her best friend arrives."

"Why isn't her bestie here?"

"He just got back to Michigan from an extended work assignment. He'll be here today."

Bailee shot Mason a skeptical look. "Her best friend is a *he*? Are you sure you're okay with that?"

Mason wrapped his arm around her neck and squeezed playfully. "Don't worry, he's good people. You'll see."

Letting out a heavy sigh, Bailee let Mason lead her into the house. She gasped as she took in the classic decor. "Oh my God, this view is spectacular." The wall of windows offered stunning panoramic views of West Grand Traverse Bay.

They stared out at the clear blue water. “I once told Mia that she’d grown up in a northern paradise.”

“You’re right. It makes good business sense to turn this into a wedding resort. It can probably even be used for a family or work retreat.”

“That’s the plan, actually. Although the original vision was for a wedding resort, the family soon realized it could be so much more. Mia’s in the kitchen. Come on.”

Bailee grabbed his outstretched hand and let him steer her toward the kitchen. Inside the gourmet kitchen, Mia stood next to a younger woman Bailee had never seen before. The two were chatting in hushed tones, until Mia glanced up and saw them. Her eyes softened and she hurried over to her.

“Bai, I’m so glad you made it.” After the two embraced, Mia turned to the other woman and waved her over. “Bailee, I want you to meet my youngest sister, Bianca. Bee, this is Mason’s sister, Bailee.”

Bailee reached out to shake Bianca’s hand, but was surprised when the other woman pulled her into a quick, but tight hug. “Good to finally meet you,” Bee said. “I feel like I’ve missed out on so much.”

Bailee remembered Mason telling her about Mia’s youngest sister, the fashion designer, and had heard about the gorgeous bridesmaids’ dresses she’d designed for the wedding. “I’m glad to meet you, too. I’m so jealous you get to study in Milan under one of the greatest designers of our generation.”

Mia smiled proudly. “She’s going to take over the fashion world.”

Bee waved Mia off. “I’m just me, MiMi.” Turning her attention back to Bailee, Bee said, “I hear you’re the best woman.”

Bailee shot a wary glance at her brother. When he'd asked her to stand up with him at the wedding, she'd assumed she'd be one of the bridesmaids. But he'd quickly doused her dreams of wearing sleek dresses designed by Mia's talented sister. "I had been looking forward to wearing that fly dress you designed for the wedding party."

"I have something even better for you," Bee said with a wicked grin.

Bailee met Mia's gaze. Her future sister-in-law was practically bouncing with excitement. "What?"

"I told Mase not to tell you," Mia said. "Bee designed a slappin' tux for you to rock at the ceremony, using the measurements you sent Mason for the plain tuxedo he wanted you to wear."

Bailee smiled. "Really? Yay!"

Bee told her that they'd meet sometime today for a fitting, and she'd finish everything up before the wedding. After a few more minutes of talking about the ceremony and the week's activities, Bee excused herself to go to her parents' place.

Once they were alone, Mia turned to Bailee. "Thank you for everything you've done for us."

Bailee had always loved do-it-yourself projects and had come up with an idea for a simple, yet elegant centerpiece for the reception tables. "It's no trouble. I have everything packed away in my trunk."

"I'll get everything out," Mason told her.

"We can have the staff do that," Mia insisted. "Show her to her room first."

Mia hugged her and then rushed out of the room, calling for someone she assumed was part of the resort staff. Mason took Bailee through the house, pointing out the library, several sitting rooms and the great room. On their way up to her room, he gave her a little history of the place. It had been built in 1998, commissioned by Anna Solomon on land that had been in her family for generations. Located on Old Mission Peninsula, the house spanned eighteen thousand square feet. It had eight bedrooms, which had been recently renovated into minisuites, each with its own en suite bathroom and an outdoor balcony or patio.

"How many people are staying here this week?" she asked.

Mason ticked off the names. "Yep, we're going to have a full house. The rest of the guests are being housed at one of the hotels in town. They'll be picked up and transported here on the wedding day."

"Cool."

They stopped in front of a closed door, and Mason pulled out a key card. "This is your room." He unlocked the door and handed her the card.

Once again awed by the view, she walked right over to the huge windows and peered out at the bay. French doors opened to a balcony, and she stepped outside. Leaning against the rail, she let out a relaxed sigh. "I needed this, Mase."

He joined her and leaned against the rail. "Are you going to tell me what's going on with you?"

She eyed him. "Don't you already know?"

With a sad smile, he nodded. "He called me last week."

Brandon was one of Mason's oldest friends. They'd played basketball together in high school and had remained friends through college. "I guess he told you how unfeeling and cold I am."

"He would never say anything bad about you to me. But he did apologize, told me he wouldn't be able to attend the wedding because it would be too hard for him to see you after everything that happened."

Bailee dropped her head. "I'm sorry for that. I guess I could have waited to break up with him until after the wedding. Now you're short a groomsman."

"You know I don't care about that. I just want you to be okay."

"I'm more than alright. Mase, he wasn't the right man for me. Once I realized that, it wasn't as hard as I thought it would be to let the relationship go."

"What changed for you?"

Everything. Bailee explained how she'd woken up one day, tired of feeling unhappy and unfulfilled in her relationship. Brandon was a good guy, but he was all about what *he* wanted for them, how *he* wanted them to live, where *he* wanted to work, when *he* wanted her to quit her job and have his kids. She'd felt like an afterthought to him sometimes.

"Brandon was so caught up in appearances, and it really started to grate on me."

"Well, baby sis, it sounds like you did the right thing. You took control of your life, which is what I always wanted you to do."

"I haven't talked to Mom and Dad," she confessed. Telling her parents that they wouldn't get their highbrow Columbus wedding wasn't something she looked forward to doing. The two families had been joined at the hip for years. Their mothers practically salivated when Brandon asked Bailee to go out with him all those years ago. "I haven't answered any of their calls, because I know the Lamberts have talked to them. I just don't want to argue with Mom about my choice."

Bailee's mother was a professional nagger. She

would more than likely take on the full-time job of convincing Bailee to take Brandon back.

"She would never understand where I'm coming from," Bailee added. "And I need her to take my side in this."

"I'll talk to them with you." He pulled her to him. "We'll spend some alone time together tonight, and we'll talk. Okay?"

Bailee nodded. "Thanks, Mase."

"What else aren't you telling me?"

Mase knew her better than anyone. "April has almost convinced me to move to Michigan."

Her brother's eyes widened, and a slow grin spread across his face. "That makes me very happy. I'm glad April is good for something."

Bailee rolled her eyes. "Stop. I need you two to get it together."

"I'm just kidding." He stood and rubbed his hands on his pants. "Let's go find Mom and Dad. When I saw them last, they were headed out for a walk on the grounds."

Bailee and Mason stepped outside just as a sleek, black BMW zoomed up the driveway. From behind her, she heard a loud screech, and soon Mia barreled out of the house toward the car.

"I guess she's happy to see whoever that is," Bailee murmured.

Mason laughed. "It's Ian, the best friend."

The name Ian gave her pause, and she turned to Mason. "Ian?"

The last man she'd met named Ian had played her body like she was his own personal instrument. She'd remembered him often since they'd parted ways. The low timbre of his voice, his hair, his skin and his smell...just the thought of her New Orleans dalliance made her skin heat with a need she knew no one else could fulfill.

When Mia flung the car door open, Bailee narrowed her eyes on the familiar man who stepped out of the car. *It can't be. It cannot be.* She blinked and zeroed in on the man again, hoping that her eyes were playing a mean trick on her.

Bailee was sure her eyebrows were touching her hairline because the man talking to Mia was none other than Mr. Hottie himself. Mia's best friend, Ian, was *her* Ian—the same man who'd pleasured her so much she couldn't forget the feel of his fingertips on her skin.

Mia gestured wildly and jumped into his arms. Bailee's gaze raked over him. *Oh, shit, I'm in trouble.*

Swallowing, Bailee scanned the grounds in search of a hiding place. She needed to think. Frantic, Bailee retreated backward, her eyes still on Ian. But before she could run away, his gaze locked on hers.

He smiled. She didn't.

"Ian!" Mason shouted across the driveway. "Get your hands off of my fiancée."

Bailee shot Mason an incredulous look. Judging by the chuckle in her brother's voice, she knew he was joking. But it felt like the joke was on her. What were the odds that the same man she'd decided to have no-name sex with was the best friend of her brother's fiancée?

Ian and Mia started toward them. *Oh God.* "Mase, I'm going to... I have to do something." Before Mason could stop her, she turned and took off toward the house.

Chapter 4

What the hell is she doing here?

Ian watched Aries make a break for it into the house, and wondered why the woman he hadn't stopped thinking about since New Orleans was at his best friend's place.

Mason met them as they approached the house, a frown on his face. "I wanted to introduce you to my sister." He turned and pointed in the direction Aries had run. "But apparently she has something else to do."

Aries is Mason's sister?

Mia slipped her arm in Mason's. "It's okay, babe. They can meet later."

"I'm sorry about that, man." Mason clasped Ian's hand and shook it. "Bailee doesn't usually act so weird."

Bailee? Ian knew she hadn't given him her real name.

"Aw, maybe you should go after her," Mia told

Mason. "I'll catch up with Ian and we can get the best woman and the man of honor together in a little while."

Mason nodded and went after his sister. *Bailee.*

"Ian?" Mia called.

He blinked. "Huh?"

"Now you're acting weird." She grabbed his hand and tugged him toward the front door. "Come on. We need to talk."

Inside the house, Mia poured two tall glasses of lemonade and cut a piece of apple pie. She joined him at the breakfast bar with two forks. "You look good, Munch." Mia ate a healthy piece of pie.

A smile tugged at the corners of his mouth. "You do, too, Big Head." He glanced around the room. "The house looks great. I noticed the improvements to the barn and the boathouse on my way in."

"I know, right? All the work finally paid off. You should see the remodeled bedrooms. Each one is a suite, for guests."

Mia had told him of her parents' plan to renovate the house and turn it into a wedding resort, available to the public. He'd championed the idea, even though she'd been hesitant to accept her parents' choice.

"I told you it would be a good move on their part. They're getting older, and this house is too big for the two of them and Nonna."

"You're right. You should see the changes they made to their house. They expanded it to include a private mother-in-law suite for Nonna. She now has her own small kitchenette, and loves it. We have to force her to come out of her room sometimes."

Ian laughed. He'd missed his second family, and planned to spend as much time with them as he could before he had to leave. "She'll come out for me."

"You'll get to see everybody at the cocktail hour later. I wanted to have something to welcome the early guests."

"Good idea." *Bailee* couldn't hide from him forever. This cocktail hour was the perfect opportunity to talk to her, if he couldn't find her before then.

"So..." Mia turned her barstool to face him. "You think I forgot about the text? You changed the subject yesterday on the phone. I want to know who you met down in New Orleans that prompted you to send me that little code message."

"Mia, I always said you should have been an attorney because you've perfected the art of badgering witnesses. Come on, now. This is your wedding week. My text should be an afterthought."

"See, that's where you're wrong. I welcome anything that can keep my mind off table settings and seating charts."

"Let it go, Big Head. It was nothing." The lie rolled off his tongue as if he really believed his short time with Bailee was no big deal. "I'm here to help you get through your big day. Give me all the details."

Mia gave him the rundown of the events he'd be required to attend that week, from the cocktail hour to the summer games to the joint bachelorette and bachelor party to the rehearsal dinner, and finally the wedding and reception. Ian got tired just listening to the long list of activities.

"Will I have time to breathe this week?" he asked.

Bumping shoulders with him, Mia said, "You will. Just not much time."

They laughed, and he squeezed her hand. "You know I'm here for you. Whatever you need, okay?"

Mia leaned her head against his shoulder. "I know. That's why you're my best friend."

"I found her." Mason entered the kitchen with Bailee walking behind him.

"Babe, you're back." Mia stood, and Ian followed suit.

Bailee still hadn't met his gaze, but he'd wait for it.

"Ian, I want you to meet my sister, Bailee," Mason said. "Bai, this is Ian."

Finally, Bailee lifted her head and nodded curtly. She stepped forward with her hand outstretched. "Hi, good to finally meet you."

He raised a brow. So she wanted to play the *I Don't Know You* game. Ian would go along with it. For now. "Nice to meet you, too. *Bailee.*"

Bailee slipped her hand from his grasp and wiped it on her pants. He noticed the cute flush on her cheeks and nose.

"Ian is a doctor at Michigan Medicine in Ann Arbor," Mason said. "If you decide to apply there, you'll probably see him around."

"Oh, really," Bailee croaked. "That's cool. Mia, why didn't you tell me your best friend was a hottie?" Her eyes widened once she realized her slip of the tongue, and Ian did his best not to laugh. "I mean…why didn't you tell me your best friend was a doctor?"

Ian covered his mouth to hide his smile. So Bailee thought he was a hottie? He'd keep that little tidbit in his back pocket for later.

Mia giggled. "I thought I'd mentioned it before. My bad."

"No," Ian said. "I want to hear about how hot I am."

Bailee covered her face with her hand. "This can't be happening."

Mia hugged Bailee. “Don’t be embarrassed. It’s cool. No big deal.”

While Mia changed the subject to dinner and the arriving guests, he took a moment to catalog Bailee. Dressed in khaki shorts and a white tank, she was a vision. Casual had never looked so good. Her mocha skin was smooth, her body toned and her hair pulled back into a messy ponytail.

His slow perusal from her Converse-clad feet to the silver hoops in her ears made him want to get her alone. Again. He really hadn’t had enough time exploring her in New Orleans. And look at God…now she’d dropped right into his lap. It must be fate.

“Ian?” A hard elbow to his gut snapped him out of his wayward thoughts.

Absently rubbing the sore spot, he forced his attention away from Bailee to Mia. When he met her knowing—and irritated—eyes, he knew he’d been caught. His best friend didn’t miss anything. They hadn’t voted her Most Likely to Solve a Crime in high school for nothing. “Yes?”

“Do you mind walking with me over to check on Nonna?”

“Of course,” he replied. For the first time, he wondered what he’d missed while he’d been checking Bailee out.

“Good.” Mia graced Ian with a hard eye roll before turning her attention back to Bailee and Mason. “What’s this I hear about you applying at the hospital?” Mia asked Bailee.

Ian wanted to know the answer to that question, too. “Are you moving to Michigan soon?”

Bailee shrugged. “I’m thinking about it,” she murmured, turning her gaze to the ceiling, to the far wall on the right, to the loose thread in her sweater, then to the floor.

"I think it's great," Mia said. "Even though he's retired, my father might be able to pull strings to get you an interview sooner."

Smiling, Bailee thanked Mia. "That would be awesome."

"My mother dragged him to the spa with her today. But I'll make sure I give him the heads-up at the cocktail party. He'll definitely want to talk to you."

"Well, it doesn't hurt to have a conversation." Bailee glanced at him before turning to Mia. "But I'm still not sure of my plans yet."

Obviously, Ian didn't know Bailee at all, but he knew a lie when he saw it. The woman in front of him was many things, but indecisive didn't seem to be one of them. He'd bet money she'd already started packing for her move. "Where do you live now?" He didn't really care about the details, but he did enjoy making her nervous.

"I live in Columbus," Bailee answered, eyeing the door.

Ian shook his head and shot her a mock glare. "You better be careful around these parts." He pretended not to notice the way Mia watched him. His best friend looked from Bailee to Ian, then back to Bailee.

Mason laughed. "Whatever, man. When Ohio State beats Michigan this year, I'll be sure to gloat."

That was the one thing Ian didn't like about Mia's future husband. Even though he worked at Michigan Medicine, Mason was still a Buckeye at heart. Ohio, Columbus, Buckeye Nation and Scarlet were all fighting words. The rivalry between the two schools was legendary, and Ian made sure he stayed far away from

Mason during football season. No sense in ruining relationships over a game. Because Ian bled maize and blue, Michigan's team colors.

"That's right," Bailee agreed. "When was the last time you guys won a game anyway?"

"Don't start," Mia said, stepping in front of him. His best friend knew that was a sensitive subject for him. "I'm declaring this a football-free zone this week. No Wolverines, no Buckeyes. How about those Tigers?"

Ian waved a hand in dismissal. The Detroit Tigers, while near and dear to his heart, were also a sore subject for him. Especially since they couldn't win a game to save his life.

"Or those Detroit Lions?" Bailee said, a gleam in her mischievous eyes.

Mason shook his head. "Bai, please. Let's not get Ian started about Detroit sports right now. He's a diehard."

"What do you do?" Ian asked Bailee in an attempt to steer the conversation away from sports.

"I'm a nurse," Bailee answered.

"Stop playing, Bai." Mia waved a dismissive hand at Bailee. "You're totally downplaying your career."

"My sister is so modest," Mason added, with a proud grin. "She's a nurse anesthetist and DNP."

Ian tilted his head. "Ah… Impressive."

Bailee's eyes flashed to him then. A frown creased her forehead before she schooled her features. "I…um. I have to go. Mase, I'll see you in a bit." She hurried off, and once again he was left watching her retreat and wondering what she'd been thinking.

Mason turned to him. "I don't get it. I'm sorry, man. She's had some things going on. I think she's just tired. I should go find her." Mason kissed Mia quickly, and took off after his sister.

An oven mitt hit Ian in the face, startling him. He blinked, then looked down at the textured gray-and-yellow mitt. Another one whizzed past his head, and he ducked, barely missing a third one. "What the—?" Next came a matching pot holder, but he caught it. "Mia, what the hell are you doing?"

"Stop looking at her like that." Mia pointed her finger at him.

"Like what?" He had no choice but to play ignorant because Mia knew what he was really thinking. She'd throw the pot at him next.

"She's Mason's sister, a good girl and off-limits to you."

"Stop trippin'. I was just looking." Mia didn't need to know the sordid details. "Bailee is a beautiful woman."

"Whatever. Don't mess up my wedding weekend. Besides, Bailee just got out of a long-term relationship."

Curiosity piqued, Ian leaned forward, resting his arms on the countertop. "Really?" *Did Bailee cheat on her boyfriend with me?* "How long ago?"

"A few weeks, I guess." Mia shrugged, and gathered the oven mitts she'd thrown. "Mase said she just broke up with the guy out of the blue, and took off on a getaway with her best friend. I don't have all the details. Their family is really close with the boyfriend's family. Well, the fiancé."

"Fiancé? She was engaged?"

Mia frowned. "Yes."

"Hmm." Ian stretched and let out a long dramatic yawn. "Maybe I should go lie down for about an hour. I'm tired. Traveling takes a lot out of ya. Can we go see Nonna later?"

"Ian, wait—"

But Ian didn't give Mia a chance to complete her thought because he had to go. Bailee had some explaining to do.

Bailee peeked around the corner, into the kitchen. *Empty.* Sighing, she headed toward the refrigerator. She'd ducked into the massive library for a half hour, and had wound up thumbing through the impressive collection. If she'd wanted to get away, she'd found the perfect safe haven. Immersing herself in a book was her favorite pastime. She read wide, enjoying several genres, from classics to thrillers to smutty romance—the hotter and wilder the better. Fortunately for her, she'd found the perfect distraction. A romantic comedy. The flirty banter and insane sexual chemistry between the hero and heroine in the first chapter had hooked her right away.

Her plan? Grab a glass of wine and a snack and retreat to her room until it was time to meet up with her parents. Opening the sleek glass and stainless-steel fridge, she sighed. *So much food.* Decision made, she pulled out lunch meat, cheese, tomatoes, lettuce and Miracle Whip.

Bailee opened several drawers before she located the flatware and pulled out a knife. On the counter stood a bottle of red wine. *That would do for now.* It didn't take her long to find the wineglasses. She filled one with the merlot and took a sip. Next, she grabbed a plate from another cabinet.

Focused on the task at hand, she prepared her sandwich and sipped her wine. Once she finished, she didn't even bother cutting it in half. No, she simply took a bite and moaned. *So good.* Bailee topped off her glass again, swiped a few paper napkins from the dispenser and picked up her plate.

"Things would have been so much easier if you would have just told me your real name in New Orleans."

Bailee yelped, nearly dropping her plate with her sandwich on the floor. She set it on the counter with a thud. "Shoot, don't scare me like that again."

Her stomach roiled, and she closed her eyes tightly. *Maybe he won't be so hot when I open my eyes again.* Letting out a heavy sigh, she cracked one eye open. Right away, she noticed several things. Not only was he *still* hot, she'd never seen a man look so good in jeans and a T-shirt. And the tattoo that stretched from his wrist to his forearm made her want to explore his body again. She didn't remember that from their dalliance in New Orleans. *And she loved tattoos.*

Ian smirked, no doubt realizing his effect on her.

Lord, help me. His smirk was so hot she felt naked under his heated gaze.

"Bailee."

A low groan escaped her lips. His voice was like Hennessy on ice, it was so smooth.

Bailee had thought about him so many times since she'd come home, even against her better judgment. But...*damn*. Her memories didn't do him justice. At all. Ian stood at least six-feet-perfect-inches tall, with muscles for days and a sexy, short Mohawk-style cut. Eyes the color of rich milk chocolate and a smile that seemed to melt her from the inside capped off the irresistible package.

He cocked his head, raising a curious brow. "Are you okay?"

She finished off her wine and set the empty glass

on the counter. "I'm fine. Just going to head to my room and read."

Ian stepped closer, and she fought the urge to retreat. "We need to talk," he told her.

"About what?" She tapped the granite with her finger. "There's nothing to talk about."

"How about the fact that we slept together? Or the fact that you lied and told me your name was Aries?"

She smirked. "Oh, please. You know you didn't believe that." Ian opened his mouth to speak, and she rushed on. "Besides, the whole point of a one-night stand is to remain anonymous. Right? I never thought I'd see you again."

"But you did." Ian let out a humorless chuckle. "We *are* seeing each other again."

"So? We agreed that it would only be one night." One night that had been seared into her brain. One night that she wanted to repeat.

"I didn't say that."

Bailee shot him an incredulous look. "You did! When we met at the hotel bar. It was implied we'd—"

"Bailee, that was you. You're the one who gave me a fake name and kicked me out of your hotel room."

Strangely, she hadn't remembered their interaction that way. But she dug in her heels anyway. "That's neither here nor there. The point is… Well, there is no point. No sense in talking about that night because it's in the past. And you can't tell anyone how we met."

"Why?" He folded his arms across his incredibly firm and muscular chest.

Bailee tried not to stare. She really did. But he was so freakin' hot it was hard not to just look at him.

"Better yet," he continued, "*who* do you want to hide it from? Your fiancé?"

Bailee reared back on her heels. "What?"

"You heard me. You were engaged to be married."

"Not that I owe you an explanation, but I *was* engaged, as in past tense." She crossed her arms and shot him a pointed glare. "And who told you that?"

"Does it matter?"

"Not really. But just so you know, I no longer have a fiancé or a boyfriend. I'm not a cheater."

"Good."

"Good," she repeated louder. "I'm going to my room."

His arm blocked her retreat. "Wait." She paused. "I'm sorry. I didn't mean to imply that you're a cheater. Mia told me that you'd just come out of a long relationship, that your trip happened after the breakup."

Bailee was going to kill Mason, then Mia, for opening their big mouths. "No need to apologize. I have to go."

"Bailee, how about we start over? Do you think we can do that?"

She craned her head to meet his gaze. "I'm listening."

"I won't say anything to anyone about us. But I won't pretend I don't find you very attractive. And I won't pretend that I'm not interested in exploring that attraction."

His confession shocked her to the bone and heat surged through her, burning so hot she braced herself with a hand on the counter. The ache between her legs intensified every second they stood near each other.

Time stretched out, and her gut twisted with want. They'd only been in each other's company for a few minutes, but it felt like she'd been with him forever. Neither of them said a word.

Sexual tension…two words that had never really applied to Bailee, never really had a place in the same sentence where she was concerned. But in that moment, she could cut it with a butcher knife. Something about Ian called to her on a primitive level, in a *do-me-baby-all-night-long* way. She had to get out of there, before she dropped to her knees and begged him to put her out of her misery.

He searched her eyes. She saw no flicker of amusement in his. "I can't pretend, Bailee."

"Ian," she whispered, unsure how she should respond. She was lost in his brown eyes, hypnotized by the *more* she swore she saw in his orbs. She couldn't quite put her finger on what shined back at her, but it was hot.

Their gazes never wavered, and Bailee couldn't look away if she tried. He was so close she could smell the faint scent of his soap. His eyes flickered to her lips, and his tongue peeked out to wet his own. He leaned forward. And she was so caught up in an Ian trance, she didn't back away.

Do it.

She should be alarmed by that inner voice, the devil on her shoulder that told her to let him kiss her, to let him do more than kiss her. But she wasn't. The only thing she wanted in that moment was his mouth on hers, his tongue stroking hers.

"Bai!"

Mason's voice snapped them out of their trance, and Ian dropped her arm as if she'd burned him.

Her brother walked into the kitchen, a wide grin on his face. "There you are."

Bailee smoothed her hair back with shaky hands. "Mase. What's up?"

"Mom and Dad are in the sunroom. I told them I'd come find you." Mason glanced at Ian, then back at her. "Ready for this?"

No. "Sure," she lied. Bailee brushed past him and picked up her plate. Exhaling, she stole another glance at Ian before turning to her brother. "Let's go, Mase. See you later, Ian." And without another word, she followed Mason out of the kitchen.

Chapter 5

Ian let out a string of incredibly nasty curse words. When he'd spotted Bailee in the kitchen earlier, the plan wasn't to let her get under his skin again. But she had. His intention was only to confront her on lying about her name and maybe get her to consider another night with him. But no…he'd acted like some sort of lovesick sap.

Who says *I can't pretend* anyway? Apparently, he did. And then she had the nerve to tell him it was only *one* night? That was his line. He left women hanging, not vice versa.

"How about we start over," he grumbled, repeating what he'd told her earlier.

What the hell was wrong with him? He'd never met anyone who made him feel like he had to prove himself. *Shit, I'm Ian Damn Jackson.* Dr. Ian Jackson.

Maybe he'd skip the food and crack open a bottle

of liquor. Mia would kill him, though. And this week was about her, not Bailee, and certainly not their *one* night together.

"What's up?" Myles stepped into the kitchen. "Talking to yourself?"

Ian looked up and grinned. "What's up, man?" He gave his brother a man hug. They hadn't seen each other in months. "When did you get here?"

His twin glanced at his watch. "About thirty minutes ago. You didn't answer the question. Since when did you start talking to yourself?"

"I was just thinking about work," Ian lied. "I had planned to at least check my emails when I got here, but Mia wanted to talk about the wedding."

"I ran into Mia and Mason outside. They told me I could find you somewhere in here, man of honor." Myles barked out a laugh. "Is your tux the same color as the bridesmaids' dresses? Will you have to hold a bouquet while you walk down the aisle? Line up to catch the bouquet instead of the garter?"

Myles's reaction basically gave him a taste of what he'd have to endure when El and Drake arrived the next morning. Ian glared at his brother. "Man, shut the hell up. Don't play me."

"You have to admit, it's funny. And if the shoe was on *my* foot, you would never let me live it down."

That part was true. "Well, it's a good thing you're not me."

"Sorry about last night, man," Myles said, changing the subject. "I got caught up at work."

Ian had expected Myles to stop by Drake and Love's house yesterday, but his brother had called to let them know he got held up at the hospital. Ian waved him off. "It's cool. You know I know the drill."

"I figured I'd hit the road early, though, and make the cocktail party tonight."

Ian clasped his brother's shoulder. "Good. You need some time away from the hospital."

"Tell me about it." Myles rubbed his face. "What did I miss?"

Ian debated telling Myles about Bailee, even knowing it wouldn't leave the room. In the end, though, he decided not to mention it.

"Nothing much. I haven't done much, just caught up with Mia and met Mason's sister."

"Ah, I feel out of the loop. I haven't made any of Mia's prewedding events. I had planned to go to the engagement party, but I was called to the hospital at the last minute."

"You know Mia understands. You hungry? I was just about to find something to eat."

Myles slid onto one of the barstools. "I could eat. I could also use a drink."

Without a word Ian went to a cabinet and opened it, revealing the stash of liquor Dr. Solomon had always kept there. "Glad to see some things never change," he murmured, removing a fifth of Johnnie Walker. Ian snagged two glasses, poured a healthy shot into each and handed one to Myles.

"Thanks." Myles took a sip. "Talk to Dad?"

"No. I figure I'll see him at the wedding. Then he'll be too concerned with appearances to hound me about medicine."

"That's smart."

Ian went to the refrigerator and pulled out the pan of lasagna he'd seen earlier. He warmed up two pieces. Once he finished, he joined Myles with his food at the kitchen table by the window.

"So," Myles said. "What aren't you telling me about New Orleans?"

While Ian was away, he'd talked to Myles often. He'd shared stories about the hospital he worked at, the city nightlife, the women he'd met and the work he'd done. But he hadn't told his twin about his plans. He guessed it was the "twin" thing that prompted Myles to call him on it.

Ian shrugged. "I've made some decisions."

"I know."

Dropping his fork on his plate, Ian glanced at Myles. "I applied to Doctors Without Borders."

Myles's head jerked back. "What?"

For years, Ian had felt unfulfilled within the walls of the hospital. He wanted to be responsible for bringing medical assistance to people in distress. What better way to do that than to join an organization whose very mission was to do that? Being in the field, working in areas of active conflict or post-conflict, felt right to him. He didn't have a wife, no children to make it home to. The opportunity was perfect for him at this stage of his life.

"You know I've wanted to do more for some time," Ian said. "My residency is over. Now is the time."

Both Ian and Myles had recently finished their surgical residencies at the University of Michigan. Ian had completed a General Surgery program, while Myles had done his residency in Integrated Plastic Surgery. Myles had immediately been accepted into the Craniofacial Surgery Fellowship, while Ian had chosen to take some time to determine his next steps.

Myles let out a slow breath. "Wow. That's…that's impressive, bruh."

"Thanks." It was high praise coming from Myles.

"Honestly, I don't know why I entertained Dad's visions of my career for so long. Plastics is not my thing. Now, Trauma? That's where it's at. Once I'm done in the field, I'll concentrate on that."

It hadn't taken long for Ian to realize that he didn't want to spend his life doing breast augmentation, lifts or reductions. He had no desire to contour bodies for cosmetic purposes. Working instead with trauma patients, running an emergency room or being called to save a patient with multiple life-threatening injuries appealed to him. Now he just had to tell his father that instead of applying for the three-year Plastic Surgery Residency program like they'd discussed, he would apply for the Critical Care Fellowship.

"I'm sure Dad won't be happy."

Of that, Ian had no doubt. Before Ian had decided to enter the General Surgery Residency program, he'd gotten into a huge argument with his father about his choice. He'd managed to convince his dad that having a general surgery background would only strengthen their reputation in the plastics industry.

Ian nodded, not surprised Myles knew what he was thinking. They had the twin telepathy thing down. "Well, it's not his life to live."

And that's what it boiled down to. Ian wasn't sure why their father felt the need to control their lives the way he did. Growing up, every single decision they made had to be run through Dr. Law. Nine times out of ten, what they wanted didn't matter. The family image, the family legacy and the forthcoming family practice had been drilled into them since they could walk and talk.

They sat in silence for a few minutes before Myles

told him, "For what it's worth, I think your way is better than his."

Ian turned to Myles. "*Your* way would be better than his, too."

"Ah, I'm good where I am."

The conversation about their careers always ended the same way. With Myles accepting his lot in life, like he had no choice in the matter. It bothered Ian, and he knew it bothered Drake and El. Hell, even his little sister, Melanie, hated the way Myles let their father control his path in life.

"I wish you really believed that."

"Look, just because you don't want to follow in Dad's footsteps..."

"Myles, this isn't about Dad. It's about you. But..." Ian stood up and took his plate to the sink. "I don't want to argue about this again. It's your life. Who am I to tell you whose dream to follow?"

His words were meant to have an impact, to spur his stubborn brother into action. But when he raised his eyes and met his brother's pensive gaze, he decided not to push the subject. Instead, he took his seat again. "Anyway, thanks for agreeing to play for Mia's wedding," Ian said.

It had taken a lot of encouragement from Ian and Mia to get Myles to agree to play for the wedding. His twin didn't usually share his gift with the public.

"No problem. Anything for Mia."

"Did I hear my name?" Mia entered the kitchen, followed by Dr. Solomon.

Ian grinned. "Pop, how are you?" He gave the older man a hug. "Long time no see."

"I know." Pop greeted Myles and turned his attention back to Ian. "Glad you could grace us with your presence."

"You know I wouldn't miss this."

Dr. Louis Solomon had devoted years to the General Surgery Department at Michigan Medicine. He'd been one of the first African American surgeons to hold the title of Chief of Surgery before Love's father, Dr. Leon Washington, took over the role. He was so well loved and respected by staff and patients alike, the hospital administrators had begged him to stay. In the end, the money thrown at him wasn't enough to keep him there.

Pop grabbed a glass from the cupboard and filled it with whiskey. "We've been running around like crazed chickens." Pop kissed Mia on her temple. "But I'd do just about anything for my baby girl."

Mia hugged her father. "Aw, thanks, Dad. I appreciate your support."

Ian often wondered how it would feel to have his father's support. But he'd always be grateful for Dr. Solomon. The older man had stepped into the role of father figure seamlessly. Not just for Ian, but for his brothers, as well. Every important event in Ian's life, Pop had been there with a smile on his face. The years had been good to Pop. He looked relaxed in a linen suit. His salt-and-pepper hair and beard were freshly cut.

Pop pointed at Ian. "Mom wants to see you, son. She's been asking about you all day."

"I know. I meant to go see her earlier. I'll make my way over in a few minutes."

"And you know my wife will be glad to see you, too."

"Where is she?" Myles asked.

"I left her at that high-priced spa she loves so much. I had to get out of there."

Pop told a story about his experience with his first couples massage and pedicure. The massage had been nice, but apparently, having another person "play with his toes" had crossed a line. They all laughed when Pop described how he snuck out of the place when the pedicurist went to the back to get hot towels.

"I hopped out of that chair so fast, I forgot my shoes," Pop explained. "Then I had to pay another worker to go back and get them."

"Daddy, you're funny," Mia said.

"Hey, I'm old school. No pedicures for me. I take care of my own feet." Pop finished his drink. "I have to go pick up your mother," he told Mia. "I'll see you three tonight."

"Well, I better start getting ready, as well," Mia announced before pointing at Ian. "And you better take your butt over to see Nonna."

Ian stood. "I'm going, I'm going."

"Don't let her smack you!" Mia shouted after him. "She's been slap happy lately. She'll leave a mark."

Ian wasn't worried, though. He'd take a slap from the woman who'd been like a stand-in grandmother to him. It felt good to be home, and neither his father nor any woman could change that. At the same time, he'd been in enough trouble to recognize it or even anticipate it. And as he headed toward the Solomon house to see Nonna, he had the distinct feeling that *trouble* had already infiltrated his mind—and his upstate haven—with her brown eyes, gorgeous smile and spitfire personality.

The day hadn't gone as planned. Bailee didn't get a chance to kick her feet up and read. Hell, she didn't even finish her sandwich after that talk with her parents. Once she'd confirmed her breakup with Brandon to her mom and dad, she'd had to sit there and listen to all the reasons she'd made a mistake. Exactly what she'd thought would happen.

Instead of having her back like he'd said he would, Mason had left her there to tend to his bride because some calamity had occurred with the wedding cake. It felt like she'd been chained to a desk for hours, being questioned by detectives for a crime she hadn't committed. But she'd escaped with her sanity and a tentative understanding in tow. Her mother had finally conceded that it was best to end the relationship sooner rather than later. The victory was short-lived, though, because Bailee had to agree they'd revisit the subject once the wedding was over.

Bailee stared at her reflection in the mirror. It had taken over an hour for her to get dressed for the cocktail party. It took even longer for her to find the right shoes. But—she twirled in a circle, paying close attention to her butt—she looked damn good. The little black dress fit her like a second skin, and the plunging lace bodice made her feel sexy.

On her way down to the party, she thought about Ian. For the last few hours, despite the many goings-on around her, she couldn't stop thinking about that moment in the kitchen. He would have kissed her if Mason hadn't walked in the room. The thought scared and excited her more than she should ever admit out loud. But she wouldn't let his dark eyes and hard body distract her. She had too much going on to get entangled with another man right now.

The cocktail party had already started when Bailee entered the great room. Soft jazz played through the surround sound speakers as people mixed and mingled with one another. Staff in all-black attire carried trays of hors d'oeuvres. She greeted Mason and Mia, who were standing near the center of the room, before heading to the bar.

When she spotted Ian near the piano with a modelesque woman, Bailee almost tripped and hit the floor. But she recovered quickly, grabbing the ledge of the bar to steady herself. Irritated at her clumsiness, she ordered a dirty martini, extra olives, extra vodka. *To take the edge off.* The flirty bartender slid her drink over with a wink, and she offered him a small smile in return.

Against her better judgment, she allowed herself a quick glance over at Ian—a quick glance that turned into a lingering stare. Dressed in a tailored three-piece black suit, he was too damn fine for his own good. His shirt and tie were gray, and he looked downright sinful standing there. Funny, Ian didn't strike her as a buttoned-up suit guy, though. He seemed like he'd be more comfortable in casual clothes. But she couldn't deny that he filled it out perfectly.

The woman—dressed in a revealing navy blue dress that was short enough Bailee swore she would be able to see the woman's behind if she bent over—let out an airy giggle and took a seat. Yet, even in her irritated state, Bailee couldn't deny the woman was stunning. She wore her hair loose, with long waves falling down her back, and had golden sun-kissed skin. And looking at the way Ian smiled at the woman, he seemed interested in hearing what she had to say. His behavior was akin to how he'd acted with Bailee at the hotel bar in New Orleans. Bailee narrowed her eyes on the two. It was obvious they had something going on over there. Body language didn't lie. And she couldn't stop watching them.

Ian laughed, and the two clinked their glasses together. *That jerk.* She watched him take a long sip of his drink and noted the way the woman then dropped her hand to his arm before she leaned in and whispered something in his ear.

Oh hell, no.

Bailee had never hated anyone for no reason, but she hated that woman. Because Ian obviously found something appealing about her. And it bugged the hell out of Bailee that he hadn't noticed her in the room, that his attention was solely on the long-legged woman. Especially when she'd picked her outfit specifically to drive him crazy, even if she hadn't admitted it to herself until now. Bailee looked down at her short legs and groaned. Knocking her martini back in one gulp, she chided herself for thinking, even if only for one second, how fulfilling it would be to push the woman off the chair.

Jealousy was a foreign emotion for Bailee, so when the tinge of envy wormed its way through her and gripped her tightly, it caught her off guard. Blinking, she turned back to the bartender and ordered another drink. *One, two, three...*

Okay, so counting to ten wasn't quelling the urge to turn around and walk right up to him and tell him what she thought of him. *Which is what exactly?*

Muttering a curse under her breath, she picked up her glass and brought it up to her lips. Bailee wasn't *that* woman. At least, she'd never been the jealous, crazy type before Ian. All because one night of bliss had apparently fried her common sense. No. There was no way she was going to let him win, let him think that he'd affected her. Pep talk complete, Bailee turned, determined to walk away, to not spare that man another glance.

"What are you going through?"

Bailee froze. The low, husky voice sounded like Ian's. But it couldn't be, because Ian was standing with the model on the other side of the room. Just in case, she ventured a glance over that way. Sure enough, he was still there flirting his ass off with the same woman.

"Bailee?"

She blinked. Had jealousy rendered her delusional? Or was it the martini? Sighing, she turned and yelped, nearly dropping her glass on the floor. She scanned the room, noting the curious glances from several people in attendance. A kind, older woman asked if she was okay. Bailee nodded that she was and turned to meet the amused gaze of…Ian?

"My twin."

"What?"

Ian pointed over to the man on the other side of the room. The man she'd thought was Ian. "I have a twin brother. Myles. That's him over there near the piano."

"Twins," she muttered, almost to herself. "Right."

"I'm assuming by your reaction that you thought that was me over there." He smiled then—a delicious, knowing half smile that made her sway on her feet.

She opened her mouth to speak, but couldn't. Because her mouth had gone dry. It should be a crime for a man to look as good as Ian, dressed in all black. His shirt was open at the collar, giving her a glimpse of his brown skin underneath. He looked…oh God, he looked incredible.

He leaned in. "I bet I know what you're thinking."

Bailee swallowed. For some reason, when Ian was

around, she had to remember to breathe. *Slow and steady, Bai.* She couldn't stop ogling him, imagining the naughty things he could do with his hands, his mouth and his—

"Bailee?"

His voice pulled her out of her vivid daydream. "Huh?" she managed to say.

He leaned closer and she smelled the faint hint of cognac mixed with lime on his breath. "Are you okay? You look a little flushed."

Clearing her throat, she let out a deep breath. "I'm fine. Just tired, that's all. I didn't know you had a twin. Any other siblings?"

He nodded. "Three brothers total, and one younger sister. Well, I should say two brothers and one uncle-brother."

"Uncle-brother?" she asked, intrigued by the term. "I don't think I've ever heard that before." Ian gave Bailee a brief explanation of the term, and Bailee was glad for the distraction. "So El is your father's younger brother, who your father raised as his own?"

"That's right. You'll meet him at the wedding. Actually, my entire family will be in attendance."

"Must have been really nice to have so many siblings. It was just me and Mason growing up. I often wondered what it would be like to have a sister."

"Mia can let you borrow a few of hers."

Bailee laughed then. "Right?"

"And Mia will be a great sister to you." Ian waved the bartender over and ordered another drink. "Would you like one?" he asked her.

She told him no thanks.

"So, are we ever going to talk about what happened earlier? Not just in the kitchen, but in New Orleans?"

His question caught her off guard, but she recovered quickly. "We already talked about New Orleans and agreed that we wouldn't mention it."

"Well, after that moment in the kitchen, I thought we should revisit."

Bailee didn't want to think about that almost-kiss in the kitchen, because nothing could ever come of it. So she did the only thing she could do in the moment. Pretend nothing had happened in the kitchen. "I don't know what you're talking about."

He studied her face with narrowed eyes. "Is that how we're playing this game?"

"No game. But I think it will be best if we leave New Orleans in the past. There's nothing to talk about. Like I told you earlier, it was just one night. And that's all it can ever be."

"What are you drinking?" he asked in a low, husky voice.

The change in subject jarred her, but she answered, "Dirty martini."

"Dirty, huh?" He chuckled, his gaze searing her skin with its intensity. "I like dirty."

Oh my. She knew he wasn't talking about her drink anymore, and the realization excited and scared her at the same time. The way he'd said *dirty* plummeted her mind straight to the gutter.

She opened her mouth, then closed it, then opened it again. To say what? She didn't know. He'd flustered her to the point she couldn't form a coherent sentence or even think a rational, nonsexual thought. So instead of saying anything at all, she set her glass on the bar and walked away.

Take that, Dr. Jackson.

Chapter 6

Smoky eyes. *Why the hell is she here?*

Ian gulped down his drink and ordered another. She'd rejected him again. Yet, even though he should let it go and move on, he wouldn't. Because he suspected she didn't want him to.

Bailee acted like she didn't want him, had told him to leave the past in the past. But the more she said it, the less he believed her. He just had to get her to admit it to herself.

He caught a glimpse of Bailee on the other side of the room. She was laughing with one of Mason's friends, a groomsman he'd been introduced to a while ago.

His gaze raked over her, from her head to her painted toes. Long, natural hair swept to the side. *Why is my body reacting to the mere sight of her?* Sexy, strappy sandals. *She's killing me slowly and softly.* Revealing cleavage. *Is that her breast?* Long legs that begged to be wrapped around his waist, while he—

A sharp elbow to his gut drew his attention away from Bailee. Myles stood beside him and pointed to the center of the room, where Mia shot a death glare his way. He must have missed something important. A toast?

Unable to keep his eyes off Bailee, he glanced her way again, lingered on her face. Those pouty, full lips. *Damn.*

"Ian?" Mia called, a tight smile on her face. She held a glass of champagne in her hand.

I did miss the toast.

It was absolutely Bailee's fault. And he didn't feel bad blaming everything on her distracting ass…and legs, and face, and hair. *I. Declare. War.*

Myles grumbled, "She thanked you for coming, bruh."

Ian plastered a smile on his face and nodded at his best friend. He held his drink in the air and Mia smiled, finishing her speech. She thanked everyone for attending and went over some of the itinerary for the rest of the week leading up to the wedding. The guests slowly started filtering out of the room. Dr. Solomon had graciously opened his restaurant to the guests if they wanted to grab a late dinner.

With his mind made up, Ian hung back, waited for the room to clear. Then he'd make his move. Bailee walked away from the older couple she'd migrated to during the toast, toward the door with her head down. Ian started to follow her, but stopped when Myles tapped her on her shoulder.

For several minutes, he watched his brother flirt with his Bailee. Wait, *his* Bailee? That thought alone would have sent him running for the hills a few weeks ago, but tonight he wasn't going anywhere. Not until he had her again. Not until she confirmed what he knew in the back of his mind. Not until she admitted that she wanted him just as much as he wanted her.

Irritated, Ian picked up his phone and dialed Myles. He watched his brother glance at his phone. Myles scanned the room, a frown on his face, before he answered, "What's up—?"

"Don't say my name."

Myles put one finger up to Bailee and told her to give him a second. "Okay. Where are you?"

"Remember that time I took a monthlong punishment because you let the air out of all of Dad's tires?"

"Yeah," Myles mumbled. "Why?"

"Remember I told you I would collect on that debt one day?"

"Yes. What's going on, bruh?"

"It's that time."

Myles shoulders slumped. "Now?"

"Now. Walk away. No questions, no more flirting. Leave." Ian ended the call and waited for Myles to make up an excuse to go anywhere else. It didn't take long, either. Within a minute, Bailee was once again standing alone. She shrugged before starting toward the door again.

Ian took that moment to intercept her before she made it to the door. He pulled her into the long hallway, in a little corner, hidden from view.

"Ian?" She crossed her arms over her chest. "What are you doing?"

"We're going to talk."

"We can't," she rasped.

He took one step closer and she retreated back. "One

thing you should know about me? I hate when people dismiss me the way you did."

"Ian, I didn't dismiss you. I simply said that what happened won't be happening again."

"I don't believe you," he told her. Ian knew he was taking a chance. She could bolt at any minute, and he would be left there with that feeling that she seemed to evoke in him. One he didn't quite understand.

She blinked. "What?"

"I don't believe you," he repeated, even though he knew she'd heard him the first time.

"Ian, you're acting crazy now. What don't you believe?"

"Everything about you reacts to me." He stepped forward, grinning when she sucked in a breath and moved back a step…then two, then three. Until she pressed against the wall.

"What do you want from me?" she whispered.

Ian opened his mouth to tell her exactly what he wanted when his phone buzzed in his pocket. But he made no move to answer it. It kept buzzing.

"Your phone," she said, a smirk on her lips. "Don't you think you should answer it?"

"They can wait."

"What if it's Mia? Or a patient?"

Ian doubted it was a patient, but it could be Mia, Still, he didn't budge. Finally, the phone stopped buzzing. "I want to answer your question, Bailee. You asked what I wanted from you. I want a conversation. One that doesn't consist of you hightailing it out of the room when things get too uncomfortable for you."

She bit her bottom lip, and Ian held back a groan. The last time they'd been together, she'd insisted they not kiss. He didn't fight her on it, because he knew how intimate the act could be. Yet, standing so close to her, taking in her scent, he wanted nothing more than to press his lips to hers, to feel her tongue against his. It seemed he was in a perpetual state of arousal over Bailee, and it was a new experience for him. No woman had ever made him feel the way Bailee did.

"Just a conversation?"

"Yes." *For now.* "Are you hungry? We can grab a bite to eat at the restaurant."

"That would feel too much like a date, and that's not something I'm comfortable with."

"Fine," he conceded. "A walk?"

She assessed him a moment before nodding. "Okay. A quick walk."

Ian finally shifted to the side and allowed her to pass him. "Quick walk it is."

Outside, they walked along a brick path, toward the gazebo. They didn't speak for a while, but Ian was fine with that.

"I've been wanting to come out here since I saw it this morning," Bailee admitted.

"Really? Is that just because you like gazebos, or is it something else?"

She looked at him out of the corner of her eye, a small smile playing on her lips. "My parents had one at their house. Growing up, it was my favorite hiding place. I could escape there with a book and not go back to the house for hours."

"I saw you with a book earlier. What's your favorite genre?"

A full smile bloomed on her face. "I can read almost anything." She giggled. "But my favorite is romance."

Ian didn't bother to hide the shock on his face. "Romance, huh? What kind of romance? Contemporary, historical, erotic?"

She eyed him warily. "What do you know about it?"

"I have a sister who makes it her business to read every smutty romance novel she can get her hands on. And my best friend is a woman. I've caught her several times with her nose in one of those books. Before she met Mason, she even dragged me to the movies to see an adaptation of one of them. The one with the shy girl and the mogul who is drawn to her for some inexplicable reason."

Ian remembered that day clearly. Mia had tricked him into going to the theater, telling him that they were going to see one of those romantic comedies he couldn't stand. He'd agreed to go only because she'd cried on his shoulder for an hour over a failed relationship.

"Seriously? I'd think it would be awkward to watch that movie with your female friend."

Ian shook his head. "If you're asking if I was turned on during the movie, my answer would be a hell no."

They made it to the fully lit gazebo and she grinned up at it. "I love it. Everything about it is beautiful—the lights, the greenery, the color of the wood."

Ian watched her as she ran a hand over the railing. She was so beautiful. The way she seemed to soak in the scenery around her, the way her eyes had lit up when she peered up at the gazebo.

Bailee took a seat on the bench and looked at him. "So tell me...what's up with you and Mia?"

He frowned. "What are you talking about?"

She crossed her legs. "I notice the way you two interact with each other, and I have questions—lots of questions and some concerns."

Ian knew what was coming next. Most women he'd

dated had a problem with his friendship with Mia. He took a seat next to her. "There's nothing going on between us. We're really just friends."

"I love my brother. And if this were some kind of *My Best Friend's Wedding* type of friendship, I might have to maim you."

Ian barked out a laugh. He knew the movie Bailee referred to. It had been one of the many movies Mia had forced him to watch. "I've seen the movie. No, that's not what this is. Mia has been a good friend to me since we were kids. I've never felt anything romantic toward her."

"It just seems kind of unrealistic."

"Are you speaking from experience?"

Bailee shrugged. "Maybe."

"Well, rest assured, I won't be blurting out my repressed love for Mia during her wedding ceremony. And I won't be pulling her aside before she walks down the aisle to tell her how much I've always loved her. I'll save that for the movies."

"So nothing ever happened between you two? In all the years you've been friends?"

Ian thought about that for a moment. Not because anything had happened between him and Mia, but because he figured it was a question many people had about his friendship with Mia. "No, nothing has ever happened between us. Not a lingering glance or anything you might read about in your romance books."

Bailee laughed. "How did I know you'd find a way to bring that up?"

"It was too easy." He chuckled, and brushed a stray strand of hair out of her face. "Real talk—I guess it's not out of the realm of possibility for two friends to be attracted to each other and suppress those feelings for whatever reason. That's not me and Mia. However, my brother Drake married his best friend a few years ago."

"Had they ever dated?"

"It's a funny story, actually. But no. They went to a family reunion in Vegas, got drunk and woke up married."

Bailee covered her mouth. "Are you serious?"

"Definitely serious."

"And they're still married?"

Ian nodded. "Happily. With a new baby and everything. Her name is Zoe and I'm smitten."

Bailee's eyes softened. "That's cute. I bet you're going to spoil her."

"I absolutely plan to."

"I think that's great." Bailee shifted in her seat, adding another inch between them. He scooted closer. She stared at him and sighed. "I know I shouldn't ask you this, but I'm curious. What made you come up to my room with me?"

Ian thought back to that night. He hadn't gone to the bar to meet anyone. In fact, that was the furthest thing from his mind. A few of his coworkers had suggested a bar night after a particularly hard day at the hospital. They'd lost several patients due to a house fire, and he'd wanted a drink, so he joined them.

When Ian noticed Bailee at the bar, he'd been immediately struck by her beauty. But when he'd sparked up a conversation with her, one that didn't make him want to run the other way, he knew he wanted more. So when she'd asked him to go upstairs, he didn't hesitate. He went with it.

"I didn't want the night to end," he answered truthfully. They'd talked about everything from politics to sports. "I enjoyed talking to you."

Bailee averted her gaze. "We did have a lot in common."

"For some reason, I think you think of me as some sort of player."

She tilted her head. "Aren't you?"

He laughed. "I have been in the past."

"Okay, then. Why can't we just leave it there? Two people who connected one night, and decided to enjoy each other's company."

Ian picked up her hand and brought it to his mouth. He brushed his lips over her palm. "Because I can't stop thinking about it."

"Before you saw me this morning, or after?"

"I hate to keep repeating this to you, but you're the one who ended the night."

She pulled her hand away and stood. "Because that's what happens after anonymous sex."

Ian stood. He wanted her to ask him to stay with her tonight, tell him she wanted him, beg him to make love to her. Because he would. He wanted to. "Bailee, don't take this the wrong way, but I'm guessing you don't have random sex often."

She frowned and crossed her arms. "What is that supposed to mean?"

"It means what I said."

"Does that mean you didn't enjoy it?"

Now it was Ian's turn to be confused. "Did I say I didn't enjoy it? Obviously I did because I told you I couldn't stop thinking about it."

"Well, you never answered my question. Before or after you saw me?"

"Before *and* after. Is that a good enough answer for you?"

Bailee swallowed visibly. "Ian, I—"

Ian took another step toward her. He reached out and took her hand again, this time pulling her toward him. Her sharp intake of breath loosened something in him, propelled him to go further. "I'm not the type of man who plays games. I want what I want, and I make no apologies for it. So you tell me..." His gaze locked on hers. "Bailee, you tell me what you want me to do."

Tell me what you want me to do.

Bailee turned Ian's words over in her head. He wanted her to set the pace, wanted her to tell him what to do next. The simple fact that he'd said those words made her feel like she held the power.

The intense look in his beautiful brown orbs, the lust shining back at her made her feel unhinged. And the heady tone of his voice, the feel of his body pressed against hers, coupled with the night air and the lights of the gazebo, made for a tantalizing scene—one that could easily be written in a book.

An appropriate response to his question would have been "Thanks, but it's better that we stay clear of one another." But she couldn't bring herself to mutter those words, because she didn't believe them. She let out a slow breath, readied herself to speak. But before she could, his mouth was on hers.

It wasn't a simple, sweet kiss, either. It was hard, possessive, all-consuming. His hands cupped her cheeks, his tongue rubbed against hers, his teeth nipped at her lips. Bailee couldn't breathe, couldn't think, could do nothing but let him have his way with her mouth. Her body felt liquid, like molten lava. And he'd done that to her with one kiss? What would happen if he got her naked again? *I might die.*

Bailee wanted to cry and laugh at the same time, it

felt so good. Her senses were tuned into him. His smell filled her nose; his husky groans vibrated through her body and heat pooled between her legs.

Ian pulled back, and Bailee fought the urge to tug him to her again. His hands were still on her cheeks as he placed soft, wet kisses over her collarbone, her jawline and finally up to her ear. His hands, those lips, made her want to surrender everything to him.

Then the heat of him was replaced with a soft breeze against her sensitive skin.

Slowly, her surroundings came into view again and she registered his whispered curse. *Damn is right.*

When she met his waiting gaze, he was grinning at her. It was that same grin that made her want to lose her mind and let him have his way with her. In every position, on every single hard and soft surface in the house.

Briefly, she wondered if she should say something. But before she could think of the words, he leaned in again, grazing his teeth over her bottom lip before he sucked it into his mouth. When his tongue swept against hers again, she groaned. Then she was lost in him.

"I can't seem to resist you," he murmured against her lips. "I couldn't then. I can't now." He kissed her shoulder, sending a new wave of shivers down her spine.

She sucked in a deep breath and nearly collapsed in a heap on the hard floor of the gazebo. He was good. He seemed to know every note of her song. And she wanted more. She wanted him. But something inside her wouldn't let her say the words. Maybe it was because she knew this wouldn't end well. One of them would end up hurt, and she was 99 percent sure it would be her.

Bailee hadn't walked away from Brandon to be sucked into a different type of one-sided relationship. This time, she'd be the one pining away for a man who didn't want her the way she wanted him.

"I don't need…" She wrenched herself out of his grasp. "I shouldn't be doing this with you."

"Why?" Ian asked.

"Because!" she shouted. "I've never done this before. You were right, I don't have sex with strangers. That night in New Orleans with you was a first for me, something I did because I wanted to go with the moment for once. But the regular Bailee, the one standing here right now, is not the type of woman who can be with someone so freely. Hell, I don't go out to bars and hang out with my friends until the wee hours of the morning."

She paced back and forth in the gazebo, torn between running back to the house and finishing this with Ian. The fact that she wanted to let loose with him was doing a number on her.

"I love to read," she continued. "I'm okay with a quiet night at home with a piece of chocolate, a beer and a Netflix binge."

"Have you watched that show with the kids and the alien invasion?"

Bailee laughed at his attempt to lighten the mood. "I have. It was so good."

"I haven't seen it, but Mia raves about it."

"Ian, we're not together, and…"

"Bailee, I know we're not together. But what happened between us is still important. You're important. No matter what happens tonight, tomorrow we'll still be running around doing man of honor and best woman duties for Mason and Mia. And if you're uncomfortable with what is obviously going on between us, I'll back off."

"You would do that?"

"As much as it would pain me, yes." With his eyes locked on hers, he stepped forward. "I can see that you're really stressed about this. And that's the last thing I want."

Bailee let out a shaky breath. "Thanks."

"But I have to warn you." His voice took on a serious tone that made her tense. "This feeling you have won't just go away. Trust me. I've tried to will it away and that doesn't work."

His words stirred something inside her, but she forced herself not to think about what she wanted him to do to her body. "It will work." Her voice sounded shaky and unsure to her own ears.

"Say what you will, but your body is telling me another story."

Her breath caught in her throat, and she looked down at her body as if she would *see* what he was talking about. "Ian, please—"

He placed a finger over her mouth. "Okay. I'm done. Let's go back up to the house. We have an early football game tomorrow."

Sighing, Bailee nodded. "Sounds like a plan."

As they made their way back to the house in silence, Bailee thought about Ian's words. They had several more days in close proximity, and if tonight was any indication, she would never make it through them without wanting to explore what she was feeling for him.

Chapter 7

The next morning, Bailee woke up sweaty and frustrated. Despite her bravado the night before, Ian had affected her. She'd tried to fight it, but it didn't matter how many times she told herself to leave him alone, to ignore him; she couldn't stop her mind from wandering to his eyes, his hands, his lips, his…everything.

Last night, he'd visited her in her dreams, looking like her own personal sex genie, ready to grant her each and every wish. And he'd brought her to one delicious orgasm after another in her vivid fantasies. *Ugh.*

Bailee stomped into the kitchen and headed straight for the fridge. Swinging the door open, she pulled out the freshly squeezed orange juice. She made quick work of fixing her breakfast, which consisted of whole wheat toast, jam and a piece of ham she found in the refrigerator. When she was done, she took a seat at the small dining table in the corner of the room. She pulled out her phone and dialed April.

"Hey, chile," April answered. "What's going on?"

"April, I need to talk."

"Everything okay?"

"I know you said you weren't coming, but you will never believe what happened."

"Girl, you're scaring me. What is it?"

"Mr. Hottie, from New Orleans. He's Mia's man of honor."

"What the hell is a man of honor?"

"Dr. Ian Jackson. Mr. Hottie. You know, one-night stand guy?"

"Shut up," April said. "You've got to be kidding me."

Bailee tucked her feet under her behind and hit the button to change the call to a video chat. A few seconds later, April's sleepy face appeared. "I wish I was kidding," Bailee said. "But I'm not. He's here and looking fine as ever. If anything, he looks even hotter."

"What did you do, Bai?" April twisted the scarf on her head and sat up in the bed.

Bailee's mouth fell open. "I didn't do anything." She scratched the back of her head. "Except let him fluster me one minute, and kiss me the next."

April shook her head. "That's it? I thought you were going to say he took you in the coat closet or something. Girl, I'm hanging up. You do realize it's seven o'clock in the morning, on my day off."

Bailee giggled. "April, you have to help me."

Before Bailee started her quest to cross off several items on her bucket list, she'd sat down with April to go over the pros and cons of each. Skydiving, snorkeling, going on an African safari and visiting Niagara Falls were easy enough goals, but the anonymous sex gave her the most pause.

"Bai, get yourself together. It's not the end of the world to kiss Mr. Hottie."

"Dr. Hottie," Bailee corrected.

"It's a bonus that he's a doctor, honestly. That makes him busy on most nights. You don't have to worry about him being a bugaboo."

"Oh my God, April!" Bailee barked out a laugh at her friend. She needed it that morning. "You're too much. So I guess you won't be coming here to be my plus one?"

"There is no way I'm stepping foot in that wedding resort. Can't do it. I'll help you, though."

Bailee pouted. "Fine, help me."

"Okay, here's my advice. Let him have his way with you, girl." April grinned. "You know you want to."

"I'm hanging up. Bye, April." Bailee ended the call, but sent off a text to April with a bear hug GIF. Her friend might be crazy, but she loved her nonetheless.

Mia strolled into the kitchen, workout gear on and her long hair piled into a bun on the top of her head. She headed straight to the refrigerator and pulled out two water bottles. Bailee watched her open one and gulp down the contents in less than a minute.

"Mia?" Bailee called.

Her future sister-in-law glanced at her and smiled. "Hey, Bai. I didn't even see you sitting in here." Mia walked over to the table and sat in the seat across from her. "I just got back from a bike ride. Woo, I'm tired."

"I didn't know you rode."

"I ride occasionally. Only with Ian."

The mere mention of Ian had her sitting straight up, feet on the floor. "Oh? He rode with you?"

Mia opened her mouth to respond just as Ian jogged into the kitchen. "Over here, Munch," Mia called.

Munch?

Ian scanned the room and spotted them in the corner. He hesitated for a moment, but then approached the table.

Bailee couldn't keep her eyes off his bare chest and strong legs. As he neared her, she noticed sweat on his brow and his chest. She imagined tracing every hard inch of his body…with her tongue. *Turn away, Bailee.*

Mia handed him the extra bottle of water she had, and he twisted the cap open. Watching the two of them and the way they interacted was like watching a train wreck. Last night, he'd mentioned they were only friends, but there was a fondness there that couldn't be denied. She wondered how they had become so close. Ian was very handsome and Mia was stunning, with her dark, silky hair and topaz eyes.

"So you two ride together?" Bailee tucked a strand of hair behind her ear.

"We do," Mia answered, smiling at Ian.

"And you call him Munch?" Bailee asked.

Ian groaned. "This is the exact reason I hate for you to call me that, Big Head."

"What?" Mia shrugged. "It's a childhood nickname," Mia told Bailee. "We've called him that for as long as I can remember."

"Why?" Bailee relaxed a bit in her chair.

Mia told the story, complete with wild hand gestures and sound effects. By the time she'd finished talking, she'd shared a few other Ian adventures and Bailee couldn't help but crack up at his antics. Ian had even joined in a few times, adding his own version to the stories.

During the entire conversation, though, Ian had

acted just as she'd asked him to—like there was no connection between them. In fact, he'd barely even looked at her. And instead of making her feel better, it made her feel worse.

"Well, I need to get dressed for the football game." Mia stood. "Bai, are you joining us? It's a Solomon family tradition."

Bailee peered at Ian, who was typing something in his phone. He looked up, met her gaze, then slid off his chair. "I'm going to head on upstairs to get dressed."

She watched him walk away, then met Mia's curious eyes. "Sure," Bailee replied. "I'll be there. No problem."

An hour later, the family and their guests had gathered at an open field on the property. Dr. Solomon instructed everyone to introduce themselves. It appeared more of Ian's family had arrived. She'd met Drake and El, and their wives, Love and Avery. Bailee felt like a fish out of water because everyone seemed so familiar with each other and she was…not. Also, she quickly realized that she was surrounded by a bunch of extremely competitive people whose sole purpose was to win. And she knew next to nothing about playing football, which was pretty much a sin in her household. Basketball? Definitely. Softball? Somewhat. Football? Hell, no.

They were split into opposing teams, with Mia and Mason as captains. Mia, of course, chose Ian. Mason chose her. She almost felt sorry for her brother because she knew she would be no help to him.

After the coin toss, it was determined that Mason's team would play offense first, and she was elected to be the wide receiver.

Shocked, she turned to Mason, eyes wide and mouth hanging open. "Are you crazy? You know I don't know what I'm doing. And if I'm not mistaken, wide receivers are integral to the game."

Mason patted her shoulder lovingly. "You'll be fine. It was a strategic move. You're a runner. We need fast people on the field."

Bailee grumbled a curse. "Good luck with that."

Dr. Solomon walked among the teams, his hands clasped behind his back. "First and foremost, this is a family game. We love each other, and we won't hurt each other." The older man cut a glare at Ian. "That goes for you, son."

Ian shrugged, and met Bailee's eyes briefly before turning away. "Hey, it's a game. We're playing to win. If Myles gets in my way, I make no promises."

Bailee glanced at her teammate Myles, standing to her right. The argument between Mia and Mason that had occurred several minutes earlier still rang in her ears. The two had argued over why the twins were not allowed to play on the same team. Apparently, they cheated when they played together.

"That's if you can catch me, Munch," Myles taunted with a smirk.

"Attention on me, teams," Dr. Solomon said. "As I was saying, we're all about family here. Let's greet each other as such."

Dr. Solomon walked away, and Bailee watched as members of opposite teams greeted each other with hugs or handshakes. She looked up to see Ian in front of her. *Oh boy.*

Determined to appear controlled, even though the sight of him brought back memories of that unforgettable kiss, she reached out, intent on giving him a handshake or an awkward side hug. But when his arms tugged her forward right into his hard chest, she froze. *Don't breathe, don't react, and whatever you do, don't...*

A low moan erupted from her throat. No, it was more like a purr. He smelled like heaven, and she couldn't help but sigh in contentment. Her body was officially a traitor because it liked everything about him.

She stepped back a little and peered up at him.

He grinned. "If you're trying to act like you don't want me, you need to stop looking at me like that."

Then he took off at a jog, leaving her right where she was.

Ian considered his options. He could either go over there, pick Bailee up and carry her off the field like some sort of urban caveman, or he could throw the football and hit Myles in the head. He chose option number two, sending the ball sailing in the air. Fortunately for his twin, he missed the noggin and connected with Myles's shoulder blade.

His twin let out a loud expletive and glared at him. "What the hell, Ian?" Myles rubbed his shoulder. "Watch where you're throwing that damn ball."

"What's going on, bruh?" Drake asked from behind him.

"That's my question, too," El said, approaching them. "You hit him on purpose."

Ian tilted his head to the sky. He should have known someone would have seen his jealous display, but he'd had enough of Myles flirting with Bailee. And he couldn't stand the fact that the groomsmen were winking and grinning at her, either.

He'd tried. He really had tried to respect her wishes and keep his distance. It had been hard to ignore her at the kitchen table that morning, hard to pretend they were nothing more than acquaintances. And he couldn't deny that she felt so good in his arms when he'd hugged her earlier. That cute little purr she let out almost brought him to his knees.

"Ian?" Drake said, pushing him out of his trance. "What's up, man?"

Ian sighed heavily. "Nothing. Let's get back to the game."

Turned out Mason knew how to handle a ball quite well, and had scored the first touchdown of the game. As the other team celebrated, Ian watched Bailee jump up and down with glee. She wasn't half bad at the game. Her speed had proved invaluable to their rivals.

"Get your head in the game, Munch!" Mia shouted from somewhere to his right. "Or I'm going to replace you with Daddy."

Fighting words. Ian had never been replaced with anyone, let alone someone's father. He forced his attention back on the game, and told himself over and over again not to look Bailee's way. Of course, that pep talk lasted only a minute because he found himself staring at the way she stretched before she got into formation. She'd dressed for the game and the weather, in Ohio State leggings and a short-sleeved matching jersey. Her hair was piled on top of her head in a messy bun. Bailee Sanders was definitely the sexiest wide receiver he'd ever played against, despite her choice of schools.

The next two plays went better for his team, though, and Drake scored a touchdown. But Ian had a new target—Mason's groomsman Charles. The man had practically leered at Bailee the entire game. And she didn't seem to mind the attention because she'd been grinning from ear to ear for the past twenty minutes.

"I repeat." Drake shoved a bottle of water in Ian's hand. Mia had called a time out to make a call to the florist. "What is going on with you? You've been distracted and downright surly."

El joined them, nodding. "I agree. You're being weird."

Ian shot his brothers a side-eye glance. "I'm fine," he grumbled.

Across the field, he noticed Bailee and Charles walk off together. And when the groomsman wrapped his arm around Bailee, lifting her up off the ground and twirling her around, he clenched his hands into fists.

Drake poked his arm. "Bruh, you ruined that bottle of water."

Ian dropped his gaze to the twisted bottle in his fist, and tossed it into an empty bucket behind him. He shook his hands out and picked up the football, ready to pitch it and break up the cozy duo. But then Bailee looked his way and smiled, and he almost forgot to be mad. Almost.

"So that's what's wrong with him," El mused. "I think Munch has his eye on the beautiful Bailee, Drake."

Ian's eyes flashed to his uncle-brother. "Don't start."

Drake nodded. "I think you're right, El."

"What is El right about?" Myles asked, joining them.

El barked out an annoying laugh. "We think Ian has it bad for Bailee."

Myles turned toward Bailee and Charles, who were now talking in hushed tones. "Ah, that makes sense." Ian shook his head, knowing his twin was putting two and two together. "You're feeling Bailee. Why didn't you just say something?"

"Better yet, why are you acting like a lovesick fool over someone you don't even know?" Drake asked.

"I do know her," Ian muttered.

Three pairs of questioning eyes landed on him, but it was Myles who spoke first. "How?"

"I met her in New Orleans," Ian admitted. "And that's all I'm saying about it." Drake laughed first, followed by El. Myles joined in, and soon all of his brothers were clenching their stomachs, cracking up at his expense. "You know what? Fu—"

"Wait, wait." Myles stopped laughing. "Don't get all sensitive, bruh. We're just not used to seeing you like this."

"Especially over a woman," Drake added.

"I would appreciate it if you kept that under wraps," Ian told his brothers, even though he really didn't need to. Although they often gave each other a hard time, it was understood that anything said to his brothers always stayed between them.

El shrugged. "Why?"

Ian sighed. "Because she doesn't want anyone to know that we know each other." That admission made it worse, as his brothers broke out in another fit of laughter. Ian pushed Myles, and his brother fell to the ground still laughing. "I can't take y'all nowhere."

Drake clutched his sides. "I'm sorry, I'm sorry."

He rested his arm on Ian's shoulder. "This is how it all starts, bruh. Jealousy. Then, next thing you know, you're in love."

"You have never lied, bruh." El gave Drake a fist bump.

Mia shouted that break was over, and Ian walked away from his brothers, eager to put distance between him and his amused siblings. His team stood in formation as he barked out the next play. On the snap, he watched as Charles winked at Bailee. But when Bailee smiled sheepishly at Charles, Ian froze in his tracks. He didn't see another groomsman coming toward him until it was too late. The hit took his breath away, and he landed hard on the grass. *Sacked.*

More than a little dazed and sore, Ian groaned. Somewhere in the distance, he heard a whistle blowing and Dr. Solomon shouting, "Flag on the play!" He rolled over on his back and waited for the world to stop spinning before he opened his eyes. Standing above him were his brothers, Mia, Mason and Bailee.

"Are you okay, Munch?" Mia asked, concern in her eyes.

Dr. Solomon was on the ground next to him. "Son, you took a big hit." Pop proceeded to do a quick exam while Ian was lying on the ground. Once he finished, he stood. "Let's help him up."

Myles stepped forward and held out a hand. Ian grabbed it and let his brother pull him to his feet. "You okay, bruh?"

Ian nodded, brushing off his clothes.

"Munch." Mia reached out to touch him, but he jerked away.

"I'm fine. I can take a hit." He glanced at Bailee,

who stood with her hands covering her mouth. She stared at him with wide, sad eyes, like she felt sorry for him or pitied him. And that's exactly what he felt like—a sorry, pitiful fool. Charles stood behind her, and Ian was hit with the urge to tug her away from the man. Instead, he made an excuse to leave and walked away.

Chapter 8

The Solomon-Sanders wedding weekend officially kicked off with a joint bachelorette–bachelor party on Thursday evening. The bride and groom had already had respective parties back home, but they both wanted one last hoorah with their entire bridal party.

Bailee had kept busy the last several days helping Mia get ready for the big day. She'd run errands, accompanied Mason to his final tuxedo fitting, finished the centerpieces and eaten so much delicious Italian food she thought she'd burst—or at least have to have her outfit let out.

Most of the bridal party and several guests had arrived early Thursday morning. Dr. Solomon had reserved a block of rooms at the Grand Traverse Resort and Spa to accommodate the wedding guests. Bailee spent the day with Mia at the hotel, welcoming family and friends.

With all she had to do, thinking about Ian should have been way down on her list. Without him distracting her with his perfect body, perfect lips, perfect everything, she'd been able to finally finish that book and work on her résumé.

But, of course, he was all she could think about—in the shower, during lunch with her parents, while she chatted with Dr. Solomon about possible positions at Michigan Medicine, at the hotel while delivering the cute little welcome baskets she'd made up for the wedding guests. He'd literally taken over her thoughts. And her dreams. Ian definitely gave good dreams.

It was almost like he'd disappeared. The estate was huge, but not so big she wouldn't have run into him in the kitchen or outside. At the same time, she tried to tell herself that he had a lot to do as well to help with the wedding. He was the man of honor, after all. But when he didn't show up for the five-course meal catered by Mia's sister Daniella last night, Bailee couldn't help but wonder what—or who—he was doing. Ian's whereabouts consumed her thoughts, and she'd almost asked Mia where Ian had been. Almost. Ultimately, she'd decided against it, for obvious reasons.

Once they left the hotel, heading toward the Solomon estate to get ready for the evening festivities, Mia turned to her. "Thanks for riding with me, Bai. It means a lot to me."

Bailee smiled at her future sister-in-law. "No problem. I can't believe you're marrying my brother in two days."

"I know." Mia had a wistful smile on her face. "I love him so much, Bai. And just in case you're worried, I'd never disrespect him or mistreat him. I know how close you two are."

Mia's assurances made Bailee happy, even though they were unnecessary. "Mia, my brother has never been as happy as he is with you. I'm ecstatic that you two found each other."

"Mason told me about your breakup, and I've wanted to reach out to you since then to let you know that you can always call me if you need to talk."

Bailee eyed Mia. "Thank you. That actually means a lot to me. I always wanted a sister."

"Well, now you have one." Mia squeezed Bailee's hand. "And once you get me, you get my family, so you'll have five sisters."

Giggling, Bailee said, "That's good. I love your family."

That was true. Since Bailee had arrived, the Solomon family had been nothing but kind and welcoming to her and her family. All of Mia's sisters were sweet, genuine women. And Dr. and Mrs. Solomon had made themselves available for anything she might need. Bailee had fallen in love with Nonna, as well. The older woman was up in age, but she could think all of them under the table, and knew a lot about everything.

"So, I've been thinking." Mia bit her lip. "How would you feel about a hookup? Nothing serious, because I know you're just getting out of a relationship. But I just want you to have fun here, maybe get to know someone."

Curious, Bailee asked, "You want to hook me up for wedding sex?"

Mia laughed. "Girl, yes. That's how I met Mason."

Bailee plugged her ears. "TMI. I don't want to hear about your and my brother's sexcapades." Though she'd already heard the story. Mia and Mason had met while they were bridesmaid and groomsman for two of their coworkers. And the rest was history.

As they pulled into the Solomon estate, Bailee's curiosity got the best of her. She turned to Mia. "Who exactly are you planning to hook me up with?" She took a sip from her bottle of water.

"Myles," Mia said simply.

Bailee choked, spraying water on the dashboard. "Oh my God. I'm so sorry." She fumbled in the glove compartment for napkins. "I didn't mean to do that."

Mia put the car in Park, laughing uncontrollably at Bailee's expense. Perhaps this was why she and Mason got along so well. They both found the humor in the most embarrassing things. "I can't..." Mia held her stomach. "What the heck was that about?"

"Nothing." Bailee scratched her ear. "Went down the wrong pipe."

The lie was obvious, but Bailee went with it. The fact that Mia wanted to hook her up with Ian's twin brother was almost laughable. But she couldn't blame Mia for trying, because no one knew of her history with Ian.

Mia covered her smile with a hand. "I'm sorry. It wasn't that funny. Are you okay?"

"Other than the fact that I could have been choking on a chicken bone and you were cracking up? Sure, I'm fine."

"It's just...you're always so serious." Mia chuckled. "It's good to see you let go of decorum."

Bailee guessed Mia would think that about her. Mason had been on her to let her hair down for years. They'd argued about her penchant for oversize sweatpants and a messy bun, her lack of a social life and daily regimen of work, exercise, dinner, book, sometimes television, bed. Her relationship, the predictability of it, had a lot to do with Brandon. And she'd just fallen into it because she thought that's what she was supposed to do as a good girlfriend. But Bailee had longed to do more, to let her hair down. Shaking that stigma was the reason she'd gone to New Orleans in the first place.

"And Myles is serious, too," Mia continued. "I saw you two talking at the cocktail party the other night and thought you'd be able to connect." She shrugged. "I don't know."

If only Mia knew that Bailee had *connected* with Myles's twin. She considered confessing everything. April wasn't around, and she needed to get it out. But Ian was Mia's best friend. It would be an awkward position to put her in.

"Thanks for thinking of me," Bailee said. "I'm not sure Myles and I would get along. We might be too similar, if you know what I mean."

"Yeah, I do. Is that why you and Brandon broke up? I mean, you don't have to tell me the details, but..."

"No, it's okay to ask. Brandon and I broke up because I woke up one day and realized that I didn't love him like I should. I knew that marriage to him would slowly suck the life out of me. Not that Brandon isn't a good guy. He is. But just not the guy for me."

It was the rehearsed explanation, the one she'd told her parents and would tell anyone else who asked. The truth was a little more complicated.

"That takes a lot of courage," Mia said. "It's hard to go against what everyone else wants you to do. Ian is actually going through something similar."

The sound of Ian's name did funny things to Bailee's insides. "What do you mean?" She tried to sound uninterested, but she definitely wanted to hear what Mia had to say.

"His father is kind of dominating. Well, not kind of. He's a jerk. I've never cared for him." Mia told Bailee about Dr. Law and his impossible standards. "Ian is on the cusp of something great. He has such a good heart, a desire to help those in need. I want him to be happy doing what he's been called to do. But Dr. Law is a nightmare. Don't tell anyone I told you this, but he was so against El being with Avery that he offered to pay off her student loans if she broke up with him. And when Drake married Love, Dr. Law rigged it so Drake could win a coveted fellowship in another state, away from her."

Bailee's mouth fell open. "Wow. That's messed up."

"Right?" Mia shook her head, a look of disgust passing over her face. "But I told Ian he needs to go for what will make him happy."

"Is that why he hasn't been around?" Bailee scratched the back of her neck. "I mean, I just noticed he wasn't at dinner last night."

"No." Mia gave her a sad smile. "That hit on the football field really did a number on his back. My dad drove him to a doctor yesterday to make sure his spine was okay."

Bailee officially felt like an asshole. "Oh no. I'm so sorry."

Mia frowned. "Why are you apologizing? You didn't hit him."

Lowering her gaze, Bailee nodded. "I know. But back pain can be awful. Will he be able to go out tonight?"

"He's not coming. I told him to skip it. I need him

tomorrow and Saturday. So I'd rather he be well rested. But he's moving better today. I saw him before we left."

"That's good. I'm glad he's doing better."

"Yeah, he hurt his back in college. That's why he didn't play football for long. He probably could have gone pro if he didn't get hurt."

"That's sad. I bet he misses the game."

Mia snorted. "I doubt it. As long as he can ride his bike, he's good. He competes all over the place."

Another thing Bailee didn't know about Ian. Just one more fact about him that made her want to take April's advice and let him catch her. "You two are very close."

"Yeah, in that brother-sister kind of way. Trust me, we've never had romantic feelings for each other. That would have been tragic."

Bailee forced a laugh past her lips. "How so?"

"We'd kill each other. Anyway, I better go on in." She climbed out of the car, and Bailee did, as well. "We'll meet out here around six o'clock. The party bus will take us downtown for the festivities." Mia wiggled her eyebrows. "Look hot! And let me know if you change your mind about that hookup."

Bailee watched Mia run into the house. As a matter of fact, Bailee had changed her mind, but not about Myles. Tonight, she'd find Ian and tell him exactly what she wanted.

Bailee thought a little liquid courage would help her make her move on Ian. But she'd had one too many shots of tequila, and Mason had insisted on riding with her back to the resort so she could sleep it off.

"Get out, Bai." Mason held his hand out, and she grabbed it, using his strength to stand.

"Thanks, Mase. I'm sorry I ruined your night out. You can go back and leave me here. I'm fine."

Mason stared at her, his lips in a straight line. "I told you to lay off the Patrón, Bai. It's not even like you."

"That's the problem!" she shouted. "Maybe I want to do something unlike me. Maybe I *have* done something unlike me."

"What does that even mean?"

"It means I need to live my life. Do you know that I'm thirty years old and I can count on one hand the times I've been drunk?"

"You can add today to the list," he murmured. "Come on. I'll make coffee."

She smacked his hand away. "I told you I'm fine. I'm not even tipsy right now." Which was a lie. She was definitely buzzed. "I can walk. Go back to Mia and your friends."

Mason hesitated a little, but relented and climbed back into the bus. "Bai, call me if you need anything. I'll come back."

Bailee knew he would. He'd always been there for her when she needed him. "I'm fine," she repeated. "Go and have fun." She saluted him.

Once the bus pulled off, she shuffled into the house, her high-heeled sandals in her hand. The place was quiet. She figured the staff had gone home and that those staying in the big house were sleeping.

One heel slipped out of her hand, and she bent down to pick it up. To her right, she heard footsteps. Turning toward the sound, she spotted Ian. Dressed in low-riding sweatpants and a tank, he looked damn good.

Without thinking, she followed him through the house, careful not to make too much noise. He walked out of the back door and down a lit path. When he froze, she hid behind a nearby tree. She gave it a minute or so before she started off behind him again.

The paved path led to an outdoor patio. Her mouth fell open at the high-end structure. She stepped under the roof, marveling at the beamed ceiling and tiled floor. It was like a little hidden oasis, almost better than the gazebo they'd been in the other night. There was an outdoor kitchen, a bar, two fire pits and lots of seating. The space allowed for a wide-open view of the pool and Jacuzzi.

Ian sat in one of the cushioned chairs that seemed more like indoor furniture than the normal outdoor furniture she was used to. As she approached him, she noticed he had a book in his hand.

"Are you following me, Bailee?" Ian asked, not bothering to turn around.

"How did you know it was me?" She rounded the chair, and...*and now he's Mr. Hottie, who looks so damn hot in a pair of reading glasses*. Bailee bit her lip, taking in his long, built frame in the chair.

"You weren't being very discreet." He chuckled.

Bailee didn't know what it was. The lighting that gave him an ethereal glow, the cool summer breeze or the tequila that made her want to abandon all of her rules. She swallowed, warring with herself over her next move. There was something to be said for living like each day was your last. But taking precautions and weighing decisions was just as important.

He peered up at her and smiled.

Damn it. That one move, that one sexy twitch of his mouth, was her undoing. Because that smirk made her mind spin and her body ache with a need she'd never felt before. In that moment, every rational thought she had was overshadowed by her desire for Ian. That very second, she wanted nothing more than to climb into his lap and let him take her out of her horny misery.

Exhaling, Bailee plopped on the chair next to him. "Oh, God, this chair is so comfortable," she blurted out.

"Are you drunk?" he asked.

"No, I'm not." *Well, not exactly.*

His forehead creased. "Aren't you supposed to be out with the bridal party?"

"My brother had a fit and made me come back. He said I had one too many shots of tequila. I only had three." *Or four.* "He's so overprotective."

"Ah, maybe you should have a bottle of water." He started to stand, but she placed her hand on his, stopping him.

"Please sit." She tugged at the neck of her dress and shifted in her seat. She couldn't seem to concentrate with him so near her. He smelled like pine and musk, orange and leather. And his lips…

"Are you sure you're okay?"

"Huh?"

"I said, are you okay?"

"I'm fine. Just hot and bothered," she added under her breath.

He laughed then, and she knew he'd heard her admission. "Bailee, you're hilarious when you've been drinking."

"So listen," she said. "I've decided that we're having sex tonight."

His mouth fell open and his eyes flickered with amused surprise. "What?"

"Come on, Ian. You heard me."

The wicked grin was back, tempting her. "I'm not

sure I did. I think I need you to repeat that. Maybe a little louder this time?"

"Okay, fine." She rolled her eyes. "We're having sex. Tonight."

Chapter 9

We're having sex tonight.

Ian couldn't believe this latest turn of events. He'd spent the last two days hiding out from everyone after the football game, only coming out to eat and go to the doctor. Even though the doctor gave him a clean bill of health, noting there was no new damage to his spine, he'd decided to relax until the wedding.

"Hey," Bailee called, snapping her fingers. "Are you going to ignore me?"

Ian leaned his head back against the cushion and turned to her. She looked so innocent sitting in the oversize chair, her knees tucked under her chin. It was clear to him that she'd been drinking, but he couldn't say whether she was drunk. He'd seen her flustered and nervous, but the woman watching him was confident, resolute.

His gaze raked over her, already turning over the

different ways he could take her in his mind. Bailee wore a short black romper, with sleeves that reminded him of a kimono. She'd straightened her hair and wore a simple part down the middle. *Stunning* was the one word that came to mind when he saw her.

On his way to the outdoor living area, he'd heard her walking behind him. He knew it was her from the moment he heard footsteps behind him. It had only taken a few seconds to register the sound, but when he did, it seemed her aroma wafted to his nose. It was distinctively Bailee, summery and fresh, with a hint of mandarin. He wanted to bury his nose in her neck and inhale her scent.

Ian knew he wanted Bailee, but he hadn't realized how much until that very moment. She looked like an angel, so sweet and pure. And she'd just thrown all her cards on the table. To hear that she wanted to be with him again, especially after she'd been so adamant against sleeping with him another time, made his body buzz with excitement. It was almost too good to be true. But she'd told him in no uncertain terms what she wanted to go down that night. He'd waited for this exact moment, had awakened every morning hard and frustrated. And now…

Bailee stood abruptly, swaying on her feet a little before glancing over at him. For a minute, he thought she was going to leave. And he was prepared to go after her. She surprised him yet again when she sauntered over to him and climbed onto his lap, straddling his legs.

"Bailee," he groaned, gripping her hips with his hands to hold her steady.

"You told me you'd stay away." She cupped his face

in her hands, forcing him to look into her pretty brown eyes. "But I don't want you to anymore."

"Is that so?" he managed to ask. It was a wonder he could even formulate a sentence with her so close.

She nodded slowly. "It is. I want you."

He raised a brow. "You do?"

Bailee kissed his chin, then bit down on it. "So much." She rolled her hips, prompting him to reaffirm his grip on them. Because if her sex made contact with his growing erection, it would be all over for him. He'd have no choice but to give her what she obviously wanted.

Maybe he was going soft, but that's not how he wanted sex with her to be. They'd had hot and heavy in New Orleans. Now he wanted slow and steady. He wanted to take his time with her. And sexing her up in a chair outside in the open where anyone could happen upon them wasn't going to work for him.

"Bai?" His breath caught in his throat when she nipped at his ear. Torture. That was the word. The woman he'd dreamed about was in his lap. "We can't do this right now."

She pouted and sat back on his knees, folding her arms over her chest. "Why?" She blew hair out of her face. "You don't want me anymore?"

Ian let out a deep breath. "That's not it, baby. But you don't really want this right now. Not here."

"There's no one here!" She held her hands out wide and turned to the right, then the left, as if she were looking for someone. "Everyone is out having a good time, and I couldn't have fun because I…" She bit down on her lip. "I couldn't stop thinking about you."

The admission caught him off guard. "That's good to know. But we're outside, Bai. In the open. What if

Mason comes home to check on you? You don't really want him to find you on my lap like this, do you?"

"Mason has sex, Ian. I want to have sex. With you."

Ian chuckled. "You've been drinking."

"I'm not drunk!" she shouted. He placed his finger over her mouth, shushing her. "I know what I want."

Before he could respond, she sucked his finger into her mouth. *Shit.* "Bai, please."

Please…what? Stop? He didn't want her to stop. In fact, the only thing he wanted in that moment was for her to keep going. Her outfit was loose enough for him to make it work without baring her to the elements. But he wouldn't.

"Bailee." He slipped his finger from her warm mouth. He was impossibly hard for her, painfully hard. So hard he felt like he would burst open from the pressure.

"Ian, tell me why you don't want to have sex with me. Is it your back?"

He frowned. "No. My back is fine."

"Mia said you hurt your back." Her hands were driving him crazy. Her featherlight touch roamed over his forehead, his cheeks, his lips and down his neck. "I can help you feel better."

"Bailee." He gently pushed her fingers away from his face. "It's not my back. I'm fine."

"I didn't know you played football in high school and college. Mase played for one year in high school, too."

"I know." Mase and Ian had bonded over the love of the game the first time they'd met. They'd even formed their own Fantasy Football league, which tended to get pretty competitive. "We talked about it."

"Do you miss it?"

"No, I don't," he admitted.

The doctor had told him to relax, but hadn't put any restrictions on him. The next day he'd been stiff, but it hadn't lasted long. Dr. Solomon and Mia were just being overly cautious. He couldn't blame them, with his history. Suffering from a herniated disc had taken him out for an entire season of football. By the time he felt well enough to play again, he didn't want to. He loved the game, but his heart wasn't in it.

To the world, Ian had caught a bad break. To the world, Ian's football career had ended before it started. Michigan football fans were devastated for him; his coaches mourned the loss as if Ian had died, and his fellow players had thrown sad looks his way whenever they'd seen him on campus. But no one knew it was his decision to stop playing. Even Mia and Myles didn't know, as he'd chosen to share his decision with only two people—his doctor and Pop. Dr. Solomon had cautioned him against making decisions based on emotion, but in the end, Ian was happier for it.

"Why? I Googled you. You were good."

Her admission that she'd done a web search for information on him brought a smile to his face. "I was okay."

"No, you were good. I read several articles that lamented the loss of your prowess on the field."

When he was a kid, his father had made all of them take up a sport. It had been instilled in him for as long as he could remember that a man should have many talents. And although his father had rarely made a game, they'd still be required to participate. Bringing a second place trophy home for anything was unacceptable and grounds for a punishment.

Luckily, football came easy for him. He already

loved the game, so getting to play it in a youth league, then in high school and finally college made his days more bearable. It was also the perfect excuse to be away from the house. Myles had chosen baseball, while Drake and El both played basketball. Melanie had joined the swim team.

Bailee tapped his forehead. “Are you still here with me?” She tilted her head, searched his eyes. “You look lost in memories.”

Even inebriated, she could still read him. He shook his head. “I’m here, Bai.”

“You smell so good.” She circled his nose with hers.

“Bailee, I—”

“No!” She sliced her hand through the air. “I just want to be with you. Why won’t you let me be great?”

Ian barked out a laugh. “You’re so damn beautiful.” He leaned back and traced the ridge of her nose. “But you’ve been drinking, and as much as I want to make love to you, I won’t.”

Cursing, he stood and lifted her in his arms. She squealed with drunken delight, wrapped her legs around his waist. He tried to pry her tight grip from him and set her on the ground, but his best efforts didn’t work. Instead, she wrapped her arms around his neck and hugged him.

Leaving his book on the chair, Ian started toward the house, grateful that he’d taken the last few days to rest his back. It took several minutes to make it to the door. Several hard minutes of her little fingers brushing over his skin and her lips sprinkling kisses over the parts of his body that were bared to her.

By the time he made it up to her room, he was on fire. Ian had never been so turned on in all his life, and unable to do anything about it. He couldn't take it. He had to get her tucked in bed, far away from him.

Ian turned the doorknob and cursed. "Bai? Where is your key card?" He hadn't seen a purse. The only thing she had when she entered the outdoor living area was one shoe. He'd spotted the other shoe along the path leading to the house. When she didn't answer, he asked again, "Bai, the card?"

"In my pocket," she murmured against his neck. "Come and get it."

Damn. "Okay, you have to get down." He attempted to set her down, but she wouldn't budge. "I can't open the door if I don't have your key card."

Bailee let out a tiny growl before she relented and relaxed her hold on him. Once on her feet, she shoved her hands in her pockets and pulled out the card. But instead of giving it to him, she held her arm up. "Are you coming in with me?"

He reached out to grab it, but she moved it out of reach. They spent a few seconds playing that game, of him trying to get the key card and her moving it away from him. Finally, he grabbed her wrist and wrenched it from her hand. "I'll tuck you in."

Opening the door, he steered her into the room, pausing at the sight of her bed. Judging by the mound of clothes on it, it had taken her a few tries to get her outfit right for the evening. He brushed past her, scooped up a pile of clothes and dropped them into an open drawer. It took him a few minutes to clear the bed, but he accomplished his task without a word. He drew back the comforter and turned to her. Her eyes were on him.

"What?" he asked.

"Nothing," she said, a somber look in her eyes.

Standing to his full height, he stepped over to her. "What's wrong, Bai?"

She swallowed visibly. "I'm sorry. I just threw myself at you. I don't know what's wrong with me. I've never done that before in my life."

Ian brushed his thumb over her cheek, enjoying the way her lashes fluttered closed. "Don't apologize. I'm glad you threw yourself at me. Now I know what you want."

"But you don't… You haven't…"

He placed his finger over her mouth again. "Bai, stop. I'm not going to make love to you when you're like this. It doesn't mean I don't want you, because I do. Very much. I would just prefer you to be sober."

"But I'm not drunk," she argued.

"You're not sober. You would hate yourself in the morning."

Her shoulders slumped. "Okay." She brushed past him, stumbled over to the bed and climbed in. "I'm going to sleep now. Will you lie with me for a while?"

Ian blinked. "Bailee, I—"

"Please? Just until I fall asleep. I don't want to be alone."

He warred with himself about the consequences of actually getting in the bed with her at that moment. If he crawled into her bed, the thin layer of control he had might snap.

"Ian?" Bailee perched herself on her elbows. "It's okay. I'm okay. Thanks for bringing me back to the room. I'll see you tomorrow." She fell back against the mattress with a low moan.

Sighing, he stalked over to the other side of the bed and climbed in with her. She rolled over to face him, a lazy smile on her face.

"You're here," she whispered. "Hi."

He laughed, turning to his side to peer into her eyes. "Hi."

"Confession time."

Ian closed his eyes tightly, steeling himself for whatever she wanted to say. He suspected it would be one more thing to endear her to him. "What is it?"

"You're only the second man I've ever been with."

Once again, she'd rendered him speechless. He stared at her, unable to respond to this latest revelation.

"I went to New Orleans to treat myself to a good time," she continued. "I haven't had many of those in my life."

"Why?" he croaked. He'd met her parents. They didn't seem cruel, or even unusual. Mason had never come across as a man who'd had a weird childhood.

She shrugged. "I've spent my life just doing what others expected of me, never rocking the boat. I met Brandon when I was five years old. He came over to my house to see Mason one day, and I fell in love at that very moment."

Ian hated hearing the words "fell in love" come out of her mouth about another man. But everything was starting to make sense. Ian was the rebound guy, the "take that" answer to her breakup. It didn't bother him as much as he thought it would. In fact, he was happy he'd been the one she'd let loose with. He wondered how this Brandon guy had hurt her feelings.

"For years I followed him around and he finally stopped running. I was a fourteen-year-old awkward kid with wild hair and braces. And he was a star basketball player and one of my brother's best friends. But he wanted me."

Ian couldn't imagine anyone *not* wanting the beauty

lying next to him. He hadn't spent any real time with her, but he already felt totally and completely drawn to her. "That's not hard to believe."

Bailee sucked in a deep breath, one he wanted to steal with a kiss. But he refrained. She smiled sadly. "I spent years with Brandon, had every first with him. He proposed a year ago, and I told him yes. I couldn't set the date, though. It didn't feel right, for some reason. It's like I woke up one day and realized that my entire life had passed me by, and I wasn't a part of it. I watched my own life from the sidelines."

A tear fell from her eyes, and he dashed them away with his thumb. "Don't cry."

She held his hand to her cheek and closed her eyes. "I'm good. I just needed to say this to someone. I've told Mason and my parents the general bits of my breakup. And I've told my best friend, April. But no one knows how this has really changed me."

"Did Brandon hurt you? Did he cheat on you?"

She shook her head, finally releasing her hold on his hand. "No. Brandon is a good man. He's kind and giving. But he's focused on his career, his ambition. He's set to take over his father's corporation, and driven to the point of pain sometimes. There were times I felt like arm candy, almost like an afterthought. And I'd given him so much of me. So much I couldn't look at myself in the mirror without wondering who was staring back."

Once again, Ian didn't know how to respond, so he remained quiet.

"Then I met you. And I made a decision based on the way we talked, the way you seemed to see inside me at the bar. It was new and different. But it was also terrifying."

"I feel the same way," he admitted.

"I know you have so much more experience with women." She smiled, a wistful look in her eyes. "But I didn't feel inexperienced with you. I felt powerful, alive. I want that again."

Ian searched her eyes, saw the truth in them. Then he made his decision. He pressed his lips to hers. Her low moan spurred him on, and he pulled her to him.

The kiss was soft, yet firm. It was everything it should have been in that moment. She needed something, and he wanted to give it to her. When he broke the kiss, he let out a deep breath and rested his forehead against hers.

"Ian?" she whispered. Her fingers swept over his neck, through his hair. "I want this. I need it."

He swallowed. "If I let you come, will you go to sleep?"

She nodded.

Without another word, Ian swept a hand up her inner thigh, under her shorts and slipped a finger inside her, moving it in and out until she was begging him to finish her off.

"Ian," she cried, rolling her hips in time with his movements and pleading with him to keep going.

Ian brushed his lips over her temple, down her nose, to her mouth, kissing her again. "You're so perfect," he murmured. "You're stunning."

With his thumb, he circled her clit at the same time he inserted another finger into her heat. It didn't take long for her to fall over the edge. She moaned his name as her orgasm pulsed through her body.

Bailee rolled over on her back, her eyes closed. She stretched and purred. The smile on her face cracked his heart wide open. If he wasn't careful, she'd be able to steal it.

"Bai?"

"Hmm," she moaned.

"I should go."

Her eyes popped open. "You're leaving? But you haven't…"

He cupped her cheeks, placed a kiss to her brow. "Go to sleep, Bai. I'll see you tomorrow." He slid off the bed and walked around to her side.

Bailee looked up at him, a lazy grin still on her lips. "Thank you," she whispered.

Leaning down, he tipped her chin up. "Don't thank me yet." He kissed the tip of her nose. "Get some sleep."

"Good night."

"Night, Bailee."

Chapter 10

"I'm so sorry I'm late." Bailee hurried down the aisle, ignoring the many eyes on her. The rehearsal had already started and she'd arrived twenty minutes late, which had been her MO all day. She'd arrived for the bridal party brunch ten minutes late, for one last alterations appointment with Bee thirty minutes late and to Mason's tuxedo fitting fifteen minutes late.

She couldn't seem to get it together. Waking up that morning and realizing she'd thrown herself at Ian the night before didn't feel as humiliating as it would have a day or two before. Because they'd shared something last night that couldn't be put into words. Yes, she'd had too much to drink, but she remembered everything about last night. She recalled the way he held on to her, the tender care he showed when he carried her back to her room, the way he'd listened to her confessions. And she remembered how it felt when he made her fall apart at the seams.

Today, when she'd seen him at the brunch, he'd watched her the entire time. But she didn't feel uncomfortable under his penetrating stare. She felt safe.

"Where have you been?" Mase asked when she stepped up to her spot beside him. "I was worried."

"I'm fine. Just moving a little slow today."

"I see," he grumbled. "I told you to stop drinking last night."

Bailee rolled her eyes. "Mase, please. I don't need your chastising right now. Mom and Dad have done plenty of that today."

Her parents had cornered her in the hallway on her way down to breakfast. Of course, her mother wanted to talk about her canceled nuptials and how poor Brandon was heartbroken and deserved a conversation. The lecture didn't stop until she'd shouted at her mother to just leave it alone, and stormed off.

The wedding coordinator announced that they would run through the ceremony again, and the wedding party headed toward the entrance of the room.

On her way, Ian stepped in beside her. "Are you okay?"

She smiled. "I'm fine. Just running a little behind."

He leaned into her as they walked. "All day?"

She froze, turning to him. "What have you heard?"

"Nothing, calm down. You were late to breakfast, and I was at the tuxedo fitting before Mason, and he mentioned not knowing where you were."

Bailee felt a flush work its way up her neck to her cheeks. "I can't exactly lie and say you're off base."

"Good, because lying is not your strong suit."

Her mouth fell open, and she shoved him playfully. "How would you know?"

"Do you even want to go there?"

Averting her gaze, she shook her head. "I don't need to. I hope I didn't..." She twisted her fingers together, trying to find the right words. "I mean... I don't want you to think I was just talking out of my head last night. I'd been drinking, but I remember everything that happened."

A whisper of a smile crept across his face. "Good. So then it won't shock you when I tell you that I didn't forget what you said, and I fully intend to finish what you started last night."

Bailee's mouth fell open, and he took one finger and tapped her chin up, closing it. But a sexy response escaped her mind at that moment.

He leaned in, his lips close to her ear. She couldn't help but scan the room, to see if anyone was paying them any attention. Surprisingly no one was. "I told you to stop looking at me like that," he said.

"Like what?" Her question came out as a breathless whisper.

The heat in his eyes made her knees feel weak. "Like you want me to pick you up and carry you out of here right now." His voice was a low growl, and it made her want to lean in for more, wedding party, wedding rehearsal, wedding ceremony and all the guests be damned. She wanted more of everything he had to offer.

"Alright, people!" the wedding coordinator shouted, pulling Bailee out of her haze. "Line up. We'll run through this a few more times before we're done."

Mia jogged over to them. "Ian, come with me."

Ian winked at Bailee before he let Mia lead him away. And Bailee grabbed hold of a chair to remain standing.

She tried to concentrate the rest of the rehearsal, to

focus. But she couldn't stop thinking about Ian. Despite her efforts to stay far away from him for the remainder of the rehearsal and avoid eye contact, she found herself glancing his way, only to find him staring at her. He'd promised to finish what she'd started, and she anticipated all the naughty things he would do to her if she let him. And she would. Oh, she definitely planned to let him.

When rehearsal ended, the wedding party and close family and friends were driven to Anna's for a rehearsal dinner in one of the private rooms in the restaurant. Dr. Solomon had closed to the public for the occasion, and the entire staff was on hand to help with the event.

Inside the dining room, place cards told everyone where they would sit. Her seat was between Mason… and Myles. Disappointment clouded her mind, and she cursed herself for it. Mia had made it very clear that she'd tried to hook her up with Myles, so she wondered if this was an attempt on Mia's part to get them to talk to each other.

Bailee glanced at her watch and took her seat. Soon, Ian entered the room with Myles and an older man behind him. The pinched expression on Ian's face told her he wasn't too happy. The three of them were standing off in the corner, and appeared to be having a heated argument. Myles seemed to be the peacemaker in the situation, stepping between the two men seemingly to keep them apart.

Bailee watched the scene unfold with rapt interest, wondering what the conversation was about and why Ian was so angry. And when his other brothers, Drake and El, approached the trio, she went out on a limb and guessed the older man was Ian's father.

"Bailee, do you mind switching seats with Bee?"

Mia whispered in her ear, drawing her attention from the corner. "She's seated next to Ian on the other side of the table. She's allergic to seafood, and the guest on the other side of her ordered the salmon. I don't want her to have an allergic reaction."

"Sure," Bailee said. She motioned to the corner of the room with her head. "Is everything okay over there?"

Mia frowned. "I can't stand him. I don't even know why he's here. He'll only put a damper on my day. I'm going to tell my daddy to step in." Mia rushed off and pulled Dr. Solomon aside.

Bailee made her way over to her new seat, and sat next to an older couple. They made small talk for a few minutes. Soon, Dr. Solomon walked over to the Jackson crew, still in the corner. In seconds, they all dispersed and Ian slid into the seat next to her.

She glanced at him out of the corner of her eye. He was focused on something beyond the table. It wasn't Myles, who'd shot her a sad look. It wasn't Mia, who discreetly dabbed at her eye with Mason's handkerchief. Maybe it was his way of centering himself, of regaining his composure. The older woman was still chatting away, but Bailee's attention was on Ian.

She fought against her instinct to touch him. Because he wasn't her problem. He wasn't even her friend really, and she didn't want to overstep. She knew more than anyone the complicated dynamics of family relationships. Especially considering she hadn't spoken much to her mother after their brief argument that morning.

Sometime during dinner, after Dr. Solomon greeted everyone and told a funny story about Mia as a child, Ian finally seemed to jolt out of his funk. He also finally seemed to realize she was sitting next to him.

Ian turned to her, and Bailee sucked in a sharp breath in an attempt to assure herself that she could actually still breathe. Her heartbeat raced faster with every second his eyes were on hers. She fidgeted under his intense stare. People chatted around them as forks clattered against plates and soft jazz played through a surround sound system. But his eyes never left hers. Swallowing, she wondered what he planned to do. At the same time, she couldn't really process what was happening around her. She couldn't think about anything but how she felt under his heated gaze, how her body opened up in anticipation.

"Bailee." His voice was low, husky.

Goose bumps pricked her skin, and her body trembled with a need that consumed her. "Yes," she said.

"I told you to stop staring at me like that."

She laughed nervously. "You started it. Are you okay?"

"I'm fine. Can I ask you a question?"

Bailee nodded. "Shoot."

Ian leaned in, so close she gripped the edge of the table. "If I were to dip my fingers in your panties, would you be wet for me?"

Her breath caught in her throat. "Oh God."

"Answer the question, Bai."

Bailee made a heroic effort not to close her eyes against the rush of warmth flooding her body right that very moment. She bit her lip, sucked in a shaky breath and turned to him. With a smirk of her own, she tossed back, "Why don't you find out?"

Ian had Bailee where he wanted her, throbbing with need for him. Seeing his father had thrown a wrench in his initial plan to get her into the coatroom before dinner started. He'd spent the first part of dinner stewing, trying to forget the harsh words his father had tossed his way. But he wouldn't spend another minute thinking about him. The only person he wanted to focus on was Bailee.

Leaning in again, he whispered, "You're already wet and ready for me, aren't you, Bai?"

"Yes," she whispered.

"You're so wet, it won't take you a minute to scream out my name."

"Yes, Ian."

His hand skimmed her thigh and she gripped it, squeezing tight and stopping his movement. When his gaze met hers, she shook her head slowly.

He looked her up and down. She wore a strapless, navy blue dress and high-heeled sandals. "You look so beautiful. So mine."

"Yes."

"Find your words, Bailee."

She turned to him. "Ian, you can't do this here."

Lust coursed through him when she let out a tiny whimper and snapped her thighs closed. He slipped his hand through them anyway, prying them open. "Just say it. Tell me you love everything about this."

Bailee stood abruptly, knocking her leg against the table, then rushed out of the room. Ian glanced at the faces around the table. Everyone was still engrossed in their own conversations. Everyone except Mia.

His best friend narrowed her eyes on him and mouthed, *What the hell are you doing?*

Ian followed Bailee out of the room. Seconds later, Mia joined him in the hallway. "Mia, go back inside."

"What is going on?" she hissed. "What did you say to Bailee? She looked spooked."

"As usual, your mind is running away from you. Bailee is fine."

"Ian, tell the truth. Something is going on between you and Bailee."

"Go back into your rehearsal dinner with your guests. I'll check on Bailee."

Mia sighed. "I've been watching you. I'm so sorry about what happened with Dr. Law."

"I don't want to talk about it, Mia. My dad is always my dad, no matter who's around."

"What did he say to you?"

Ian didn't want to relive the moment. He just wanted to find Bailee. "He found out about my application to Doctors Without Borders and basically had a fit. He called me a joke. But what else is new, right?"

Mia's chin trembled and tears filled her eyes. "I didn't want to invite him. I swear, he's only here because of my parents."

Ian squeezed Mia's shoulders and kissed her forehead. "I'm fine. I should be used to it by now."

"He's still your father. Part of you will probably always want to please him."

In less than five minutes, his father had charged into the place and knocked him off his square. And it'd pissed him off that he'd let him. "I should know better, though."

"Aw, I'm so sorry." She sighed. "Find Bailee and come back to dinner. Are you sure nothing's going on between you two?"

Ian laughed. "You're relentless, Big Head. What would happen if I told you yes?"

Mia's eyes widened with shock. "Is that what you're telling me?"

"No. I just asked a question."

"Okay, so if you told me yes, I'd wonder why and how it happened. Then I guess I would have no choice but to accept it. With a firm warning not to hurt her," she added with a growl.

"Mia, I love you. Thank you for always having my back."

"Way to change the subject, Munch." Mia winked and pulled him to her in a tight embrace. "You know that will never change. Even once I'm married to Mason." She peered up at Ian. "I love you. You're my best friend, for life."

Ian snickered. "Or until Mason tells you to stop seeing me."

Mia smacked him on the arm. "Not going to happen."

"It won't." Bailee approached them, her arms crossed over her breasts. She looked at Ian. "My brother would never tell Mia to dump you."

"Bai? Are you good?" Mia asked, squeezing Bailee's hands. "I was worried when you stood and bolted out of the room. I blamed Ian."

"It wasn't his fault," Bailee said.

"See." Ian gestured toward Bailee. "She told you it wasn't my fault, so let's drop it."

"I just had to get some air." Bailee made a show of fanning herself. "It was kind of hot in there."

Mia nodded. "I know, right? I thought it was just me. I'm going to have the staff adjust the thermostat." Mia went back in the room, leaving Ian and Bailee in the hallway.

"Bailee, I'm sorry."

"For what?"

"I didn't mean to be so forward with you."

"Ian, don't apologize. You were right. I loved every minute of it."

A bolt of lust buzzed through him, and he stepped closer to her. Tracing the hem of her short dress, he hiked it up just a little. Her eyes were hazy with desire, and pride coursed through Ian. He'd made her feel that way. He'd succeeded in his quest to drive her crazy with need for him.

The air around them crackled, even as they heard loud laughter and the clink of glasses in the dining room behind them. Ian feathered a finger over her collarbone. "Your call. Tell me what you want me to do."

Bailee's mouth fell open. "Oh," she breathed. "I..." She swallowed visibly and shifted her weight from one foot to the other before dropping her gaze.

"Ian?" Mason poked his head out of the door. His eyes lit up when he saw Bailee. "Bai? There you are." He joined them in the hallway. "I wondered where you went. You got up so fast. Everything okay?"

Bailee nodded quickly. "I'm fine. I needed air."

And Ian needed to get her alone. Now. "How about I take you back up to the house?"

"I can't leave," Bai said. "And you can't, either."

"Yeah, Ian," Mason agreed, as he took Bailee's hand in his. "Come on, Bai. Mom and Dad want to take family portrait number three thousand, four hundred and fifty-seven." Bailee laughed and followed Mason into the dining room without another word.

After fifteen million toasts, countless hugs and one too many pinches on his cheeks, Ian finally made it back to the main house. He'd spent the rest of the night dodging his father and watching Bailee smile at everybody except him. Then he noticed her slip out of the room, never to return.

"You good, bruh?" Myles held the door open for him, waiting for Ian to step into the house before he closed it.

"I'm fine. Tired."

"Is it your back?"

Myles followed Ian into the kitchen. Ian knew his brother was concerned, but he wasn't in the mood to talk to anyone about anything. The fact that Bailee had left before they could finish the very important conversation they had started before Mason interrupted them, pissed him off. And to think, the day had started off with so much promise.

"Nah," Ian said, grabbing a couple of beers out of the refrigerator. He popped the tops off, and handed a bottle to Myles.

"Dad?"

Ian waved Myles off. "No." He refused to give his father any more power over his day. Hell, over his life. "Dad is being himself. Nothing to talk about."

Seeing his father that evening, listening to the man berate Ian for daring to spend time serving the community, had cemented his desire to do just that. The more his father pushed, the more Ian wanted to do the opposite. Not out of spite, but because it was right. Life was more than galas, remote island getaways, name-brand clothes and fund-raising for the sake of appearances. The people Ian wanted to help needed more than a check. They needed someone to care enough to be there, to give their time to causes dear to him.

"I'm sorry about tonight," Myles said. "I had no idea he would even be here so early."

Ian glanced at his brother. "Stop apologizing for him, Myles."

"Yes, Myles." His father stepped into the kitchen.

"No need to apologize for me. I'm not sorry for what I said."

"Exactly," Ian agreed, taking a long pull from the bottle. "Dad has never been sorry for anything he's said."

"Look, I'm tired of being in the middle of you two," Myles said.

"Nobody told you to stand in the middle," Ian told his brother. "I'm capable of talking—or not talking—to Dad."

"Myles, I need a moment with your brother."

Ian said his goodbyes to Myles before his brother left him to face his father.

"I believe we were having a conversation before you had your unfortunate temper tantrum earlier." Ian's father stepped up beside him. "I'm not happy with your plans."

"Well, it's a good thing you're not living my life," Ian retorted.

"Watch how you talk to me, Ian." The tone in his dad's voice was unmistakable. When he was a kid, he knew that particular tone meant he should tread carefully. But Ian didn't care.

"When are you going to watch how you talk to me? I'm not sure why you even care what I do anyway. You never did before. The only time you even looked my way was when you needed me to escort a colleague's daughter to some gala or show up to one of your award ceremonies like a good little son. The fact that you're upset with me because I'm choosing to do more with my medical degree than simply earn a paycheck is ridiculous."

His father leaned forward, his hands braced on the

counter between them. "I think you better consider your next words very carefully."

"Why?" Ian had never heard his father raise his voice, but he always remembered the fear that raced through his veins at the idea that he had upset his dad. But today? He wouldn't give Dr. Law the satisfaction.

"I've worked very hard to ensure that my sons would be the best. You had the best education, the best of everything. I've groomed all of you to be strong members of the community. After everything I've done, I'll be damned if you and your brothers think you're going to disrespect me and speak to me like I'm some punk off the street. Now, you will respect me."

"Respect is earned, Dr. Law," Ian said between clenched teeth. He'd wanted to hurt his father by calling him by the name everybody else did. But his dad didn't even flinch.

"That's right. My name is Dr. Law. You would do well to remember that."

Ian snorted. "It used to upset me, how you treat us. I wondered why you made such a big deal about us playing sports, but never showed up to a game. Then I wondered why you stayed on us about our grades, but never attended a parent-teacher conference. I always knew that you thought you were better than most people. I just didn't realize that *we* were those people. You treat us like we're nothing more than the people who work for you. I'm not your assistant, I'm your son." Ian slammed his bottle onto the granite and stepped around the countertop until he was face-to-face with his father. "It would be nice if you remembered that, too." Without another word, he walked away.

Ian raced up the stairs, taking two steps at a time. In the past, any argument with his father ended with him drowning his sorrows with booze, a bike ride, food or women. It was too late to ride, the beer he'd had did nothing for his temper, he wasn't hungry and the only woman he wanted would rather smile at stupid-ass Charles than him. He rounded the corner, mumbling a string of curses about his life at that very moment when he saw her, standing in front of...*my door.* Bailee's head was down, and she seemed to be talking to someone. *Herself?*

Then she looked up, her eyes meeting his. "Ian." She twisted her purse in her hand.

"Bailee."

She tucked a strand of hair behind her ear. "I'm sorry about..." Her voice trailed off, as if she were trying to figure out what to say.

With every second that passed of her not speaking, not doing anything, Ian grew more impatient. Bailee wanted him to make the next move, and under normal circumstances he would have no problem doing so. But this wasn't a normal situation. Bailee wasn't just a random woman. And Ian wasn't in the mood to try to figure her out. He'd had enough.

"Bailee, if you have something to say, you should say it now. Because I'm tired, and I'm ready to put the day behind me." He brushed past her, pulled out his key card and unlocked his door. But before he went inside his room, he turned to her. "I'll see you tomorrow, B—"

"Ian, shut up." Bailee looked at him then, fire blazing in her brown eyes. "I'm sorry for skipping out on you tonight. I know what I said last night. I know what we talked about this morning. But, Ian..." She stepped forward, until they were nearly touching. Peering up at him, she placed her hand over his heart. His eyes flickered from her brown eyes to her full lips. "When you touched me, I lost myself again. I can't seem to help myself with you. I'm so turned on by you, so consumed with you…it scares me, honestly. At the same time, I just want to feel it."

His mouth was on hers in an instant. The minute their lips touched, he groaned. Anyone could turn down the hallway or step out of their room and see them, but he didn't care. Because she tasted like a dream. Her body molded to his like they were meant to be like this with each other. He couldn't explain it, but he wouldn't question it. Without breaking the kiss, Ian pulled her into his room and kicked the door shut.

Chapter 11

God, I can't breathe.

Ian was on the edge, dangling by a thread. And Bailee was holding the string. Everything about her was too much. Because this? Her? He'd never wanted anyone so much his body ached with need. Never before had he wanted to claim any woman. Not until Bailee Sanders came into his life. Not when she kissed him with a fire that matched his own. Not when her scent wrapped around him like a vine. She was so beautiful, and felt so good in his arms. And he wanted to give her everything he had so she'd know that no one would ever make her feel the way he did.

Her skin was so warm, so smooth he couldn't stop touching her. He ran his fingers back and forth over her neck, across her shoulders and down her arms. The way she shivered, the way she reacted to his touch by leaning closer told him that she wanted his hands on her.

Finally, breaking the kiss, he sucked in a deep breath and leaned his forehead against hers. "Damn, I need it."

Ian didn't even realize he'd said it out loud until she said, "Then take it."

He didn't need another invitation. In less than a minute, with her dress now in a puddle on the floor, he ordered, "Bra. Take it off."

Bailee let out a low moan, but did as she was told. With her eyes locked on his, she unhooked the front clasp and let it fall open, then down to the floor.

"So beautiful," he whispered.

Her nipples were hard, ready for his attention. He cupped her breasts in his hands, placed soft, wet kisses down her neck until he took one hard bud into his mouth. Her knees buckled, but he snaked an arm around her waist to hold her upright.

"Ian, you're killing me."

"Join the club," he murmured against her skin.

"What are you doing to me?"

"Patience, Bai. I'm not done touching you, tasting you." Her breath caught in her throat, and he smiled. "I'll give you what you really want in due time." Ian traced his lips over her ear before he bit down on it lightly. "You're mine." He didn't even bother to add "for the night" to his statement because he doubted he would be satisfied with one night.

"Oh," she breathed.

He stepped back and raked his gaze over her. "Panties. Take them off."

Once again, Bailee did as she was told, sliding the thin, lacy fabric over her hips and down her legs slowly.

His breath hitched in his throat at the sight of her, naked and ready to give herself to him. A low growl pierced the air, and he realized it was him. Not her.

He was so hot for her, so consumed by her beauty, he couldn't think or see straight.

"Come here," he commanded.

Bailee bit her bottom lip and approached him. "Your turn," she said, her voice low.

Ian gripped her hips, nipped her chin, her collarbone, her shoulders, as she removed his shirt. She pushed his pants and underwear over his hips.

"Now we're even." She tugged him to her, kissing him passionately.

Lifting her in his arms, he carried her over to the bed and lowered her to the mattress. He kissed his way down her body, until he was at the apex of her thighs. She squirmed under him, but he held her still. Then he darted his tongue out to taste her finally, closing his eyes at the feel of her against his tongue.

"Bailee," he murmured against her bundle of nerves. "Give me everything. Let go."

It didn't take long before Bailee stiffened, and then shuddered with her orgasm as he worshipped her with his tongue. When she collapsed against the bed, he slid a condom on and crawled up her body.

Bailee wrapped her legs around his waist and pulled him into a possessive kiss. "Now," she whispered.

He bit her chin lightly before he pushed inside her warmth, swallowing her gasp with another searing kiss. Ian could feel her muscles tense as he moved inside her. Her stomach quivered, her legs trembled, her arms flexed…every part of her responded to him, to what he did to her and how they were together. Which was good. So good. And he was close. So close to exploding inside her.

Need twisted in his spine as they raced to completion. Bailee let out a tiny little whimper, then a sexy purr right before she came, unspooling around him. She groaned his name over and over again as she climaxed. Then he was done, coming so long and hard he could hear nothing but the wild pulse of his heartbeat in his ears.

Minutes later, Ian rolled over to his back. After he discarded the condom, he climbed back in bed and pulled her against him. She burrowed into his side as if she belonged there. And, he thought, maybe she did. They didn't speak for a while, and Ian thought she might've fallen asleep.

"Ian?" Bailee traced the muscles of his stomach with her fingers.

"Hmm?"

"Thank you."

His eyes popped open, and he leaned back to peer at her face. Frowning, he said, "I'm not sure how to take that."

Bailee giggled and dropped her forehead onto his chest. "It's not what you think."

"What do you think I think?" Ian wasn't even sure what he thought she meant by her words. He just knew it didn't make him feel as good as it should have.

Shrugging, Bailee perched her chin on his chest. "I'm just glad that you didn't give up on me. That's why I'm thanking you."

"Ah, I get it now."

"I'm very stubborn. It takes a lot to get me to budge."

Now it was his turn to laugh. "I figured that out… Aries."

"Oh no. I hated that I gave you that name. It was so obviously fake. And even when you called me on it, I couldn't bring myself to let it go. See! Stubborn."

"True." He tapped her nose. "But I like that about you."

"You do?"

"Yes, I do." He rubbed her bottom lip, smiling when her eyes fluttered closed.

"Ian?" she whispered.

"Yes?" He leaned in, circled her nose with his before he brushed his mouth against hers.

"I should probably go," she said. "We have a long day tomorrow."

"Bailee?" Ian sucked her bottom lip into his mouth until she groaned. "Just so you know, I have no plans to let you out of my sight anytime soon. I'm not done with you yet."

"Oh my God."

"Bailee."

Her name on Ian's lips, in his low and husky voice, made it worse. It made her want him even more. Which was impossible, right?

"I can't," she breathed.

Bailee had already climaxed three times. There was no way she'd be able to do it again. But his touch was so gentle, his tongue was so talented, she wanted to weep.

"I meant to ask you if you finished your smutty book?"

His voice was so quiet, so muffled, she wasn't sure she'd heard him right. "Huh?"

She felt his body tremble with laughter, right before he drew her clit into his mouth.

"Oh God."

"You said that already."

Technically, she hadn't said that. But the argument died on her lips as he licked and sucked, driving her crazy with his attention, with the way he worshipped her body.

"I did finish it," she managed to say. She clenched the sheets in her hands.

"Tell me about it."

Bailee couldn't concentrate on anything, let alone a book that had held her attention a few days ago but now paled in comparison to the real deal. Because Ian was the stuff romantic heroes were made of.

"Uh, it's a friends-to-lovers book."

"What's that?"

"Oh." She gripped his shoulders and rolled her hips in time with his movements. "Uh, it's when the hero and the heroine are friends first, then they fall..." Two fingers dipped inside her. She moaned, unable to finish her thought.

"In love," he finished for her.

"Yes." She dug her fingernails into his skin. "Ian, please."

Still, he didn't stop and Bailee was delirious. In the best way, of course. And soon, she was riding the waves of pleasure over and over again.

When she came down from the high of her orgasm, she felt boneless, weak. Woozy. She could barely keep her eyes open, but didn't want to fall asleep, either.

"Sleep now," she heard Ian whisper before sleep pulled her under.

Several hours later, after an early-morning orgasm, Bailee tiptoed out of Ian's room, careful not to slam the door. She'd added a lot of things to her forgotten bucket list, but the walk of shame wasn't one of them. Bailee still couldn't believe she'd let Ian talk her into spending the night with him. Well, the lure of multiple orgasms had definitely helped make her decision.

Bailee rushed toward her suite, praying that no one

would see her. Because if someone caught a glimpse of her, they'd know what she'd been doing. She'd seen herself in one of Ian's mirrors before she walked out of his room, and "hot mess" had been the first phrase to come to mind.

"Bai?"

Shit. Bailee turned slowly, and smiled brightly at her future sister-in-law. "Mia? Hi!" That *hi* came out just a little too loud.

Mia frowned. "Where are you going?"

Bailee scrunched up her nose. "Um, to my room."

"From where? You look… Didn't you have that dress on last night?"

"Oh." Bailee dropped her head and smoothed a hand over her dress. "Well, I had to run out this morning and just threw it back on."

Mia tilted her head, her eyes narrowing. "Really?"

Nodding, Bailee said, "Yes. I had to run to my car." It was officially official. Bailee was a horrible liar.

"Were you with Ian?"

"What?" Bailee blurted out. "I mean, why would you ask me that?"

Mia sighed, shaking her head. "I'm going to kill him." She turned on her heel and started toward the other end of the hallway, where Ian's room was.

Bailee caught up to Mia and grabbed her arm, halting her movement. "Mia, wait. Please. Don't say anything to Ian."

Mia folded her arms over her chest. Her mouth was a grim line. "I told him to leave you alone."

"Seriously, Mia. I am a grown woman. And why would you assume I was with Ian? I could have been with Myles. Or any one of the groomsmen."

Mia raised a brow. "Are you really going to lie to me

after I've caught you with bed hair, smeared makeup and swollen lips?"

"Fine. I was with Ian."

"That settles it, then. I'm going to kill him."

"Mia, stop. I was hoping you'd be a sister I could talk to about things like this. I don't need another overprotective person in my life."

"Oh, Bailee." Mia's eyes softened. "That's not my intention. It's just that I know Ian."

"And you told me he was a good man."

"Yeah, he's one of the best men I know. But you're Mason's sister. If things don't work out, it will be extremely awkward."

"Why? We're not together. It's just sex."

Mia gasped. "Wow, do you really believe that? I've actually seen the way he looks at you, and the way you pretend not to look at him. It's not just sex."

"It is. So I'd appreciate it if you don't tell Mase. I don't want him to worry."

"I'm worried." Mia rubbed her face. "But…I won't say anything. Just be careful. Sometimes, even with the best intentions, things can take a turn so quickly. Look what happened with me and your brother. I didn't go to my friend's wedding thinking I'd meet my future husband."

"There is nothing to worry about, Mia," Bailee assured her. "Ian and I have an understanding." She wrapped an arm around Mia's shoulders. "Now, you have to get ready to marry my brother. And I have to get showered and ready for my hair appointment."

Bailee hugged Mia and hurried off to her room. *So much for discreet.*

Ian strolled into the bridal suite at his designated arrival time. Since he didn't need to be primped and prodded, he was told to arrive fully dressed. He draped his tuxedo jacket over a chair and headed toward the bathroom.

"I'm here," he announced, his hand over his eyes. "I hope everyone is dressed."

"It's just me," Mia said.

Ian peeked through his fingers. Once he was satisfied he wouldn't see his best friend in her underwear, he dropped his hand. "You're beautiful, Big Head."

Mia stood at the mirror, dabbing a tissue under her eyes.

"Are you crying?" Ian joined her at the mirror. "What's wrong?"

"Just emotional." Mia fanned her face. The makeup artist had already done her up, and her hair was pinned in tiny ringlets with little silver clips. The sink was crowded with various makeup containers, powder, blue sponges and white towels.

"Why are you by yourself?" he asked.

"I knew you wouldn't be late, so I asked the ladies to leave me alone for a bit."

Ian leaned against the sink, his eyes on his best friend. "You good? Need me to bust you out of here?"

Mia let out a half wail, half laugh. "No. I'm fine. Just nervous."

"That's normal, from what I hear. It supposedly goes away once you see Mase."

"Since when do you know anything about jitters?"

"Since my best friend asked me to be her man of honor."

During the rehearsal the day before, Ian had agreed to walk down the aisle like everyone else. But he'd drawn a hard line at handling the bustle thing in front of the church. Instead, Bee would take charge of that job, since she'd designed the dress. Also, he'd told Mia that he would not, under any circumstances, hold her bouquet.

Mia eyed him in the mirror. "What if I'm not a good wife, Munch? I love him so much. I want to be good for him. I want to be the wife my mother is to Daddy."

"First of all, you're not your mother. And he's not Pop. The only person you can be is Mia, the woman he actually proposed to."

She shot him a lopsided smile. "I knew you'd be what I needed right now. See? You're a good man of honor."

Ian shook his head. "Yeah, there is a first and last time for everything."

She laughed for real this time. "You're crazy."

"Seriously, you're a beautiful bride. Mason is lucky to have you, Mia."

She hugged him, and he let her. After today, things would change between them, despite what she'd told him yesterday. And he'd expect nothing less. It was time for Mia and Mason to make a life together. "Love you, Munch."

"Love you, too, Big Head." After a moment, Mia pulled away, sniffling. He handed her a tissue. "Stop crying. I'm no expert, but doesn't that make your eye shadow run?"

"You mean mascara?" She bumped into him with her hip. "You need help. Speaking of, I ran into Bailee this morning."

Busted already. Ian dropped his head. "Really?"

"Ian, what are you doing?" Mia asked.

He met his friend's worried gaze. "What do you mean?"

"She's Mason's sister!"

"So?"

"Ian, what if things don't work out between you? Don't you think it will be awkward at my baby's christening when we name you both godparents?"

"You're pregnant?" Ian asked.

"Shh," Mia said, scanning the area. "We haven't told anyone yet."

Ian smiled. "Get the hell out of here. You're having a baby?"

"Yes, why do you think I've been crying so much?"

"Hey." Ian held his arms out in surrender. "I didn't want to say anything, but I wondered why you were being a crybaby. But then I read an article about wedding jitters."

"You're the first person I've told," Mia said. "I haven't even told my sisters." Ian wondered if Mason had told Bailee, but Mia answered that question when she said, "Mase hasn't even told Bailee."

"Okay."

"So you see why I'm panicking, right?"

Ian shrugged. "No. It's not a relationship, Mia. Bailee and I are just having fun."

"Why her?"

"She's beautiful. Why not?"

"Again, she's Mason's sister."

"And? We're both adults capable of having a fling."

Mia pinned him with her *don't play with me* glare. He stepped back out of habit. "I don't think it's *just* a fling. Like I told her, I've seen the way you look at her."

He sighed. He hadn't wanted to tell Mia about New Orleans, but he did. When he finished his story, Mia gaped at him. "Close your mouth, Mia."

She snapped her mouth shut. "Oh no. You and

Bailee? She's the woman from New Orleans? You just made my point."

"How so? If anything, that should prove that we can peacefully coexist in a family situation."

"Except you didn't peacefully coexist. You took her to bed again!"

Ian turned to Mia, squeezed her arms. "I love you for caring about me. I love you for caring about Bailee. But we're fine. We both know what this is. Now, suck up those emotions and finish getting dressed. I'm getting you down that aisle no matter what." He kissed Mia's brow and stepped away from her, pointing at her. "Last chance to bail."

Mia laughed. "No bailing."

"Good to know. I'll go find your entourage."

Ian left Mia in the bathroom, and tried not to think about his best friend's warnings. Because after last night, after spending the night wrapped up in Bailee, he knew Mia was right.

There was a need in him that compelled him to go toward Bailee, to be near her. He'd told her that first night that he couldn't get enough of her. At the time, it was just something he'd said in the heat of the moment. Now he knew that it was more than that. He couldn't stop wanting her.

Which meant *peacefully coexisting* was a long shot.

Chapter 12

Mason and Mia were married at sunset, on a bluff overlooking Lake Michigan, surrounded by family and friends. The bride and groom shared personal vows that made every woman, and some men, tear up. Bailee swore she'd even seen Ian wiping a tear from his eyes. Once the pastor said, "Introducing Mr. and Mrs. Mason and Mia Sanders," the crowd erupted into loud cheers.

The ceremony was beautiful, and the little touches Mia had insisted on were well worth the trouble. The bridesmaids looked lovely in their coral gowns, and the groomsmen were handsome in navy blue tuxedos. But only one man had held her attention through the entire ceremony.

Ian commanded the room as he'd strolled down the aisle by himself. Although his tuxedo was gray, to set him apart, Mia had arranged for Ian's suit to have pinstripes. He also didn't wear a vest like the other groomsmen. He looked so good, so smooth with his swagger and his dimpled grin, she had to bite her lip to stifle the groan that seemed to always want to escape when she saw him.

Even now, as they posed for pictures, she felt her face flush as she imagined him inside her, his hands roaming her body. She wondered if he felt it, too. Was he just as aroused as she was simply from the nearness of him?

"It's driving you insane, isn't it?" Ian whispered in her ear, jolting her out of her thoughts.

Bailee bit the inside of her cheek. His scent washed over her, like fresh water and woods. She turned her attention back to the photographer in front of them. "You should probably go back to your spot. On the other side," she muttered.

"I'm supposed to be here, right behind you." He leaned forward and whispered against her ear, "I can't keep my eyes off you, Bailee. The way those pants hug your hips, the tiny glimpse of your breast in that jacket. I've never been so attracted, so hot for someone in a tuxedo before."

She fought the urge to lean into him. Smile. Click. Smile. *Oh my, what am I going to do?* "Really?" she said.

"When I saw you standing at the end of the aisle, next to Mason, I wanted to pull you onto my lap and let you ride me." Smile. Click.

His words…the way he talked to her drove her wild with anticipation. Ian hadn't even touched her yet, but she felt his fingers on her skin as if he had. She wanted him in a way that was foreign to her. No man had ever made her want to abandon her code of conduct just to get a taste of him.

Maybe it was the champagne? Or the sweet treats Mia had brought in for the wedding party to enjoy before and immediately after the ceremony? Bailee had tried them all—chocolate-covered strawberries, chocolate pretzels, chocolate almond bark, chocolate and caramel apple slices. Or better yet, it might just be the wedding effect. *Yep, that's definitely it.*

The romantic setting, the candles, the sweet floral fragrance...no wonder she seemed to be in a perpetual state of arousal. Mia and Mason had set the mood with their whimsical and romantic decor and heartfelt vows and alcohol and chocolate. Yes, it was a flimsy excuse at best, but if she kept repeating it to herself, she might actually believe it.

She sucked in a breath. Funny pose. Click. "Ian." She looked around at the other members of the bridal party, but everyone was in their own little world, trying not to look bored at the countless pictures Mia wanted them to take.

"Don't worry about them. Just focus on me. Pretend you're not wearing panties under your pants."

"I'm not."

A soft burst of air in her ear, followed by his low groan, made her want to climb him like a tree, touch him all over, shower him with kisses. "You're so damn beautiful, Bai. So sexy." His voice was raw, hoarse. His hand brushed against her behind, and she pushed back against it. She felt him then, hard against her butt, ready for her.

The photographer ordered the pairs to act like they could stand each other, and Ian snaked his hand around her waist, pulling her close to him. With his hand splayed across her stomach, she plastered another smile on her face. Click.

The feel of his breath on her skin, the brush of his lips on her ear and finally the back of her neck ramped up her arousal even more. She tried to wrench herself out of his hold, but he held her in place. "Don't move."

Weird face. Click. "Ian, you have to stop. Someone will notice." She tilted her head back to look at him. They held each other's gazes for a beat, before his dropped to her mouth. Click.

The sound of the camera drew her attention back to the photographer. And when Mia announced she wanted to take pictures with just the women, Bailee let out a relieved breath.

An hour later, they walked the lit path toward the reception area. The music was playing in the distance, and guests could be heard talking, laughing and even singing with the music.

Thank goodness for traditional head table etiquette. Bailee took her seat next to Mason, away from Ian. Dinner went by in a flash, and before she knew it, it was her turn to toast her brother and new sister.

Bailee stood, and glanced at the crowd before her. She started her toast with a funny story about the time Mason tricked her into cursing in front of her parents. And then she paid him back by telling their mom that he'd taken the car on a joyride while they were asleep one night. The guests laughed.

"Mason, I love you," Bailee said, swallowing around a lump that had formed in her throat. "We've always been there for one another. I don't expect that will change, but I'm glad that you have someone else looking out for you now. Someone who will care for you, someone who will love you through every hardship, every victory you face for as long as you both shall live. To the bride and the groom." The crowd clapped and Mason stood, pulling her into a tight hug. He whispered he loved her in her ear, and she took her seat.

Ian stood next, and told the story of how Mia and Mason had met. Bailee watched him woo the crowd and noticed quite a few women in the audience fixated on him while he gave his toast. Then his gaze softened and he smiled at Mia.

"Seriously, my life wouldn't have been as bright without you. I'm thankful that you and your family accepted me into your life and immediately treated me like I was one of your own." His eyes then focused on the table where his father sat with his family, before he turned his attention back to Mia. "If I had one wish for you, it was always for you to be happy. And I can see that Mason does that for you. Love you, Big Head. Mason, welcome to the fold." Mia wiped tears from her eyes and stood, embracing Ian. When she was done, Ian shook Mason's hand, before giving him a quick man hug.

The bridal party took the floor next in the traditional bridal party dance. Bailee fought back a smile as Ian approached her with a sexy grin on his face. He pulled her close, and they swayed to the music.

She wrapped her arms around his neck. "Nice toast. Touching."

Ian shrugged. "It was nothing but the truth."

"I have to admit, I was a little worried when I saw you and Mia interacting. But now I can see that you genuinely love her like family."

"She is my family. I'd do pretty much anything for her."

"I can see that. It's great."

"Bailee, I don't know what to do with this."

Jarred by his change in subject, she asked, "What?"

"This desire that I have to find a dark room somewhere and have my way with you."

When she bit her lip, his eyes darkened. Bailee couldn't look away from the hungry look in his eyes if she wanted to. She was thoroughly under the control of his heated gaze. It went on like that for a few moments, neither of them looking away. The air around them crackled with electricity.

"Where would you take me?" she asked, finally.

"There's a coatroom near the front of the building. I'd take you there. Or the bathroom toward the back of the building. Anywhere I can touch you, taste you."

Bailee wanted to tell him she would follow him wherever he wanted to go, but the song ended and Mia and her sisters pulled Ian away for more pictures. While Ian laughed with his family, Bailee took a moment to speak to several of her own family members. Soon, she'd relaxed with them, reminiscing about old times and even making preliminary plans for a reunion next summer.

The DJ cooperated with her when he shifted the music from love songs to party anthems. When her favorite song blasted through the speakers, she used the music to center her, to keep her mind off Ian.

Bailee allowed Charles to pull her onto the dance floor for a few songs. Mason joined them, and they spent a few minutes doing old dances and going down the Soul Train Line.

A little while later, the waitstaff served the wedding cake. Bailee snagged a piece off the tray, thanked the young waiter and immediately dipped her fork in and stuffed a fat piece into her mouth.

"You like sweets, don't you?" Ian said, taking the seat next to her, his own piece of cake in hand. But he'd grabbed a slice of the chocolate, while she preferred the white cake.

Bailee nodded. "I do."

"You remind me of Love."

She knew that Love was his brother Drake's wife, but the woman didn't look like she had a sweet tooth, let alone a baby. "Really? She's so tiny."

"Genetics, I guess."

Bailee looked out on the dance floor and noticed Drake and Love swaying to the music. "They look happy."

Ian watched them for a minute. "They are. I'm happy for them."

"Your father didn't stay long."

Earlier, Bailee had seen Dr. Law leave the reception after saying his goodbyes to the Solomon family. She'd also noticed Ian deliberately ignore his father when he'd walked out.

"He never does," Ian grumbled.

Sensing he needed a subject change, she pointed to his cake. "How's the chocolate?"

He turned up his lips. "I don't like it. Should have picked up the white cake."

"We can share." She took another bite of her cake. "If you want."

He scooted his chair closer and took a piece of her cake. "It is good," he said. "We should get another piece, don't you think?"

Bailee was either greedy or she just wanted to spend more time with Ian, because she agreed. Ian waved over a server and pulled another piece of cake off the tray.

"So," she said after a few moments. "The coatroom. Where is it?"

A slow smile spread across his face, and he pointed to a closed door on the other side of the massive space. She stood on shaky legs and made her way over, turning back for just a second to find him staring at her with his fork still in midair. She winked and then continued her journey.

Inside the coatroom, she waited. It didn't take long—Ian joined her within three minutes. He reached out, traced the opening of her suit jacket.

Bailee held out her hands. "We're here. Now what?"

He smirked. "Let's start with you stepping out of those pants and bending over. I want you to let me kiss every inch of your body. I want to hear your low moans and know that I'm the one driving you crazy, that I'm the only one who can make you feel like this"

Quite a while later, he helped her get dressed while she fixed her hair the best she could with limited lighting and lack of a mirror. They exited the coatroom and she hurried toward the restroom, hoping no one noticed what she suspected was a dazed look in her eyes, or the sated, yet cocky gleam in his.

"Superman or Batman?" Ian asked.

"Superman, of course," Bailee answered with no hesitation. "I can't stand Batman with his punk self."

Ian agreed with Bailee. Batman sucked.

"But if I had to choose comic universes?" Bailee added. "I'm shouting Team Marvel all day, every day."

Ian pointed at Bailee before giving her a high five. "That's what I'm talking about."

They'd just finished a round of This or That, and he'd learned quite a bit about her in the five minutes he had to bombard her with questions. Bailee loved horror movies and preferred beer over wine. She was a morning person, would rather listen to music than play it and shared his love of all things Marvel.

"So you were in a cotillion in high school?" Bailee asked after Ian had fed her another bite of the cake he'd boxed up from the reception. They were entangled in each other on her bed, after making love on her private balcony.

Ian nodded. During her turn in the game, he'd admitted that his disdain for formal dances had a lot to do with the annual ball his father had made him participate in during high school. "We were all forced to go. It's sort of a rite of passage for my father's set of acquaintances. They've been doing it for years, under the guise of scholarship and charity."

Every year, the wealthy African American society of Ann Arbor hosted a Beau-Debutante ball for high school seniors. The goal of the program was to develop youth transitioning from one life stage to another, and to prepare them to be contributing members of society. The organization required each participant to attend workshops on civic involvement, etiquette or social graces, and charitable activities. They'd competed in several categories, such as talent and entrepreneurship. Because his father served as a board member, Ian and his siblings were expected to participate. Ian had resented the experience, but he'd donned his formal wear and performed the waltz with his date anyway.

"And you don't believe that's the motive?" she asked.

"No, I don't."

"Why not? You mentioned scholarship was part of it. That's a good cause. So many young people can't afford to attend college."

"I know," he said. "But they awarded the big scholarship to someone who didn't need the money, to someone whose father is the CEO of a Fortune 500 company. It would have made more sense to choose someone who couldn't afford to attend a university."

"True, but it's not like there aren't other charities to support. The ball and the mission are obviously important to your father. Why else would he insist you participate?"

"My father doesn't do anything out of the goodness of his heart. He does things that benefit his bank account and his reputation." All of the charities, the surgeries and the lectures only served one purpose. Personal gain.

"That's pretty awful."

He brushed the backs of his fingers across her cheek. "He's not a nice guy."

Ian didn't know how they'd started talking about his family, but he found that she was easy to converse with. She didn't judge him, and when he talked, she listened intently. In so many ways, his interactions with Bailee reminded him of his friendship with Mia, with the added bonus of a physical attraction. It was the best of both worlds. Something that he hadn't realized he'd wanted in his life until now.

"My parents belong to a similar society in Columbus. Mason and I grew up attending the community and volunteer events. It was all about the club, as they called it." She held up air quotes when she said "club." "It's the reason I hate long, poofy dresses to this day. New season, new ball gown. I'm glad Mason asked me to be his best woman. It was cool to wear something totally different and unexpected. But don't tell him I told you that, because I gave him a hard time about it initially."

Ian laughed. "The tux you wore suited you."

"Bee is very talented." She rolled over on her stomach, and he smacked her butt.

When Ian had spotted Bailee earlier, in her suit, he'd nearly tripped on the aisle runner. The navy blue tuxedo she'd worn was simple, fitted. Bee had cut it in such a way that he'd been able to see Bailee's ample curves. Bailee had rocked the look like a runway model, in four-inch coral sandals.

"That she is," he agreed, running a finger down her spine. "But I don't think it was the suit as much as the woman wearing it."

Bailee smiled and rolled over on her back. She had on his dress shirt and nothing else. He couldn't resist pulling it open to bare her breasts to him. Leaning down, he took one pebbled bud into his mouth.

"Ian?"

He glanced up at her. "Hmm?"

"What are we doing?"

The serious tone in her voice told him he'd better stop and listen. He sat up and met her gaze. "What do you mean?"

Bailee shrugged. "This. The fact that we keep having sex like we're not leaving tomorrow."

Those two words—*leaving* and *tomorrow*—weren't ones he wanted to hear in that moment. As far as he was concerned, he hadn't spent enough time with her. Still, she had a point. The wedding was over, and he'd be making the drive back home to Ann Arbor in a few short hours.

She sighed. "We've already established that I've never been in a casual relationship. And I'm not asking you to be more," she added in a rush when he opened his mouth to respond.

"Can I ask you a question?"

She nodded.

"What kind of man do you think I am?"

"I don't know." She gestured to him. "You're Ian."

"Who do you think Ian is?"

"Initially, I thought you were a player. I figured one-night stands might not be so uncommon for you."

She wasn't wrong. He'd done a lot of playing the field in his early twenties. In the past, he wouldn't have thought twice about taking a beautiful woman back to his place and waving goodbye in the morning. But the man he was now wasn't interested in meaningless flings with women he couldn't stand in the light of day. At the same time, he couldn't say he was ready for a commitment.

"I'm not that man anymore," he admitted.

"I know." She averted her gaze. "Just in this short time, I can see that you're a man who knows what he wants, and takes steps to get it. But you're not conceited or selfish. You're not the typical trust fund baby that I've run across, rich and entitled. You don't treat me like I'm incapable of making adult decisions. I appreciate that."

"Is that how Brandon was?"

"Sort of. We grew up taking simple things for granted. But I quickly learned that life isn't easy for everyone."

"That's true."

"Brandon doesn't get it, though. He didn't learn that lesson."

"Sometimes I think that you have to take yourself out of a situation to appreciate where you were. Which is why I applied for Doctors Without Borders."

Her eyes widened. "You did? That's great."

Ian smiled at her enthusiastic response. "I think so, too. I'm excited."

"No, Ian, that's awesome. It takes a lot of guts to step outside of our comfort zone and change our circumstances. You're doing things that people just talk about. I knew so many nurses who trotted out the idea of volunteering or doing meaningful jobs, with no intention of ever sending in the application. And you've done the hard part."

"I've wanted to do it for a while. When I finished my residency, I spent some time going over my options. For a long time, I wondered if I even wanted to be a doctor. Volunteering in New Orleans, though, confirmed I do. I don't want to spend my days performing cosmetic surgeries for people like my mother."

"Ouch," she muttered.

"Enough about my parents. Back to the topic at hand."

"Right. I'm just going to be blunt."

He frowned. "Okay."

"I enjoy spending time with you. But I'm not ready for a relationship. I don't even have a job. I have no idea what I want to do with my life right now."

"Does this mean I have to get out now?"

She giggled. "No. I just felt like you should know where I'm coming from."

He cupped the back of her neck and pulled her into a quick kiss. "I'm okay with that." He patted his lap. "Come here."

Bailee straddled his lap. "So we're good?"

"I thought you said you didn't do casual relationships?" Ian gripped her thighs and pulled her closer.

"I don't. But I'm going to go out on a limb and categorize this as one moment in time. And after tonight, I think we should just be friends."

"Friends. So no regrets?"

She shook her head. "No regrets," she repeated.

He pushed his shirt off her shoulders and kissed her smooth skin. "Then we're definitely good."

Chapter 13

Bailee had spent a lot of time pretending. She'd pretended she was happy with Brandon, pretended she loved her job, pretended she didn't want to eat that glazed doughnut for breakfast instead of the cup of yogurt she ate and pretended she knew exactly what she was doing when she'd decided to have sex with Ian. Again. And again.

The bravado she'd managed to pull out of her behind while in Traverse City faded as soon as he'd walked out of her room the morning after the wedding. They didn't say dramatic goodbyes or make promises to look each other up in the future. He didn't save his phone number into her phone or even ask for hers. The sexual bubble they'd been in just popped. And her good mood flew away with it.

Telling Ian that she didn't want a relationship was the right thing to do. Even though it wasn't the complete truth. Bailee knew she needed time to be by herself, but her feelings weren't as clear-cut as she'd like them to be. Ian understood her in a way no one had before. He got her. And that made him even more attractive to her.

Giving voice to her true feelings wasn't something she had been prepared to do at that point. So she'd decided to play it cool and *pretend* she could do casual with him. She'd chosen to settle for the physical connection between them. And now she was left with an ache in her stomach that couldn't be soothed. Not with a doughnut, not with a book and not with her vibrator.

"Girl, I told you to eat that damn doughnut." April yanked her earbuds out and jogged in place, waiting for Bailee to catch up to her. "You look pitiful."

It had been a week since her brother and Mia tied the knot. One week since Ian had made love to her so hard, so good that she couldn't remember sex before him.

Bailee bent over, sucking in several deep breaths. "I'm not pitiful. You're running too fast. I told you I ate a lot last week."

"I call BS. All the sex you had last week should have burned those calories right off."

"Shut up." Bailee shoved her friend playfully. "It wasn't a lot of sex."

"Seriously. You have to get your head back in the game, Bai. Your interview is in three hours."

With the decision made to finally move to Michigan, Bailee had spent the last several days cleaning out her house. She'd hired a property management company to handle the rental contract and maintenance on the condo, and rented a storage unit to store her furniture and other items. Bailee had arrived on April's doorstep, suitcases and boxes in tow, last night. And her best friend had showed her to the guest room where Bailee would stay until she found her own place, and then demanded details on the wedding week and Ian.

"I still don't understand how you ended things with him," April said. "You just chucked up the deuces and kicked him out of your room?"

Bailee finally plopped down on a nearby bench. "April, we're not a couple. We talked about it and agreed to leave our fling in Traverse City."

"And New Orleans."

Bailee glared at her bestie. "You make me sick."

Shrugging, April bent and stretched. "What happens when you see him again? Especially now that you're here and applying for a job at his hospital."

Bailee had thought about what she'd say when she saw Ian again. The only strategy she could come up with was to treat him with respect and try not to climb him like a tree. "I'm not worried about that," she lied.

When April arched a brow, she knew her friend didn't believe her. "I'm going to let you keep telling yourself that. Do you think you'd want to have sex with him again?"

Bailee would like to say no and mean it. But who was she kidding? Of course she wanted to be with him again. Just the thought of him made her want to take off her clothes and let him have control of her body. The real question was, *would* she be with him again?

Standing up, Bailee took off at a run. Anything to avoid more questions from April. Or maybe she was simply trying to outrun her feelings.

Later, Bailee arrived at the hospital thirty minutes early for her interview. Dr. Solomon had arranged for her to meet Love's father, Dr. Leon Washington, who was also chief of surgery at Michigan Medicine. As a favor to both his daughter and his friend, Dr. Washington had agreed to meet with her today. According to Dr. Solomon, the interview was a formality. She pretty much had the job if she wanted it. Which she did.

I guess.

Michigan Medicine was one of the largest healthcare systems in the country, and was owned by the University of Michigan. Bailee had visited the hospital before with Mason, but the impressive renovations made it seem like a different place. She'd read up on recent additions when she wasn't busy moving or daydreaming about Ian. They'd done a lot to improve the patient experience, including bringing in cutting-edge medical equipment and updating patient floors.

The only thing she didn't like was the horrendous parking situation. It had been a nightmare driving onto campus in the middle of the afternoon, and even worse trying to find a spot in the crowded parking structure. After driving around every single floor, she'd given up and used the valet service. Now she was cranky and sleepy and pissed off. Not a good combination if she wanted to remain composed and professional at the hospital.

When she arrived on the surgical floor, she felt a little better. The candy bar she'd grabbed on her way up helped. The walls were painted with warm, bright colors, not the drab gray or white walls she'd seen at other hospitals. Bailee tucked her leather binder under her arm and approached the desk.

"Hi, I'm here to see Dr...." Her voice trailed off when she spotted Drake to the right, talking to Myles and Ian. She took a moment to watch their interaction, noting the ease they shared with each other, the genuine smiles on their faces. The brothers looked relaxed, happy to be around each other. And Ian…

She drew in a shaky breath as she cataloged every single detail about him she could make out. Ian in regular clothes was fine, but Ian in dark scrubs? *So damn hot.*

Even though they hadn't been together in days, she still felt his kisses on her mouth. She couldn't stop thinking about his lips, his tongue on hers. She wanted him; she needed to feel that again. Decision made, she started toward him. But then she stopped in her tracks when a stunning woman joined the fellas.

The woman had on the same color scrubs as Ian and Drake, so Bailee figured she was a surgeon. Ian wrapped an arm around the woman and grinned at her. It was the same, sexy grin he'd shined on Bailee only a week ago.

"Excuse me?"

Bailee jumped at the voice behind her. When she turned, she met the cool eyes of the receptionist and realized she hadn't even told her who she was there to see. Had the woman been trying to get her attention this whole time? Bailee swallowed, and tried not to glance over at Ian again. "I'm sorry. I'm here to see Dr. Leon Washington. I have an appointment with him at two o'clock."

The lady gave her a curt nod, before giving her directions to the doctor's suite, where his administrative assistant would let him know she was there. Bailee spared Ian another glance. The woman had disappeared, but the brothers were still there. And Ian was looking right at Bailee.

Taking a deep breath, she walked toward them. She greeted Myles and Drake with a sincere smile and hugs.

Then she turned to Ian and gave him a plastic, stiff embrace. He smelled good—like the sun and the beach and mandarin.

"Hi, Ian," she breathed. Her voice sounded foreign to her own ears. Her gut twisted as she awaited his response.

"Bai," he rasped.

Vaguely, she heard movement behind her, felt the breeze of someone passing her. But her eyes were only on his. Until she remembered the woman and the dimpled smile he'd thrown at her. Anger simmered in her gut. Not at Ian, but at herself for being *that* woman. Bailee had never been the jealous type. Why the hell did she even care who he talked to anyway? Ian wasn't her man. They'd only shared a couple of hot and heavy sexcapades. No promises. No expectations. *Ugh.*

Ian held out his arm when she tried to walk past him, effectively blocking her movements. "Hey."

"Move, Ian."

"You're just going to walk away from me like that?"

Bailee met the curious gazes of Myles and Drake, scanned the area and noted a few nurses watching the scene unfold. "I'm not doing this with you right now. I have an interview." At that moment, the beautiful doctor he'd been talking to earlier breezed past them and waved. "Why don't you go talk to your little friend over there. Maybe she'll scratch that itch you always seem to have."

Without a word, he gripped her arm and steered her into an empty exam room. Whirling around, he pointed at her. "Seriously, Bai? I don't date women I work with. That's a surefire way to lose my job. And what the hell is your problem? *You* told me that we should just be friends."

She snorted. “And I bet you couldn’t wait to get your flirt on with the next available woman.”

“Are you crazy? Did you forget you’re the one who said you didn’t want to be in a relationship?”

“I didn’t forget, okay? But this is the reason I said that.”

“You’re killing me. Make up your mind. One minute you’re acting like you’re cool with the boundaries *you* set. Then next week you’re acting like you caught me cheating on you.”

“Listen, you said you don’t date people you work with. I’ll be working here soon enough, so that should solve the problem.”

She brushed past him, yanking the door open and hurrying down the hall.

Ian pounded his fist into the wall. *Ouch.* He shook his hand out. He couldn’t believe what had just happened. Not only did she accuse him of messing around on the job, but she’d walked away from him. Again.

He thought they’d moved past the BS in Traverse City. They’d parted on friendly terms, even though Ian didn’t need another friend. Mia was enough. Thoughts of Bailee had followed him all week, on his bike rides to work, during rounds, at lunch and especially overnight.

When he’d seen her in the lobby, looking so beautiful in a black pencil skirt and silk blouse, he’d wanted to march over to her and brand her. Because she was so damn fine—all golden and tight and serious. Everything that had never been attractive to him before, and now he couldn’t stop thinking about her—in his bed, on his floor, in the car or even in a tree. He’d take her any way he could, anywhere she’d let him.

Stalking toward the door, he froze when it swung open and Bailee stood in the doorway. "Bailee, you—"

She entered the exam room, a shy smile on her face. "I'm sorry. I…I was a maniac."

Ian closed the distance between them, pulling her into a deep kiss. "You were," he said when he broke the kiss. "But you're forgiven."

Bailee sighed. "I have to go to my meeting with Dr. Washington. I just couldn't walk away without telling you that."

She backed away from him, but he yanked her forward, groaning when her body crashed against his. "Have dinner with me."

"Just dinner?"

Desire, lust and something else he couldn't name surged through him. Ian wasn't naive. He recognized his dilemma. He'd known everything was different when he got home from Traverse City and realized he missed her. He wished he could say it was just the mind-blowing sex that he missed, but he knew it was more than that. It was their connection, the way they seemed to fit together in ways that went far beyond the physical attraction.

"A date." He placed a kiss to her cheek, then her mouth. "Whatever that entails."

Bailee shot him a lopsided grin. "You want to date me?"

He peered up at the ceiling, pretended to think over her question. But when her fingers grazed his arms as she clenched his sleeve, he looked down at her. "Yeah, I do. I know we agreed to just be friends, but—"

Bailee placed her index finger over his mouth. "Newsflash. We've already passed the just friends stage. I don't even know why I said that because, like I told you, I don't do casual relationships."

"Good." He kissed the tips of her fingers. "Because we're doing this." He gripped her shoulders and stepped away from her. "You better go. I'll pick you up at seven."

"Don't you need to know where I'm staying?"

"Text me your address."

With a frown, she said, "I don't have your phone number."

"Yes, you do. I wrote it on the little piece of paper you used as a placeholder in the book you borrowed from Dr. Solomon."

Before Bailee had left the Solomon estate, she'd borrowed a book from the library—one she'd wanted to read for quite some time.

Bailee giggled. "You didn't."

"I sure did. I guess you haven't finished it yet."

"I haven't had time."

"Well, you better get to it. Talk to you later."

She beamed. "Okay. Later."

Dinner consisted of Caribbean food at Bahama Breeze Island Grille in Livonia, Michigan. Ian had chosen the spot because they played live music on the deck, and he knew from their time together that Bailee enjoyed reggae. He'd ordered the Jamaican Jerk Chicken, while Bailee picked the Braised Short Rib & Oxtail entrée. At some point—he wasn't sure when—Bailee had stolen a piece of his chicken.

He dropped his gaze to his plate, then brought it back to Bailee.

She bit into the piece of chicken she'd taken and moaned. "So good."

Ian tried to be mad, because he really wanted that last piece. But the way she did a little dance while she ate was too cute. She'd dressed in ripped jeans, a tank and one of those sheer kimonos he'd seen his sister, Mel, wear from time to time. Her hair fell wild and free, which he liked.

"If you weren't so damn sexy, I might be a little upset that you took my last piece of chicken."

Bailee stopped dancing. He hooked his foot around the leg of her chair and pulled her closer to him. When she was next to him, he picked up the hand that was holding the pilfered piece of chicken and took a bite.

She let out a shaky breath. "Hot," she breathed.

He raised a brow. "The chicken?"

"The man," she admitted.

Ian sucked the sauce off one of her fingers. "So good."

"The sauce?"

"The woman wearing it." He grazed her thigh with his other hand, traced the skin between the tiny rips in her jeans.

"Ian." She bit her lip as her gaze dropped to his mouth. "Just so you know, I don't put out on the first date." His eyes snapped to hers, and he caught the hint of a smile in them. Then she outright laughed. "You should see your face right now."

He joined her, chuckling. "You got me."

"Seriously, though." She leaned back, peering into his eyes. "I spent a lot of time in a relationship that wasn't good for me. I don't want to make any drastic decisions or jump into something so blindly. But there's something about you that makes me want to rip out every page in my rule book."

He thought about his response, tried to figure out

how he could say what he felt without really saying it. Ian knew what she meant, though. He couldn't remember the last time he'd wanted to take a woman on a date. But he'd found himself worrying over the details. Did she like casual or fancy, Italian or steakhouse? In the end, he went with his gut. Bailee came from money like he did, but she wasn't pretentious. She was down-to-earth and appreciated the small things in life, like a good book or a turkey sandwich. She loved to be outside and eat dessert. And he wanted to give her those things. He wanted to give so much more.

But he wasn't sure he was ready to tell her how crazy he was about and for her. He didn't think it was the right time to tell her that he hadn't felt so consumed by another woman. Ever. After all, this *was* only their first date. They hadn't discussed anything other than the fact that they wanted to see each other, that *he* wanted to date her. That was a huge feat in and of itself. Ian didn't date, or have girlfriends. Not because he was a jerk or a player, but because he didn't have the time to devote to another person. He'd never met a woman who made him want to make the time for her. Until now.

So he did something that shocked the hell out of him. He told her the truth. "I think we should take our time with this. I don't expect you to do anything that makes you uncomfortable. I just want to get to know you, to take you out." He brushed his thumb over her chin, then swept the back of his hand down her neck, enjoying the way her eyes fluttered closed. "I've never met anyone like you before."

"And you never will again." She winked at him.

He chuckled. "I don't doubt that."

"Ian, I hope you know I didn't mean what I said

about not putting out. I think it's pretty obvious how this night is going to end."

"Does this mean I get to take you home?"

"Only if you let me set the pace. It's my turn to drive you wild."

Bailee liked to be in control of her emotions. That was very obvious. Which was why he'd relished the act of seducing her. But he wouldn't mind giving her control over his body. In fact, he wanted her to take it.

"Really?" he asked.

She leaned in closer. "I want to touch you everywhere. I want to taste you on my tongue. All of you."

"You do?"

Nodding, she said, "I do. I want you naked and ready for me." She dropped her hand to his erection and squeezed.

Damn. Ian scanned the restaurant, spotted the waiter near the register and waved him over. When the man in the yellow tropical shirt had made his way to their table, Ian told him, "Check, please."

Chapter 14

Bailee had enjoyed the last month getting to know Ian. They'd spent most nights together, reading, eating, sitting outside on his patio. They'd talked about anything and everything, gone to a jazz club with Drake and Love, attended a movie premiere with El and Avery. Mia and Mason had invited them over for barbecue and beer last Sunday.

She'd learned about his obsession with chess, how Dr. Solomon had taught him the game. Ian had been in the chess club in high school. He'd taught her how to play, and even let her win sometimes. Bailee discovered her daring side when they went and got tattoos together. He added to the elaborate design on his back, while she decided to get a tiny daisy behind her ear. It hurt. But he'd held her hand the entire time, and rewarded her for her bravery later with his tongue. Ian had taken her on bike rides and she'd cheered him on at his last race. Bailee had gladly taken his one hundred dollars when she'd beat him in a swim challenge.

And now she knew what it meant to be totally and completely enamored by another person. Ian was funny, generous and caring. He'd sat through a marathon of her favorite rom-coms without even complaining. He'd even admitted—reluctantly, of course—that Tom Hanks and Meg Ryan won the contest for best couple in *You've Got Mail*, her favorite movie.

And sometime between the late dinners and the games of chess, she'd fallen in love. And every day, she fell a little more. At this point, he could do just about anything and she would think it was adorable.

The realization that she loved him made her feel sick and elated at the same time. Sick because they hadn't defined what they were to each other or made any promises. Elated because she felt better with him near her, and she slept better beside him.

Bailee was a planner, though, and it had started to bother her that they still hadn't talked about his plans for his career, or their plans for each other. Ian wasn't content working in the hospital. He wanted to be out in the field. She loved that about him, but she wasn't sure if his goals aligned with hers.

Dr. Washington had offered her a job at Michigan Medicine, but Bailee had turned it down. Instead, she'd applied for an Adjunct Professor position with the university. Unbeknownst to Bailee at the time, she'd met the Dean of the Nursing School at Mason and Mia's wedding. The older woman and Mrs. Solomon were close friends. Mason's in-laws pulled a few strings to get her an interview, and she was awarded the position. She would start her new appointment in August. Being off work during the summer had allowed her time to enjoy Michigan. She'd put down a deposit on a condominium in Ann Arbor and was just waiting on a close date. In hindsight, having her mini–midlife crisis on her thirtieth birthday was just the thing she'd needed to get her life together. She only hoped her heart didn't ruin it for the rest of her. Because if things didn't work out with Ian, she knew it would wreck her.

Tonight, they were at a pregnancy reveal party for Mia and Mason. Her brother and new sister-in-law were ecstatic to become parents, and had planned the reveal for the start of Mia's second trimester. The news that she would soon become an aunt had shocked Bailee, but Ian didn't seem all that surprised. She'd figured Mia had told him beforehand.

Her brother's backyard had been transformed for the intimate dinner party, complete with a long table under a tent, lots of lanterns and plenty of food. For the reveal, Mia and Mason gave everyone gift boxes wrapped in pretty pastels. Everyone opened their box at the same time, and the room erupted in loud cheers. In Bailee's box, there was a picture of Mia and Mason's joined hands holding tiny little booties and a T-shirt that said Auntie's Baby. Happy tears had pricked Bailee's eyes as she embraced her brother and Mia, and whispered her name to her nephew or niece.

The news was a welcome surprise, and Bailee enjoyed hanging out with her friends and family. Even April, who was out of town for work, texted several happy dance GIFs when Bailee had shared the good news with her. Now Bailee was seated on a lounge chair watching everyone mingle and laugh. Four people were playing Spades at a card table, her parents had flanked Mia and Mason to iron out plans to travel to Michigan once the baby was born. And Ian…he looked so adorable playing with his niece, Zoe. He'd spent several minutes flying the cutie-pie around the backyard and making airplane sounds. He'd played patty-cake and talked baby talk. And Bailee felt her heart open up a little more and her body react to the scene before her.

She couldn't stop ogling him, and she knew she should because they were in public. Her parents were mere steps away, for goodness' sake. But she couldn't help it. She wanted him. It was his fault, really. He'd started it in the car on their way over, with his dirty, filthy words and his roaming hands. And he'd continued it over the course of dinner, with his whispered promises of cake and orgasms later.

Bailee just needed to get his attention. She needed him to walk over to her and say the two words she wanted to hear.

"Profiterole, ma'am?" A waiter held a tray full of assorted cream puffs in front of her.

Those aren't the words.

Bailee nodded and took the offered dessert. She bit into the tiny pastry and moaned at the burst of cream that filled her mouth. *Yum.*

When she looked up, Ian was staring at her, a hungry look in his eyes. He handed his niece to Drake and walked over to the wine table. As he poured her a glass, he looked her up and down. The heat in his eyes took her breath away, and she felt arousal pool between her thighs. Would she always want him like this? Would her fingers always itch to touch him? Would the sound of his voice, the feel of his eyes on her always make her feel weak and strong at the same time?

She sat up straighter, watching him as he stalked toward her. A slow smile spread across his face, lighting up the room and squeezing her heart. He had a beautiful, genuine smile. One that made her want to hold on to him forever.

Ian leaned down once he'd closed the distance between them. "Stop looking at me like that." His voice was a low rasp, almost a whisper. "You should know better by now."

Bailee swallowed, and held out her dessert. "Cream puff?"

He took a bite, chewing slowly, his eyes never leaving hers. Bailee swore she was about to go up in flames. He was so close she felt his breath on her lips, smelled the cream filling on it. She wanted to lick him. And he hadn't even touched her yet. Which was a good thing because if he did, she might explode. In the middle of the pregnancy reveal party. In front of everybody.

Ian kissed her bare shoulder. Then her neck. Then her lips. She let out a whimper when he took her mouth like there was nobody else in the room. She remembered the first time he'd kissed her in public. They'd spent the day on the Detroit River with his brothers, and listened to Boney James as he played to the crowd at Chene Park, an outdoor concert venue. And as the saxophone pierced the night air, they'd danced on the deck. When Ian had leaned down and placed a sweet kiss to her lips, she'd frozen. But that didn't last. It never did when his mouth was so close to hers.

Pleasure wrapped around her spine, then moved down to her core. She wanted nothing more than to have him inside her, making love to her the way only he could. Bailee cupped his face in her hands, giving herself to him. She didn't care what anyone had to say. She just wanted his lips on hers.

"Bai?" he said when he pulled back. "Let's go."

It was a good thing that Ian's house was literally

seven miles away from her brother's house. Because she was wound tight, burning with need and yearning to be touched. Once they made it to his place, it took only seconds for him to strip her bare, lay her on the bed and sink inside her.

Pure bliss. Two words, so much meaning. Bailee didn't know how she would get over how it felt when he filled her, when he made love to her. Each and every time felt new, like he was completing her puzzle, providing a missing piece of her that only he had. It was so good, so hot.

As if he'd read her mind, he grumbled, "It's so good. I can't stop wanting it."

"Yes," she breathed.

It didn't take long before she cried out her release. It felt like he'd stolen her breath, almost like he'd pushed her over the edge without her realizing it. He fused his mouth over hers, sucked on her bottom lip until she whimpered. Then his fingers dug hard into her hips and he was coming, too, groaning her name over and over again.

Bailee fell back against the mattress, sated. She turned to Ian, who was lying next to her, staring up at the ceiling. He reached out to her and pulled her into his arms.

"I don't know what I'm going to do with you." Ian kissed her brow.

"Keep doing this." She stretched, and hooked a leg over his waist. "This is good."

Bailee had never been with someone she could have fun with. For the first time, she didn't feel weird about being silly, or simply enjoying the moment. She'd never smiled as much as she'd smiled with Ian.

He shifted, turning to his side. "Doctors Without Borders emailed me."

Bailee's heart dropped. "Really?"

"They want me to fly out to New York for an interview."

"Oh." They'd talked about his application before. She knew how much an opportunity like this meant to him. But it felt like a ticking time bomb ready to explode.

He wrapped his hand around the base of her neck, kissed her nose. "This is the first step in the hiring process."

Bailee knew that. She'd read up on the organization herself. Once he was accepted to the program, he would have to go through a rigorous training in a faraway destination. Then he'd wait until they placed him somewhere. A typical assignment could last from nine months to one year.

"That's good," she said, trying to sound supportive and happy for him. "You've worked so hard for it."

Ian rested his head on her shoulder. "Yeah, I have." He pulled her close to him, wrapping his arms around her tightly.

Bailee swallowed rapidly as her heart pounded hard in her chest. She should probably say something else, but she couldn't bring herself to talk, sure her voice would betray her. It felt like Ian wanted to say something, too. Something important. Was it so much to hope for that he felt the same way as her? As happy as he probably was to get the call, could he be regretting the timing, too? Several moments passed, and Bailee's loud thoughts threatened to unravel her.

But then Ian pulled back, peered into her eyes. "Come with me to New York."

Relief surged through Bailee as she searched his face for a sign. His brown orbs pleaded with her to say yes, but they were also filled with something else. It felt like hope, and maybe even more than that. *Love.*

She nodded. "Sure. Let's do it."

New York City was one of Ian's favorite places to visit. He'd spent a lot of time there during college, making little weekend trips with Myles or Mia to explore the city. So he was surprised Bailee had never been to the Big Apple.

They'd arrived early in the morning the day before his interview. Although the organization offered to pay for his travel expenses and hotel stay, he'd opted out. Because once Bailee had admitted she'd never experienced Manhattan or Brooklyn or Harlem, he knew he had to make this trip count. He'd splurged on first-class tickets, and had reserved a suite at the Four Seasons.

The money he'd spent, the plans he'd made, the favors he'd called in were all worth it to see the smile on Bailee's face when they stepped into the gilded lobby of the hotel that morning. And she'd shouted with glee and jumped into his arms, showering him with kisses, once she'd seen their suite. The Central Park Suite featured oversize windows that offered panoramic views of the park. The suite also included a separate living area and a private terrace with outdoor furniture.

Ian had arranged for room service to deliver breakfast, and they'd enjoyed pancakes, fresh fruit, thick bacon and mimosas on the terrace. Then Bailee had pulled him into the room and let him make love to her for a few hours.

The hotel was situated in Midtown Manhattan, so there were several sites he wanted to show her. Since he'd listened to her when she'd told him about her favorite romantic comedies, he figured he'd surprise her and take her on a tour of the places she'd only seen in her favorite movies.

He'd started with a cab ride to the Empire State Building, and more specifically, the eighty-sixth floor Observation Deck, where his boy Tom Hanks won Meg Ryan's heart in *Sleepless in Seattle.* That's when Ian had discovered Bailee was just a little bit afraid of heights and wouldn't get too close to the railings.

After they left the Empire State Building, they'd visited the 91st Street Garden, where once again Tom Hanks revealed himself as Meg Ryan's online suitor and sealed the deal with a kiss. And because Bailee was such a huge *You've Got Mail* fan, she'd nearly cried when the Uber dropped them off in front of the park.

"Oh my God, Ian. This is awesome."

They'd stopped right in front of the sign where her favorite on-screen couple pledged their love for each other.

"I can't believe you did all this for me."

Ian shrugged. It wasn't rocket science. The only thing he'd done was listen to her. He'd spent time getting to know her, learning what made her happy, what made her sad and what made her want him.

"You deserve it, Bai." He stepped into her, traced her lips with his finger before he kissed her. "Haven't you figured out that I'd do anything for you?" Because Ian didn't have any control over his actions or his heart.

Tears filled her eyes. "Ian, this is...everything."

He kissed her cheeks where the tears fell. "Don't cry."

"I can't help it. No one has ever done anything like this for me."

In the back of his mind, he realized this interaction was eerily similar to the one in the movie she loved so much, which was corny and so not him. But in that moment, he didn't care. Seeing her so happy made him happy. Bailee had shared a lot of things with him over the last several weeks. He couldn't believe Brandon had never spoiled her, never made it a priority to make her smile. *Punk.* There was no excuse for Bailee to not have been to New York or Hawaii or Jamaica or Paris.

"I still can't wrap my brain around that," he said. "Did I tell you he was a punk?"

She giggled, leaning her forehead into his chest. He wrapped his arms around her. They swayed to silent music as he contemplated how to tell her what she meant to him. Although he hadn't officially given her the title of girlfriend, he felt like she was his. And he'd acted accordingly. He hadn't seen anyone else, or even wanted to see other women. He knew that she wasn't dating anyone else, either. But with Doctors Without Borders looming over his head, he didn't want to make a promise he couldn't keep.

Long-distance relationships worked only sometimes. Ian didn't want to hurt Bailee, and he didn't want to be hurt. And he didn't want to ask her to wait for him, especially after everything she'd gone through with the punk. She'd finally taken control of her life, made lasting changes that she was happy with. He didn't want to throw a wrench in any of that.

He loved her. It was real and all-consuming. It was everything. A lump formed in his throat when she pulled back and graced him with her perfect smile.

They held each other's gazes. She traced the line of his jaw, sending sparks straight to his heart. His veins hummed with a need to claim her. But he'd stick with his plan for the night.

"Where are we going?" she asked.

"What if I wanted to surprise you?"

She groaned. "I've had enough of surprises. I want to know what you have planned for me."

"Tickets to *Cats* the musical."

Her eyes lit up with glee, and his heart opened up a little more. She wrapped her arms around his neck and kissed him. "Ian, you didn't."

"I did."

Bailee had told him that her father had promised to take her to see the musical when she was a kid. She'd held out hope for the day she'd be able to see the play, but the tour ended and her father had forgotten. Mr. Sanders had been apologetic, had even taken her to see *The Lion King* in Chicago, but it wasn't the same.

Ian had called in a favor from a friend who worked as a real-estate developer in in the city. Cedric came through at the last minute with excellent tickets. Ian wanted her to meet his friend, so they'd decided to get together for drinks before the show.

He set her down on the ground and she beamed at him. "You're spoiling me." She grabbed his hand and pulled him out of the garden. "I might have to keep you."

Her words stirred something inside him. Tugging her to him, he asked, "Might?"

She stood on the tips of her toes and kissed him. "I'll amend that to say I will definitely keep you. As long as you keep giving me what I want."

"Ah, I get it. You'll keep me around as long as I keep making you scream my name?" Her smile...*damn*. He sucked in a deep breath, because breathing seemed to be a chore right then.

"Something like that," she said with a wink.

Ian wanted to say more. He wanted to tell her he loved her and he wanted her to be his forever. But the loud blare of a horn scared her, ruining the moment.

Later, Ian and Bailee met Cedric and his date for cocktails at Ty Bar, off the main lobby of the hotel. They enjoyed bar bites and Hudson Bourbon, which was created specifically for the bar. Bailee had surprised him when she'd ordered the bourbon neat, instead of one of her preferred fruity cocktails. Ian loved watching Bailee step outside of her comfort zone more and more.

Surprisingly, *Cats* the musical was good. Ian enjoyed the show. Bailee held his hand the entire time, squeezing it when the actors jumped out of the shadows. When the show was over, he took her to a dessert bar Cedric had recommended.

Back at the hotel, they were barely in the room before Bailee tackled him. Clothes flew off, her skirt behind his head, his shirt behind hers. She unbuckled his pants and pushed them down. He fumbled with the ties of her blouse, tempted to rip it to shreds to get to her.

Bailee steadied his hand. "You better not rip my shirt, Ian. It's my favorite."

Ian growled, hooking his hands under her butt, lifting her in his arms and carrying her to the bedroom. He dropped her on the bed and crawled on top of her. He savored the way they fit together, like she was made for him. Their lovemaking wasn't hot and fast. Instead, it was slow and tender. And when they finished, coming in tandem, he knew he'd never love anyone the way he loved his Bailee.

* * *

After his interview the next day, they spent time in Central Park. They visited Bethesda Fountain, walked The Mall like another couple in one of her favorite movies, *Brown Sugar*, played chess in the Chess & Checkers House and rode the Carousel. On Saturday, they lazed around the hotel suite until dinner. He took her to Dinners in the Dark at Camaje, where they enjoyed dinner blindfolded.

"Where did you come up with that idea?" Bailee asked once they were back in the suite. She was curled up in his lap on the terrace.

He shrugged. "One of the doctors talked about it at work one day, and I figured why not."

"I loved it."

The idea was to enjoy dinner without sight, which was supposed to heighten other senses, like smells and textures. "It was intense."

"Sensual," she agreed. They watched the skyline for a few minutes before Bailee hopped up.

He gripped her wrist. "Wait, wait, wait...where are you going?"

She bent down and brushed her lips over his. "I'll be right back." True to her word, Bailee was gone only for a few minutes. When she returned, she held a box in her hand. He opened his arms and she climbed into his lap again. "I got you something."

Ian took the offered box. "What is it?"

"Open it."

He lifted the top off the Tiffany Blue box, and wondered when she had time to go and purchase something from the jewelry store.

"I ordered it online, and picked it up while you were gone on your interview yesterday."

He eyed her as he pulled the white ribbon and lifted the top off the box. His heart tightened in his chest when he pulled the silver key chain out. It was a rook.

"It's stupid, but I thought it was cute."

He ran his finger over the metal, touched by her thoughtfulness. Although it was small, the fact that she'd listened to him, that she'd thought of him, made him love her even more.

She bit her lip. "Do you like it? I remember when you were teaching me how to play chess, you mentioned the rook was your favorite piece."

Ian remembered the conversation. He'd spent some time explaining each piece and its role in the game. And when he got to the rook, he'd confessed that he loved how the piece had simple movement, but it played an important role in game play. The rook threatened the king, supported the queen and sometimes sacrificed itself for a bishop or knight. And in the end, rooks were often the last pieces standing, aside from the kings.

He'd often equated chess to real life. Pop had taught him many lessons while they'd played—focus on the board and not the opponent, be creative, don't read more into other players' moves, be flexible, look after the little guys because they matter, and think three moves ahead. Most people liked the queen, because it was the most powerful piece on the board. But the rook represented the value of support and sacrifice, giving of himself for others.

"Thank you, Bai. I love it." He pulled her into a kiss. *I love you.*

Chapter 15

Bailee started her job and moved to her new condo the same week. It was now the end of August, and she'd settled into her new life in Michigan. Classes would start after Labor Day, and Bailee was enjoying the preparation. She'd thrown herself into lesson plans and presentation materials. She wouldn't say she'd never go back to nursing full-time, but she liked the idea of training the next generation of nurses.

Tonight, Ian was coming to her place for the first time before she flew down to Florida for the holiday. They'd watch movies and chill, preferably naked. After their trip to New York, they'd grown closer, spending lots of time together. Still, they hadn't made a commitment, although she'd never dream of dating someone else. She was hopelessly in love with Ian. She wanted him, and only him.

Bailee stirred the meat on the stove. Steak and

shrimp fajitas were on the menu because Ian loved them. And he deserved to be spoiled since he'd single-handedly coordinated her move. Last week, they'd rented a truck and driven down to Columbus to pick up the rest of her things. And he'd insisted on unpacking everything in one day. Then he'd helped her set everything up.

"Bai?" Ian called from the front of the house.

"In here!" She dropped the onions and peppers in the pan just as Ian rounded the corner and entered the kitchen. Her heart pounded in her chest at the sight of him in his scrubs. *So fine.* And a sight for sore eyes. He'd just worked two days in a row, and the only interaction they'd had was several flirty—more like dirty—texts and a hurried video chat. She smiled when she noticed the tiny smirk that formed on his face when he saw her.

"Hey, beautiful." He massaged her shoulders. "Smells good in here." He kissed the back of her neck, then her jaw, then her lips.

"You know I had to hook you up, to thank you for everything you've done."

He sat down on one of the barstools. "No need to thank me." He yawned.

"You look tired."

"I am. But I'm hungry, too."

"Dinner is almost ready. Why don't you go relax on the sofa?"

"Sounds good." He gave her another quick kiss and disappeared a few seconds later.

Once the fajitas were finished and his plate was made, she took it to him in the living room. She chuckled at Ian curled up on the couch—fast asleep. She set the plate on the coffee table and pulled a blanket over him.

His eyes popped open. "I'm up."

"No, you're not. Go back to sleep."

Ian gripped her wrist, pulling her down on the sofa with him. He wrapped his arm around her. "Stay with me. I just need a quick nap, and then we can eat and watch a movie."

She turned in his arms, ran her fingers through his hair. "The food will be here when you wake up."

"I'm sorry," he muttered.

"Don't apologize."

"Is this going to stop you from doing me? Because if so, I'm up. I feel great. So good I could run a marathon."

She laughed. "Ian, go to sleep. I'll be here when you wake up."

"I missed you." Then he buried his face in her neck and promptly fell back to sleep.

An hour later, Ian woke up and smiled. Bailee set her book down. "You're up." She stood. "Ready to eat?"

"I'm hungry, but not for food." He waggled his eyebrows.

"You're silly." She shoved him playfully.

"I'm serious." He grabbed her ankles and tugged her forward.

Bailee cracked up when he pulled her pants and shirt off. "You're crazy."

"About you," he murmured before he kissed her. His phone rang and he groaned. "I hope it's not the hospital."

"It's fine. Answer it." She scooted off the couch and walked into the kitchen to reheat his food. A few minutes later, she came back with his plate. "Hey, are you okay?" He was sitting on the couch, staring at a spot on the wall. "Ian?" She sat next to him. "What happened?"

He looked at her then. "That was Doctors Without Borders."

Bailee swallowed. "Okay. Did you get accepted?"

Ian nodded. "Yes. They want me to fly out for training next week."

"Next week?" she repeated. "Wow."

Knowing he'd applied for a position was one thing. But being faced with him actually going away was quite another. His eyes bored into her, waiting. For what? She didn't know. If he was waiting for her to ask him to stay, he'd be waiting forever. Because she couldn't do that. She couldn't tell him not to go.

"I don't know when I'll actually be assigned a post," he said. "It could be two weeks, or two months."

She nodded. "I know."

"I don't even know how long the assignment will be."

"At least nine months," she said.

"Can we...?"

She looked at him then. "I'm excited for you. We need to celebrate."

"Bai? Don't you think we need to talk about this?"

"Why? There's nothing to talk about. We both knew this was coming. The interview was just a formality. Your résumé is impressive. I knew they'd hire you." But she was ashamed to say she'd hoped they wouldn't. Because even though they'd spent so much time together and it felt like they were on the same page, she knew they weren't ready for long distance.

Bailee stood, but he grabbed her hand. "Sit."

She sat.

"You're going to tell me to leave and not give us options?"

Shrugging, she said, “What options? It’s not like we’re together.” His face fell, and she knew she’d hurt him. She forged ahead anyway. “Ian, we didn’t make any promises.”

“Is that it?”

“What else is there?”

“Bai, I can’t even believe you’re saying this to me after everything. I’m supposed to walk away like what we have doesn’t matter to me? And be okay with it? I can’t do that.”

Glancing at him, she asked, “Why?”

“Because!” He stood and paced the floor. “You’re my… You’re mine.”

His admission had simultaneously filled her heart with joy and trepidation. “Ian, you’re leaving. And I want you to go because I know it means so much to you.”

“You mean something to me, too. I didn’t expect it. I definitely didn’t plan for it.”

“Me, neither.” Her voice broke, and she squeezed her eyes closed. Tears wouldn’t help the situation. “But it’s not like you’ll be gone forever. You’re going to come back. Look, Ian. The way I see it is our timing just sucks. And that’s life.”

“Is it because you don’t trust me to be gone and not cheat on you?”

Her gaze snapped to his. “No.”

“I would never hurt you like that.”

“I believe you. But sometimes getting hurt is inevitable. Especially when a situation is hard. I’d rather walk away now than invest more time and effort into a relationship that won’t work.”

“Straight up? How do you know it won’t work?”

“I doubt that it will. It’s only been a few months. I

stayed in a relationship for over fifteen years waiting for things to get better. Or accepting that they sucked. I don't have it in me to do that again. What if you go away and love it? What if when you get there, they love you so much they want you to go on more assignments? Where does that leave me?"

"Okay, so you're scared. That's understandable."

"I'm not just scared, Ian. I'm being realistic. Why don't you just concentrate on your new job right now? Because this is probably confusing things for you."

"Don't tell me how I feel, Bailee," he snapped.

"How about I tell you how I feel, then?" She folded her arms over her chest. "I already care so much about you it feels like I'll burst open from the intensity of these feelings. Being with you like this took a lot for me."

Hurt flashed in his eyes. "So you regret being with me?"

Her shoulders fell. "No. Ian, I've loved being with you." *I love you.* "But you're me in this situation."

Ian looked thoroughly confused. "What?"

"You're at a crossroads in your life. You have to go with a clean slate. Without me and expectations and commitments that don't align with the vision you have for yourself. Because if you don't—if we try to make this work—one day you might realize you've wasted time trying to make a relationship work that was doomed from the beginning."

"That's the craziest thing I've ever heard!" he roared. "You left Brandon because he was a selfish punk who didn't put you first."

"I left him because I wanted more for my life. And you want more for yours. So go. We're good. We can be friends."

Ian stepped back as if she'd slapped him. "Friends?"

"Yes." She turned on her heel and walked into the kitchen. *What am I doing?*

The same thing they'd bonded over was the thing that could tear them apart. Their ambition, their need to be understood, their desire for something more. When she'd started this, she never expected to love him. Hell, she didn't even feel like she could love anyone after Brandon. What had happened between Bailee and Ian was anything but casual, and more serious than she ever anticipated. Yet she wouldn't change a single thing.

Doubt clouded her mind, and panic welled up inside her. How was it even possible to be a wreck over Ian when she hadn't shed a single tear over Brandon? *Because I love him.* Ian was right. The situations were different. He wasn't Brandon. And she wasn't Brandon's Bailee anymore.

Bailee wanted Ian, more than anything. "Ian," she whispered. Bolting out of the kitchen, she called his name as she entered the living room. But he was gone. She opened the door just in time to see him speed out of the subdivision.

Closing the door, Bailee leaned against it and sunk to the floor. Burying her face in her knees, she finally let loose the tears that had been threatening to fall.

It had been only two hours since he'd left Bailee's house, but Ian felt like he'd been thrown into hell. The conversation replayed in his mind on a continual loop. Even the whiskey he'd downed hadn't dulled the ache.

"Why didn't you just tell her how you feel?" Myles asked as he refilled Ian's glass.

"Right?" Drake said, glaring at Ian. "That doesn't even make any sense."

"Oh, shut up." Love smacked Drake on the arm. "Like you haven't made stupid decisions before?"

After he'd left Bailee's house, Ian drove to El and Avery's place. One look at him, and El called in reinforcements. His siblings had descended on the house in minutes.

"You should have fought for her," El said.

"Says the man who didn't fight for me," Avery deadpanned.

"Hey," El said. "This isn't about me."

"I thought we were building something," Ian said. "And she was so flippant about it. Then she called us friends. I'm not her freakin' friend."

"Listen, Ian," Love said, squeezing between Drake and Ian. "I'm not going to tell you that you did the wrong thing. We all know that Doctors Without Borders isn't a death sentence for a relationship. I'm sure even Bailee knows that. But she's scared, so she said some things I'm sure she's regretting right about now."

Avery plopped down on the other side of him. "Love is right. Sometimes we women can be a little hasty."

"Exactly," El chimed in.

"As I was saying," Avery said, blowing El a kiss, "she messed up. And she'll realize it. Sooner rather than later. Have faith, brother. And stop drinking so much."

"And when she does come to you," Love said, "tell the girl you love her. Jeez. Get it together. I'm not sure why you haven't told her before now."

"That's what I said," Myles said, jumping in. "It was pretty obvious to us. Since when do you spring for extravagant vacations in New York City for anybody? I can barely get you to buy me dinner, and we were in the womb together for nine months."

And that was when Ian finally laughed. "You're dumb as hell. But thank you. I appreciate the support."

When Ian got home later that evening, he was surprised to find his father waiting for him inside. How he got a key to Ian's place, he'd never know. He dropped his keys on the table next to the door.

"What are you doing here?"

"I heard you were accepted into the program," his dad said.

"Is this when you tell me you won't support my decision? Or when you let me know how disappointed you are in me?"

His father sighed. "I don't want to tell you any of those things, son. Our conversation has played in my head many times since the wedding."

"And you're just now coming to clear the air with me?" He'd gone practically the entire summer without seeing his father. Ian knew Dr. Law's schedule was generally packed, but he also knew his dad had been in town for weeks.

"I figured you needed time."

Ian stared at him incredulously. "Really? Almost three months?"

"Look, son. I'm an asshole. What can I say?"

"How about I'm sorry?"

"I'm sorry."

Ian stared at his father in disbelief. An apology was the last thing he'd expected from his father. "What?"

"I apologize. You were right. I should be proud of the man you've become. I *am* proud of you. Of all my children, you're the one most like me."

As far as Ian was concerned, that wasn't a compliment. "I'm not sure what to say about that," he grumbled.

Then his father laughed. It had been years since he'd seen his dad smile, let alone laugh. "You've never backed down from a fight with me. Not even when you were a little boy. You go after what you want. That's something to be proud of. It's something to respect. The fact that you're willing to lose momentum in your own studies to give back to communities in need is commendable. And something I've never had the courage to do."

Ian was speechless. And since he didn't know what to say, he walked to the fridge and pulled out a bottle of water. "Did you want something to drink?"

His father nodded. "I'll have a beer."

A beer? Ian had never seen his father drink anything but bitter scotch. But he grabbed a Modelo out of the refrigerator, popped the top and slid it across the table to his father. They sat for a few moments, him guzzling his water and his father sipping his beer.

"That woman," his father said. "The one you've been hanging out with? Where is she?"

"Again, how do you know what I've been doing?" Ian laughed. "I haven't seen you." It seemed his father knew everything.

"I've seen you."

"Bailee," Ian said. "Her name is Bailee."

"That's right. Mason's sister."

"Yeah. We broke up."

"Really?" His father took another sip from the bottle. "I actually like her."

"How do you even know her?"

"I ran into her when I was leaving the Solomon estate. She told me it was a shame I couldn't see what a good son I had. Then she said I should spend more time supporting you instead of tearing you down."

That was news to Ian. Bailee had defended him to his father. Damn, he loved that woman.

"When do you leave for training?" his father asked.

"Next week, after the holiday. The recruiter told me they wanted me to start as soon as possible because they're short on qualified doctors."

"Good." Dr. Law stood. "I better get home." He clasped Ian's shoulder. "You'll do well, son." His father walked to the door. "Oh, before I go." He pointed to a box on the coffee table. "That was sitting outside when I got here."

"How did you get a key to my place?"

His father laughed. "Good night." Then he was gone, without answering Ian's question.

Ian picked up the box on the table and opened it. A new chess set, the one he'd told Bailee he wanted weeks ago, was inside. But it wasn't just a chess set. It was hope. He picked up the card and opened it.

Ian, I had planned to give this to you tonight. I hope you love it.

Ian did love it. Even more, he loved her.

Chapter 16

Pregnancy reveals, gender reveals… Ian knew Mia was going to take this being-a-mother thing too far. His best friend had texted him while he was in Montreal at training, and let him know that she'd scheduled the reveal so that he could be there. But he had no idea it would be on the day he'd returned from training.

The moment Ian walked into his best friend's house, Mia screamed and ran over to him, pulling him into a tight hug. "You're here. Thank you for coming."

"Did I have a choice? Because I could have sworn I got a message on my phone threatening me if I didn't make an appearance."

Mia laughed, shoving him lightly. "Fine. So you didn't have a choice. I'm just glad to see you. How was Montreal?"

Ian spent a few minutes telling Mia about training. It was rigorous, but he'd loved the challenge. Except for the nights when he'd tossed and turned, missing the feel of the woman he loved next to him. Every time he closed his eyes, he saw her. Every time he breathed, he smelled her. She lingered on him as if she'd doused him in her essence. Being away from her shined a light on how incomplete he felt without her. He missed her. He missed the sound of her laugh, the way she bit her lip when she was concentrating on something or when she was turned on. He missed her smile. He missed the feel of her in his arms, the warmth of her body against his.

Bailee had left for Florida the morning after their argument, and then he'd left for Canada. He'd sent her a few texts while he was away, which she'd responded to. But the things he'd wanted to say to her couldn't be said over text or on a phone call. He needed to see her.

"Is she here?" he asked.

Mia smiled. "She's out on the patio."

Ian kissed his friend on the cheek and headed for the patio door. Bailee was sitting outside, a beer dangling from her fingers. She wore black jeans and a T-shirt. Her eyes were closed. *Perfect.*

"Bai?" Her eyes popped open and she whirled around, nearly falling out of the chair. He rushed over to her and held the chair steady. "Are you okay?"

"Ian?" She jumped up, shook her hand. "I spilled beer on my jeans." She grabbed a paper towel off the table next to her chair and wiped her pants, growling in frustration. "Shoot, these are new jeans." Then she looked at him and smiled. "Hi."

"Hi."

"When did you get here?"

"Just now. Mia told me you were out—"

"I'm sorry," she said, interrupting him. She inched closer to him. "I'm so sorry, Ian. I was so wrong.

There's so much I want to say to you. Things that couldn't be said over the phone."

"I know," he said.

"Do you want to sit?"

"Let's go to the gazebo."

She smiled, and they walked toward the structure Mia had recently added to the backyard. Inside, she leaned against the rail, peered up at the sky. "It's a beautiful night."

He stared at her. "Yeah, beautiful."

She shot him a shy smile. "How was Montreal?"

"Can we talk about that later?" He picked up both of her hands. "I hate the way our last conversation ended. And I'm partly to blame. Because I didn't tell you how I really felt. I didn't communicate what was on the line for me. I left without letting you know how much I love you."

Bailee gasped.

"That's my fault. I won't make the same mistake again. I love the idea of Doctors Without Borders. I enjoyed learning and training to go out in the field. But being up in Canada, not knowing where *we* stand, was a special kind of torture. Because you mean more to me than any job, any opportunity."

"Oh, God," she breathed.

"What?"

"Can we back up just a little bit?" She let out a shaky breath. "Because you love me?"

He pulled her to him and kissed her. She tasted like beer and cookies, and something distinctly Bailee. When he broke the kiss, he pressed his forehead to hers. "Of course I love you. Isn't that obvious? I love you so much I can't even think straight." Ian was a transformed person when she was in the room. It didn't matter who was there; Bailee commanded all of his attention. "And I couldn't go another day without telling you."

Grinning, she brushed her thumb over his bottom lip. "I love you, too."

He closed his eyes and let her words wash over him. He cupped her cheeks and brushed his lips over hers.

"Does this mean you accept my apology, that you forgive me for tripping out?"

"There's nothing to forgive." He grabbed her hand, led her over to a nearby bench and pulled her down on his lap. "I need you to know that we can make this work. Because I—"

"Ian, I know. I won't pretend that I don't hate that you'll be so far away, but that's what planes are for. And vacations."

He chuckled. "Bai."

She babbled on about frequent flyer miles and Marriott points before she asked, "Do you have an idea of when you're going to be assigned to a post?"

He sighed. "Next week, but—"

"Aw, I won't get much time with you." She gave him a lingering kiss. "But it's okay. We'll make the most of the time we have now."

"Bai, stop." He pinched her mouth closed. "If you'd let me get a word in edgewise, I could tell you something very important about my assignment."

She nodded.

"My assignment is in New Orleans."

Come to the hotel bar. I'll be waiting.

The text had been short, but Ian's words had stoked a fire in Bailee. Her arousal was at a tipping point by the time the town car pulled up at the luxury hotel, the same one she'd stayed in all those months ago, the same hotel where she'd met him. Bailee thanked the driver and slid out of the vehicle.

It had been a month since Bailee had seen him, and she was anxious to lay eyes on him. They'd talked nearly every day since he'd left, sharing their days with each other via video chat. He'd told stories of long days working in the inner-city hospital and on the streets. The latest hurricane, a category three storm, had devastated the city. But everyone on his team had been working hard to help rebuild the medical system. He worked hard, but always made sure to check in with her, even when he was exhausted. Sometimes he'd even fall asleep while they were on the phone, and Bailee listened to his soft snores, taking comfort in the sound of his breathing in her ear.

The technology at her fingertips helped, but she'd missed the face-to-face contact. She'd missed his touch, his lips. Every minute of the day, she'd been aware of his absence. She was so gone over Ian.

Memories of sweaty sex, slow or fast lovemaking with Ian only made her cranky. Dirty texts and phone sex paled in comparison to the real thing, even though Ian was good on the phone. Last night, Ian had sent her a five-word text saying, Get on a plane. Now. A minute after she'd received the text, her phone buzzed with another notification—an email. He'd sent her a gift card for the airline. So she did as she was told, booking a flight and throwing a few outfits in a carry-on. She couldn't get a flight out that same night, but she'd found one for the next day.

Bailee pulled out her phone once she stepped into the lobby and made one call. To April.

"Guess where I am?" she said when her best friend picked up.

"Where?"

Bailee hadn't told anyone she was leaving, since she'd be back in two days. "I'm in New Orleans."

"Get out. When did you leave? And why didn't you tell me?"

"It was a last-minute thing. Ian sent for me."

"You are so spoiled," April said. "I'm jealous."

"Don't be. You're pretty spoiled yourself." For the last month, April had been happily dating one of their college friends, and had even admitted she might love him.

"Right? I can't believe it."

"I have to go, but I just wanted to let you know that I'll be off the grid for two days. We'll do lunch when I get back, so we can catch up."

"All right, Bai. Love you. And don't come back here with child."

Bailee laughed. "Shut up. Goodbye." She ended the call and sent a quick text to Mason, letting him know she was with Ian. Then she turned off her phone and walked into the hotel bar. She spotted Ian right away, sitting at the end of the bar, a drink in hand. Her eyes narrowed when she saw a woman cozy up to him. But then her heart soared when he shook his head and sent the woman away.

She slid onto the seat next to him and gestured for the bartender. When the man asked for her order, she told him to bring a bourbon for her and another for the gentleman next to her. Once her drink was in front of her, she took a sip, enjoying the smooth taste.

"Thanks for the drink," Ian said.

Bailee swiveled her bar seat around so she could

face him. He was dressed in dark jeans and a white button-down shirt. She was sure he could feel her gaze, but he didn't acknowledge her or even react to it. But that was okay. She could play this game, too. "Come here often?"

He arched a brow, shot her a sideways glance before turning to face her. His eyes traveled over her body, like he was memorizing everything about her. "No. But I needed a drink and figured I'd try it."

She crossed her legs and watched his gaze drop to her bare legs. Bailee had chosen a wine-colored strappy-back skater dress that showed just enough skin to drive him crazy. Bailee tipped her head up to the ceiling, noticed the little touches she hadn't noticed before. "I just flew in for the weekend," she told him. "To see my *friend*."

"Must be a good friend for you to wear a dress like that to see him."

Smirking, she nodded. "The best."

"Is he, now?" He slid off the seat. Ian inched closer to her and gripped the edge of her seat, caging her in with both arms.

"Yes," she breathed, staring into his eyes—eyes that seemed to see inside her, eyes that made her want to give in to the burn that worked its way through her body.

"What's your name?" he asked.

"Aries." He dropped his head to her shoulder, chuckling softly. "What's yours?"

"Ian. And this game is over." He traced the V of her dress with one finger. "I missed you, Bai."

"I missed you, too. Now kiss me."

Leaning in, he whispered, "You're bossy." But then his mouth was on hers, and she was lost. His kiss was full of need, and when his tongue slid between her lips, she moaned.

Too soon, he broke the kiss, and Bailee felt desperate for more of him. "I need you."

He brushed her knee with his thumb, and slid his hand up her thigh slowly. The feel of his fingers on her skin almost made her forget where they were. Almost.

Bailee snapped her legs closed. "What are you doing?" she asked. "We're in a public bar."

She knew Ian had chosen this spot at the bar purposefully, because it was off to the side, and hidden from most of the customers. But still…

He pressed a kiss to her shoulder. "Staking my claim," he murmured against her skin. "I wouldn't want your friend to come back and think he has a chance with you."

"Are you jealous?"

"Are you mine?"

Bailee raised a brow. "What do you think, Ian?"

"I want you to say the words, Bai." He nipped at her earlobe before pulling it into his mouth. "Your hands." He kissed the palms of her hands. "Your mouth." He pressed a soft kiss to her lips. "And your body." Ian slipped his hand under her dress and it wasn't long before tips of his fingers grazed her sensitive core. She gasped. "Tell me, baby. Tell me you're mine." He slipped his thumb under the band of her panties.

"I'm yours," Bailee whispered. She couldn't take it. His touch lit a fire in her that wouldn't be doused.

"Good. Now, tell me that no one makes you tremble or shiver or tingle the way I do."

"Nobody. Only you."

"You're mine." His voice was a low, husky growl.

"Yes."

"Not only is your body mine, but your mind is mine and your heart is mine."

Bailee shuddered. "Everything, baby. Everything is yours. And you're mine," she added.

"All yours." He caressed her cheek with his other hand.

"Ian?"

"Hmm?"

"Take me to bed."

It took less than five minutes for them to get to her room. Ian nearly tore the door off its hinges when the key card didn't work at first. Finally, the door clicked and he pushed it open. With hands roaming, lips nipping, they undressed.

"Get on the bed," he ordered. "Now."

Bailee didn't need to be told twice. She ran to the bed and jumped on it, laughing when he followed suit. Soon, they were in the throes of passion, moving together, giving and taking.

Ian gripped her hips, sinking all the way into her. "I'll never stop," he whispered. "I'll always make you feel this way."

Her orgasm burst through her with a fury, so intense it felt like she'd split in two. And he joined her soon after, moaning her name.

When Bailee came down from her orgasmic high, she opened her eyes to find Ian staring at her. He circled her nose with his. She loved his tender side. She loved how he took care of her, how he made sure she was always good.

Bailee kissed him, pouring her heart and soul into it. And when she pulled back, her breath caught at the love shining back at her through his eyes. "Ian." She traced his jaw, peppering kisses over his face. "I don't ever want to lose this feeling."

"We won't. I promise. Because of you, I know how to love."

Tears filled her eyes. "Stop making me cry, man."

He kissed her tears away. "My poor Bai. Don't cry. I love you."

"I know. Love you, too."

Chapter 17

Eight months later

Bailee waited outside the Detroit Metropolitan Airport. Ian's flight was due in any moment. The last two days had been a nightmare of flight delays and missed phone calls. But she'd finally received the call she'd been waiting for that morning. Ian told her to be there by eleven o'clock.

She glanced at her watch. It was now eleven thirty. No Ian. Grumbling a curse, she rested her forehead against the steering wheel. She yelped when someone knocked on the passenger-side window. Bailee jumped out of the car when she realized it was Ian. She ran into his waiting arms, into a delicious kiss.

When he set her down on the ground, she wiped her gloss off his lips. "You made it."

"Finally." He hugged her again. "You look good, baby."

"So do you."

Ian had shipped most of his belongings ahead of time, so he didn't have to carry so much luggage. It had been a long eight months of weekend visits, phone calls, emails and FaceTime. She'd visited him in New Orleans several times, and he'd flown home for the birth of Mason and Mia's baby.

When his assignment ended, Ian had turned down the opportunity to extend his employment and booked a flight home. He hadn't even told her about the offer until he'd purchased his ticket to come back to Michigan. His explanation had simply been, "I'm coming home. No more questions. I love you."

Ian tossed his bag in the trunk and hopped in the driver's seat, and soon they were on the road. He made a quick stop at his house to read his mail, eat and make love to Bailee. Then they hit the road to Traverse City. Dr. Solomon had planned a huge birthday celebration for Nonna, and Ian hadn't wanted to miss it.

They arrived at the Solomon estate early in the evening. It was still as beautiful as it had been the first time she'd seen it. And she couldn't wait to spend time there with Ian. When she entered the house with him right behind her, she was thrilled to see the Solomon family, the Jackson family and the Sanders family had already arrived. And...April?

"April!" Bailee exclaimed, hugging her friend. "What are you doing here? I thought you had a work thing this weekend."

Her bestie shrugged. "Mia invited me. Who turns down a minivacation at a beautiful resort?"

More hugs were exchanged, high fives were given,

cheeks were pinched and kisses were planted on foreheads.

Bailee's heart swelled in her chest at the love in the room. Everyone had taken time out of their busy schedules to gather and enjoy one another. She'd never grow tired of this. She eyed Ian, who was swinging Zoe in his arms. He looked incredible, with his tanned skin and bulging biceps. And the happy toddler in his arms loved her uncle "Een," as she called him. He met her gaze and winked, before he continued to make buzzing sounds against a delighted Zoe's belly.

Once they were settled in their room, the same suite Bailee had stayed in during the wedding week, they gathered for dinner in the outdoor kitchen. Dr. Solomon barbecued pork ribs and ribeye steaks, while Mrs. Solomon and her mother zoomed around, readying the table with the settings and dishes full of corn on the cob, macaroni and cheese, greens, fried potatoes and coleslaw. All of Bailee's favorite dishes.

Bailee snuck a cream puff from the dessert table before taking her seat next to Ian. There were tiny boxes on each place setting that they were all instructed not to open until after dinner. She wondered what type of reveal they would be treated to tonight. Mia was a new mother and Avery had recently announced her pregnancy, so it couldn't have anything to do with them. Love could be pregnant with Zoe's little sister or brother, but Bailee didn't think so. They'd recently had a conversation about babies, and Love had made it very clear that she wanted more time between the babies.

While Ian had been away, Bailee had grown very close to the Jackson clan. Even Ian's sister, Mel, had become a dear friend to her. It was Bailee who had encouraged Mel to follow her heart and attend business school instead of medical school like her father and brothers. And Bailee had been there when Mel broke the news to Dr. Law that she was moving to New York City next year to attend Columbia University. He'd taken the news surprisingly well, but that was likely because he didn't believe Mel would follow through—he had said as much. Yeah, he was still Dr. Law.

Dinner was served, and she piled her plate with tender ribs, a small piece of steak and a little bit of everything else. "This is so good." She cut into her steak and popped a piece into her mouth. "So tender."

Ian eyed her, a gleam in his eyes. "Yeah, except that's not your steak. You think you're slick."

Bailee giggled. She'd swiped Ian's steak off his plate a few minutes ago, while he was making funny faces at Zoe. "I'm sorry. I should have grabbed a bigger piece, and now it's all gone."

He smiled at her. "It's fine."

Once all the plates were cleared and everyone was full, Mia announced that it was time to open the gifts. Bailee picked up her box and shook it. It couldn't be a T-shirt because the box was so small. Maybe it was a key chain? Or a trinket from Nonna? A souvenir from Dr. Solomon's trip to Florence?

Everyone tore open their boxes, and Bailee watched for reactions. Except everybody's box was empty. Frowning, she finally opened hers and gasped. Inside her box sat a beautiful, clear, sparkling diamond. A ring. "Oh my God." She turned to Ian. "What is this?"

Ian turned to her. "You told me that you didn't want an out-of-the-ordinary proposal. But—"

"Did I tell you that?" Bailee thought proposals

should be intimate, either between the man and the woman or with a small gathering of close family and friends.

"You did. And stop interrupting me while I'm trying to be sincere." He mimicked the act of zipping up lips, before he pulled her chair closer to him.

Vaguely, she heard some "Aws" and "Oh my Gods" somewhere around her. But she couldn't look at anyone else but the man sitting in front of her.

Ian picked up the box—her box—and pulled the ring out. "I didn't need months to tell me that I want to be with you for the rest of my life. This past year, getting to know you and love you, has been the best year of my life. I don't regret taking the opportunity to serve my community, but I've also realized that being so far away from you for an extended period of time doesn't work for me."

Tears streaked down her cheeks, and he gently wiped them away with a tissue.

"I know beyond a shadow of a doubt that my life is nothing without you," Ian continued. "I love you so much, Bai. I want you to be Mrs. Jackson. Will you marry me?"

Bailee didn't need to think about it. She already knew what she wanted, so she shouted "Yes!" before climbing into Ian's lap, wrapping her arms around his neck and kissing him. She heard the applause and cheers, but Bailee couldn't stop kissing her future husband.

Soon, she heard the clearing of throats and realized she might have set the record for the longest kiss at a semipublic proposal. She pulled away and whispered to Ian, "Your hand is on my butt."

Ian chuckled and kissed her nose, then her chin. "I know." Then he smacked her butt for good measure. "I love you, Bai."

She traced his jaw with her finger. "I love you, too."

* * * * *

SPECIAL EXCERPT FROM

HARLEQUIN

KIMANI ROMANCE

Rita feels an instant connection to homegrown hunk Keith Burke. A hot fling with the sweet-talking Realtor could be just what she needs. Until an unexpected arrival shatters the fragile bond between Rita and Keith...and their trust in a future together.

Read on for a sneak peek at
Undeniable Passion,
the next exciting installment in the Burkes of Sheridan Falls series by Kayla Perrin!

As Rita watched Keith carry her two large suitcases from the trunk, she couldn't help thinking that he was seriously attractive. He was the kind of guy she could enjoy gazing at. Like someone on a safari checking out the wild animals, she could watch him and not get bored.

However, she knew that wouldn't be wise. Keith wasn't a man on display. And he was the kind of man that she knew would be risky to get close to. If she had him pegged right, he had an easy way with the ladies, and how many times had Rita seen women fall for guys like that during vulnerable times? She knew her heart was especially weak after her breakup with Rashad a few months ago and the reality that their wedding would have been just weeks away. The fact that her mother was getting married on top of that only made her heart more fragile.

Vulnerable women looking for a way to forget or ease their pain often brought on more heartbreak. Rita read about it in the various stories sent to her for her magazine, *Unlock Your Power*. The magazine was a voice for women who'd endured devastating situations but were picking up the pieces of their lives. Sharing their stories was a way to help ease their pain and let others in similar situations know that they weren't alone.

So Rita definitely knew better than to think of men as a distraction. She could look at Keith or any other man and leave it at that. It was a matter of choice, wasn't it? Knowing the risks and behaving accordingly.

The first rule of guarding your heart was to not get involved on any level. Keith was simply a man who wanted to help her out—a good guy doing the courteous thing. No need to let herself think that there might be more motives to his actions.

Keith exited the bedroom, where he had brought her two big suitcases.

"I know it's a lot, but considering I might be here for a while…" Her voice trailed off. "Speaking of which, are there laundry facilities?"

"Excellent question. Forgot to mention that. There is a stacked washer and dryer in the cupboard in the kitchen. You'll see it."

"Perfect, thank you."

Keith headed to the door again, and Rita said, "I can get the rest."

"You don't have too much more. I'll get the big box I saw in the back seat. Plus, wasn't there a case of water?"

"Yes, but—" Rita stopped when her phone rang. She pulled it out from the back pocket of her jeans and glanced at the screen. It was her best friend, Maeve.

Keith jogged down the steps, and Rita swiped to answer the call. "Hey."

"How's it going?" Maeve asked without preamble.

"Good. I got here okay."

"You said something about a mishap," Maeve said, concern in her voice.

"Yeah, but… It's not really a big deal. It was a small fender bender, but the situation's been resolved."

"Someone hit you?" Maeve asked.

"Actually, I hit someone."

"What?"

"I was distracted for a second when I was pulling up to the coffee shop. And…it was barely a touch. No real damage."

"Did you leave a note for the owner?"

"Actually, he was in the car," Rita said as she watched Keith make his way back up the steps with the box of food items. "There was just a bit of paint transfer." He gave her a little smile as he passed her, and Rita smiled back. Then she stepped outside the unit to continue her call. "I offered to pay. He refused. Everything's good."

"Okay, that's great to hear. Just make sure you follow up. You don't want the guy to start claiming back pains tomorrow."

"I doubt that's going to happen. Something tells me that people in small towns like this are honest, not opportunistic. And from the sense I got from the guy…I highly doubt he would do that."

"All right, if you're sure, then I trust your judgment."

"I am sure," Rita said. She didn't bother to tell her that the very man whose car she'd hit was currently helping her move in.

KPEXP0719